Thundering Pines

Thundering Pines

Rita Potter

SAPPHIRE BOOKS

SALINAS, CALIFORNIA

Editor - Tara Young
Book Design - LJ Reynolds
Cover Design - Fineline Cover Design

Sapphire Books Publishing, LLC
P.O. Box 8142
Salinas, CA 93912
www.sapphirebooks.com

Printed in the United States of America
First Edition – March 2022

This and other Sapphire Books titles can be found at
www.sapphirebooks.com

Dedication

For Terra: My stability and my reason
For Jae: My mentor

Acknowledgment

First, thanks to Sapphire Books and Chris. I'm grateful that you've given me the perfect landing place.

To my editor, Tara. This is our first time working together, but I couldn't ask for a smoother process.

I'm going to focus on the special circumstances surrounding this book, which I wrote during my time in the GCLS Writing Academy.

Thanks to the amazing GCLS instructors, Finn, Karelia, Anna, Penny, and the guest instructors. I learned so much from all of you.

Thanks to my fellow students in the class of 2021. A special shoutout to Lori, my first buddy in the class, and partner in crime. Actually, crime fighting and superheroes, but that's a topic for another day. Also, my feedback group deserves a special mention, Nan, Cade, and Michele.

My biggest thanks must go to Jae, who served as my mentor. I've run out of words to express my gratitude. I'm still in awe of the amount of time and effort you put into improving me and *Thundering Pines*. You went above and beyond anything I could ever have imagined. I truly received a private Master Class in writing. I may never be able to repay you for all you've done and continue to do for me, but I will certainly pay it forward. You will always be the role model I look to emulate as I interact with other authors starting out. One day, I hope I can give back a fraction of what you've given me and the entire Sapphic writing community. And I will always smile whenever I think of your explanation to how Germans give feedback and take your praise times ten.

I can't go without thanking Terra and Chumley. You guys are my world. And for anyone who's read my previous acknowledgments, I still haven't asked Terra to marry me, even though we've been married for nearly eight years. Try and wrap your brain around that.

And lastly, to my readers. I continue to learn and hopefully improve, so I can write a better story for you.

Chapter One

Dani Thorton flipped through the pages of a two-year-old magazine without registering what she was looking at. She ran her fingers over the well-creased cover and squirmed in the cold leather chair.

The receptionist looked up and gave her a sympathetic smile.

Dani returned the smile and focused on sitting up straighter and minding her posture.

The décor was at least two decades out of style, but the waiting room of Patterson, Clifton, Dunhurst, and Johnston was immaculate. The dark wood paneling and the burgundy and gold furnishings made the already small room seem smaller, and the walls closed in on her.

Her natural inclination to arrive excessively early was a blessing and a curse. On one hand, it afforded her the opportunity to get comfortable with her surroundings. On the other, it gave her time to overthink, a skill she was exceptionally good at.

Shouldn't be here. She leapt from her chair and pushed open the door. When she burst out of the tiny room into the much larger atrium, a loud exhalation escaped her lungs.

How embarrassing. When she returned, she'd have to face the receptionist after her mad dash to freedom. She needed to get a grip before she made a fool of herself. It would be bad enough to let Shelby see her this way, but she would *not* act this way in front of the Prodigal Daughter.

She'd greeted Brianna Goodwin in her mind at least a dozen times, but none seemed quite right. Walking toward the coffeemaker in the far corner, she ran through her practiced lines. Maybe she should stick with the simple. *Hi, I'm Dani Thorton. I worked for your father.* If she tried to say more, she'd come off like a babbling fool. *Who invites the hired help to the reading of a family will, anyway?*

Caffeine was the last thing her nerves needed, but maybe she could find green tea, anything to keep her hands occupied. *Paydirt! Hot chocolate.* She grinned as she heaped mini marshmallows into the dark liquid, then dunked them with her spoon to cram more into her cup.

She wasn't ready to go back inside, so she circled the atrium and browsed the exhibits on the walls. All the paintings and photographs were from local artists, most of whom she knew, which made the artwork more interesting.

Dani studied a painting of a cow and pig dancing the tango in a partially harvested cornfield. She grinned. The artist had a unique aesthetic.

A draft from behind made her turn. A very tall blond woman marched confidently through the door.

The woman's porcelain skin was ruddy, not holding up under the cold from outside. Her long wool coat hung open, revealing a perfectly tailored business suit. Her outfit likely cost more than a small-town lawyer earned in a week. Who wore heels in the middle of winter?

Just inside the door, the woman paused and

gave a perfunctory glance around the atrium. A frown etched her brow, and her nose crinkled as if she'd smelled something offensive.

She wasn't a local. Clearly, she must be Brianna, Donald Goodwin's daughter.

Dani pulled her sweater down and ran her hands along her slacks, smoothing out the tiny wrinkles she'd gotten from sitting. *I'm underdressed.* There was nothing she could do about it now.

She put on a smile, squared her shoulders, and ambled across the room, trying her best to appear casual. When she reached the woman, Dani held out her hand. "Hello, you must be Brianna."

The woman looked down at her hand but made no move to take it. "No, I am not."

"Oh, sorry, I just thought…So sorry." Should she get more marshmallows, or did the situation require her to explain herself?

Before she could decide, the woman said, "Caroline, Caroline Dirst. Brianna will be along shortly."

"Hi, Caroline. I'm Dani, Danielle Thorton, but everyone calls me Dani. You must be Brianna's lawyer."

"No." Caroline's look of distaste deepened. "I am a lawyer but not Brianna's."

"I just assumed. I'm sorry. I'm afraid I'm a bit nervous today." Dani flashed a smile, hoping to defuse the uncomfortable interaction.

"Really?" Caroline looked down her nose at Dani. "And who are you exactly?"

"I'm, um, I am…" Dani wasn't sure how to answer the question.

A blast of frigid air granted her a reprieve as the door opened again. A darker replica of Caroline stood in the doorway.

Where do women like this come from? Their clothes were nearly identical, only in a different shade of gray. If the three-inch heels they sported were any indication, neither woman was self-conscious about her nearly six-foot height.

Caroline's blond hair appeared white while the newcomer's chestnut brown hair bordered on black. *Yikes, they must have headaches by the end of the day with their hair pulled back so severely.* Dani gratefully touched her own hair that hung loose. Though they resembled models, their plasticity was a turnoff to her.

The woman stamped her heels on the mat, knocking off the grime she'd picked up from the sidewalk, then glided toward them.

"There you are, sweetheart." Caroline lightly pecked the woman's lips.

The dark-haired woman flinched. She recovered and smiled but took a half step back. "Um, I just dropped you off at the door like two minutes ago."

"Such a kidder," Caroline said with an unnatural giggle.

The puzzled look on the brunette's face deepened.

Dani watched the awkward exchange and debated if she should deliver her practiced line since this must be Brianna.

"Apparently, this woman was looking for you. I have yet to ascertain why. Her name is Danielle Thorton."

Dani wanted to say, *Really, I am standing right here, maybe you could address me,* but instead she reached her hand out. "Dani, Dani Thorton, and you must be Brianna Goodwin."

"Hello, Dani." Brianna shook Dani's hand.

Hmm, firm handshake. It wasn't the dead fish

variety Dani had expected. *Okay, good.*

"Yes, I'm Brianna Goodwin. Have we met?"

"I highly doubt it." Caroline rolled her eyes. "Danielle thought I was you."

"No, we haven't," Dani answered, ignoring Caroline. "I worked for your father."

"Why would your father's lawyer invite the hired help?" Caroline asked.

"How should I know?" Brianna said. "I have no idea why the hell I'm here, so how would I know why Dani's here?"

Heat rose on Dani's neck and settled on her cheeks. She took a cleansing breath. Nothing good could come out of a confrontation, so she pushed back her ire.

"Well, look who the cat dragged in," said a loud brassy voice from across the room.

Could this day get any worse?

Shelby Twait walked toward them. Her short, tight, black dress, which seemed more appropriate for a nightclub, clung to her hips. It was hard not to stare at her exposed cleavage since a large gold cross fell between her breasts.

"Should I bow to the golden child?" Shelby said to Brianna.

"I think a handshake will suffice," Brianna answered with a forced smile.

"Holy hell, doesn't that hurt?" Shelby poked at Brianna's hair. "How do you get that shit pulled so tight?"

Brianna pulled away. "What flavor of Kool-Aid do you use to get your hair that shade of red?"

Dani stifled a giggle, happy the attention had shifted away from her.

Shelby's glare remained on Brianna, but she stepped back and draped her arm over Dani's shoulders. "Dani, I see you've met my sister."

"Half," Brianna said.

"What?" Caroline shot her a look.

"Half sister," Brianna clarified.

"Really? And why is it I didn't know about her?" Caroline asked.

"I embarrass her." Shelby winked at Caroline.

At the same time, Brianna said, "It didn't seem important."

Shelby dropped her arm from around Dani's shoulders and stepped forward. She stopped just inches from Brianna. Dani suspected Shelby wanted to get in Brianna's face but fell short since Brianna stood at least eight inches taller. Shelby's face reddened, and the vein in her temple throbbed as she looked up at the much taller woman. "You think you're so fucking superior, don't you? Newsflash! You and your, whatever she is," Shelby glanced at Caroline before turning back to Brianna, "you ain't shit. You might think you're a big deal because you live in the city, but you came from here. So you're just like me."

Without missing a beat, Brianna responded, "Trailer trash?"

Dani didn't know whether she should laugh or hide because this was about to get uglier. Shelby may have met her match, which Dani previously didn't believe possible. Dani gripped her hot chocolate more tightly. She didn't want to be in the middle of what might happen next.

"You bitch." Shelby bumped Brianna with her expansive chest.

"Please." Brianna rolled her eyes. "Don't tempt

me."

"Oh, poor little Brianna trying to act tough, but we all know why you and your momma left here, don't we?" Shelby smirked.

Ouch, low blow. Most everyone in town had heard the rumors, but only Shelby would be willing to throw it out in this setting. Dani almost felt sorry for Brianna.

"I don't believe everyone does. Why don't you tell them?" Brianna's voice was calm, only the set of her jaw gave her away. "Caroline and Dani, would you like to know?"

It was hard for Dani not to giggle seeing Brianna call Shelby's bluff. By the scowl on Shelby's face, the dig she'd planned to level was rendered useless by Brianna's reaction.

Shelby's face turned red, and she stammered a couple of times before she spit out, "You are such a bitch."

Brianna let out a half laugh, half snort. "That the best you've got?" She turned away from Shelby. "Come on, Caroline, let's go inside."

Shelby stood gaping, speechless, which might have been a first.

Brianna had taken several steps before she turned around. "It was nice meeting you, Dani."

"You too," Dani said, watching her walk away. *The day just got more interesting.*

Chapter Two

*B*rianna focused on her heels clicking on the tile floor as she and Caroline made their way across the atrium. She glanced to her left and smiled at a painting of a cow and pig dancing in a cornfield. *Gotta love Flower Hills.*

Back in town for less than half an hour, and she already wanted to leave. *Why did I agree to this shit? Masochist?* She'd been asking herself this since she'd gotten the call from Mr. Dunhurst three weeks earlier. She hadn't been able to explain it to Caroline, either, despite Caroline's relentless questioning.

"Why the hell didn't you mention a sister?" Caroline asked between clenched teeth.

"I don't know."

"No, you're not getting away with that. Spill."

"Honestly, I don't know." Brianna's shoulders sagged. "This is a place I wanted to leave in the past. Still do."

"Then maybe we shouldn't have come."

"I didn't have a choice," Brianna said as she stopped outside the law office.

"You know the reading of the will is a thing of the past."

How could she not know since Caroline had been harping on it for the past two weeks? She repeated the line she'd heard at least a dozen times out of Caroline's mouth. "Yes. It was necessary when literacy rates were low and methods of communication much less reliable."

Caroline nodded with a smug smile. "Exactly. So I fail to understand why we needed to come to this place."

"Because Donald Goodwin was a control freak." Brianna yanked open the door, thankfully putting an end to any further conversation.

꧁꧂꧁꧂

When Thomas Dunhurst joined them, Dani secretly blew out a breath. Despite the room being eerily quiet, tension lay just under the surface. She suspected it wouldn't take much for it to erupt.

He set his file folders down at the head of the large mahogany conference table but remained standing. His gaze landed on Brianna and Caroline. Since he'd been friends with Donald Goodwin for years, he would probably be able to identify his daughter.

"Ms. Goodwin, I presume." He reached his hand out to Brianna and ignored the huff from the other side of the table. "I'm Thomas Dunhurst, your father's attorney."

Brianna clasped his hand with a firm grip. "Mr. Dunhurst, please call me Brianna. And this is Caroline Dirst."

"She shouldn't be here," Shelby said. "No one invited her."

"She's an attorney," Brianna answered smoothly.

Slick. Brianna hadn't lied. She never said Caroline was *her* attorney, and judging by their earlier interactions, there was much more to the relationship.

"Very good." He extended his hand to Caroline.

"So glad to meet you. Your offices are so quaint." Caroline put her hand against her chest. "I just love the old-time charm."

Laying it on thick. Was Thomas falling for Caroline's schtick?

"Thank you, Ms. Dirst."

"Caroline."

"Very well, Caroline. I'm happy to make your acquaintance." He turned his attention to the other side of the table. He nodded but didn't extend his hand. "Hello, Shelby, nice to see you."

"I bet. Plan on calling the cops on me again?"

Whoa. Dani hadn't heard anything about it on the local grapevine. That was what happened during the off-season; none of the campers were around to keep her in the know.

"That depends on how you behave."

"It wasn't my fault," Shelby said. "Your receptionist is a bitch."

"I'm afraid I will have to ask you to leave if you continue to disparage my staff."

Brianna laughed. "Well played, Mr. Dunhurst."

Thomas ignored her and made his way to the far end of the table. When he stopped in front of Dani, she sprang from her chair.

"Dani," he said with a genuine smile.

"Thomas." She wrapped her arms around him. "Thank you so much for helping Aunt Helen the other day. She couldn't stop talking about how understanding you were."

"Any time. She's a lovely lady."

"Do we have to listen to this drivel?" Shelby asked. "Don't you think we should get down to business?"

"Of course." Thomas smiled at Dani. "Thank you for coming."

Strange. She could have sworn she detected a twinkle in his eye before he turned away.

Meticulously, he explained the applicable laws surrounding estates, trusts, and wills in the state of Illinois. He talked for nearly ten minutes, and Dani's eyes started to glaze over at the legal jargon. Caroline was the only one in the room who intently focused on his monologue.

"Can't you just cut to the chase?" Shelby said.

For once, Dani agreed with Shelby. This was tedious.

"Sorry, Ms. Twait, but I do not want it to be said later that I did not fully explain the proceedings here." He ran his finger down the notes in front of him and continued his speech. When he finished, he put both palms on the table and looked up. "Does anyone have any questions?"

Caroline made a few cursory inquiries while Shelby glared.

Dani shifted in her seat. She had no idea why she was being subjected to this torture. She had no desire to know any of Shelby's business; it could only lead to trouble. "Thomas, I mean no disrespect, but I really don't think I should be here. This sounds like a family thing to me."

"I appreciate your concern, Dani, but I assure you that your attendance is not a mistake. If there are no further questions, I will move on to the reading of the will." He slowly glanced around the room before continuing. "As you are aware, we are gathered today to settle the estate of Donald Steven Goodwin. Your father." He nodded to Brianna and Shelby. "And your employer," he said to Dani. Thomas flipped open the top folder and removed a document. "Three years ago, Donald placed all of his assets in the Donald S. Goodwin trust. At that time, he was the sole trustee, but he named a successor in the event of his death."

Shelby smiled broadly, nodding as Thomas talked.

"I have prepared a list of all the assets held in trust, and it will be included in the packet that I will give each of you before you leave. The major assets that we will be discussing here today are his main residence, the Thundering Pines Campground, and his stock portfolio valued somewhere in the neighborhood of three million dollars."

Holy shit. Dani had no idea Donald had been sitting on that much cash. He'd been excessively frugal; some might say cheap. He still drove a dented old pickup and wore clothes from the thrift shop. She assumed he was barely making ends meet by the way he acted, but then again, he'd never involved her in the finances, nor did she want to be.

Thomas opened another file and extracted a document. He licked his fingers before turning the page. "Mr. Donald Goodwin has named Ms. Brianna Goodwin as acting trustee of the Donald S. Goodwin Trust."

There were a couple of beats of silence before Shelby slammed her palm on the table. "What the fuck kind of joke is this?"

"I assure you, it is no joke, Ms. Twait."

Brianna stared at him, her mouth open. "Mr. Dunhurst, for once, I have to agree with Shelby. Is this some kind of sick joke? I hadn't spoken to my father in nearly fifteen years."

"If you are unable or unwilling to take on this responsibility, Mr. Goodwin did name a secondary trustee."

"Now you're talking." Shelby snatched a pen off the table, pulled her notebook closer, and sat up straight. "Turn it down, Brianna, so we can get on with this."

"Not so fast." Brianna smirked at her. "I need to think this over before I do anything."

"You bitch! I see what you're doing. You just want to watch me squirm."

"I think this conversation may be moot," Thomas said, interrupting the exchange. "Should Ms. Goodwin want to relinquish her role, the next named trustee is Ms. Danielle Thorton."

"Are you fucking kidding me?" Shelby slammed her pen on the table.

Holy hell, now what? Dani felt Shelby's gaze on her, but she sat stock-still, staring straight ahead. Donald had never told her any of this, and she certainly didn't suspect. Would the Goodwin sisters believe her?

Brianna laughed. "Well played, old man, well played."

"Real fucking funny," Shelby said. "I've been the one here taking care of him all these years while you were off doing God knows what with God knows who, and this is how the bastard repays me."

"Yeah, I can see your compassion knows no bounds."

"The asshole listed me third?" Shelby said to Thomas.

"Well, no, you aren't listed at all."

Shelby whipped around in her chair and leveled

her gaze at Dani. "And how the hell did you weasel your way into this whole thing?"

Dani shrank back into her chair, hoping to disappear. "I have no idea."

"Right, and you expect us to believe that? Sweet Dani, so fucking innocent." Shelby looked at Brianna for the first time and pointed at Dani. "I wouldn't be so smug. She's coming for your shit, too."

"Ladies," Thomas said, raising his voice. "I would like to continue. There is still some information that you need to know."

Shelby continued muttering under her breath, but the room quieted enough for him to continue.

"There's a stipulation in his trust that none of the assets are to be distributed for six months after this reading, which means the trust must remain intact until at least August 11 of this year."

Brianna groaned. "If I accept the role, I won't be able to liquidate for at least six months?"

Shelby cackled and shot a satisfied grin in Brianna's direction.

"That is correct, Ms. Goodwin." Thomas opened the last file and pulled out another document. "I would like to conclude by reading the last will and testament of Donald Steven Goodwin." He quickly read the legalese and slowed when he said, "To my daughter Shelby Twait, I leave my residence and everything therein. To my daughter Brianna Goodwin, I leave the Thundering Pines Campground."

Before he could continue, Shelby was on her feet. "No way, Thundering Pines is mine."

"I'm afraid not, Ms. Twait. Your father left that to Ms. Goodwin. If I could finish, that leads us to the final substantial asset, his investment portfolio." Thomas shuffled through the pages and held the document close to his face as he read, "I leave my stock portfolio in three equal parts to my two daughters, Brianna Goodwin and Shelby Twait, and the remaining third of the portfolio to Danielle Thorton."

Dani gasped. *A million dollars?*

Shelby, still standing, jabbed her finger at Thomas. "You did this. You always hated me. You made him do it, and you're not going to get away with it. Isn't there a law against being your best friend's lawyer? Conflict of interest or something."

"I assure you, Ms. Twait, that everything was done legally and ethically."

"Bullshit!" Shelby shouted. "Just give me my fucking packet."

Thomas picked up a folder and held it out to her.

She snatched it from him and stormed toward the exit. With her hand on the doorknob, she whirled back around. "None of you are going to get away with this. Thomas, you will be hearing from my attorney." She yanked open the door.

"Bye, Shelby, have a wonderful day," Brianna said with a gleam in her eye.

Dani winced, waiting for more fireworks.

Shelby stomped back into the room, her face bright red. "You are so fucking full of yourself. It must be such a burden for the big-city girl to have to deal with us simpleton country folk."

Brianna grinned but said nothing.

"You think you are so much better than us, don't you?"

"After this display, how could I not?"

"Whatever! I hope when you fall off your pedestal, there's someone there to catch you." She glanced toward Caroline. "But somehow, I don't think there will be."

Brianna leaned back in her chair and crossed her arms over her chest. Her lips curled in a haughty smile.

"Smirk all you want." Shelby shrugged, and an unnatural calm replaced the fire in her eyes. "You might think your life is so much better than mine, that you have so much more, but anyone can see it's not real and probably never has been."

Dani's breath caught when Shelby's attention shifted toward her. "Good luck, you're going to need it with your new employer."

Before she could answer, Shelby left the room.

"What a piece of work," Caroline said, breaking the silence.

"Who asked you?" Dani snapped, tired of the entire circus.

"Oh, great, are we going to be schooled by another redneck?" Caroline said.

Dani looked past Caroline to Brianna. "Do you have anything to say?"

"No, I'm just trying to take it all in, Dani. It's a lot."

"Well, I have plenty more to say," Caroline said.

Brianna shook her head. "No, too much has been said already. Let's just get this finished, so we can go home."

Home. Exactly where Dani wanted to be. This meeting needed to be over.

Chapter Three

Brianna considered turning on the radio but settled on listening to the rhythmic beat of the windshield wipers. The steady thump, thump, thump soothed her, which she needed after the scene in Dunhurst's office.

Caroline stared straight ahead, her expression wavered between boredom and anger. The silence was a blessing, even though it meant she was in a snit.

Images from earlier swirled in Brianna's head, but the worsening weather pulled her from her contemplation. The sleet came down fast and heavy, causing it to clump on the wipers. The ice-coated blades created wet streaks across the glass and limited her visibility.

"I can't believe you sided with that redneck bitch." Caroline finally broke the silence.

Since she strained to see the road in front of her, it took a moment for Brianna to register that Caroline had spoken. "What?"

"You aren't even listening to me."

Caroline's gaze bore into her, but she continued staring through the windshield, trying to maneuver through the slush. "You haven't said anything for the last twenty minutes. Did you think I was just sitting here waiting on pins and needles for you to honor me with your commentary?"

"Don't get pissy with me. You're the one that

dragged me out to that godforsaken place."

"Bullshit!" Brianna shot a glare at Caroline before turning her gaze back to the road. "I never asked you to come. You just assumed that I wanted you to."

"You didn't?"

"No, I never invited you."

"I meant you didn't want me to come?"

"I don't know." Brianna sighed. She'd give anything to be curled up in her bed right now, instead of having this conversation with Caroline. "I don't know what I want."

"What's that supposed to mean?"

"It means that this whole situation sucks, and I don't need my girlfriend giving me shit." Brianna blinked back tears. "My dad's dead. I'm in charge of an estate I never wanted, and—"

"Don't play the 'my dad's dead' card on me," Caroline interrupted. "You hadn't talked to him in years."

"Really? Listen to yourself."

"What? You'd written the man off years ago, so don't pretend you're mourning." Caroline crossed her arms over her chest. "How do you think I feel?"

"When did this become about you?" Brianna gripped the steering wheel more tightly, not sure whether it was in response to Caroline's words or the sleet that seemed to have gotten heavier.

"You just inherited property worth several million dollars from a man you couldn't care less about, yet you're edgy."

I'm not doing this. Brianna turned on the radio. Caroline had been in a mood the entire drive to Flower Hills, and it seemed the trip home would be more of the same. Brianna's thoughts were a jumbled mess, and she needed time to think.

Caroline turned the radio off. "So I shouldn't be upset that my girlfriend threw me under the bus?"

"How did I throw you under the bus?" She was getting exasperated by the conversation but knew Caroline would never relent until she won her oral argument. One of the perils of being in a relationship with an attorney.

"I was getting ready to unload on that bitch, and you stopped me."

"Is that why you've been pissed off ever since we got in the Jeep?"

"You embarrassed me, worse yet, in front of that mountain woman."

"Mountain woman? If you hadn't noticed, there are no mountains in Illinois."

"Well then, lumberjack or whatever the hell she is."

"Are you talking about Dani?"

"Yes, Danielle," Caroline corrected. "The only good thing is that your psycho sister was already gone by the time you made a fool of me."

"I was not trying to make a fool of you." Brianna kept her voice calm and refrained from saying that Caroline was acting like a fool now. "I just didn't think starting something with Dani was necessary. She has nothing to do with this whole ugly mess."

Brianna's shoulders stiffened at Caroline's snort. She braced herself for what Caroline would say next.

"You really think Danielle is so innocent? She weaseled her way into a million dollars of your money, and now she's trying to find a way to take the campground from you. Wake the fuck up and smell the coffee."

I can't do this right now. Brianna slumped against her seat and took a deep inhalation. "You're right Caroline, I'm sorry."

"That's better." Caroline smiled. "I knew my girl would come around."

"Yep, I always do." Brianna forced herself to smile.

෴෴෴

"I cannot believe you defended that woman." Aunt Helen pulled open the oven.

Dani's mouth watered, and her stomach growled as she breathed in the yeasty scent. "And that's the first thing you have to say after everything I just told you?" Dani leaned against the kitchen counter, staying out of Aunt Helen's way. Over the years, she'd learned not to mess with Aunt Helen when she was in a cooking frenzy.

"You know how I feel about Shelby. I'm just shocked you defended her."

"I know, right?" Dani shrugged and shook her head. "Trust me, I was as shocked as you, but I kinda felt sorry for her."

"Really?"

"You'd understand if you'd met Caroline. She's a piece of work. She looked at us with such contempt. Like we were gum on her shoe." Dani ran her hands through her hair, drawing it into a ponytail and wrapping a tie around it. With her hair off her shoulders, she felt more like herself.

Aunt Helen wielded her bread knife. With practiced strokes, she cut the bread into perfectly uniform slices. "Sounds like a lovely woman. What about the daughter? Was she nasty, too?"

"Brianna, her name's Brianna. Would you stop calling her *the daughter*?" Dani edged closer. When Aunt Helen turned to put the knife in the sink, Dani grabbed a piece of warm bread and slathered butter on it. Before Aunt Helen could protest, she shoved it in her mouth and took a bite. She closed her eyes, savoring the melting butter and the taste of yeast.

"Danielle Thorton, would you stop being a cave person? I am making us sandwiches."

Dani smiled and chewed dramatically. She decided to speak before swallowing, just to get under Aunt Helen's skin. "She's slightly better than Caroline. The jury is still out on how much better."

"I am not going to talk to you with your mouth full." Aunt Helen turned from Dani and piled roast beef and cheese on the fresh bread, creating two oversized sandwiches.

Dani swallowed the bite in her mouth and thought about taking another, but she knew Aunt Helen would be true to her word.

Dani was still weighing her choice when Aunt Helen turned, holding two full plates. *Damn, that sandwich looks good.*

"You know you're going to have to work hand in hand with her, don't you?"

"Don't remind me." Dani groaned and pretended to tug at her ponytail. "I just want to forget this whole damned day."

"Even the million dollars?"

"Yep, even that." Dani rubbed her chest, hoping to loosen the tightness. "You know I've never been about money."

"But money can buy you freedom. You don't have to work for that woman if you don't want to."

"Brianna, not *that woman*." Dani shot her a look. "You know I love Thundering Pines. I'd give all the money back if I could just stay and manage it."

"Buy it."

"Sure, I just need another three or four million. Can I borrow it from your piggy bank?"

Aunt Helen laughed. "You said that wom… Brianna might not be all that bad. Maybe she'll be okay to work for."

"Maybe." She knew Aunt Helen wanted to be positive, but she didn't want to think about any of it right now.

"Once you eat, you'll feel better," Aunt Helen said as if reading her mind.

"I want to get out of these clothes."

"Eat first." Aunt Helen dropped a handful of Doritos onto the plate next to the sandwich.

She wouldn't win an argument with Aunt Helen, so Dani took the large jug of sweet tea out of the refrigerator and poured two glasses.

❧ ❧ ❧ ❧

Dani breathed in deeply as she stepped off the porch, her exhale created a plume of steam, which quickly dissipated in the heavy sleet. She tightened the hood around her face and walked the short distance to the wooded path that led to Thundering Pines.

Thankfully, Aunt Helen's property butted up against the campground. She preferred being outdoors, but in this weather, the mile-and-a-half trek could prove treacherous.

Her pace increased once the trees flanked her. They acted as an umbrella against the heavy sleet, so it no longer stung her cheeks.

With each step, her head cleared more, and her thoughts became less jumbled. She wasn't going to allow herself to think about the events of the day. Years ago, she'd read about walking meditation, and it had been a lifesaver. She practiced it now, focusing on identifying each tree as she passed. She scanned the bark and branches, looking for any sign of distress or disease. By the time she arrived at the campground, she'd identified three trees that she'd need to watch as spring approached.

Dani made a beeline to the campsite area. It had grown to over two hundred fifty permanent lots with an additional one hundred fifty for short-term renters. The campsites sat empty this time of year, which made it eerily peaceful. Come spring, it would be teeming with campers, but for now, she took solace in the quiet.

She wove her way through the campsites, toward her favorite part of Thundering Pines and its namesake. She smelled the pine trees long before she saw them through the thick forest. Her breathing became heavier as she climbed the steep hill to the pine grove, which sat on the highest part of the grounds and overlooked the river. Once she arrived at the top, she stopped and inhaled the overpowering scent.

Pinecones crunched under her feet as she walked toward the center of the grove. Stopping occasionally, she searched for the spot that gave Thundering Pines its name. She knew she was getting closer when she heard the river below and corrected her course when the sound became fainter. With each step, the sound that started as a whisper turned into a murmur, then a roar until she found the spot where it could only be described as thunder.

She remembered her awe when Donald had brought her to hear the thunderous rumble for the first time. Shortly after, she'd asked him if she could purchase a plaque to mark the spot in the woods. He'd laughed and told her about the lightning bolt he'd carved into the trunk of a tree to pinpoint the location. Later when he'd brought a girl he was trying to impress to the spot, he was shocked when there was only a low rumble. Dani had learned the sound moved around the grove, depending on factors they'd never quite identified.

Dani stopped when she found the sweet spot. Closing her eyes, she let the sound wash over her. The noise thudded in her chest like a drum. Normally, she stayed for only a couple of minutes because the reverberations became overpowering. It gave her a feeling of claustrophobia. Today, she remained much longer because the uneasy feeling somehow brought her comfort.

She walked out of the pine grove into the clearing that overlooked the river below. The picnic tables were stored for the winter, but the clubhouse remained. Dani considered going inside to warm up, but she wanted to get to her destination. Since the days were still short, she'd have about an hour before she'd need to head back. Walking in the dark usually didn't bother her, but in this weather, it was a recipe for a fall.

Myriad emotions washed over her, and the tightness in her chest returned. This was the first time she'd been to the tower since Donald's death. As she approached, she admired its sheer size. The juxtaposition of the heavy steel structure next to the pine forest only enhanced its grandeur. It stood six stories tall and looked out over the river below.

She smiled, remembering Donald's obsession with building a tower. For years, he did nothing but talk about it and doodle sketches on whatever paper was in front of him. He insisted that one day he would build it once he hit on the perfect design, but as the years passed, she figured it was just an old man's ramblings.

Then one day, he excitedly called her into his office. His eyes were wide, and he didn't speak; instead, he pointed to his computer screen. A picture of an enormous tower labeled the Sirveta Observation Tower, Didziasalis, Lithuania, filled the screen. He'd found his tower.

It was one of Donald's few splurges, and he spared no expense. She always wondered what it cost but probably didn't want to know. He'd hired a contractor who modified the blueprint but kept a similar feeling to the Sirveta Tower. The memory was bittersweet since Donald insisted that one day he'd see the tower in person. He never did.

Dani shook the memory from her mind as she climbed the spiral staircase that wound up to the observation deck five stories above. The open-air stairs and structure did nothing to block the wind, so it grew colder with each step.

She longed to be in the place where Donald's design diverged from the original, so she quickened her ascent. On the top floor, she walked across the observation deck and reached the imposing steel door marked private. The door was decorated with several scratches, scuffs, and gouges, likely put there by drunken campers determined to see what was inside. As far as she knew, the door held, and no one had ever been able to breach the sanctuary.

She put her key in the lock, turned it, and waited for the panel to flash three times before she punched in her security code. A melody played when the lock released. Warmth hit her when the door swung open. Climbing the stairs to the loft, she smiled at the luxurious surroundings.

The walk had made her thirsty, so she grabbed a bottle of water out of the refrigerator. When she turned on the television, country music greeted her. Music might be what she needed. Her favorite chair beckoned, the one that had the best view of the river. She plopped down and immediately felt as if she had fallen into a cloud. The sleet pelted the windows, making it more difficult to see the raging river below.

Dani squinted, trying to make it out, but gave up and sank farther into the comfort of the chair. Mesmerized by the water that streaked down the window, she thought of nothing else. After several minutes, she pulled herself away from the view.

Could she work with Brianna for the next six months? And if she did, would she still have a job after that? After fifteen years, Thundering Pines remained the great love of her life. She never imagined working anywhere else, but she may have to. She blinked multiple times, forcing back her tears. She knew she should try to remain optimistic, but after meeting Brianna and Caroline, it was difficult.

She sat and continued to watch the frozen rain hit the glass. Part of her wanted to curl up and spend the night here, but she knew Aunt Helen would worry.

She sighed and stood from the solace of her chair. After being so warm and comfortable, she knew the walk home was going to be brutal. She didn't want it to be dark, as well. Besides, she had six months to figure it all out, there was no sense in driving herself crazy tonight.

Chapter Four

*D*ani twirled the business card between her fingers. As she flipped it, Brianna Goodwin's name appeared and then disappeared with each turn.

Just get it over with. She had a list of things they needed to discuss regarding Thundering Pines. At this point, she likely wouldn't even have a job.

She dropped the card onto her desk. Maybe she should straighten up her office before she made the call. She glanced around at the tidy room and sighed. Her office at Thundering Pines was immaculate. Donald had instilled this in her. He hated clutter and referred to her desk as a pit of squalor. Dani didn't consider herself sloppy, but to Donald, more than three files out and not precisely stacked constituted a mess.

She knocked over the neat pile of files and let them scatter. *Childish much?* The downed branches from the last storm needed to be picked up. That was what she should do. After all, she took the job to be outside, not to sit behind a desk.

She began to rise, but the business card caught her eye. *Shit.* She picked up the card. Was it appropriate for her to reach out, or should she wait for Brianna to call? Dani had shared her number at Thomas's office, but it had been three days and still no contact.

Even though it was only the middle of February, much work needed to be done before the campground opened at the end of April. If Brianna wanted to make any improvements for the season, they'd need to get to work on them soon.

She picked up the receiver of her desk phone, then set it back on the cradle. Maybe she should use her cellphone. They would likely need to talk regularly, so she might as well establish her cellphone as her preferred method of communication. Would Brianna think it unprofessional?

Stop overthinking! Why did she always do that? The only way to discover how best to communicate with Brianna would be to get to know her better. And the only way she could do that was to talk to her.

She snatched her cellphone off the desk, punched in Brianna's number, and hit the call button before she could second-guess herself.

"Brianna Goodwin," the voice said on the first ring.

Dani hadn't been prepared for such a quick response. "Uh, yeah...um, hi..."

"Hello?" Brianna said.

"Sorry, I wasn't expecting you to answer so quickly." *Jesus.* Could she come off any more clueless?

"To whom am I speaking?"

"Brianna. No, you're Brianna. I mean this is Dani...Dani, Danielle Thorton from Thundering Pines." *Wow!* If Brianna had doubts about her competence, she'd have no doubts now. She'd know she was inept.

"Dani, hello." Brianna's voice was warm, almost chipper.

"Hello." Dani paused. "Is this a good time to talk?"

"Can you hold on one minute? I was just finishing up a meeting."

"Oh, God, how presumptuous of me. I shouldn't have called. You're busy. I'll just email you to set up a time to talk."

"Relax." Brianna chuckled. "I'll be with you in a minute. Hold tight."

The line went silent. Brianna must have muted herself.

Dani looked down at the card she'd continued flipping between her fingers. It read *Brianna Goodwin, Executive Vice President.*

What the hell does an executive vice president do? It sounded like a lofty, slightly pretentious corporate title to her. But then again, it wasn't as if she was well versed in corporate America. She'd been perfectly happy in her little corner of the world for the past fifteen years and had no aspirations of becoming executive vice president of anything.

"Dani?"

Brianna's voice jolted her out of her musings. "Yes. I'm sorry I caught you at a bad time."

"Not at all." Brianna lowered her voice. "You gave me an excuse to get the hell out of that meeting. It'd been dragging on for two hours, so you saved me."

Dani smiled. "Glad to be of assistance."

"What can I do for you?" In person, Dani hadn't noticed how pleasant Brianna's voice was. It had a lower register but was still feminine.

"I'd like to talk about your plans for Thundering Pines."

"Of course," Brianna said. "I guess we need to figure something out since I can't sell it for six months."

Dani's back stiffened. "Oh, so you've already decided to sell?"

"Well, yeah." Brianna inhaled deeply. "I thought it was a given."

"Maybe for you!" *Stop.* She must be coming off like an insolent child. "I mean. I guess...well, I thought maybe you'd want to talk with me about it. And possibly see Thundering Pines before you made a decision."

"I'm not sure what I'd do with a campground," Brianna said.

Even though Dani wasn't happy with Brianna's response, she didn't detect any animosity, so she pushed forward. "I just thought maybe there would be a sentimental tie from childhood."

"I can assure you, Ms. Thorton, there are no sentimental ties." Brianna's voice hardened, and her delivery was clipped.

"Sorry, I didn't mean any offense."

"Are you aware of my past?"

Shit. Everyone in Flower Hills had heard about Donald's many indiscretions and his daughter's hatred toward him. How did she answer? She was formulating a response but struggled to come up with an appropriate one.

"By your silence, I'm assuming that's a yes," Brianna said. "Unfortunately, there is nothing in Flower Hills that has any value to me."

Ouch. "I understand." What else could she say? At least she knew where she stood.

"Wow! That came out bad, didn't it?" Brianna's voice softened.

Was that a trick question? Was the polite thing to say *of course not,* or was she supposed to tell the truth? "Well, maybe a little," Dani said, settling on the truth.

"I'm sorry. I shouldn't take it out on you. It's just been a lot to take in." Brianna let out a heavy sigh. "I have another meeting in ten minutes. How about we schedule a time to talk tomorrow late afternoon? Would that work for you?"

"Yes, that would be perfect."

"Why don't I send you a Zoom link? I prefer face to face."

No! "Sure," Dani said. Her future lay in Brianna's hands, whether she liked it or not. Maybe she could convince Brianna not to sell. Even if she couldn't, she still had to decide if she wanted to work for Brianna for the next six months.

Who was she kidding? She loved Thundering Pines. She'd stay until Brianna forced her out. A lump caught in her throat; the thought of leaving behind the woods and the river made her queasy. The view from the tower flashed in her mind. *Stop.* This wasn't doing her any good.

⚜ ⚜ ⚜ ⚜

Dani paused in front of the door but didn't lift her hand to open it. This was a bad idea. She was about to turn and walk away when the door flew open. Without thinking, she grabbed it before it smacked her in the face.

"Whoa, sorry," the man coming out said. "You okay? I didn't gitcha, did I?"

"No, I'm good." Dani flashed him a smile. "Not your fault. I wasn't paying attention."

He put his hand on the door and gestured for her to enter. "Please, let me hold it for you."

Crap. She didn't want to go in, but if she didn't, it might make him feel bad. As if he'd scared her off. "Thanks." She entered the Spotted Owl.

It was only eleven thirty, a little early for the lunch crowd, so the bar was nearly empty. Hopefully, she could get in and out before it started to fill up. She couldn't believe she was here before noon.

Oh, for God's sake, it wasn't as if she stopped in to tie one on. After her phone call with Brianna, she'd found herself pacing around her office, unable to focus. She needed something to ease her nerves.

Sliding onto a bar stool, she smiled at Frank James.

A smile lit his face. He sauntered over and tossed down a coaster in front of her. "Hello, stranger."

"Hey, Frank. How's it going?"

"Can't complain. Just celebrated my twenty-fifth anniversary here. Twenty-five glorious years at the Spotted Owl. I'm living the dream, I tell you."

Dani laughed. "Holy shit. You can't be a day over thirty-five," she teased. Although it was true. He'd aged well and could easily pass for much younger than his years. There wasn't a hint of gray in his jet-black hair or his trim beard.

"Started bartending when I was ten." His blue eyes twinkled. "What can I get you?"

"I want a big thick cheeseburger, medium rare, and the greasiest fries you've got."

"Rough day?"

She nodded.

"What do you want to drink? Pick your poison, and it's on me."

"I'll have a glass of sweet tea."

He winked. "I see you're still a party animal."

While Frank put in her order and waited on other customers, she scrolled through her phone. Anything to distract her from thinking about her phone call with Brianna, even if it meant skimming through the news, which was normally depressing.

"Here you are. The thickest burger we could make and the greasiest fries I could find." Frank set the full plate in front of her.

"You're the best." The grease oozed off the fries. She glanced at her napkin, tempted to place it over the fries just to see the oil saturate the paper, but instead she squeezed a fry between her fingers, letting the grease seep out over her fingernails. Satisfied, she put it in her mouth. *Heaven.*

"I'm not sure how you stay so trim eating like that." He put a handful of napkins next to her plate. "You're gonna need these."

"Wait until you see me eat my burger. I'll probably need a bigger stack of napkins."

He laughed. "I hear there's some drama going on at Thundering Pines."

She was about to put another fry into her mouth but stopped. "What did you hear?" She hoped she sounded casual.

"I hear you got a new boss."

"Yep, that's true. What else?"

"And I hear you have a new enemy."

Dani studied him, weighing her words carefully. She wasn't too keen on the entire town knowing about her million dollars, but she wouldn't put it past Shelby to be shouting it from the rooftops. "And who might that be?"

"Maybe she's not your enemy, but Shelby sure can't stand Donald's other daughter."

Dani's shoulders relaxed. "To say the least. She was a little upset that Donald left Thundering Pines to Brianna."

His eyes widened. "A little? Try a lot."

"You sound like you have some news. Anything I should know about?"

Frank glanced around the bar and leaned in closer. "She was in here a couple nights ago with her cousins Nicky and Tommy."

Great, the twins. They made Shelby look like a picture of stability. "I'm thinking they aren't planning on throwing Brianna a welcome party."

"Hardly." Frank leaned in farther. "Those two aren't right. I'd just watch my back if I were you, and you better tell Brianna the same."

Before she could ask for clarification, another customer shouted his name.

"Duty calls." He winked. "Don't be a stranger."

Damn it. She wanted to know more, but the bar was filling up. She thought of sticking around until the crowd dwindled, but she knew he wouldn't tell her much more, anyway. He hadn't kept his job at the Spotted Owl all these years by having loose lips. Something they'd said must have disturbed him, or he never would have said this much.

She dropped her money on the bar top, leaving a generous tip. Now that she'd had her fill of grease, maybe she could focus on her work. She'd forgo desk work today and get outside where she felt the happiest. How could she bear to lose Thundering Pines? Tomorrow her conversation with Brianna would be what it would be. There was no sense dwelling on it.

≈≈≈≈≈

Brianna slipped her feet out of her heels, brought one foot to her lap, and rubbed the arch. When her thumb hit a sensitive spot, she groaned. What she'd give to be able to wear sensible shoes. Whoever invented high heels was the devil.

For the last two hours, she'd been prowling the boardroom, pitching a digital marketing plan to an up-and-coming microbrewery. She suspected she'd closed the deal, but her feet had paid the price. All she wanted was to go home and stretch out on the couch and watch a mindless comedy, but she still had the meeting with Dani.

Dumb. Why had she scheduled it for late Friday afternoon? *Too late now.* She glanced at the clock. It was still ten minutes before meeting time, but she suspected that Dani would be early.

After their email exchange, she better get in before Dani. It was clear by her questions that she wasn't well versed on virtual meetings and would panic if she arrived first.

Brianna clicked on the link. At least Dani hadn't arrived yet. She muted her sound and shut off her camera while she waited. It was a habit she'd gotten into because she never wanted customers to pop in and see her before she was ready for them.

She picked up the binder from her earlier presentation and flipped through the appendix. Her team had put together one hell of a report. If she scored this account, it could solidify her promotion.

"Shit," a voice said.

Brianna jerked, startled out of her thoughts. She glanced up.

Dani's face filled her computer screen.

Holy shit. How close to the camera was she?

Just as she thought it, Dani pulled away. Dani took the tie out of her hair and shook it out. Tilting her head forward, she ran a brush through it a couple of times before gathering it into a ponytail and reinserting the tie.

An errant strand she'd missed stuck out on the right side of her head. Dani leaned in, squinted, and reached for the left side of her face. Frowning, she dropped her hand, then brushed it along her left side again. She made the gesture a few more times before she sat back in her chair and scowled. She moved toward the camera until her face filled the screen.

In slow motion, she reached toward her left side. When her fingers were nearly to her forehead, she stopped. She stared as she inched them across her forehead to the right side, where her thumb grazed the loose hair. In a flash, she seized the strand as if she were capturing a bug flying around her head. With a look of triumph, she tucked the hair into her ponytail.

Brianna laughed. *Priceless.* Dani didn't realize the camera showed everything in reverse, nor did she know that Brianna could see her. Should she let Dani in on the secret? Maybe she should, so she didn't repeat the mistake with someone else. First, she needed to stop laughing.

Dani sat back in her chair with a satisfied smile.

Brianna took the opportunity to study her since she'd barely looked at her at Dunhurst's office. The only thing she'd remembered was the thin streak of gray that ran down the middle of her dark brown hair. It was less noticeable with her hair pulled back.

She didn't wear any makeup, but her skin had the healthy glow of someone who spent their time outside. Small wrinkles were beginning to form around the corner of her large hazel eyes. Her high cheekbones elevated her from average to attractive.

Before Brianna could flip on her camera and announce her presence, Dani leaned in again and parted her lips, so Brianna was closeup with her straight white teeth. *Oh, God,* now she was checking to make sure she didn't have anything stuck in her teeth.

She needed to stop this *now*. Brianna clicked on the camera icon and unmuted herself. "Hi, Dani."

Dani flinched and pulled back.

Brianna stifled a giggle. "Thanks for joining me."

"Um, were you here all along?" Dani's cheeks reddened, and she put her hand over her mouth.

"No, no, I just..." Brianna started to say. "Yes, I have been."

"Oh, God." Dani lifted her gaze to the ceiling and shook her head. "The whole time?"

Brianna smiled. "If you're asking if I saw the hair fiasco, then the answer would be yes."

"Seriously?" Dani laughed. "I'm just going to crawl under the desk now."

Brianna couldn't help but laugh, too. "It was a classic. I take it you don't use Zoom much."

"What was your first clue? I'm confused, though." Dani narrowed her eyes and intently studied the screen. "You weren't here, it was just an empty black box with your name. I thought it was like a seat, waiting for you to get here."

"Nope, I was here. I just hadn't turned my camera on."

"You can turn your camera on and off? How?"

"There's a little camera icon on the bottom of your screen, or my camera has a flap on it that I can just close."

Dani leaned in and appeared to be searching. She disappeared, reappeared, and disappeared again before coming back on screen. "Wow, cool. But I don't see a flap."

Dani's hand shot out and looked as if it were going to come through the screen. Brianna shrank back and then laughed.

"Oops, sorry," Dani said. "I didn't mean to poke you in the eye."

Brianna laughed again, something she rarely did at work. "It kinda felt like you were going to."

"I don't think I have a flappy thingy." Dani's fingers continued to fill the monitor.

Flappy thingy. Fingers. Stop. She didn't need to react like a twelve-year-old boy and turn this sexual. Dani worked for her, at least for the time being. She put on a professional face. "Are you on a laptop?"

"Yeah, does that make a difference?"

"Yep, most of those don't have a flap. I usually put a Post-it note over my camera."

The screen turned yellow. "Did it work?"

"What you see on the screen is what I see, so, yes, it worked."

"Oh, shit, seriously?"

"Yeah, why?"

The yellow disappeared, and Dani was back on screen with a panicked look. "You mean everyone on the meeting can see me?"

Brianna nodded.

Dani put her hand over her face. "I'm so embarrassed."

"What did you do?"

"I've been taking these online business courses for campground managers. I didn't think they could see me."

"Ah, they probably can't if they're in training mode. Can you see any of the other participants?"

"No."

"Then you're probably safe, but I'd be more careful in the future." She spent the next several minutes giving Dani a lesson on how virtual meetings worked.

"I'm so sorry. I'm sure giving me computer lessons is the last thing you want to do late on a Friday afternoon."

"It's no problem," Brianna said and realized it was true. Dani amused her with her naïve innocence. "But I suppose we should get to the business at hand."

Chapter Five

*D*ani laid out the quotes on her desk before picking up her cellphone.

"Hi, Dani," the now familiar voice said.

Dani smiled. Over the last couple of weeks, she'd begun to look forward to hearing Brianna's voice. "Hey. Is now still a good time?"

"It's perfect. I see you've been busy."

"That I have. What do you think of the quotes?"

Paper rustled on the other end of the line, and Brianna made a humming noise. Dani pictured her poring over the documents. "I didn't realize tractors were so damned expensive."

"Right? Did you get my notes on the various features each one has?"

"Which one is the green one?"

"What?"

"The green one, you know. Which one is green?"

"You are not seriously going to buy a tractor based on its color, are you?"

Brianna laughed. "Had you going, didn't I?"

On more than one occasion, she'd been surprised by Brianna's sense of humor, but now she'd come to expect it. "I personally like the red one."

"Good thing I'm the boss."

"Maybe we could get both, ya know, compromise."

"Absolutely not. Green and red, we'd look like a

Christmas tree farm."

"Fine," Dani said, pretending outrage.

Dani glanced at the clock. They'd been going over business for nearly forty-five minutes, but it seemed like ten. They'd developed such an easy interaction, moving from business to joking and back to business again. These phone calls were the highlight of her day, but she feared the last topic on her agenda would ruin the good spirit.

Dani cleared her throat. "I have one more thing I'd like to discuss with you."

"Why am I not liking the tone of your voice?"

"Uh-oh, now I have a tone?" Dani hoped her teasing would keep things light, so Brianna wouldn't react badly. "Actually, I have more of a request."

"Okay." There was hesitation in Brianna's voice. "What's the request?"

"I know you want to sell Thundering Pines, but I'd like you to consider waiting until the season is over to make your final decision."

"When's the season end again? October?"

"Yep, our tradition is to end it with a Halloween bash. So it would only be a couple months extra."

"Why do you want me to wait?"

Dani considered the best response, but she decided on the simplest. "Because I want time to convince you not to sell."

"I see. What do you think the extra time will do?" Brianna's tone had turned serious.

"I'm not sure," Dani admitted. "I'd like to start by getting you out here. Have you given any more thought to a date?"

"Oh, crap, I'm sorry. Didn't I tell you I'd like to come out next weekend? I already took Friday off, so

I'll have an extra day."

"Really?" Dani sat up straighter, and adrenaline surged through her. It had been nearly a month since Brianna had inherited the campground, and Dani had begun to fear that she would never visit. "That would be perfect."

"I'd wanted to come this weekend, but apparently, Caroline's planned a celebration."

"Sounds fun." *If you like those kinda things.*

"That almost sounded convincing." Brianna laughed. "It'll be okay."

"Now who sounds convincing?"

"Touché." Brianna yawned. "I'd just like to stay in and watch Netflix, but I guess we need to be seen."

Every now and then, Brianna would say something so removed from Dani's world she couldn't relate. Now was one of those times. "Does that mean you won't be able to make the meeting tomorrow?" She was surprised how disappointed she was.

"Why are we having a meeting when opening day is over a month away?" Brianna asked.

"Because the weather is starting to warm up, and the campers are getting restless. They like to come out to the grounds, check out their campers, and get together with the others." How true that was. After a long winter, they all wanted to get outside, including her. "I implemented it about eight years ago."

"I thought you sent out a packet in early February."

Dani snorted. "Yep, I did. It has all the information that I'll give them tomorrow."

"Then why do it?"

"If I didn't, they'd be blowing up my phone. This way, I can tell them all at once. They feel better, and it gets them excited for the new season. It's a win-win."

"Smart."

Sweet. Brianna's compliments felt good. "So you won't be able to make it?"

"It's at ten in the morning, isn't it?"

"Yep."

"The city doesn't come to life until ten at night." Dani could hear the smile in her voice. "I'm looking forward to it."

Dani let out the breath she hadn't realized she was holding. "Good."

"I wouldn't miss it for the world. I want to see you pluck your eyebrows and pick things out of your teeth."

"Huh?" Dani said, and then realization dawned. "Very funny. I only did that the first time. Now I'm a wizard of virtual meetings."

"Okay, wiz. So you've got it all set up."

Dani smiled. "I hired one of the campers' daughters to run it."

"Let me guess, college student?"

"High school," Dani admitted, knowing it would elicit a reaction from Brianna. She loved to make her laugh.

"Priceless." Brianna chuckled.

They talked for another twenty minutes before the persistent ringing of Brianna's office phone ended their call. Once Brianna was gone, Dani kicked back in her chair and closed her eyes, replaying the funny moments from their call.

❧❧❧❧

Brianna moved her laptop back a couple of

inches on her desk. Since she would be the only one on the screen, she didn't want to sit too close. The meeting wasn't set to start for another half hour, but she clicked in now to alleviate Dani's anxiety.

She had already talked to Dani three times this morning. She'd been so cute. Despite her nerves, she'd still had her signature sense of humor. That wasn't quite true. At first, she'd been rigid and jumpy until Brianna was able to tease her out of it. Funny how quickly they'd developed such rapport. At least her dad picked good employees.

Wanting to enjoy the meeting, she shoved her father out of her mind. All thoughts were extinguished when a giant room filled her screen. *Wow!*

It was the first glimpse she was getting of the campground. The meeting was taking place in the clubhouse, where, apparently, the campers sometimes held parties and celebrations. She hadn't expected such a gigantic room. When she'd heard the word campground clubhouse, she thought of a tiny shack in the middle of the woods, but this place was impressive.

She leaned in toward her screen to see better. The room had to be big enough to hold at least two hundred fifty people. The walls looked to be made of logs, but she couldn't tell if they were real or just décor. Two large fireplaces adorned each side of the room, and a bar sat off in one corner. She was still methodically studying the layout when her thoughts were interrupted.

"Hey, Creeper," Dani said. "I know you're there."

Brianna clicked on her camera. "Quick learner. I was just taking in the majesty of the room."

Dani spread out her arms as if gathering it all in. "And it's all yours."

Shit, it is. Why was it still so hard for her to wrap her mind around? "Care to give me a tour?" Her request served two purposes. She wanted to see more of the room, but she also knew it would calm Dani's nerves if she had something to do.

Dani rewarded her with a big smile. "Absolutely. Hey, Debbie, can you follow me with the camera?"

The picture bobbed, and a young voice said, "Certainly."

"Awesome," Dani said. "Debbie, I want to introduce you to Brianna." She pointed at the far wall where Brianna assumed her face was projected. "She's normally not that big and scary."

The camera flipped, and a young blond girl's face appeared, and she waved.

She looks twelve. When had she hit the age where high schoolers looked so young?

"Hi, Debbie. It's nice to meet you." Brianna smiled.

"You too," Debbie said.

The camera switched again, and Dani was back on screen. She looked adorable in her casual clothes, which Brianna assumed was standard campground wear. She had on a flannel shirt and blue jeans, but it was the hiking boots that sealed it. Her hair was pulled up into a ponytail, and Brianna suspected she was wearing a trace of makeup, but on camera, she couldn't be sure.

"Ya ready for the tour?"

"How big am I?" Brianna asked.

"Bigger than the Kardashians," Dani replied quickly.

"Smartass, that's not what I meant. I thought I'd be projected on a fifty-inch screen or something smaller, but looking at this setup, I'm thinking I might be bigger than that."

Dani smirked. "Debbie, do you want to show her?"

The camera swung around, and Brianna gasped. "Holy shit, that looks as big as a movie screen."

"Not quite, but close."

"Donald was a cheapskate. I can't believe he sprung for something like that."

"He didn't. The campers took up a collection and bought it. It's their hangout, so they wanted something nice."

"Nice is an understatement." Brianna leaned in. "Holy fuck, my pores are going to look like canyons."

"I hope you exfoliated," Dani said. "But I'd be more worried that your nose hairs will look like tree trunks."

"Stop." Brianna laughed and put her hand over her face. "I'm going to have to sit twenty feet away from my camera now."

"Stop your complaining. I have a tour to give you."

"Fine, but if I scare away the campers with this scary mug, it's your own fault."

The camera shifted back to Dani. By the look on her face, she wasn't aware that Debbie had switched the view. A slight smile played on her lips, and her eyes were soft. "I think it'll be okay. You're not too hard on the eyes."

"Gee, thanks."

"Oh, shit," Dani said. "What time is it?"

Brianna glanced at the clock. "About a quarter till ten."

"You did that on purpose, didn't you?"

"What?" Brianna asked, genuinely puzzled.

"Kept me distracted, so I wouldn't freak out."

Brianna smiled. "Oh, that."

"Don't give me *oh, that.*" Dani's voice was playful. "The campers have started to arrive."

"You're on then," Brianna said. "I'm gonna turn off my camera until everyone gets there and just sit back and watch."

"Creeper," Dani whispered before turning toward the door. "Agnes and Pete, I'm so glad you could make it."

Brianna watched in awe as Dani greeted the campers. There was no trace of the nervousness from moments ago. As more people streamed in, Brianna couldn't make out the conversations, but that almost made it easier to witness Dani's magic. Everyone who walked in the door greeted Dani with a large smile and a hug. Dani reciprocated and said something that brought on a bigger smile or a laugh before she moved on to the new arrivals.

The camera pulled back, and she was once again viewing the entire room. There must have been nearly a hundred people milling around.

"Can I get everyone to fill the tables near the front of the room?" Dani had to call out a couple more times before she could be heard over the din.

Brianna's gaze shifted to the time in the corner of her screen. *What?* It was nearly ten after ten. How had twenty-five minutes disappeared? She'd been mesmerized watching Dani work the crowd. Apparently, there was more to the small-town girl than she first thought. After what she'd witnessed, she had no doubt that Dani could hold her own in any boardroom in the city. *Impressive.*

❧ ❧ ❧ ❧ ❧

Dani flopped into the chair and groaned. She looked up at Brianna's huge face. *God, she's gorgeous.* Where the hell did that come from? "I need a beer."

"You were perfect," Brianna said. "Let me know if you're ever looking for a job. I'd hire you in a heartbeat."

"I already have a job." Dani grinned. "And I'm already employed by you."

"I mean a real job." Brianna sucked in a breath of air. "Shit, I didn't mean it that way. I know running the campground is a real job. Sorry."

Dani's shoulders relaxed. *And then that mouth.* Every now and then, Brianna's bias still slipped out. Should she respond, or should she just let it go?

"Oh, Dani," Brianna continued. "I don't mean to be offensive."

"But you do it so well," Dani said without thinking.

"Ouch, does that make us even?"

Dani wasn't sure if it was Brianna's extra-large face that made her smile so disarming or if it were Brianna herself. "I'll call it even."

"Seriously, you were amazing with the campers. It's obvious they all adore you. How do you do it?"

"Are you asking me for my trade secret?" Dani winked, but she wasn't sure if Brianna saw it. Debbie had left with the last of the guests, so she was on her own with the technology.

"If you get to see my face the size of King Kong, I should at least be able to see your expressions."

Dani pulled the camera closer. "Better?"

"Much. But don't think you're going to get away with not spilling your trade secret. How do you keep everyone straight?"

"I got the technique from the woman that cuts my hair. I was always amazed at how she remembered little things I told her three months earlier, so one day, I asked her. She pulled out an old ratty notecard box, flipped through it, and handed me a couple notecards that were clipped together." Dani smiled remembering. "The first card had basic information about me and my hair. The rest of the cards had a line for each of my visits with one thing I'd talked about. Cat died. Aunt Helen's kitchen remodel. Flood at the campground. Cubs game."

"I can't believe she showed you."

"I asked," Dani said. *That's how small-town people are.* "Then it became a game. I'd make sure to talk about something ridiculous, just to make my card interesting. I'll have to have her show it to me some day. Alien abduction. Lobotomy. Guinness record for most marshmallows eaten in thirty seconds."

Brianna shook her head, but the smile never left her face. "So you have a large notecard file on all the campers?"

"Yep. That's why I always have them RSVP for an event like this. Then I know which cards to review."

"Brilliant. But you know, they make databases for information like that. Then you could have it in the cloud and be able to access it from your cellphone."

Dani held up her hand. "Whoa! I'm still trying to learn how to use this technology." She picked up the camera, brought it to her face, and pointed it up her nose.

"Gross. Now whose nose hairs look like tree

trunks? And you better get a tissue. There are some boogies way up in there."

Dani laughed and pulled the camera back.

"Do you have a few minutes?" Brianna asked.

"Sure, I've got nowhere else to be. What's up?"

"I realized you probably know a lot more about me than I do you." Brianna smiled. "I'm sure you have a notecard on me at least."

"Several," Dani lied. Judging by her widening smile, Brianna knew it was a joke, too.

"Who are you, Dani Thorton? And where did you come from?"

"Is this a job interview?"

"Could be." Brianna's light brown eyes danced.

Those eyes. They were even more mesmerizing on the large screen. Dani's earlier impression of her as cold didn't match the warmth she saw there.

"It feels like I've been at Thundering Pines my entire life. I guess you could say I grew up here."

"When did you start working for Donald?"

"I was nineteen."

"So you weren't kidding. You did grow up there. You weren't raised in Flower Hills, were you?"

"Nope. My dad and I came to live with my aunt Helen when I was eighteen. We'd been living in North Carolina."

"Who in their right mind would move from North Carolina to Flower Hills, Illinois?"

"My dad got sick."

"Oh, God." Brianna's face dropped. "I am so sorry. I didn't know. I don't mean to pry."

"It's okay." *Wow. I mean it.* Maybe it was seeing Brianna's sympathetic eyes on the giant screen that made her seem more compassionate, but she wanted to tell her story.

Dani took a sip of water before continuing. "He was diagnosed with ALS when I was seventeen. We stayed in North Carolina, so I could finish high school. We probably should have moved sooner because we needed the help, but Dad was a trouper and wanted me to be able to graduate with my class."

"How sweet. I'm assuming..." Brianna stopped, and her lips pursed. "Um, where was your mom?"

"She left us when I was three." That was a story she wasn't going to get into. "But Aunt Helen has been like a mom to me. She's my dad's older sister. She's amazing. She took us both in, which couldn't have been easy. With him being sick and me being a sullen teenager, she had her hands full." Dani took a deep breath. "I still remember the day the doctor gave us the diagnosis. I call it the day my life changed forever. It's permanently etched on my brain. Weird, but it always replays in slow motion when I think about it."

"I can't even imagine how hard that was." Brianna's voice was soft.

She hadn't expected Brianna to be so compassionate. Then again, even though she didn't know all of Brianna's story, from the things she'd heard, Brianna's life hadn't been all sunshine and roses.

"It was. I still feel guilty about my reaction. I locked myself in my bedroom and refused to come out. I was destroyed and had no idea how to cope. Any time he tried to talk to me, I burst into tears and ran from the room. When he needed me most, I acted like a spoiled brat."

"Give yourself a break. You were seventeen. That's a lot for anyone, but especially someone so young."

"That's what Aunt Helen tells me." Dani smiled. "She was so patient with me. I was angry that I had to leave my home in North Carolina and even more angry that my dad was sick."

"Hence the sullen teenager comment?"

"Yep. I didn't know Aunt Helen all that well. We tried to visit her once a year for the holidays, but that's different than seeing someone on a regular basis. In a way, she nursed us both."

"How long, um…? How long did he…? Um…" Brianna struggled to get her words out.

"How long did he live?" Dani asked.

"Yes."

"Four years, three months, and ten days," Dani answered without having to stop and think. "It was the longest four years of my life and the shortest."

"That's an interesting way to explain it, but I think I understand what you mean." Brianna's eyes looked as if they were misty.

"I watched him get weaker and weaker, and his decline seemed to go on forever. Four years watching someone suffer can seem like a lifetime."

"Why the shortest then?" Brianna asked.

"Because in a blink of an eye, he was gone." Dani angrily wiped away a tear that escaped down her cheek. "It's been thirteen years, you wouldn't think I'd still do this. I don't like losing control."

"It's okay. I'm sorry I brought up such painful memories. Besides, I don't think one tear can be labeled as losing control."

"Thanks." *Odd.* Had she started to consider Brianna a friend? *Maybe.* She didn't normally open up to people so quickly, but they had been talking almost daily for a while. *Interesting.* She looked at the screen for several beats before continuing. "I haven't shared that story in a long time. When it was happening, the locals and campers were always wanting updates, so I feel like I've told it a million times. I guess I got good at telling the facts but learned how to keep the emotions out of it, or I would have been a blubbering wreck the entire time."

Brianna brushed back her hair and bit her lip. "For the record, that tear doesn't qualify you for blubbering wreck status. But I feel bad that I brought up something so painful."

I need to lighten the mood. It was hard enough having conversations like this in person, but virtually made it seem more awkward. Dani grinned and held her arms up to the big screen in front of her. "How could I not want to share? Nothing says comforting like a twenty-foot *face.* I thought I was talking to the Wizard of Oz."

"Not God?" Brianna feigned shock.

The tension broke, and they both burst out laughing.

"Oh, crap," Brianna said. "What time is it?"

Dani glanced at her watch. *Shit!* "It's almost twelve thirty."

"Caroline just got home. I was supposed to pick up the dry cleaning for tonight. Oops."

"Uh-oh, I better let you get to it." Dani couldn't believe they'd been talking so long. She could have sworn it had only been twenty minutes, but all the campers had been gone by quarter after eleven, so it'd been over an hour.

"Yeah, I need to look sharp tonight. And..." Brianna paused. Dani was getting used to seeing Brianna's playful face on the big screen, but a more serious look took its place. "I just wanted to say, I've really enjoyed talking to you."

"Same here," Dani said, realizing how much she meant it. "Have fun tonight."

"Thanks. I'm looking forward to coming out next weekend."

"Me too. Do you mind if I call you this week?" Dani looked away from the camera and forged on. "Or I can just wait until next weekend when you're here."

"I'd like that," Brianna answered.

Dani tried not to show her disappointment. "Okay."

"No, I mean I'd like it if you called. That is, if you had something you needed to talk to me about," Brianna said in a rush.

"Apparently, I'm setting up a new database, so I'll probably need some technical assistance."

"Nice. I'm pretty sure I can help out."

Dani heard Brianna's name being called. "Sounds like you're needed."

"Yep, I'll talk to you later. Have a great weekend."

"You too." Dani watched the screen until Brianna's face disappeared.

Chapter Six

Dani threw down her pencil and pushed her hair behind her ear. She'd been at the books for several hours and couldn't get the account to balance. Even though she knew it was ridiculous spending so much time looking for a twenty-cent error, she hated it when things didn't add up. Logically, she knew taking a break would do her good, but her stubborn streak kicked in. She kept thinking a couple more minutes and she would find it, but she had been saying that for over two hours now.

What is wrong with me? It was Saturday night, and here she sat in her office at Thundering Pines poring over the books. Brianna was probably getting ready to head out on the town. Clubbing in Chicago had never sounded like fun to her. She wasn't much for bars, but a bar in the city seemed like pure torture.

Interesting. She wasn't sure why Brianna came to mind. The meeting with the campers had gone well, and she'd enjoyed talking with Brianna afterward. She was starting to have hope that maybe they could work together and, more importantly, that she could convince Brianna not to sell.

Maybe she should live a little and head into Flower Hills to the Spotted Owl. She smiled to herself. *Sure I will. Who am I fooling?* There was no one at the Spotted Owl that she wanted to see; she was much more comfortable here in her sanctuary. Besides, she'd had more than enough socializing at the meeting with the campers.

Even though it was still cold outside, she'd cracked the window to let the fresh air in. She could smell the damp earth from the melting snow and knew it wouldn't be long before spring would come. Would this be her last spring at Thundering Pines? She couldn't think that way. *Brianna will come through.*

The pompous city girl she'd met at Thomas's office was fading. Their easy banter came almost immediately, but it was the depth of their conversations that surprised her. She had no idea how large chunks of time disappeared when they talked, but it had happened too frequently to be an anomaly.

She picked up her pencil and stared at the ledger in front of her without really seeing it. *This could work out.* Maybe she wouldn't have to leave Thundering Pines after all. Brianna was already proving to be much different to work for than her father. Brianna was logical and weighed everything whenever they talked while Donald had always done everything he could to cut corners and save a buck. It had worked well for him over the years since he'd amassed a lot of money, but now Thundering Pines was starting to show the effects of his penny pinching. Dani had done much of the work herself to keep the place up, but to fix the years of neglect, Brianna needed to put significant money into the campground.

As soon as she found that damned twenty cents, she'd work on the proposal outlining the work that needed to be done. She needed to have it ready for when Brianna came out next week unless she died of starvation looking for her error.

One more time. She printed out a fresh copy of

the register and statement, so she would have a clean slate and began the process all over.

After only a few minutes, a heavy pounding jolted her out of her thoughts.

What the hell was that? It seemed to be coming from the front of the building.

She got up from her desk and made her way through the store. It was closed for the season, so the shelves were nearly bare. Who in the hell was pounding on the door at nine o'clock on a Saturday night? A small silhouette stood outside. If she lived in the city, she would probably be more cautious, but in Flower Hills, she wasn't too concerned.

Dani flung open the door and was almost hit by a fist that was raised to pound on the door once again. "Jesus, what the hell are you doing?"

"Oh, fuck, sorry," Shelby said, lowering her hand.

She was dressed in a tight, low-cut blouse that left little to the imagination, and her jeans appeared to be painted on. Dani searched her face, trying to find a resemblance to her half sister. They would have had the same shade of dark brown hair had Shelby not dyed her hair a brassy red. Both had brown eyes, but Shelby's were a shade darker.

Dani was reluctant to admit that both were pretty in their own right. Shelby's attractiveness was ruined by her overdone makeup and overt sexuality while Brianna's had been muted by her rigidity. *Hmm.* Had been? Dani didn't have time to analyze her thoughts with Shelby standing in front of her.

"What do you want?" Dani didn't try to hide her irritation. The last thing she wanted to deal with was Shelby's drama, again.

"Can I come in?"

"What for?"

"I need to talk to you." When Dani didn't move to let her in, Shelby said, "Please."

"Fine." Dani stepped back to let Shelby pass.

Shelby staggered as she entered, and the smell of alcohol wafted in with her. It seemed not to be just on her breath, but oozing from her pores.

Great, wasn't it too early to be drunk? A sober Shelby was enough of a handful, but a drunken Shelby was even more unpredictable. Tonight, Dani didn't have the patience to ride Shelby's roller coaster of emotions. Crying. Laughing. Back to crying.

Dani sighed. It was too late now that she'd opened the door. If she tried to get Shelby to leave, it would no doubt trigger a tirade.

"Come on back to the office. Would you like a pop or water?"

"Ya got anything stronger?" Shelby put her arm around Dani and pulled her closer, rubbing her breast against Dani's side.

Holy shit! The whiskey stench was enough to get Dani drunk. "'Fraid not." She wiggled out from under Shelby's arm.

"I'll take a Coke then."

"Go ahead into the office. I have to go to the storage room." Dani watched Shelby weave her way toward the back before turning away. She so didn't need this tonight.

When Dani returned, her confidence that she could get Shelby in and out quickly dwindled. Shelby had already made herself at home. She'd tossed her shoes off and sat on the couch with her feet under her, wrapped in the blanket that was normally draped over the back of the couch.

Dani handed Shelby her soda and deliberately sat on the opposite end.

Shelby patted the cushion next to her. "I don't bite," Shelby said with a drunken drawl and a large smile. She giggled. "Unless you want me to."

"What is it you want?" Dani said guardedly.

"Oh, I get it. We are going to be formal, is that it, Ms. Thorton?"

"Cut the shit. What do you want?" Dani wanted this conversation to be over, so she could get back to her numbers.

"For you to stop treating me like a stranger. Would it hurt you to sit down here?" Shelby patted the couch again.

Dani's jaw tightened. "It's not going to happen."

Shelby laughed. "Lighten up, Dani. If anyone should have an attitude here, it should be me."

"Really?"

"Yes, really. I'm not the one that took a million dollars from you."

"Is that what this is about?" Dani relaxed. She was prepared to deal with Shelby's ire, but she didn't want to get put in the middle of the feud between her and Brianna. "I had no clue he was going to do that."

"I believe you. Cold bastard."

"I'm sorry."

"I actually believe you are." Shelby's eyes glistened with unshed tears.

"What can I do for you?" Dani asked. Even though she wasn't up for dealing with Shelby, she felt sorry for her. Underneath the rough exterior, the heavy makeup, and anger, there was a damaged little girl. Despite her sympathy, Dani knew better than to allow herself to be drawn in again. She'd watched for years as Shelby did everything she could to get her father's attention. When doing something to make him proud didn't work, she'd gone the opposite direction and rebelled. Apparently, negative attention was better than no attention, and Shelby had gotten a lot of that. But she knew too much kindness would give Shelby the wrong idea, so she remained guarded.

"That was the final fuck you from the fucker, wasn't it?"

"What was?"

"Not letting me have Thundering Pines."

Dani wrestled with a response. Over the last couple of weeks, she'd thought a lot about why Donald had given the campground to Brianna, knowing that Shelby wanted it more than anything. It was yet another move in the sick father-and-daughter dance that Dani had witnessed for years. Donald's final attempt to control his children from the grave. *Sad.*

Dani decided her best bet was the truth. "I don't know. He didn't tell me anything. I was as shocked as you."

"Did he hate me?" Shelby was no longer able to hold back the tears that welled in her eyes.

Dani shifted in her seat, wanting out of this conversation. "I don't know what he felt." She wanted to throw a bone at Shelby but had none. "I worked for him, that's all. It wasn't like we had a personal relationship."

"Yet he left you a million dollars."

"I know. I wouldn't believe me, either, but our relationship was all about the business."

"He never told you about the golden child?" Shelby sneered.

Dani wanted to lie but instead said, "Yes, he did

tell me about her."

"So it wasn't all business then?"

"No, I guess not. I think he talked about her to me more because I didn't know her."

Shelby snorted. "Figures. I'm sure you heard everything about the successful daughter that made him so fucking proud. Not the one that was a big disappointment."

"I'm sorry." Dani responded without truly answering, but the meaning was clear. Shelby was right, she'd heard about Brianna for years. Donald raved about his successful daughter who graduated magna cum laude from Northwestern University. She wasn't sure where he got his information, but he seemed to know Brianna's every move.

Shelby opened her mouth, but no words came out. Instead, tears streamed down her face. Without the angry sneer, it was easy to see her beauty. Her dark eyes looked blacker because of the heavy mascara. Shelby's straight white teeth made her smile her best feature, but she was not one to smile easily. Her hair was overworked with too much product. When left alone, it had a slight wave that gracefully framed her face. Dani wondered what Shelby saw in the mirror and why she masked her natural good looks.

"I'm sorry." Dani didn't know what else to say. She fought her instinct to go to Shelby and offer comfort. She wasn't going to make that mistake again. Instead, she sat quietly, waiting for Shelby to react.

"Are you going to help me?" Shelby asked after several minutes of silently crying.

"Help you how?" Dani asked suspiciously.

"Let's bring that bitch down."

Yep, this was the Shelby she'd been waiting for.

She figured it would take a little longer for the switch to flip, but Dani felt on firmer ground dealing with her like this. It made Dani nervous when faced with the sympathetic version of Shelby. "I'm not getting in the middle of this."

"Why?"

"It's not my battle to fight."

"You'd rather work for Miss Thing than me?"

"That's not what I said." It was true, but Dani had no intention of telling Shelby. She knew she was walking through a minefield and had to work her way through this conversation carefully. "I have no choice in the matter. Your father made the decision."

"Bullshit!" Shelby's eyes narrowed. It felt as if Shelby's gaze was boring into her soul, so she shifted in her seat. "What the fuck? You like her, don't you?"

"I don't even know her," Dani said, trying to deflect the conversation.

"Have you talked to her since Dunhurst's office?"

"Well, yeah, the campground will need to open soon."

"Son of a bitch, you do like her." Shelby sprang from the couch. "The one person I thought I could trust has chosen the enemy."

"Cut the drama. I haven't chosen anyone. She's my boss, so I have to talk to her about campground business."

"Like you only talked to my father about the campground?" Shelby stood over Dani and glared down at her. "Oh, but that's right, you had extensive talks with him about the golden child."

"It's not like that. You're just pissed and trying to take it out on me." Dani rose from the couch. Shelby didn't step back, so Dani was forced to push past her.

"Oh, you will never know how pissed I am." Shelby shoved Dani in the back. "Or maybe you will."

"Don't threaten me," Dani said warily. She continued across the room, ignoring Shelby's shove. She sat on the corner of her desk and measured her words. "Let's not do this again."

"Fuck you, Dani. I'm outta here."

"No, you've been drinking. Let me drive you home. We can talk about this after you get some sleep."

"Fine." Shelby looked at the ground sheepishly.

That was almost too easy. "Thank you. I'll go get my coat and keys."

⁂

When Dani returned to the office, Shelby was gone. She walked into the store, but Shelby wasn't there, either. She peered out the door into the night; Shelby's vehicle was no longer parked outside.

"Damn it." Dani turned away. There was no sense chasing Shelby.

Dani went back to her desk and picked up the statement. In less than five minutes, she smiled when she saw the sixty-cent entry that should have been forty. Her twenty cents were found, but now the victory felt hollow.

Chapter Seven

Brianna held open the door for Caroline. When they entered, a blast of warm air hit them.

Only a handful of people lingered around the bar. At ten p.m., it was still early, which suited her fine. It would give her time to settle in before the crush hit and women stood shoulder to shoulder.

The dance floor was empty. Soon, it would be pulsing with sexual energy as couples came together, as well as strangers. For her, the ritual was unnerving, so she avoided dancing here, even though it was something she had once enjoyed.

The only thing she liked about the club was the splendor of the décor, but it would soon be masked by the swarming crowd. The predominate color was silver that shone like polished chrome with the accent trim in matte black. A few mirrors were interspersed, which gave a startling contrast to the distorted images reflected off the chrome. The old-school disco ball spun over the dance floor, sending flashes of light in all directions, creating an epileptic nightmare.

The music was loud. The bass reverberated off the walls and pounded in her chest. Brianna smiled at Caroline, who let the music wash over her. Caroline half danced and half walked to the bar, her long arms raised in the air as she seductively swayed from side to side. It was rare for the conservative Caroline to let down her hair, so Brianna certainly wasn't going to complain.

She followed Caroline and moved her hips awkwardly, hoping nobody noticed her discomfort. Out of the corner of her eye, she glanced at the few people standing around. She was relieved not to recognize anyone she passed.

"Doesn't look like anyone is here yet," Brianna said loudly when she arrived at the bar.

"I ordered you a rum and Coke," Caroline answered. "You need to let loose and relax tonight. They're in the loft."

God, it was loud. Couldn't they turn down the music until it filled up? "What?" Brianna shouted over the music.

"I ordered you a rum and Coke."

"I heard that. Who's in the loft?"

"The whole crew. Didn't I tell you we rented the loft for tonight?"

"Who rented it?" Brianna cupped her hand over her ear.

Caroline leaned in. "We did, you and me. We can actually hear each other up there."

What the fuck was Caroline thinking? "Are you kidding me? The whole thing?"

"Of course the whole thing. There's nothing worse than having to share it with strangers." Caroline danced seductively against Brianna's side. "Besides, if I want to make partner and you want to get that promotion, we need to schmooze the right people."

Image is everything. They'd always been the power couple, so why did it feel hollow now? Her trip back to Flower Hills must be messing with her brain. They'd vowed they'd meet their goal by forty, which was only a couple of years off. She needed to focus. "It must have cost a small fortune."

"What do you care? You're a millionaire now." Caroline ground her hips against Brianna and put her lips next to Brianna's ear. "Tonight, you are going to show me a good time."

Before Brianna could answer, their drinks arrived. It wasn't lost on Brianna that the bartender liked what she saw, and her hand lingered as she took the money from Caroline. Apparently, Caroline noticed, as well, because she ran her tongue over her bright red lips and gave her a provocative smile. "Keep the change."

The bartender leaned in and said something to Caroline, but Brianna couldn't make out her words.

Caroline tilted her head back and laughed, exposing her long slender neck.

Brianna was used to the way people reacted to Caroline's beauty, so she'd learned to take it in stride. The flirtation was certainly nothing of concern to her, so she smiled and took Caroline's hand. "Our friends are waiting for us."

Caroline winked at the bartender and allowed Brianna to lead her away.

They were still holding hands when they entered the loft. Before she could get her bearings and determine who was there, a loud scream pierced the air.

"Caroline," Kylie yelled as she ran across the room and wrapped Caroline in a bear hug. "I thought you would never get here."

"You are such a drama queen." Caroline smiled and hugged her back.

"Oh, hi, Brianna," Kylie said over Caroline's

shoulder, feigning indifference while still hugging Caroline.

If only all Caroline's friends were like Kylie. Not only was she the best of the bunch, but she brought out something in Caroline that no one else did. Brianna chuckled and wrapped her arms around both women. "Great to see you, too, Kylie."

"Come on, girls." Kylie took their hands. "Drew's already at the table."

Ugh, not the most uninteresting woman in the world. Brianna thought they'd broken up, but apparently, they were back on again. She'd never understand what someone as dynamic as Kylie saw in Drew, other than her model looks. It was almost as if Kylie didn't want to find a real relationship.

"Looks like we've got that one." Caroline pointed at the large table that overlooked the dance floor.

A large sign in the middle said reserved. *At least we got a prime spot for our money.* It took them nearly fifteen minutes to reach the table as they were greeted with hugs and air kisses along the way. Apparently, everyone wanted to be seen here because the loft was already filling up. There were more people crammed into this space than in the club below.

Brianna slid into a chair near the railing, already drained from their trek to the table. Caroline was in her element and seemed to draw energy from the attention. It was what they had dreamed of since they got together. Nearly all their conversations revolved around how they'd take the city by storm or sex.

When can we go home? She wasn't sure when this had become old. *Power couple.* They'd been working their plan for years, so why had it begun to feel hollow?

Once seated, Caroline pulled her chair close to Brianna's and lightly rubbed her fingertips over the back of Brianna's hand.

A waitress appeared out of nowhere and asked them if they needed anything.

Caroline ordered another martini while Brianna declined since she'd only taken a couple sips of her rum and Coke.

Brianna leaned over and whispered in Caroline's ear. "At least we're getting good service for two hundred fifty dollars an hour."

Caroline swirled around the last liquid in the bottom of her martini glass. "It's in your best interest to keep me in martinis." She slowly drew her finger up Brianna's arm.

Brianna flinched at the electricity that traveled through her. "Don't think I didn't notice what you're drinking." She smirked.

Caroline continued caressing Brianna's arm, drawing tiny circles with her finger. "It's been a rough couple of weeks. You haven't been right since we went to that Podunk town of yours, so I thought you could probably use a little release."

"You need liquid encouragement to have sex with me?" Brianna teased.

"Nope, I just want to ensure you aren't disappointed. It might take a while to work out all your stress." Caroline seductively licked her lips.

Brianna smiled. No doubt, martinis revved Caroline up. Caroline rarely drank them, but when she did, Brianna knew she was in for a wild evening.

Caroline put her hand on Brianna's thigh. "Honey, keep plying me with drinks, and I might have to do something about it right here."

"Hey, you two, get a room," Drew said. "But before you do, we want to hear all about Hicksville."

"It's Flower Hills." Brianna shot a look at Caroline. "Would you please stop telling everyone my hometown's name is Hicksville?"

"That's what it should be called." Caroline rolled her eyes. "You guys should see this place. I felt like I was in the backwoods of Tennessee. I was just waiting for the banjos to start playing."

The women sitting around the table laughed as Caroline began her monologue about their trip.

Brianna tried to keep her expression neutral. Most of the faces around the table she knew well, but there were a few she'd only met at Caroline's office parties. It was bad enough their friends were hearing the story, but she cringed that Caroline's colleagues were.

"And the people were even worse," Caroline said after she finished her description of the town.

"Tell us about the mountain girl and the train wreck," someone called out.

"Apparently, you've been talking?" Brianna said, barely moving her lips.

"It made for a great lunchtime story at the office." Caroline brushed off Brianna's ire with a wave of her hand. "Where should I start?"

"Start with the train wreck," one of their friends said.

"You mean my sister?" Brianna said through clenched teeth.

"Oh, for fuck's sake, she's just your half sister. I'll stop talking if you can honestly tell everyone here that she's not a train wreck." Caroline stared at Brianna until Brianna looked down at the table.

"Where was I?" Caroline resumed her story, finishing with a flourish as she described Shelby's dramatic exit from Dunhurst's office.

"Wow, that's the kinda shit you see in the movies," Drew said. "And she's your sister?"

"Half." Nobody seemed to notice her irritation or simply didn't care. Brianna sighed; it wasn't worth ruining the evening over. "I haven't seen her in years. We didn't grow up together. She was from my dad's other family."

"Divorce can be so ugly." Kylie placed her hand over Brianna's. Her eyes were warm and sympathetic. "You know my dad left us, too, and remarried within a year. It was like me and my brother didn't exist after he had his second set of kids." She raised her glass. "Fuck him and fuck your dad."

Brianna looked into Kylie's eyes and raised her glass. "Fuck 'em."

"That's the spirit." Kylie squeezed her hand. "Let's leave Brianna's family be and talk about something else."

"Oh, my God, the mountain woman was the worst," Caroline said.

Brianna wanted to shout, "Let it go," but didn't. Ever since Dani's so-called slight, Caroline had been merciless. She knew she should keep her mouth shut. If she antagonized Caroline, it would only make her more relentless.

"She wasn't that bad." *Wrong thing to say.* She knew it as soon as she saw the look that crossed Caroline's face.

"Stop defending your girlfriend." Caroline thrust out her hand and turned away from Brianna. "I swear since the reading of the will, Brianna talks to her like five times a day."

"I've got a campground to open," Brianna said. "Oh, God, I never thought I would hear those words come out of my mouth. What have I become?"

Everyone laughed, and Brianna shook her head. At least the laughter seemed to neutralize Caroline.

"I should be jealous, but it's pretty hard to feel threatened by someone that looks like Danielle. I'm fairly sure the outfit she wore came from JCPenney about fifteen years ago."

"Seriously? She wore a sweater and a pair of black slacks. How can you say that's dated?"

"Hmm," Drew said. "I don't know, Caroline, maybe you should be worried since your woman recalls exactly what the mountain woman was wearing."

"Right." Caroline made an exaggerated shrug. "Honey, did you see the pattern on that sweater and the pleats on those pants?"

"I didn't notice."

"For a gorgeous woman, you have no fashion sense. Good thing I dress you." Caroline kissed Brianna on the cheek.

She wasn't sure if it was the martinis or their friends that put Caroline in a better mood, but she'd take it. "I'm going to focus on the gorgeous part and ignore the rest." Brianna smiled. She noticed that Caroline's drink was nearly empty and waved the waitress over.

Once the drinks were ordered, Caroline resumed her onslaught. "And her hair, I think that was the worst."

"She has pretty hair. Now you're just being mean."

"If you're into skunk hair," Caroline said.

"What the hell is skunk hair?"

Caroline ignored Brianna's question. "They make dye, you know? There's really no reason for someone to walk around looking like that. And I can guarantee nobody would put those ugly gray streaks in on purpose."

"Can we talk about something else?" The conversation made Brianna edgy. She'd been in contact with Dani daily, and talking behind her back like this made Brianna uncomfortable.

Kylie grabbed a knife off the appetizer platter and hit it against the side of her bottle.

Brianna cringed. If she hit it any harder, it was likely to shatter, but she did appreciate Kylie's attempt at distraction.

"Come on, we're here to celebrate, not roast Brianna," Kylie said.

"Fine. I thought it might do Brianna some good to see it through the eyes of her friends," Caroline said.

The conversation felt wrong. Mean spirited. Brianna's jaw clenched. "What are you getting at?"

"You're here in civilization, with real people, successful people, not the backwards crap you came from."

"I left Flower Hills when I was ten. You act like I'm going to become one of them if I spend any time there." *It might be more fun than here.* Where in the hell had that come from?

"What's that lyric from *Rent* about taking the girl out of Hicksville?" Drew said.

"Not helping." Kylie shot Drew a look. "Caroline, you said you wanted Brianna to have a good time tonight, but by the looks of it, she isn't." She shifted her attention to Brianna. "She knows how stressful it's been for you, that's why she got everyone together tonight."

"It's true." Caroline flashed her an innocent smile.

"I know, thank you, Caroline. And thank you, too." Brianna put her arm around Kylie, thankful that Kylie always knew how to defuse any situation. "I just want to get this all settled, so I never have to go back to that hellhole again. Too many shit memories." That was what she wanted, right?

"It's settled then, no more talk of the shithole for the rest of the night, or there will be hell to pay." Kylie raised her glass.

Everyone toasted to the end of the conversation.

Brianna sighed and sat back in her chair. *Only a few more hours.*

❧❧❧❧❧

After another round of drinks and a heated political debate, Caroline put her hand on Brianna's arm and smiled impishly. "Are you gonna dance with me tonight?"

"I'm gonna leave the dancing to you and Kylie. I don't have it in me." *Nor enough alcohol.*

"Suit yourself. Are you at least going to watch?" Caroline whispered into her ear, her lips brushing Brianna's earlobe.

Brianna shivered. Caroline knew her ears were almost as sensitive as her nipples. "Why is it when you drink martinis you can make anything sound sexual?"

"I doubt you'll be complaining about it when we get home." Caroline winked before she grabbed Kylie by the arm. "Come on, girl, we have some dancing to do."

Kylie jumped up, not asking if Drew wanted to join them.

Great, alone with Drew, should be fun—not!

At least tonight they had something to talk about. Brianna was leaning toward honoring Dani's request to wait until the end of the season to put the campground up for sale, but she doubted she'd keep it. She could at least plan for afterward.

"Do you think your firm could sell a campground?" Brianna asked.

"Sure, we cover the entire state. We've got plenty of rural agents."

"I can't sell yet because of the will, but I'd like to be ready to roll when the time comes."

"I can take care of it." Drew pulled out her cellphone and began typing. "I'll just need to get some information from you."

"Seriously? Thanks." Guilt washed over Brianna. Maybe Drew wasn't that bad. "What do you need to know?"

They'd been discussing real estate for too long, and Brianna's eyes were beginning to glaze over. She glanced around for a diversion and spotted Caroline and Kylie on the dance floor. They appeared to be the leaders of a conga line. Their hands were raised over their heads, and they shook them. *Jazz hands.* Then they brought their arms down and flapped them like eagle wings before they thrust their hands over their heads again. Each new gesture was more exaggerated than the last. Brianna swore she could hear their laughter from the loft, which was impossible with the driving music.

Brianna pointed over the rail. "Look at those two. I swear they act like grade school kids when they're together."

"Looks like Kylie's cutting loose. If her hair is any indication, she's having a blast." Kylie's wiry mop of hair looked more out of control than ever. Kylie was the most animated person Brianna knew, and the more she talked, the more she ran her hands through her hair until it splayed out in all directions. Obviously, she'd been doing it while she danced.

"It's the worst when my parents stop by and think we've been rolling around in bed in the middle of the day."

Did Drew just make a joke? She didn't think she had it in her. "Bozo hair and sex hair have a lot in common." Brianna looked around, hoping no one overheard. She didn't want anyone to think she was being mean. Bozo hair was a term Kylie had coined long ago.

"But Caroline doesn't have a hair out of place." Drew gestured toward the floor. "You've got one gorgeous woman on your hands."

Brianna frowned, not sure how to answer. "I think we've both found ourselves beautiful women."

Drew waved her hand. "Would be if she lost a few pounds."

Seriously? Sure, Kylie was constantly trying to shed twenty-five pounds, the same ones she'd been trying to lose since college, but when she flashed her dimpled smile and pulled someone in with her expressive green eyes, nobody even thought of it. "I think she's perfect just the way she is."

Drew shrugged, and Brianna wanted to slap her. *Relax.* Starting something with Drew wouldn't be prudent. The best course of action was to change the subject. Brianna chuckled. "What kind of dance moves are those two doing now?"

"It looks like a combination between the chicken dance, the Macarena, and the electric slide." Drew shook her head. "How do you live with someone like that?"

Brianna's jaw clenched. She hoped she could keep the bite from her voice. "Like what?"

"Somebody that's always having fun and goofing around. Acting like that." Drew gestured as Caroline dipped Kylie and nearly dumped her onto the floor. "Dating Kylie is fun, but I'm not sure I could ever live with her."

Wow! Did Drew just call Caroline fun? Brianna hoped her reaction didn't show on her face. Was Drew on drugs? Drew was staring at her; she needed to answer. "Um, well she…um, she has her serious side."

As she spoke, realization dawned. Drew had only seen Caroline when she was around Kylie. There was no doubt that Kylie was the only one who brought out her playful side. Caroline wouldn't be caught dead being silly on the dance floor with Brianna.

Brianna felt a pang in her chest and chastised herself. *Really?* They didn't need to have frivolous fun to have a good relationship. It was fine the way it was. She glanced around the loft. Look what they'd built together. Some of the most successful women in the city were here tonight at their party. It was what they'd worked for. The power couple had arrived, so why did she feel so empty? *Damn it.* She must just be exhausted from dealing with Donald's crap. Once it was over, she'd feel more like herself.

"I suppose Kylie has a serious side, too." Drew

stared at her.

Shit. She'd missed whatever Drew said before that. "Yeah." Brianna nodded.

"Anyway, as I was saying, the suburban housing market has really changed over the past decade…"

Brianna sighed. It was going to be a long night.

Chapter Eight

It was still too cold to take the top off her Jeep, but it wouldn't be much longer. Brianna cruised down I-55 without having to fight the traffic. Her decision to wait until after rush hour was a good one.

Whenever Chicago got too confining, she popped the top off and headed west out of the city. She could drive for hours, letting the wind rush through her hair and the sunshine heal her. At least now she'd have a destination and a place to wear her Jeep clothes, as Caroline called them. She pushed up the sleeve of her flannel shirt, letting the sun warm her arm. She thought she looked cute in her Jeep clothes, but she didn't have much occasion to wear them in the city.

The trip to Flower Hills should take her about three hours. Dani expected her by noon, which gave Brianna plenty of time even if she decided to stop and stretch her legs. She listened to Garth Brooks's greatest hits and felt nostalgic. She chuckled to herself. Caroline would hate her music choice and accuse her of infusing the country back into her bloodstream.

She wouldn't have admitted it to anyone, but she'd been nervous the last couple of days. Today, she would visit Thundering Pines, her campground. It still sounded strange to her ears, so she couldn't blame her friends when they laughed every time the topic came up, but the redneck jokes had worn thin.

Last weekend, after Caroline had come off the dance floor, she'd insisted they mingle. It was good for their careers, but Caroline hadn't been happy when the conversation turned to the campground. She saw it as an embarrassment, certainly not a good way to get ahead. Even though the business grossed well over two million dollars a year, everyone Brianna talked to saw it as a quaint country thing.

She turned up the music, not wanting to think about anything but the wind rushing in through the windows. Today, she planned on returning to Flower Hills on her own terms.

⁂

The butterflies that danced in Dani's stomach surprised her. They'd been there since she'd woken up this morning and had only gotten worse. She caught herself looking at the clock for what must have been the tenth time. *Stop.* Brianna was probably at least an hour out.

Focus. There should be enough time for her to run through the books one last time and review the itinerary she'd created. A lot of ground needed to be covered the next three days. Between bankers, lawyers, and contractors, they had a full plate, but Dani also wanted to give Brianna time to enjoy the grounds and get reacquainted with Flower Hills.

Aunt Helen cautioned her against overthinking and reminded her Brianna was just a person, not royalty. Funny how her perceptions had changed. A month ago, she would have called Brianna a princess. Someone who thought she deserved to be put on a pedestal, but now Dani had to admit she was giving

Brianna the majestic treatment because she wanted to make her feel welcome.

After shuffling the same papers for the third time without really seeing them, she gave up. She left her office and busied herself with unpacking the boxes that had arrived yesterday afternoon. The store shelves were starting to fill up now that camping season was approaching. She usually waited a few more weeks to order supplies, but she hadn't wanted Brianna to see a completely empty store.

Truth be told, she was nervous and needed to do something with her pent-up energy. Brianna texted nearly half an hour ago saying she was stopping for gas and would be there soon. *Why the hell am I so jittery?* Sure, she wanted to impress the boss, but it was more than that.

Their phone conversations, which started out strictly business, had recently turned more friendly. While she had plenty of friends, she wasn't one to share her innermost thoughts with anyone, except maybe Aunt Helen. She'd been surprised by some of the stories that easily spilled out of her mouth when talking to Brianna. Probably because she wasn't a local. *Made it easier.*

She'd just finished breaking down the last box and searched for something else to do when a car door slammed. She straightened her shirt, brushed off her jeans, and adjusted the tie in her hair. She was a few feet from the door when it swung open.

Dani hoped the surprise didn't show on her face when Brianna walked through. There was no mistaking it was Brianna due to her nearly six-foot height, but in all other ways, she didn't resemble the uptight woman she'd met at Thomas's office. She wore blue jeans and a red and black flannel shirt; her heels had been replaced by a pair of Columbia hiking boots. Her dark brown hair fell loosely over her shoulders, instead of being pulled back. She wore little makeup, but her thin eyeliner made her light brown eyes pop. The look suited her. Dani quickly pushed it from her mind.

"Brianna," Dani said with a genuine smile. Brianna's complete change in looks was throwing her off, and the witty opening she'd prepared was suddenly forgotten, so she settled on polite small talk. "How was the drive?"

"Can't complain." Brianna returned the smile. "I couldn't have asked for a more beautiful day."

"Weather forecast is calling for three days of beautiful, just for you."

"You must have connections."

"Yep, nothing but sunshine every day here at Thundering Pines."

"I think we should use that on our marketing material."

"Sure thing." Dani laughed. "What's a little false advertisement if we can draw in more campers?"

"Exactly."

"So should we get down to work?" Dani never cared much for small talk, but she hoped she didn't come off too abrupt. She studied Brianna but didn't detect a negative reaction.

"Lead the way."

"I hope you don't mind my office. It isn't much, but I like it."

❧❧❧❧❧

"Wow, I'm not sure I can put much more information in this tiny brain of mine." Brianna closed the last file and sat back in her chair. Who knew a campground could be so complex? She wasn't easily impressed, but Dani's grasp of the business was notable. Almost immediately, they'd fallen into a good working rhythm as if they'd been doing it for years. "How long have we been at it, anyway?"

"Holy shit. It's after three," Dani said.

"Oh, no." Brianna intentionally widened her eyes and gasped. She frantically grabbed the file to the left of her and rifled through the papers. "We've missed three things on our itinerary already."

"Very funny, jerk." Dani swatted at the folder.

Brianna clutched it to her chest. "Back, brute. I will not relinquish the sacred itinerary." When they had started working, Dani presented a detailed agenda for the entire weekend, and Brianna had been teasing her about it since. Brianna laughed and dropped the papers to the desk. "So, boss, what's next on our agenda?" Brianna asked.

"Whoa, I thought you were the boss."

"Oh, crap, I am. I think there's a memo about that around here somewhere." Brianna pretended to shuffle through the piles of scattered folders.

"Are you trying to insinuate that I might be a touch overprepared?"

Brianna put her thumb and forefinger close together. "Maybe just a tad. Hmm, what is the word for that?" She pretended to be deep in thought. "Anal."

"Fine. What's next on your unwritten, haphazard agenda?"

"I'm starving. Let's get something to eat."

"I can get you a bag of chips from the front if

you'd like. But I am not feeding you."

"Why not?" Brianna whined.

"You may be my boss, but I am much more afraid of Aunt Helen. Even my dad was afraid of her when it came to mealtime." Dani opened the file and pointed at the itinerary. "See here, Aunt Helen is serving us dinner at five thirty sharp. And you damned well better be hungry, or I will have hell to pay."

"I certainly will not cross your Aunt Helen, but are you sure she's okay with me staying with you guys?"

"I would never hear the end of it if you didn't stay. Besides, you know Flower Hills doesn't have a hotel, and there is no time in my itinerary for excessive driving."

Brianna threw her arms up in surrender. "I have to tell you, I'm looking forward to a home-cooked meal. Unfortunately, I don't get many in the city."

"Too bad it's spring, or you would get a meal fresh from Aunt Helen's garden."

"Do I get a raincheck?" Brianna said without thinking. *Where the hell did that come from?*

Dani's eyebrows raised, and she sat up straighter. "Sure, if you want one. I didn't think you'd be coming back out once the season started."

Neither did she. Since when did an offer of fresh veggies become a big enough draw to bring her back to Flower Hills? Lately, she'd not understood herself. If she didn't know better, she might think she was enjoying working on Thundering Pines. But that was ridiculous. A campground in the middle of nowhere couldn't compare to the career she'd built in the city. Sure, Dani made her laugh, but that wasn't reason enough to come back. *Was it?*

She needed to stop. Flower Hills had stirred up so many hidden emotions that she wasn't thinking straight. It was probably natural. Once she worked out her feelings, she'd be back to normal. In the meantime, it probably wouldn't hurt to visit again sometime. "I guess I might come back." Brianna shrugged. "So what's next?"

Dani picked up the agenda and studied it. "Oh, hell!" She crumpled up the itinerary and threw it on the desk. "You've already messed it all up."

"Hey now, we might need this." Brianna opened the ball and did her best to smooth it out on the desk. She carefully folded it and put it in her front shirt pocket.

"What do you say we take a tour of the grounds?"

"Are you sure?" Brianna took the schedule out of her pocket. "You rebel, that's not on the agenda until tomorrow. Can we really do that?"

"I see how this relationship is gonna work." Dani pursed her lips. "I think I'll need to talk to HR about the abuse I'm subjected to by the owner."

"Oh, great, I have myself a litigious employee. Good thing I have a lawyer on speed dial."

"Now you're scaring me straight. I don't think I want to tangle with her." Dani's eyes got big, and her face reddened.

Oops. That obviously had slipped out of Dani's mouth. Brianna snickered. "She scares me, too. Just don't tell anybody."

Dani audibly exhaled. "Let me put these files away first, then I'll give you the grand tour."

Since the meeting in Dunhurst's office, Brianna had only seen Dani on the computer screen. Now being in person, she studied her as Dani meticulously gathered up the paperwork. Her weathered face suggested she spent a lot of time outdoors. The tiny wrinkles in the corner of her eyes were even more pronounced in person. They accented the twinkle in her hazel eyes. Her high cheekbones and muscular neck gave her an athletic look but didn't take away from her femininity. Her shoulders were slightly broader than her slender waist and compact butt. "Do you work out?"

Dani stopped putting the files into the drawers and glanced at Brianna. "What?"

"Um, I was just wondering how you stayed so lean and trim." *Dork. Just telegraph that you were checking her out.* Brianna's face felt hot.

Dani smirked. "I have a membership, but I rarely go. The best exercise I find is working with these." Dani held up her hands. "I help with much of the outdoor work around here. Not because I have to but because I want to."

Change the subject. She didn't need to be asking about Dani's body. "Wait, so I pay you the big bucks to do something I could pay half as much for?" Brianna hoped it came out jokingly but feared it didn't in her awkwardness.

"I'm salaried, so you're safe." Dani winked and continued stuffing files into the drawer.

Oh, good. Dani didn't seem upset. "In that case, how do you feel about painting?"

Dani grinned and shook her head. "You don't want me painting. I wear more than what I get on the walls."

"Good to know."

❧ ❧ ❧ ❧

When they stepped outside, Brianna stopped and lifted her face to the sun.

Dani smiled at the joy on Brianna's face, the up-tight woman she'd met over a month ago seemingly gone.

"Ah, listen to the birds chirping," Brianna said. "I rarely hear that sound over the drone of the city."

"Wait until later in the season when the crickets come out."

"That's the best. I had an app on my phone that played the sound of crickets chirping, but Caroline complained about the god-awful noise, so I removed it."

"They get boisterous sometimes, so you might wish you could uninstall them."

Brianna laughed. "Point taken. So where are we going?"

"It's a little over half a mile to the maintenance barn. Do you want to walk, or should we take the truck?"

"It's too beautiful out not to walk. Besides, I'm looking forward to stretching my legs after being bent over a desk for the last few hours." Brianna did an exaggerated stretch, putting her arms out and bending backward.

Wow. Dani did a double take; Brianna's gesture accented her height and showed off her long limbs. She quickly looked away, hoping her face hadn't colored.

Dani pointed to the path that went off to the left. "The maintenance barn is through the woods. It's hidden back in the northwest corner."

They began walking along the winding path. "Why so far away?" Brianna asked. "Shouldn't the equipment be closer to where it's needed?"

"In theory, but none of the campers want to know how the sausage is made."

Brianna shot her a look. "Huh?"

"They want the grounds to look pretty. The machinery appears out of nowhere, does its job, and disappears."

"Ah, brilliant. The magic of Thundering Pines."

Dani scowled. This was the worst possible time for Brianna to be seeing the grounds. Being so early in the season, the bare trees held no buds or leaves. Only a hint of green could be detected in the brownish yellow grass, and the remaining snow, once a pristine white a few weeks ago, was a dingy brown.

"I know it's ugly this time of year." Dani hoped her voice didn't come out as self-conscious as she felt. "But give it a few weeks, and it will be magnificent."

"I believe you." Brianna smiled. "This time of year, it's ugly in the city, too."

Dani pointed at a deep rut on the side of the path. "I hate that. When the snow melts off and the ground is too saturated, the runoff creates a mud bog."

"Looks like someone doesn't know how to drive very well." Brianna gestured at a deep groove on the side of the road.

Dani crinkled her nose. "No doubt. The rut is bad enough, but look at the muddy track in the middle of the gravel. It makes everything look dingy."

The woods had the damp, earthy smell of early spring, and Brianna took a deep breath, pulling the air into her lungs as if she were toking on a joint.

"Nothing like the fresh air out here, huh?" Dani asked.

"Oh, sorry, I thought I snorted in the air subtly."

"Wow! Remind me not to come to you if I want subtle. I've heard elephants sucking up circus peanuts quieter than that."

"Now who's doing the harassing?" Brianna laughed, but her face turned serious, and a frown creased her brows.

Something was wrong. Maybe she'd taken the teasing too far. "Is everything okay?"

"Sure," Brianna said too quickly.

What the hell just happened? She studied Brianna's face but couldn't read her. "Why am I not believing that?" When Brianna didn't answer right away, a sinking feeling washed over Dani. "I'm sorry. I'm not being a good host."

"No, you're fine. If you want the truth, I was thinking how much I like bantering with you."

Brianna's revelation caught Dani off guard. It certainly wasn't what she expected to hear. "And that made you frown?"

"No, it made me think of how long it has been since I've had a friend like that. Last one was my old college roommate. Our friends now are a little more *adult.*" Brianna mimicked air quotes.

Dani wrestled with her reply. She struggled to merge the woman she'd met last month with the one walking next to her wearing blue jeans and a flannel shirt. Settling on a less personal response, she said, "Being an adult is highly overrated."

"You're telling me. The only one in our circle of friends who refuses to be an adult is Caroline's best friend, Kylie."

"What about your best friend?"

"I don't really have one." Brianna fidgeted with the bottom of her shirt. "When I moved to Chicago with Caroline, I kinda lost touch with most of my old friends."

"That's a shame. Well, I can be your non-adult friend then." Dani wanted to kick herself. *What's my problem?* This was her boss. The same woman who'd breezed in like a princess not long ago. Sure, they'd shared a few laughs over the last couple of weeks, but that didn't mean they'd become buddies.

Brianna had stopped and knelt to tie her boot.

Dumbass. Brianna had left Flower Hills in the dust years ago. Now she was an executive vice president of something. What would she have in common with a lowly campground manager? She certainly wouldn't want Dani as a friend.

Brianna stood. "It's a deal. You can be my non-adult friend." She flashed her white teeth at Dani.

The smile made Dani forget her self-doubt, and she grinned back.

✥✥✥✥

With Dani's love of hiking and Brianna's long legs, their pace was brisk. They arrived at the large structure that housed all the equipment and supplies needed to run Thundering Pines. As they approached, Dani used the door remote to open the center bay of the barn.

Dani stood back, wanting to enjoy Brianna's reaction. The door rumbled up slowly, revealing a variety of machinery parked bumper to bumper.

"Holy shit." Brianna's eyes widened. "I had no idea it took all this to keep the place up."

Dani swept her arm forward. "And it's all yours."

"Sweet." Brianna ran her hand over a large tractor. "This should look nice in my garage. Shit, I don't think it'll fit in my parking space. Do you think they'll allow off-street parking?"

Dani laughed. "Maybe you better keep it here for now."

"Buzzkill." Brianna's brow furrowed. "This doesn't seem very efficient. Shouldn't we think about building a bigger barn?"

"Why? This barn has more than enough room."

"But everything is crammed in tighter than sardines. What if I wanted to use that mower back there?" Brianna pointed to the back of the barn.

Dani smiled, finally understanding Brianna's confusion. "This isn't how the barn looks during the season. We're still in winter storage mode. We spread all this into the other two bays once the season starts." She led Brianna through a door to the left and switched on the lights. "See."

The space was nearly full. At the back, racks held canoes and kayaks of various sizes and colors. In the middle, benches and picnic tables were piled three high, and Porta Potties lined the front.

Brianna crinkled her nose. "Shouldn't we store those outside or at least in the way back?"

"Do you smell anything?" Dani tried to hide her smile. Watching Brianna was like watching a child at the zoo.

"Well, no," Brianna said. "But eww."

"All yours. Would you like to take one of them home, too?"

"Oh, God, I would love to see the look on Caroline's face." Brianna pulled out her phone and snapped a couple of pictures.

Warmth spread across Dani's chest. Brianna's

enthusiasm was infectious. "Gonna send her a photo?"

"No, I'll save them for when the time is right." Her eyes twinkled as she took a selfie with the line of outhouses in the background. "Evidence that I've gone full-blown country. But seriously, why don't they smell?"

"At the end of the season, they're all power-washed and sanitized. You could eat a meal off them."

"I'll pass, but go ahead and be my guest." Brianna chuckled. "Any time you're wanting a fine dining experience, you are welcome to borrow one of my outhouses."

Dani clapped her hand to her chest. "Your generosity knows no bounds. Let's go to the other side, so we can get to the main attraction."

"Better than this?" Brianna said with mock surprise. She swept her hand toward the Porta Potties like a game show assistant showing off the prizes the contestant could win.

"I know, hard to top, but I think I might be able to pull it off." Dani shut off the light and weaved through the maze toward the other side of the barn.

Brianna followed close behind, letting out a few oohs and aahs as they went.

As they approached the far side, Dani could already smell the scent that awaited them. She started to go inside but stopped and stepped aside. "I'll let you do the honors."

Brianna sniffed the air and looked at her suspiciously, but she pushed inside without saying anything. When the door swung open, the aroma assailed them.

Dani reached around Brianna and flipped on the light switch.

"Wow, where did all this come from?"

Various-sized bays along the back and sides of the large area were each chocked full of chopped wood piled at least fifteen feet high.

Dani breathed in deeply, taking in the intermixed scents from the types of wood. To Dani, the smell was better than the finest perfume. She glanced at Brianna, hoping that she didn't find the scents overpowering. "We sell firewood."

Brianna approached the largest pile. "How much did all this cost?"

"Not a cent, except for labor." Dani joined her. "Most of this came from Thundering Pines."

Brianna spun around with a look of horror. In an accusatory tone she said, "You're cutting down our trees to sell for firewood?"

"Relax! This is all from downed or damaged trees. We keep everything cleaned up in the woods, so when you get the chance to walk around out there, you'll find very few trees littering the ground." Dani pointed to the corner. "Over there is our log-splitting machine. All the logs are cut right here."

"Sorry, I didn't mean to accuse you of pillaging the grounds."

Dani laughed. "You're forgiven. It was a city girl mistake."

Brianna groaned. "I'm gonna show my city girl-ness again. Why are there so many different bins?"

"Different types of wood." Dani picked up a log from the pile they were standing in front of. "Here, smell."

Brianna took a deep whiff. "Oh, my God, that's pine."

"Yep, hence the name Thundering Pines."

"So all the bins are different?"

"Mostly. A couple of the smaller bins have the same type. Come on, I'll give you a tour."

They spent the next ten minutes going from one bay to the next. Dani let Brianna smell each wood and educated her on the various trees it came from.

When they finished their tour, Brianna said, "I'm so stupid. I never thought of wood having different smells."

"Never heard of Pine-Sol or cedar planks?"

"I know, dumb, right?" Brianna shook her head. "A picture won't do this place justice. I need one of those scratch-and-sniff stickers."

"I'm sure they'd be big sellers. So are you ready for the main attraction?"

"You mean there's more?"

"You were so enthralled by the wood, you missed these beauties." Dani walked to the front of the area. Four side-by-side ATVs were lined up in front of the large overhead door.

Brianna's eyes widened. "These belong to the campground?"

"They're all yours."

"And they're green." Brianna gave her a cheesy smile. "Just like the tractor I want."

"All Gators are green." Before Dani could explain the relation to the tractor, Brianna interrupted.

"This is so cool. I've ridden one with handlebars." Brianna reached inside and gripped the steering wheel. "But this is like a mini-Jeep."

"I guess you could say that." Dani laughed. "Do you want to drive your own, or would you rather ride along with me?"

"Are you kidding me?" Brianna answered.

Dani studied her, trying to figure out what the right answer was.

"I don't drive a Wrangler for show. I'm an off-roader at heart."

"Really? You continue to surprise me, Bri." Dani noticed the look cross Brianna's face. "I'm sorry. You don't want to be called Bri, do you?"

Brianna looked contemplative for a couple of beats. "You know what, I like it coming from you. Only adults need to call me Brianna."

"Bri it is then."

⁂

Brianna struggled to focus on Dani's ATV operation lesson. She knew the instructions were important, but she just wanted to get behind the wheel and go.

"Are you listening?" Dani asked.

"Um, sorry." Brianna patted the hood of one of the ATVs. "Was it that obvious?"

Dani shook her head. "You're just like a kid at a go-kart track. Good thing I didn't have you sit in it, or you would have kept letting off the brake and edging forward."

"What can I say? I have a need...a need for speed."

Dani pointed at the ATV Brianna had been admiring.

Yes! It was the one she wanted. "I love the cool bumper thingy on this one."

Dani shook her head. "It's not a bumper thingy. It's a brush guard."

"Brush guard?"

"It protects the grille, the hood, and the lights

when you drive through brush." Dani held up her hand. "Before you ask, I'm not taking you through any brush."

"You're no fun." Brianna jumped into her ATV. "You're just jealous that mine looks cooler than yours."

"That's it." Dani got in her own ATV and fired up the engine. "Follow me."

It was a short drive down the service road until they arrived at the campsites. Dani drove slowly, but Brianna still felt the rush of excitement being behind the wheel.

Pulling to a stop, Dani pointed to the right. "Over there is where all the transitory campers park. See the short towers? That's for electric and water hookup. Let's take the road through the middle of the permanent campsites."

"Those are the people that sign annual contracts?" Brianna asked.

"Yep, good memory. Let's go."

They drove slowly, side by side, as they wound through the park. Brianna marveled at the number of campers parked relatively close together, but she noted how the trees and vegetation gave a feeling of privacy. Despite being shuttered for the season, they were decorated like homes, with intricate landscaping, decks, and gazebos.

"Holy shit," Brianna yelled over the engines. "Some of these sites are impressive. It must have taken a long time to get them looking like this."

"They are impressive. Some of the campers have been here since your dad opened the place. These lots are at a premium. We have a waiting list for people wanting one." When they came to the edge of the campsite area, Dani stopped. "So what do you think?"

"I don't remember much from when I was a kid, but I know this place didn't look like this. When I think of camping, I think of tents."

"Oh, we have those, too, but they're on the other side of the grounds. The people on this side don't like having tent campers wandering around their lots, so we try to keep that area separate."

Nice. "I'm sure the campers appreciate it."

"Why do you think we have a waiting list? You ready to see the rest?"

Brianna started to edge forward but stopped. "One more question."

"What's that?"

"Do we really have to follow the ten-miles-per-hour speed limit signs?"

Dani smiled. "When the campers are here, definitely. But we're alone today, so let's hit it." Before Brianna could respond, Dani jammed the throttle forward and was off. She sped down the trail, shooting gravel as she maneuvered around the winding curves.

Sweet. Brianna hit the gas and matched Dani's speed, staying right on her tail.

When Dani glanced over her shoulder, a shocked look crossed her face.

Priceless.

Dani kicked up her speed.

Brianna grinned. Apparently, she didn't like a city girl keeping up with her.

They sped down the straightaway toward a sharp curve ahead. Dani let off on the gas and spun around the curve.

Brianna followed suit.

The river came into view. *Beautiful.*

Dani kicked up her speed and headed toward it. They bounced along the path, but Dani wasn't slowing down despite getting closer to the water. She peeked over her shoulder, and Brianna flashed her a cheesy smile. Braking hard, Dani turned her wheel and slid to a stop a few yards from the river.

Brianna gripped the wheel tightly, and her tires skidded over the gravel as she came to a stop a few feet from Dani. "Is that all you've got?" Brianna shook her hair out as she exited her ATV.

"Holy shit, Bri. You're full of surprises." Dani jumped out of her ATV. "Aren't you a city girl?"

"Transplant, at least that's what our friends say every time I do something that embarrasses them."

"So I'm thinking they wouldn't be impressed with your ATV driving skills?"

"Afraid not. What about you?"

"What about me?" Dani asked.

"Are you impressed?"

"Not yet." Dani smirked. "I've got a lot more where that came from."

"Challenge accepted."

"Slow down, Danica. Let's check out the river first before I run you through your paces."

⚕ ⚕ ⚕ ⚕

Dani walked along the riverbank with Brianna, neither speaking. It was companionable, not uncomfortable. In Dani's experience, people wanted to fill every quiet moment, so this was a rare treat. It would have been difficult to talk over the din of the rushing water, anyway.

The birds announced the arrival of the new season with their excited chirping. Damn, they were loud, especially since the water threatened to mute them.

When a splash sounded, Dani whipped her head around but was too late to catch a glimpse of the fish that had jumped out of the river before it pierced the choppy water.

Movement from above caught Dani's eye, and when she looked skyward, an eagle circled the river in search of a meal. Dani grabbed Brianna's arm and pointed.

A huge smile broke out on Brianna's face as they stood and watched, mesmerized by the majestic bird.

Eventually, they moved on and continued east along the river. The ground was spongy, and with each step, their feet sank into the terrain. It was too early for any blooms, but Dani preferred the earthy scent to the smell of flowers.

After walking for another ten minutes in quiet, Dani said, "We better turn back if we're gonna finish the tour. Aunt Helen won't be happy if we're late."

"I'm sorry, I didn't hear a word you just said." Brianna turned to Dani.

Dani repeated herself, then added, "You like it out here, don't you?"

"Could you tell?" Brianna looked to the ground. She rolled her shoulders a few times. "I've been tight all week, but I think the knots are loosening just being out here."

"It has that effect. You never missed it?"

"I suppose in a way." They took several steps before Brianna continued. "Life just happens sometimes. I was busy building my career and a relationship, so I didn't think about it much. Being out here makes me realize how much I've missed. Spring was always my favorite."

"Mine too. I love how the melting snow causes the river to rage with such power. It won't be the same later in the season."

Brianna nodded. "The frenetic surge of water is exhilarating. Makes me feel alive."

Profound. Brianna got it. Maybe she should say something brilliant, but she settled on silence.

When they arrived back at the ATVs, Dani grabbed the roll bar and swung herself into the seat. She fastened her seat belt and reminded Brianna to do the same. "Are you sure you're up for this, city girl?"

Brianna climbed into her own ATV. "Bring it on." She still fumbled with her seat belt when Dani fired up her engine.

Dani jammed the ATV into gear and punched the accelerator. She giggled as she sped along the trail. She'd probably have to circle back around since she'd gotten such a big head start.

A few minutes later, Dani looked back. *What the hell?*

Brianna was right behind her.

Game on! Dani tightened her grip on the steering wheel and shot off the trail down a much narrower path through the woods. She used it often and could probably drive it with her eyes closed, even though it was tight and, in some parts, overgrown.

An errant branch smacked her in the face. *Shit. Reflexes are rusty. Better learn to duck, dumbass.* Her cheek stung where the branch lashed her, but no way would she rub it in case Brianna was watching.

She'd started out at medium speed, but maybe she should kick it up a notch. She looked back.

Brianna drove with one hand, pretending to

stifle a yawn with her other.

"Now you're asking for it," Dani yelled over the roar of the engines and throttled down.

They sped through the trees, the wind whipping through their hair.

This is what freedom feels like. Dani expertly threaded through the trees and made a sharp hairpin turn, pushing it harder than she would have if she were alone. A rush of adrenaline coursed through her as Brianna continued to challenge her. All her senses were heightened, and she entered the zone where everything around her slowed. The trees zipping past were no longer a blur; instead, she clearly saw the moss growing up the sides.

This is it. Brianna is toast.

The fork in the path was nearly upon her. She could turn left and go back to the office or go off to the right to give Brianna one more challenge. Dani turned right.

The sounds of the engines reverberated through the trees. She headed toward the creek that cut the property in half. This time of year, there was no telling how soggy the banks would be, but they would soon find out.

Dani stayed in the tree cover, wanting to keep the impending creek hidden from Brianna as long as possible. *Fair? Maybe not.* But there were no rules in ATV warfare.

When she darted out of the trees, the creek was only twenty feet away. She gunned the engine, hitting the raging water at full speed. The wheels slid under her. A spray of water and mud flew off in all directions. A shockingly cold dollop landed on her cheek.

When Dani made it across the creek, she slowed

to a crawl and turned to watch.

With a determined look on her face, Brianna turned the steering wheel hard to correct for the current.

Brianna's done. She overcorrected. Victory is mine.

Brianna loosened her grip on the steering wheel and let the natural momentum of the ATV take her across the rest of the creek. Laughter shook her, and even the mud-splattered windshield couldn't hide the exhilaration on her face.

Damn it, who the hell is this woman—Danica Patrick's cousin?

"Is that all you've got?" Brianna called out as she skidded to a stop next to Dani.

Unbelievable. Without a word, Dani thundered away. She still had one more challenge up her sleeve before she admitted defeat.

They rocketed alongside the creek for some time until they arrived at a shallow section.

Dani raced down the small bank and hit the creek again. This time, instead of crossing, she drove down the center, weaving around the rocks and muddy areas she knew so well. Hopefully, Brianna followed in her tracks, or she would end up stuck in a sandbar. Dani smiled at the thought.

She didn't bother looking back because she could still hear the rumble of Brianna's engine. *It could probably use a tune-up.*

Dani rapidly approached the pond that fed the creek. *Now I make my move.* She couldn't resist peeking behind her before she turned her wheel to the left to climb the bank. She realized her mistake immediately. *Fuck!*

She'd turned about five feet too soon.

Her tires hit the thick mud, and the steering wheel sent a jolt up her arms as she tried to power through. Although the engine was much too loud to hear anything, in her mind, she heard the suck of the mud pulling her in.

The tires spun.

She gunned it one more time but sank farther into the mucky water.

A blur shot past her and climbed the bank about ten feet from where she struggled. Brianna made a show of spinning around and coming face to face with Dani, who was only burying her ATV deeper every time she hit the throttle.

Brianna killed her engine, grabbed the roll bar, and pulled herself up out of her seat. She laughed so hard tears streamed down her face.

Dani tried to glare but was soon laughing, too. "Get your ass down here and help me."

"Before I do, I have one question."

"And what would that be?"

"Impressed now?"

"Yes," Dani said in a near whisper.

"What? I didn't quite hear that," Brianna teased.

"Yes," Dani yelled. "Now shut up and help me."

Chapter Nine

can't believe I have to meet your aunt looking like this." Brianna touched the crusty mud in her hair. *I must look hideous.*

"It's your own fault." Dani removed her boots and shook out the mud.

"Mine? You started it."

"Aunt Helen, we're home," Dani called out.

"What are you doing?" a pleasant voice answered from inside. "I'm in the kitchen."

"Um, you might want to come out to the garage."

"What are you doing in the garage?" Helen walked through the door, and her eyes widened. "Good lord, child, what did you do?"

Dani's resemblance to Helen was unmistakable. Helen's snow-white hair, the only thing that hinted at her age, didn't match her youthful face. Doing the math in her head, Brianna figured she had to be in her mid-sixties. She hadn't expected her to be so beautiful or statuesque. Weren't aunts supposed to be dowdy?

"Where's your manners, Aunt Helen?" Dani smirked. "I'd like you to meet Brianna Goodwin."

"What did you do to her?"

Brianna reached out her hand. "It's nice to meet you."

Helen took her hand. "I'm normally a hugger, but pardon me for passing this time."

Brianna turned to Dani. "Now look what you

did. I don't even get a hug."

"Not my fault." Dani picked mud out of Brianna's hair and motioned toward her face. "You might want to wipe off your face, too."

Helen pulled a towel out of her apron and handed it to Brianna.

"Thanks." She scrubbed at her face, but only a little dried mud flaked off. "I'm afraid I'm gonna need some water."

"Of course," Helen said. "But first I want to know what you did to her, *Dani*."

"She fell in the mud."

"Trying to push your ATV out." Brianna turned to Helen. "And this is the thanks I get, a mud bath."

"Oh, heavens. Danielle Thorton, how did you get stuck in the mud?"

"How about we tell you over dinner? I can smell your stew cooking from here."

"You are not eating dinner like that. And how did you get covered in mud, too?"

"Um, that would be my fault," Brianna said sheepishly.

Helen's eyes narrowed, and she frowned.

"Well, you see, I was putting all my muscle into pushing Dani out. I was leaning on it hard when she got traction, and I fell face first into the creek."

"Oh, my." Aunt Helen put her hand on her chest. "I still don't get how Dani got so dirty."

"She came to see if I was okay and offered her hand. So in the process of standing up, I might have accidentally pulled her into the mud with me."

"Oh, hell, don't lie to Aunt Helen. It was definitely no accident, especially when she pulled me down and rolled me a couple times."

Helen giggled. "I certainly hope none of the campers saw you."

"Your reputation is safe," Dani said. "No one saw."

Helen rolled her eyes. "You two, go clean up. I'm going to put the bread in the oven. You have half an hour, so get moving."

⊱ ❦ ❦ ❦ ⊰

Dani left her hair down, not bothering to fully dry it. Hopefully, she'd gotten all the mud out, but she wouldn't bet on it.

She arrived in the kitchen as Aunt Helen sprinkled rosemary into the stew. The aroma wafting from the stove reminded Dani of her beloved pine forest. Maybe it was why she loved rosemary so much.

When Dani reached for the spoon, Aunt Helen slapped her hand.

"It needs a little more slurry before you go tasting it. Nothing's worse than runny stew." Aunt Helen stirred the flour and broth mixture a few more times before pouring it into the pot.

"Your stew is good, runny or not."

"Last time I saw you that muddy, you must have been ten. You were catching frogs in the creek." Aunt Helen continued stirring.

Dani's mouth watered, and her stomach growled. The exertion of the day made her ravenous. "If you would've told me yesterday that my day would turn out like it has, I would have said, 'no way.'"

Aunt Helen stopped stirring and looked at Dani. "Meaning?"

"We had a blast. I haven't laughed that hard for

a long time. I certainly wasn't expecting that."

"What were you expecting?"

"I'm not sure." Dani placed silverware next to the three bowls she'd already put on the table. "I guess someone a lot more rigid, certainly not someone that would roll up her sleeves and play in the mud with me."

"Maybe you've met your match."

"I'm hoping I'm the match you're talking about," Brianna said, entering the room.

"You are. Speak of the devil, as they say." Aunt Helen removed the bread from the oven and set the pan on the stove. "Now I'll take that hug."

Brianna was across the room in a couple of strides, easily wrapping her arms around Aunt Helen. Aunt Helen was tall for an older woman, standing 5'8", but Brianna still towered over her, so she bent slightly as they hugged. When they broke the embrace, Aunt Helen said, "You smell much better than when you came in."

"Gee, thanks, I think." Brianna smiled.

Aunt Helen is right. Brianna smelled of sandalwood with a hint of musk. When Dani walked past her to grab napkins, she couldn't help but inhale deeply. Figured, not only was Brianna a knockout, but she smelled good, too.

"Let's eat." Aunt Helen carried the steaming bowl of stew to the table. "Grab the bread, Dani."

⁂

Brianna studied Dani while she told the story of their earlier exploits. Her gaze was drawn to the thin streak of gray that ran down the center of Dani's dark brown hair. Caroline had unkindly labeled it skunk hair, but Brianna found the look intriguing. She'd once heard that if someone suffered a shock, a section of their hair could permanently turn gray. What was Dani's story?

Now wasn't the time to ask.

While Dani talked, she pushed her hair behind her ears and revealed the wispy hair around her temples, which was also streaked with gray. When her hair slid from her ears and fell back around her face, the gray disappeared.

The animated way Dani told the story highlighted her best feature. Her hazel eyes twinkled and danced as she talked about the race through the woods. Crow's feet etched the corners of her eyes, her face showing the weathered look of someone who spent most of her time outdoors. She would never be considered beautiful, but her looks were interesting, almost alluring.

"Don't forget to tell Helen that I skillfully avoided getting stuck in the mud," Brianna said.

"Well, yeah, there was that. But that's not the point here."

They took turns filling in the details. Helen looked back and forth between them as if she were at a tennis match. Each tried to paint the story in their favor, adding a touch of exaggeration, which caused Helen to cackle.

As they transitioned to other topics, Brianna marveled at the effortlessness of their conversation. It was as if she'd sat at Helen's table for years, sharing her day. It had been a long time since she'd felt anything like this. *Family?*

Was there something about being in Flower

Hills that made her feel this way, or did it have to do with Dani and Helen? Caroline certainly wouldn't understand, but she'd been born and raised in the city. She could hear Caroline in her mind: *Why are you cavorting with the hired help?*

Brianna didn't think of Dani that way. She obviously still had enough small-town girl left in her to find this natural. It felt right, so who was she to question it?

Brianna used the homemade bread to sop up the last of the stew. "That was amazing."

"Thank you, honey." Helen beamed. "Are you sure you don't want some more?"

"As tempting as it is, I think I'd burst if I ate another bite."

"But I baked Dani's favorite for dessert."

"No, not coconut cream pie. Why didn't you tell us before we had seconds?"

"Obviously, all those shenanigans made you forget who your aunt is. Have you ever known me not to serve dessert when we have guests?"

"Touché. Can we have it when we get back from the movies tonight?"

"I suppose it will keep. When do you girls need to leave?"

"The movie doesn't start until nine fifteen, so we'll leave around eight thirty," Dani answered.

"Oh, good," Brianna said. "Gives me plenty of time to sit here with my pants unbuttoned, so I can breathe."

Helen patted her hand. "Why don't you girls go sit on the porch? I'll join you in a bit."

"No way," Brianna said. "My mama taught me better. I'm helping with cleanup."

Dani and Aunt Helen always made quick work of cleanup, but with Brianna added to the mix, they were done in no time. Dani sipped on her sweet tea while they watched the last light of the day fade. The sun had already disappeared, but a hint of light still glowed on the western horizon.

Aunt Helen had chosen her old farmhouse largely because of its wraparound porch. In the evenings, they usually elected to sit in front, so Dani could enjoy her favorite time of day, twilight. The days had been getting longer, but it was still dark by seven o'clock.

Like many farmhouses, it sat well off the road, so in the dim lighting, she was hardly able to make out the bare field on the other side of the street. Dani strained her eyes, hoping to spot deer feeding so she could show Brianna, but with the light nearly gone, hope faded, too.

Dani and Brianna sat on the two-person swing and moved their legs to put it in motion.

Aunt Helen rested in her well-worn rocking chair. It rhythmically creaked each time it rocked back.

"You mentioned your mom," Aunt Helen began.

Don't do it. They'd been having such a good time, but knowing Aunt Helen, she'd ask a question that would be better left unasked.

"We obviously knew your dad, but tell us about your mom."

"Well." Brianna shifted in her seat and gazed out into the dusk.

Dani shot Aunt Helen a look. "You don't have to answer if it makes you uncomfortable."

"It's okay. I'm not sure what stories you've heard, but knowing this town, I'm sure you've heard a few."

"You've got that right." Aunt Helen was obviously ignoring Dani's glare. "That's why I wanted to get it straight from the horse's mouth."

"Thank you," Brianna said.

Dani thought she saw a look of surprise cross Brianna's face but couldn't be sure in this lighting.

Brianna took a deep breath before continuing. "My mom and I left town when I was ten. It was a big scandal at the time. Apparently, half the town knew what was going on, but they kept it from my mom."

"Oh, dear, so the rumors are true?"

"Really? Aunt Helen, I think you're making Brianna uncomfortable." Dani glowered at Aunt Helen before she turned to Brianna. "I'm sorry. Please forgive her. She's old."

"Danielle Thorton, I am not old. Don't listen to her, Bri."

"It's okay, really." Brianna put her hand on Dani's arm. "I'd rather you hear the true story from me instead of from the Flower Hills grapevine."

"So it's true that your dad snuck around and had a second family on the side?" Aunt Helen asked.

"For fuck's sake, Aunt Helen, you can't just ask her things like that."

"You watch your language, little missy. You know how much gossip goes on around here. I wanted to get the scoop directly from Brianna."

"No worries." Brianna smiled. "Yes, that part is true. He had another child right under my mother's nose. Sadly, almost everyone knew, even Mom's closest friends."

"Oh, good lord, that's terrible. And that other child would be Shelby Twait?"

"The one and only. She's only two years younger than me. We went to the same grade school and rode the same bus. For eight years, my dad kept his little secret."

"Unbelievable." Aunt Helen shook her head. "How did your poor mother find out?"

"That's a little murky to me. My mom claims that she found love letters, but when I came back to town, I heard otherwise."

"I do remember now. I'd been living here for about ten years when I heard that Donny Goodwin's daughter was back in town." Aunt Helen turned to Dani. "I'm afraid we were pretty preoccupied with Dani's dad."

"Oh, that's right," Brianna said. Without warning, she wrapped her arms around Dani. "I've been wanting to do this ever since the other day."

At first, Dani stiffened, surprised by Brianna's reaction, but then she relaxed into the hug. It felt natural, even comforting. *Odd.* Since when did she become someone who could be soothed by an embrace? Dani had the reputation of being fiercely independent. Aunt Helen must have been having similar thoughts. Dani had to divert her eyes for fear of bursting out laughing. It was rare anyone caught Aunt Helen off guard, but by the shocked look on her face, Brianna had.

"Thanks," Dani said.

"Apparently, Danielle told you about her dad," Aunt Helen said.

Danielle, nice. She was being subtly scolded. "Oh, Aunt Helen, stop being butt hurt. I told Brianna the other day, and I just forgot to tell you."

Aunt Helen's eyes narrowed, and she nodded. "I see." She gazed directly at Brianna. "You must be pretty special."

Heat rose up Dani's neck into her cheeks.

Brianna gave Dani's shoulder another squeeze. "Well then, I feel honored." Brianna met Aunt Helen's gaze. "But I hear you were the true hero of the story."

Was that on purpose? Somehow, Brianna must have sensed her discomfort and shifted the conversation. Dani patted her leg and smiled.

Aunt Helen waved her hand in dismissal. "No. I was just doing what anyone would do."

"I was a sullen teen when I came to live here, but she loved me even when I was unlovable."

"And look at her now. She's become a sullen adult." Aunt Helen grinned.

"Gee, thanks." Dani shot her a fake sneer.

"But enough about Dani," Aunt Helen said. "I want to hear more about you."

Dani groaned. "How many times do I need to tell you, she's our guest? Stop the inquisition."

"But I'm having trouble figuring," Aunt Helen waved her hand back and forth between Dani and Briana, "*this* out."

Dani's heart raced. What the hell was Aunt Helen getting at? "Figuring what out?" Dani pursed her lips, flared her nose, and made eye contact with Aunt Helen.

Aunt Helen locked gazes with her for a second before turning to Brianna. "You don't seem like the same cold fish that Dani described from Thomas's office."

Dani nearly spit her beer out but swallowed hard. Too hard. It went down the wrong way, and she choked. After several seconds of coughing, she said, "Jesus, Aunt Helen."

"Do not use the Lord's name in vain. I've taught you better."

Brianna sat with an amused smile but said nothing.

"You cannot say things like that to people," Dani said, raising her voice slightly.

"But I'm old." Aunt Helen's eyes danced.

"You're only sixty-five. You're not *that* old."

Aunt Helen shifted her focus to Brianna. "See what I have to put up with? Didn't she just say earlier that I was too old to know what I was saying?"

"She did." Brianna smiled and nodded. "Apparently, you can't win for losing with her."

"Really, Brianna? Don't encourage her."

"But seriously." Aunt Helen dropped her smile. "You seem so much more down to earth. More than I expected you to be."

Brianna brought her hand to her chin and rubbed it. "It's hard to explain. I'm not sure I even understand."

"Try," Aunt Helen said.

Dani thought about protesting but sat back in the swing. *I give up.* If Brianna got offended, she'd clean up the mess later, but there was no stopping Aunt Helen at this point.

"I came from here. Flower Hills." Brianna looked out into the night. "Maybe part of it is still inside me. I left long ago, not of my own accord. For a long time, I hated this place. I thought I still did when I came for the reading of the will, but now I don't know."

"What changed your mind?" Aunt Helen leaned forward in her rocking chair and gave Brianna an encouraging smile.

"I'm not sure." Brianna's eyes filled with sadness. "Thundering Pines. Dani. You. Just being back in this town. It's so familiar. More familiar than the life I've had the last ten years." She stopped and shook her head. "I know that sounds crazy."

"Not at all, honey. We all need to find the place we belong. And sometimes, it's coming home again."

"I don't know if I'd go that far." Brianna sat up straighter, and a wall descended. "Just the ramblings of someone feeling too much nostalgia. It'll pass."

Aunt Helen must have sensed the change, as well. "You'll figure it out. But Dani and I aren't going anywhere, are we, Dani?"

"Nope." Dani glanced at her watch. "But Brianna and I are. If we don't get moving soon, we won't make it to the movies on time."

Brianna stopped moving her legs in rhythm with Dani, and the swing lurched. "Oh, sorry." Brianna gave Dani a sheepish look. "I'm kinda enjoying the fresh air and the conversation. I'd be fine staying right here."

Aunt Helen smiled. "We're gonna make a country girl out of you in no time."

Chapter Ten

"Whose idea was it to sit out on the porch half the night?" Dani said as she pulled her pickup into a parking spot and killed the engine. "Now I'm tired."

"Oh, stop your whining." Brianna playfully swatted at Dani's arm. Yesterday had been perfect, even though they'd stayed up until nearly one in the morning. "You're the one that packed our itinerary so full."

"I'm afraid I was overly ambitious. Unless we forgo eating, we're not going to get everything done."

Brianna's stomach growled in protest. "It's my first weekend here. It's not like I can't come back."

"When? I'm not letting you fool me that easily."

"Sheesh, doesn't this look like an honest face?" Brianna batted her eyelashes.

"Nope. Not going to work."

"Fine." Brianna pulled her phone from her pocket. *Damn.* "I have something I can't get out of next weekend. What about the following one?"

"That'll work. It's settled then." Dani broke into a large grin. "Let's get something to eat."

"I still can't believe there's a sushi joint in town." Brianna shoved the pickup door open with her foot and hopped out.

"Obviously, Flower Hills is no longer a small town."

"I'm not sure sushi in a strip mall qualifies as big city."

"Stop being a snob." Dani held open the door for Brianna as they entered.

Brianna stopped dead in her tracks just inside the door. Once crossing the threshold, she was transported to another world far away from the parking lot. She'd been in five-star restaurants with less ambience than the Sushi Palace.

The recessed lighting around the dining area was low and the walls dark, which made a visitor's gaze travel to the brightly lit stainless steel sushi bar in the back. It was ultramodern, and all the fresh ingredients lay under glass that spanned the length of the counter. Three chefs, dressed in white, cut and rolled for everyone to see. Above their heads hung various wooden and bamboo instruments used to make sushi, along with a few large knives. The artistic renderings made from chopsticks gave the décor a note of whimsy.

"Holy shit," Brianna said. "This place is amazing. If the food is anywhere near as good as the ambience, you found a keeper."

"I know how to pick winners." Dani winked. When the hostess greeted them, Dani held up her fingers. "Table for two, please."

Once seated, Brianna pored over the menu. She flipped through the pages, trying to take it all in. It was the most sushi she'd ever seen on a menu. And she found it in Flower Hills. Brianna looked up from her menu. "Aren't you going to look at it?"

"Nope, I always get the same thing."

"That's not very adventurous. It's time to kick you out of your comfort zone."

"Do I detect a challenge?"

"Take it any way you want." Brianna smiled.

Dani scowled but began perusing the menu.

"Why don't we order three?" Brianna said. "You pick one, I'll pick one, and we'll let the waitress choose one for us."

"Sounds good. My pick is the dragon roll."

"Is that the one you always order?"

"Yup," Dani said with a triumphant grin.

"Nope," Brianna answered. "Did you miss the part about stepping out of your comfort zone? Try again." She didn't wait for a response and buried her face back in the menu.

"But…"

Brianna held up her hand and shook her head.

"Fine, I'll pick something else."

"Are you pouting behind that menu, Danielle?"

Dani glared over the top of the page. "I'm working on my choice."

"Hurry up, I'm starving."

⁂

It'd been a long time since Dani had been out with a woman. *Oh, God.* She couldn't think of Brianna as a woman. *Of course, Brianna is a woman.* But when she thought of a woman and going out to eat, she thought date. This certainly wasn't a date. It was a business lunch, nothing more. *Get a grip, Thorton.* She grabbed her glass of water and took a large gulp, hoping Brianna wouldn't notice the blush that heated her cheeks.

After ordering, they got down to business and reviewed their earlier meetings.

"Enough shop talk." Brianna pushed her notebook and pen aside. "I consulted the agenda and didn't see anything about how you're planning on entertaining me tonight."

"You mean my sparkling personality isn't enough?"

"Hardly. Where's the local hotspot?"

"You don't want to go there."

"Why not? Afraid I won't fit in?"

"You might fit in too well. The guys in town aren't used to seeing a six-foot-tall woman in their midst."

"I'm only five-eleven."

"Well then, you should be fine."

Brianna's expression turned serious. "You know I'm a lesbian, don't you?"

Dani squirmed in her seat and became extremely interested in arranging the sliced ginger on the top of her sushi. Sexuality wasn't something she cared to talk about. *Why did people have to put labels on these things?* She didn't know how she was supposed to respond, so she played it safe. "Yes, of course."

"Oh, good, I was afraid this was going to get awkward."

Dani laughed, but Brianna didn't. "Sorry, I didn't mean any…"

Brianna burst out laughing, "Sorry, I couldn't resist screwing with you."

"Nice. Stop talking to me, so I can eat my sushi." Dani made a show of putting a whole piece of sushi in her mouth and chewed slowly.

"Good try, but I can still talk while your mouth is full. You didn't think that one out, did you?"

Dani tried not to laugh for fear of choking

but ended up snorting a piece of rice, which led to a coughing attack.

A smile tugged at the corner of Brianna's mouth as she took an exaggerated tiny bite of her sushi.

The sushi was long gone and the bill paid, but they were still sitting and talking when Dani said, "I think you have an admirer."

"What?"

"That woman over there keeps staring at you."

"Where?"

"Over by the window. She's eating alone. Maybe she thinks you're cute."

"Really?"

"Or maybe she's just staring at the big piece of spinach stuck in your teeth."

Brianna casually dropped her napkin on the floor and leaned over to pick it up. "Nope, she doesn't look familiar."

"Wow, that was subtle."

"Brianna?" the woman called.

"Oh, great, I think she thought you were flirting. Here she comes," Dani said.

Brianna's eyes narrowed as she watched the woman cross the floor, but by the look on her face, she was drawing a blank.

"Brianna, it's me," the woman said.

"Molly?" Brianna's eyes widened. "Oh, my God, it is you."

"The one and only."

Brianna leapt out of her chair and wrapped her arms around Molly.

Dani watched as they hugged. She half expected them to burst into tears. *A former lover?* Surely Brianna would have recognized her if that were the case. Besides, what would it matter?

"I didn't recognize you," Brianna said, still holding on to Molly.

"I can't imagine why."

"You cut off all your hair, and you went blond." Brianna held Molly at arm's length but still didn't let her go. "Your hair used to be down to your ass."

"Almost."

"You look great."

"Thanks. Nice move with the napkin by the way, real subtle." Molly giggled.

They'd finally let go of each other, but Brianna grabbed Molly again and hugged her.

When they separated, Brianna finally glanced at the table where Dani still sat. "I'm sorry. Molly, have you met Dani?"

"I don't believe I have, but I'm assuming you're the Dani that runs Thundering Pines."

"That would be me." Dani stood and reached out her hand.

"This is Molly Chambers." Brianna draped her arm over Molly's shoulder. "Molly was my best friend in grade school before we split town."

A smile finally broke out on Dani's face as her stomach settled. *Good, not a former lover.* "It's nice to meet you, Molly."

After a couple of minutes of small talk among the three, Molly said, "How long are you in town?"

"Just until tomorrow."

"Damn, it would have been so nice to catch up with you."

Brianna's face fell. "Maybe next time."

Dani studied Brianna for a few seconds before turning to Molly. "What are you doing right now,

Molly?"

"I was just out running a few errands."

"Why don't you two catch up now?" Dani said.

Molly broke into a broad smile. "I have the time if you do."

"Why don't you join us?" Brianna turned to Dani.

"No, Bri. You guys go ahead."

"But don't we have more work to do this afternoon? And you were going to take me to the pine forest so I can see how Thundering Pines got its name."

"Nothing I can't handle. And I'll take you there tomorrow."

Brianna glanced at Molly, then back at Dani.

Seeing Brianna's hesitation, Dani said, "I insist, get out of here."

"But—" Brianna started to say, but Dani cut her off.

"I'm out of here. Aunt Helen is planning dinner for five o'clock, so give me a call if you're gonna be late."

"I promise I'll have her home before then," Molly said. "I know your Aunt Helen, and there is no way I'm going to mess with her."

Dani nodded. "All right, it's settled. You kids have fun."

"It was nice meeting you," Molly said.

"Nice meeting you, too." Dani turned to leave but stopped when Brianna called her name.

"Thank you so much." Brianna caught Dani off guard when she wrapped her in a hug.

"You don't need to thank me. Go have fun." Dani squeezed her, enjoying the feeling of Brianna's body against her.

"Don't think I've forgotten."

Dani searched her mind. *What am I forgetting?*

Brianna made a grand gesture of pulling the itinerary out of her pocket and pointed to the handwritten note that she'd added to the bottom of the page. "Right here, it says take Brianna out for an entertaining evening."

Dani shrugged. "Sorry, I'm afraid that's null and void since you aren't sticking to the rest of the schedule."

"Danielle Thorton, you are not going to get out of it that easily."

"Take her to the Spotted Owl," Molly said. "There's nothing more entertaining than that."

"Is that the place we were talking about earlier?" Brianna asked.

"Yes, but I'm not taking you there."

"Yes, you are. It's settled."

Dani groaned. "We'll talk about it later."

⚛⚛⚛⚛

Get over yourself. Dani kicked a rock as she walked back to her truck. She couldn't believe she felt sad. It should make her happy that Brianna would get to spend the afternoon with her friend, but damn it, she was going to miss her.

Bad idea. She didn't want to become attached to Brianna. She was perfectly fine with lots of acquaintances. Besides, all the campers thought of her as a friend, so she had hundreds. Her notecard box proved it.

Why did a conversation with Brianna feel so different? Small talk was so inane. Talking to Brianna didn't feel that way, though. The conversation came easy, the teasing natural, and most importantly, Brianna held her interest. They hadn't stopped talking since Brianna had arrived, and here she was sad that she would have to spend the afternoon not talking to Brianna.

Brianna probably wanted to get away from her. But she hadn't acted like it. They'd had a blast today, laughing and joking the whole time. If anything, it felt as if their friendship was deepening.

She was acting like a grade school kid. The next thing she knew, she would be sending Brianna a note saying, *Will you be my friend, yes or no?*

The image made her smile. She could imagine Brianna if Dani passed her a note like that. Brianna would have something sarcastic to say.

Really. When did I become an expert on Brianna Goodwin's reactions? Dani forced herself to shove Brianna out of her mind as she started her truck.

Chapter Eleven

S o where do you want to go?" Brianna asked after watching Dani drive away. She felt a twinge of sadness when the pickup turned the corner. *Really? What's my problem?*

She couldn't deny she enjoyed Dani's company, and last night had been intense, but she was only here for the camping season. Then she would never return. Why did she feel more comfortable talking to Dani than the friends she'd known for years?

She was just nervous about catching up with Molly since things had been strained between them when Brianna had returned to Flower Hills the last time. Had it really been nearly thirteen years?

Brianna relaxed now that she had an answer for her edginess, which had nothing to do with Dani.

"Would you mind taking a walk with me? The older I get, it seems harder to keep this up." Molly ran her hand down the sides of her body.

"I'd love to. You look amazing, by the way."

❧❧❧❧

"And the rest, as they say, is history," Molly said. "I threw his ass out and never looked back."

"Good for you. Nobody should make you feel bad about yourself."

"I'm sorry, Brianna." Molly touched her arm. "I

was stupid. I know you were just being a good friend and saw what a jerk he was. I wasn't ready to hear it. But you planted the seed, and even though you never knew it, you were the catalyst that gave me the courage to get away from him. Thank you."

"I was young and arrogant when I came back here. A bulldog." Brianna squeezed Molly's shoulder. "I could have gotten my point across better. I'm just happy to be here with you now."

"It's great to see you, too." Molly smiled. "I'm sorry I let the jerk come between us. It's amazing how much he messed with my self-esteem."

"Don't let him. You're one of the best people I've ever known." Brianna looked Molly up and down. "Plus, you're a knockout."

"Are you flirting with me?" Molly teased. "I have a boyfriend."

Brianna laughed. "Nah, I've been with Caroline for ten years, but if I weren't, you'd have to watch out."

"Don't you know, you're not my type." Molly waited a beat before finishing. "Too tall."

Brianna bumped her hip into Molly as they walked. "God, I've missed you," Brianna said, realizing how true it was. "You're real."

"That's an odd compliment." Molly shot her a sideways glance. "Care to elaborate?"

"I'm not sure." Brianna shoved her hands into her pockets. What was it about this town that caused her to lose her filter? Who tells someone they're real?

"Oh, no, you're not getting off that easily. I just spent the last half hour telling you my saga."

"Damn, has it been that long?" Brianna had been so engrossed in Molly's story that she hadn't paid attention to their surroundings. It finally registered that they were walking around the lake where she'd loved to fish as a child.

"Nice try, but changing the subject isn't going to work."

"Honest, I wasn't trying, but you know how much I love the lake." As she gazed over the smooth surface of the water, Brianna's vision blurred as her eyes misted. Some of her best childhood memories had taken place here. Molly's family had brought them to the park often for picnics.

She had been too young to notice that her parents never did that sort of thing. In hindsight, they had never done anything as a family, probably because Donald had been too busy wooing other women. *Wooing, what a nice word for what he truly did.*

"Why do you think I brought you here? Now spill."

"It's different in the city. Everyone I know creates an image of themselves. Nobody's real."

"Even you?"

"Shit, you're going to go right at it, aren't you?" She looked at Molly. "Unfortunately, yes, even me." The people here were different. Molly and Dani were different. *Real* was the word that kept coming to her mind. In the city, everyone hid behind a façade. *Impression management.* "Nobody shows who they are, just who they want everyone to think they are. There are no warts or scars, just perfect lives."

Molly held out her arm and nearly knocked Brianna off balance. "Whoa, watch the duck poop."

Brianna did a stutter step around the piles. "Christ, you just about pushed me into it."

"Sorry." Molly smiled and shrugged. "Perfect

sounds boring and dishonest."

"Check and check." Brianna made imaginary checkmarks in the air. "It's been a bit of a mind fuck being back here. I've had more real conversations in the last two days than I've had in years. I'm not sure how I feel about it."

"I do. I'm elated that you're here." Molly grabbed Brianna, nearly throwing her off balance again.

"Whoa, you're going to throw me into the duck poop yet. Then I might not be so happy to see you."

"You still would be." Molly winked. They began walking again. "I'm a bit shocked that you sold out. The Brianna I knew was always so real."

"I know, right?" Brianna stared off at the lake, not wanting to make eye contact with Molly. Her emotions bubbled just under the surface. A fish jumped, disturbing the still water. Ripples went out in all directions. "I think the universe is sending me a message."

"I must have missed something."

"My life was like that lake, clear and undisturbed, but then the fish jumped. It just took one little action, the ripples started, and there was no way to stop them. That's how I'm feeling. The ripples started due to something beyond my control, and I'm not sure what direction they will end up going."

"Let me take your metaphor a little deeper, pun intended." Molly smirked. "The lake may seem clear and undisturbed, but obviously, something was going on under the surface to make the fish jump in the first place." They stopped walking to watch the ripples approach the shore. "And you, my friend, have a lot more going on under your surface than meets the eye."

Brianna smiled. "Well, haven't we become quite poetic and philosophical?"

"Poet, let's walk back into town, so you can buy me a beer."

❧❧❧❧

There were only a few people in the Spotted Owl when they walked in. *Wait until I tell Dani where I've been.* Brianna offered to order their drinks while Molly found a table.

Peanut shells crunched under her feet as she walked to the bar. Some were ground so deeply into the floor, she suspected they'd been there since the bar opened. A waitress halfheartedly pushed a broom around the tables. It was a losing battle as the patrons threw more shells as soon as the broom passed.

She tried to take it all in without being obvious. It was imperative that she remembered a few details, so she could throw them out in conversation with Dani.

The walls were scuffed and marred with large sections of peeling paint on the outer wall, where the booths were located. The lighting was unintentionally low with nearly half the bulbs burned out.

The bartender ran a wet rag over the bar, but it did little to improve its appearance. The surface was marked by deep cigarette burns from long past when it had still been legal to smoke inside.

All three of the men at the bar gaped at Brianna, not bothering to hide that they were checking her out. The one sitting on the stool closest to her looked as if he had been there for a while. It seemed the liquid courage in front of him made him bolder.

When he said, "darlin'" several times, Brianna ignored him. As soon as the bartender set down her drinks, she dropped her money on the bar and walked away.

"Is this where I insisted Dani take me tonight?"

"Afraid so. Be careful what you wish for." Molly laughed and took the beer from Brianna.

"Are the men here always this charming?"

"Afraid so, but tonight, they will at least be a little younger."

"Great. How come I don't remember the Spotted Owl?" She ran her hand over the nicked-up tabletop. "This place looks like it's been here for a while."

"You were ten when you left here, so I doubt it was one of your hangouts."

"Good point." She took a big gulp of her beer and held it up. "I can't believe how cheap these were. They'd have cost three times as much in the city."

"So," Molly said, suddenly looking serious. "Tell me more about Thundering Pines."

"What's that look for?"

"The grapevine is alive and well in Flower Hills, but I want to hear about it straight from you."

"There's not much to tell. I inherited it. This is my first time visiting, so Dani is showing me around. It's too soon to say what I'll ultimately do."

Molly narrowed her eyes. "So what do you think of her?"

"She's been great." Brianna studied Molly. "What aren't you telling me?"

"I just want to make sure you're being careful."

"Do you really think I'm going to let you get away with saying something like that without elaborating?"

Molly smiled. "I don't know her. You know how

small towns are. I don't want to go repeating stuff that might not be true."

"Come on, you need to tell me if there is something I should be concerned about." *Do I really want to hear this?* It was probably nothing, so why did her chest tighten? *Betrayal?* The thought of talking about Dani behind her back didn't seem right. She would share it with Dani tonight to alleviate her guilt.

"Apparently, she likes to play the field." Molly leaned in, so only Brianna could hear.

Brianna's breath caught, but she didn't want Molly to notice. "What does that have to do with Thundering Pines?" *It's not my business. Dani's an adult, so she can do what she wants.*

"Rumor has it that she has quite the following with the women at the local gym. The married ones." When Brianna remained quiet, Molly added, "She sleeps with them."

Wow. That hadn't been anything she'd expected. *Be cool.* She didn't want Molly to catch her reaction. *Hell.* She didn't even want to think about the thoughts racing through her mind. *Focus.* "Seriously, that's it? I thought she was embezzling or selling drugs or something. So she can't keep it in her pants. It's not really my concern unless she's doing it with the campers."

"I think she steers clear of them. At least that's what I've heard. Apparently, one of the women threatened to give up her campsite so she could get a piece."

"Wow, she must be pretty good." Brianna hoped her voice remained steady and carefree. Why hadn't Dani mentioned being a lesbian earlier when they'd talked? *Stupid.* Just because she'd slept with women didn't mean she identified as a lesbian. She was an adult, so she could sleep with whoever she wanted. "Doesn't sound like it should be any concern to me."

"I just thought..." Molly stopped.

Brianna tilted her head and stared.

"Well, seeing you together today, watching you from across the room, I thought maybe there was something going on between the two of you."

"Oh, God, no." What did Molly think she saw? "You're so sweet. You were afraid I was being drawn in by a player."

Molly exhaled and visibly relaxed. "I'm sorry. I didn't want to gossip, but..."

"But you didn't want my heart broken." Brianna patted Molly's hand and smiled. It touched her that after all these years, Molly felt the need to protect her. She wondered if any of her friends in the city would do the same.

"Exactly, I just thought, well..."

"You thought, Brianna is a lesbian, and Dani sleeps with women, so it must be," Brianna teased.

"No, it's not like that. I'm not..."

Brianna watched in amusement as Molly stumbled over her words.

"Earlier, I thought I picked up some vibes between you two, some chemistry. And she didn't look very happy when I came to the table until you told her who I was."

Chemistry? Molly probably picked up how much Brianna and Dani enjoyed teasing each other, then mistakenly thought it was an attraction. *That made sense.* "Is it weird that I already consider her a friend? I've told her more about myself than I've told any of my friends in Chicago, so that's probably the vibe you felt."

"After what you've told me about your friends, I wouldn't call it weird at all." Molly sat back in her seat and took a drink from her beer, looking relieved that she'd gotten it off her chest.

"I'm just happy it wasn't something horrible. I'm afraid I wouldn't have handled it well." Brianna realized how true the statement was. She would be crushed if her assessment of Dani turned out to be wrong. Tears welled in her eyes, and she pointed at herself. "See, I don't know what the hell is happening to me."

"The ripples have just begun." Molly winked at Brianna. "Since I'm being protective of you, I think you should know that Shelby is on the warpath."

"Is that supposed to be a surprise? The reading of the will wasn't pretty."

"Seriously, please watch yourself. Word on the street is she and her cousins have been scheming."

"Oh, great, Shelby and the twins. The story just gets better and better."

"I don't know what they're up to, but she's telling anyone that'll listen that she's going to make your life a living hell like you made hers."

"Seriously? Can you tell me what I did to her?"

"You exist." Molly flagged down a waitress to order another beer. "Your daddy loved you best."

"Right, like he was father of the year to me. I hadn't talked to the man in nearly thirteen years. Exactly how is it that I interfered in her relationship with him?"

"Maybe she's jealous that you got away. She's spent her whole life chasing after his love."

Brianna finished the last swallow of her beer and set the bottle down harder than she intended. "Yep, I was showered with love."

"In her eyes, him giving you Thundering Pines confirms he loved you more. I know it's messed up, but she and her mom never got over being the second family."

"Well, fuck them," Brianna said. "Maybe if the slut had kept her legs together, I wouldn't have lost my family."

"Do you actually believe that?"

"No." Brianna sighed and twirled her empty bottle. She'd spent too many years overcoming her anger; she wasn't going to let it take hold of her again just because she was back in town. "If it wasn't Shelby's mom, it would have been someone else."

"Apparently, before he died, it was three or four someone elses."

"I can't talk about him anymore. Makes my skin crawl." Brianna gave an exaggerated shudder and ran her hand down her arm, as if she were wiping him off her skin. "Why do you think Dani didn't tell me that she was a lesbian?"

"I'm not sure if she labels herself as one."

"You mean she's bisexual?" Brianna's guilt rose again. She should be asking Dani these questions, not Molly.

"I think she had a boyfriend a long time ago but haven't heard her linked to anyone recently. Then again, she hasn't exactly been openly running around with any of the women, either."

"Interesting. I wonder if she'll tell me about it."

꧁꧂

"Tell Dani thanks for letting me steal you for the

afternoon," Molly said. They were standing by her car outside of Dani and Helen's house.

"Will do," Brianna said. "Is it stupid I'm afraid to say goodbye to you again?"

"It's not going to be that way this time. We're older and wiser."

"And you're more confident and hotter." Brianna smiled.

"Sheesh, stop flirting. Don't you remember you're too tall?" Molly joked. "You have my number, and I've got yours, so it's all good."

"You're right." Brianna fought back tears. *What's wrong with me?* Two days here and she was becoming an emotional wreck.

"It's okay." Molly wiped the tear off Brianna's cheek. "I'm sure being back here has opened up all kinds of old wounds." She put her arms around Brianna and hugged her tightly.

"I'm still not going to say goodbye," Brianna said when they ended their hug.

"Okay, until next time then."

"Until next time."

Chapter Twelve

Butterflies danced in Dani's stomach. She'd barely been able to eat in anticipation of Brianna seeing the loft.

"How many damned stairs do we have to climb, anyway?" Brianna looked up at the tower.

"It's only six stories. Good exercise," Dani said. "Trust me, it'll be worth it."

"I'm not sure. Not when we could have gone to the Spotted Owl." Brianna started up the stairs, exaggerating heavy breathing as she did.

"You have to admit, it's pretty impressive." Dani stayed right on her heels, goading her on.

"It's a big steel structure in the middle of the woods. It's cool, but I still don't see why you rushed us through dinner to get out here."

"You'll see. Just climb."

At the top, Brianna feigned exhaustion and panted heavily. "Now what?"

"We go in that door over there." Dani pointed.

"That's an ugly door. Look at all those nicks. I think you should paint it."

Dani turned the key, entered the code, and swung open the door.

"No, not more stairs," Brianna whined.

"You are such a drama queen." Dani pushed past her and bounded up the stairs.

Brianna trudged along behind, muttering to

herself.

Dani hurried to the top, wanting to see Brianna's face when she finally saw the loft.

"Holy shit," Brianna said when she entered the room. Her mouth hung open. "Why the hell didn't you tell me this was here?"

"I wanted to surprise you." Dani smiled.

Brianna made a beeline to the floor-to-ceiling windows that spanned three of the four walls. "I can't believe the view." Her gaze darted from window to window as she took it all in. Sitting at over six stories, they could see nearly all the campground.

Her light brown eyes shone with a childlike wonder that warmed Dani's heart. She wore her dark brown hair down, as it had been all weekend, and the natural curls cascaded around her shoulders. The softness of the fading light made her even more beautiful somehow.

The realization caused Dani to look away and begin straightening the books she'd left on the table the last time she'd visited.

"Wow." Brianna looked out over the river. "This is amazing. I'm not sure I ever want to leave here."

"I come here every chance I get." Dani sneaked a glance at Brianna, who now had her face inches from the glass. "If it weren't for Aunt Helen, I would live here, but I'm afraid she would get lonely."

Dani joined Brianna at the windows. Both gazed out without speaking for several minutes. They watched as the sun crept toward the horizon and the birds made a final pass over the water.

Brianna put her hand on Dani's shoulder, but neither broke the silence.

The heat from Brianna's touch radiated through

Dani's shirt. Having Brianna's hand on her shoulder felt right somehow as they watched the light of the day fade. It was Dani's favorite time of day. She preferred sunsets to sunrises. Something about the close of a day that was well lived touched her in a way that the start of a day never could.

The sky was a combination of purple and orange. Dani once heard the color was caused by pollution, but she never sought to discover whether it was true. She didn't want anything to taint the beauty of watching the light fade from the sky.

Both inhaled slowly and deeply, their breath synchronizing as a peaceful calm descended over them.

The light was nearly gone when Dani said, "Can I get you something to drink?"

Brianna jumped at the sound of Dani's voice.

"Sorry, I didn't mean to frighten you."

"No, it's okay."

"You were a million miles away. Are you wanting to escape from here, Bri?"

"Actually, just the opposite." She turned to Dani, and they locked gazes. "I'm trying to figure out how I can keep this feeling forever."

"It does have that effect, doesn't it?" Dani reluctantly turned from the window since there was nothing left to see but darkness. She strode across the room to the kitchenette. "Pick your poison."

"I don't suppose you have a nice bottle of merlot, do you?"

"I'm not sure how good it is, but I do believe I have a bottle or two." Dani pulled a bottle from the wine rack built into the small pantry.

"Sold."

"Still mad that I wouldn't take you to the Spotted

Owl?"

"I've forgiven you. But don't think I've forgotten about it."

"I still can't believe you had Molly take you there." Dani suspected Brianna enjoyed getting a rise out of her when it came to the Spotted Owl. She also knew Brianna wouldn't stop badgering her until she got her way.

☙❧❦❧

Brianna yawned and stretched her legs.

Damn, she has long legs. Dani tried not to stare. They reclined on opposite ends of the oversized couch, facing each other. Dani's legs were tucked under her, while Brianna stretched her legs down the length of the couch. Occasionally, her feet grazed Dani when either moved.

"Tired?" Dani asked.

"No, just really relaxed. I just love your Aunt Helen," Brianna said out of nowhere.

"She is a character." Dani smiled. "I say that with the utmost affection. But I'm sorry she put you on the spot last night."

Brianna stretched her legs out farther, arched her back, and lifted her hands over her head. Something popped. "I think she's charming. Saying what's on your mind is a dying art."

"Well then, she's certainly an artist." Dani shook her head. "She's also a chatterbox. I never got the chance to ask you about your afternoon with Molly."

"It was nice." Brianna's voice was low. "She took me to her house. It's a cute little bungalow. I'm so happy she finally got away from her asshole boyfriend. She seems so much happier."

"I'm glad you had fun."

"I'm going to meet her for breakfast next time I come back. It's nice to have a friend here."

Dani's chest tightened. *Really? Not again.* She needed to accept that Brianna didn't think of her as a friend.

"And thank you for making me feel so welcome."

"It's been my pleasure." *It really has.*

"Now I have two friends in Flower Hills."

Dani's chest unclenched, and she could breathe again. "You're not so bad to have around."

"Gee, thanks. Such a ringing endorsement." Brianna smiled.

"Do you mind if I ask you a question?"

"Go for it."

"Last night, you were telling us about your parents before Aunt Helen hijacked the conversation. Would you mind finishing your story?" Dani glanced out of the corner of her eye and was happy to see a slight smile part Brianna's lips.

"What do you want to know?"

"What happened? What's the real story?"

"To be honest, I'm not sure I have the real story." Brianna's voice was full of sadness. "I was ten years old, too young to understand what was going on. All I knew was my life was uprooted overnight, and my parents hated each other."

Dani's heart ached for Brianna. Losing her mother had been hard on Dani, but she was glad that she was too young to remember anything. It would have been brutal to be ten years old and watch her mother walk away. "That sucks," Dani said. *Wow, really helpful.*

"It happened to you, too."

"I don't remember a thing. I was only three."

"You don't remember your mom at all?"

"Nope, I don't even know what she looks like." Dani had spent years trying to remember but finally gave up. In her mind, she created a vision of what her mom looked like, but she was probably completely off base.

"You don't have any pictures of her?" Brianna raised her eyebrows.

"My dad destroyed them all when she left." As much as Dani loved her father, in this case, his actions had been selfish.

"Brutal. I'm sorry."

"Nah, it's better that way."

"How does the conversation keep getting turned back on me? I want to hear your story."

"Fine," Brianna said after several seconds.

꧁꧂꧁꧂

Brianna took in a deep breath. She couldn't believe she wanted to tell her story. That hadn't happened before. Maybe it was just because of her earlier conversation with Molly.

No, that wasn't it. She couldn't lie to herself. There was something about Dani that made her want to talk. She felt safe. *Odd choice of words.*

"You don't have to tell me if you don't want to. I understand."

"Sorry, it's just hard. But I want to. Where do you want me to start?"

"Wherever you'd like." Dani shot her a smile.

"Until my mother loaded me into our car in the middle of the night and drove away, I didn't know there were any problems between them. Not that many ten-year-olds have a clue about their parents' marriage."

"That must have been tough." Dani's voice was full of compassion.

Brianna shifted her gaze to the large window across the room. "I never got a chance to say goodbye to my friends or teachers. Not even my father. We lived in a motel for a couple of weeks and only left to get food. There are only two things I remember clearly. Even though Mom packed light, she'd loaded up a backpack with all my favorite books. We sat in that hotel room and took turns reading every single one aloud to each other." Brianna smiled, remembering how her mother did all the animal voices in *Charlotte's Web*. She could still hear the perky voice she used for Charlotte and the deep voice for Wilbur the pig.

"And the second thing?" Dani asked when Brianna hadn't spoken for several minutes.

"She cried a lot." Brianna felt Dani's gaze on her, so she turned away from the window. "It would have been a great vacation if it weren't for that."

"What happened next?"

"We moved into an apartment. We didn't have any furniture for the first couple of weeks, but eventually, a moving truck arrived with all our belongings. Being a dumb ten-year-old, I was sure my dad would come with the movers, but he didn't. I didn't see him again for eleven years."

"Ouch. Did you know why you left?"

"Nope, I was a teenager when I found out what the son of a bitch did." Brianna ran her hand through her hair. "What kind of man has two families? He ruined a lot of lives."

Dani held up her wineglass. "I could use a little

more. How about you?" Before Brianna could answer, Dani sprang from the couch and grabbed the bottle off the counter.

Dani's lack of response stung; no, it hurt. Brianna stood and walked to the window. *Stupid.* She shouldn't have allowed this conversation, especially with someone who was a big fan of the late great Donald Goodwin.

Dani returned with the wine and motioned toward Brianna's hand.

Brianna held out her glass. "Oh, well, water under the bridge. What's first on our agenda in the morning?"

Dani flinched, and the wine splashed onto her hand. "I'm sorry, Bri."

"Nothing to be sorry about." Brianna stared out the window. "Is the bank the first meeting of the day?"

"Please look at me." Dani touched her arm.

Brianna turned, ready to shut Dani down with her professional glare, but stopped when she saw the look of sadness on Dani's face. *Damn it, who is this woman?* Brianna had mastered the art of indifference but didn't seem to be able to channel that part of herself around Dani. She nodded toward the wine droplets on Dani's hand. "Are you going to drink that or save it for later?"

Dani licked the wine off her hand. "Please don't think I'm dismissing your story because I'm not. I'm just trying to wrap my brain around everything. I absolutely hate that your dad hurt you."

"But?" Brianna said a little more defensively than she'd planned.

"But he was always so kind to me." Dani's face was full of anguish. "Obviously, he did terrible things to you and your mother. It would be easy for me to sit here and say, 'what a son of a bitch,' to stay on your good side, but it would be dishonest. I respect you too much to do that."

Brianna didn't speak as she processed Dani's words. She absentmindedly ran her finger around the rim of her glass. Her first reaction was to be angry, but it quickly faded. She lived in a world where everyone agreed with you to your face, then talked about you behind your back. It took courage for Dani to say what she did, especially since Brianna held Dani's career in her hands.

Before Brianna could respond, Dani said barely above a whisper, "I'm scared to death that I just messed up a nearly perfect weekend."

"No, you didn't. I appreciate your honesty. When I came back to town, it made me so angry when everyone told me what a wonderful man he was." Brianna could feel the rage rising in her again. "Wonderful men don't have two families. And wonderful men do whatever they can to stay in touch with their ten-year-old daughter."

"Agreed," Dani said. "I'm trying to understand how someone who was kind to me could have been so unkind to his own daughter."

"Donald Goodwin was a charmer." Brianna shivered. "He collected people and wanted everyone to adore him."

"Can I press my luck a little more in the honesty department?"

"What the hell, why stop now?" Brianna smiled. She was surprised how quickly her earlier defensiveness faded. Dani's genuineness put her at ease.

"I understand what you're saying because I

watched what he did to Shelby." Dani looked at Brianna warily.

"It's okay, I'm not going to bite your head off. Explain."

"He was cruel to her. Sometimes, I felt sorry for her, but then I'd brush it off, knowing how *delightful* Shelby can be."

Interesting. "So you're asking if Shelby is naturally delightful, or if she's a product of Donald's cruelty?"

"Maybe. I hadn't really thought of it that way, but I've seen glimpses of a decent person under the bitchy exterior."

A pang of jealousy gripped her. It was unexpected, but what surprised her more was the realization that it had nothing to do with her father. Of course Dani would know Shelby. They might even be friends. "Donald Goodwin screwed up two daughters." Brianna tried to sound lighthearted, but she knew she missed the mark.

"No! It's...well...I mean," Dani stammered. "It's not exactly what I meant."

"But it's probably true. I guess I'm the lucky one since I didn't return until I was twenty-one. He didn't have as much time to screw me up."

"I'm assuming things didn't go well when you came back?"

"Hardly." Brianna leaned closer to the window, trying to get a glimpse of the river.

"I'm sorry, I'm prying too much."

"No. You have no reason to be sorry." Brianna tried to give Dani a reassuring smile, but she knew it fell short. "I'm just not very good at this. I haven't talked about this to anyone since college."

"Fifteen years?" Dani didn't hide her surprise.

"Caroline knows my parents were divorced but not much more."

"You never told her?"

"She never asked."

"Did you want her to?"

"Damn, you ask some tough questions. Yeah, I guess I did. But you must understand, that's not how we are. Not how our friends are. We don't talk about things like this."

"Is it okay if I ask?"

Brianna twirled her wine in her glass and watched it for several seconds before responding. "I can't believe I'm saying this, but yes, it is. Thank you."

Dani motioned to the couch as Brianna launched into her story.

"I was young and stupid when I came back to town." Brianna took her place back on the couch. "I had this fantasy of how it would be. I guess I watched too many reunion movies. Funny, they used to be my favorites, but now I can't stand them."

"What made you decide to come back then?"

"I was in college. I had a really good friend who'd been adopted. She found her birth mother, and it turned out to be life-changing for her. I was inspired, and she encouraged me to reconnect with my dad."

"So at twenty-one you stroll into town. Did he know you were coming?"

"Nope." Brianna smiled. "I told you I watched too many reunion movies. They always walk in unannounced."

"How did it go?"

"At first, it was okay. Until I asked about his

other family. He said my mom knew all along, so he was shocked when she ran away. When I pushed him, he told me what consenting adults agreed on wasn't anyone else's business. I lost it on him," Brianna said. "I remember screaming that when consenting adults have children, that bullshit doesn't fly. Because I certainly didn't consent to having my family torn apart. Do you know what the asshole said?"

"I'm afraid to ask."

"He said it was unfortunate collateral damage." Brianna pulled her legs up and hugged them against her chest. "What the fuck kind of person tells his daughter her life being ripped apart was unfortunate collateral damage?"

"Wow." Dani's jaw clenched. "So that was it then?"

"I wish it were, but I was young and craved a relationship with him." Brianna rocked in her seat and rubbed her hand up and down the arm of her sweatshirt. "How pathetic is that?"

"No, Bri, it's not pathetic. That's what all kids want."

"Did you?"

"I thought we were talking about you," Dani said. Brianna shot her a look and didn't say anything, so Dani continued. "Yes, I spent so many nights wondering why my mom didn't love me enough to stay or come back."

"How long did it take you to figure out it had nothing to do with you?"

"You mean I was supposed to figure that out?" Dani said with half a smile.

Aww. Brianna recognized the pain behind Dani's smile and wished she could say something to bring the spark back into her eyes.

"Seriously, on my worst days, I still think it must have been something I did." Dani pointed at her head. "Up here, I know it wasn't me." She moved her hand to her chest and patted it. "But my heart doesn't necessarily believe it."

"We're quite the pair. Maybe that's why you're so easy to talk to."

"Aww, thanks, I feel the same way about you." Dani smiled.

Brianna considered letting the subject drop but realized she wanted to tell her story. It had been buried inside for so long, maybe it was time for it to come out. "I left town and didn't return for six months. It should have been a clue when he never tried to contact me after I left. But I was a glutton."

"The second time turned out as bad as the first?" Dani lightly touched her arm.

"Ironically, no. He said all the right things. He told me what a rotten father he was and that he wanted to be the father I deserved. He even paraded me all over town introducing me to everyone. I left town at the end of that weekend feeling on top of the world." Brianna shook her head.

"It didn't last?"

"Nope, I don't think it was ever real. It was a bunch of empty words. There's something to the saying that actions speak louder than words." She'd been looking down at her lap when she spoke, but she stopped and looked into Dani's eyes.

Dani gave her a reassuring nod.

"I wanted to matter," Brianna said sadly. "I wanted to be a priority in my dad's life. When I told him that's what I wanted, he laughed and said it was easy because I would always be a priority."

"He couldn't sustain it?"

"Never even tried. I just kept giving him passes and making excuses for him. I got used to him forgetting my birthday and Christmas. I even forgave him when he didn't send me a card when I graduated from college or when I got my first professional job. He never remembered any of my friends' names, regardless of how many times I talked about them. He never asked me any questions about my life or showed any interest in anything I enjoyed."

Even though her chest ached, it felt good to share what she'd buried for so long. "I tried to convince myself that he wasn't really rejecting me because he didn't even know me. When I called with exciting news, he would change the subject as soon as he politely could. I pretended that he was interested in my life, despite all the evidence to the contrary. After a couple years of that, I knew I would never be a priority."

"Is that when you walked away?"

"No." Brianna was embarrassed by her own naïvety. "I justified his behavior, and decided it was just who he was. If I wanted a relationship with him, I needed to suck it up and accept him as-is."

"What was the final straw?"

"Are you sure you want to hear this?" *Do I really want to tell it?*

"Definitely, but only if you're comfortable."

"I'm comfortable with you." *Wow.* It was true. She liked the way Dani looked at her while she talked and seemed genuinely interested in what she had to say. "I'm just embarrassed."

"No need to be embarrassed with me."

"This couch is huge. I feel like you're a million

miles away." Brianna patted the seat cushion next to her.

Dani slid toward Brianna and stopped a couple of feet away. She tucked her legs under her and faced Brianna.

"Better," Brianna said. "I was on my way to work, and some idiot passed me on the interstate. He must have been going at least ninety. I found out later he was drunk. When he whipped back into my lane, he clipped the front of my car. I spun out of control into the left lane and was T-boned by an oncoming truck. The car flew off the road and slammed into a concrete embankment."

"Oh, my God!" Dani gasped and touched the faint scar on Brianna's forehead. "Is that where this came from?"

"Yes," Brianna answered softly. She pulled back the collar of her shirt, revealing a three-inch scar on her left clavicle. "Amazingly, this is the only other evidence I have."

Dani brushed her fingers against Brianna's other scar.

Brianna shivered, and Dani started to pull her hand back. Brianna put her hand on top of Dani's and pressed it against the scar. "It's okay." She closed her eyes and held Dani's hand against her skin.

When she opened her eyes, Dani was looking at her with watery eyes.

"You're lucky you survived," Dani said.

"That's what the paramedics said, too. They were shocked when they arrived, and I was awake and alert." Brianna released Dani's hand. "My mom and stepdad were on their dream vacation, a Mediterranean cruise. I didn't want to ruin it for them, so I told the paramedics to contact my dad."

"I don't like where this story is going."

"The next thing I know, I'm waking up in the hospital, barely able to move, bruised from head to toe. I should have known that something was up when I asked the doctor about my dad, and he couldn't get out of the room fast enough. Eventually, the nurse had to tell me he wasn't coming."

"He didn't come?" Dani said, the anger clear in her tone.

"I thought it was a mistake, so I asked the nurse for a phone. It was no mistake." Brianna's chest tightened, but she refused to cry. The son of a bitch didn't deserve her tears. "He said he was too busy with the campground to come. I was in the hospital for five days, and he never once called or visited."

Dani took Brianna's hand.

The warmth from Dani's hand was comforting. Brianna squeezed it. "I was so embarrassed that I didn't tell anyone, except to call in to HR at work. I spent the longest five days of my life alone in the hospital."

"I'm so sorry, Bri. What an asshole." Tears welled in Dani's eyes. "Someone should have been there for you. You never should have had to have gone through that by yourself. I'm sorry."

Brianna looked down at her lap. She blinked back tears. *Don't cry.* "And until today, I have never told anyone that story."

"Would it be wrong to say that I'm honored?"

"No." Brianna looked at Dani's face. She'd waited years to see the compassion she saw there.

"I wish I could come up with something profound to say, but words don't seem enough. Can I give you a hug?"

"I'd like that." Dani slid over and wrapped her arms around Brianna, who finally let her tears flow.

❧❧❧❧

Brianna hugged Helen one last time and picked up the heavy bag of food from the kitchen table. "You're gonna spoil me."

"That's my intention, so you'll keep coming back." Helen nodded toward Dani. "We like having you around."

Dani feigned a yawn. "Except for the lack of sleep."

"It's your own fault, keeping me up until two a.m.," Brianna said. "Besides, I planned on leaving this morning. If I'm not mistaken, you're the one that begged me to stick around."

"Seriously, begged? Aunt Helen, are you going to let her get away with this slander?"

Helen shrugged. "I do recall you whining at breakfast because you hadn't gotten the chance to take her to your favorite fishing hole."

Brianna chuckled and nodded. "That's how I remember it, too."

Dani crossed her arms over her chest and glared.

"Pouting doesn't become her." Helen winked. "Seriously, it was lovely to have you. Please, come back any time."

"I'll be back in a couple weeks. If that's okay with you."

"Perfect." Helen clasped her hands together.

"I better hit the road. The sun will be setting soon, and I'd like to make it to the interstate before it does."

"I'll walk you out." Dani picked up Brianna's duffel bag.

At the Jeep, Brianna shuffled from foot to foot. Since when did she get nervous saying goodbye? A hug was in order, wasn't it?

Dani smoothed the bottom of her shirt for what must have been the fifth time. Was she as uncomfortable as Brianna?

An awkward silence hung in the air. Brianna couldn't believe how ridiculous she was being. She probably suffered from a disclosure hangover since they'd shared so much this weekend. *Relax.* Putting on her most casual smile, she said, "Thank you so much for everything. I had a great time."

Dani smiled. "Me too. See you in two weeks?"

"Yep. And I'm sure I'll talk to you before that."

"Good. We still have some business to take care of." Dani fumbled with the zipper on her jacket.

Oh, for God's sake. Had she forgotten all her social graces? Brianna stepped forward and opened her arms. "I better hit the road, so I don't have to drive the whole way in the dark."

Dani walked into the hug and squeezed. Brianna breathed in deeply. Dani smelled of outdoors. *Nice.* Surrounded by the city, it was rare for her to experience the scent.

Dani stepped back and smiled. "You drive carefully. Please, text me when you get home."

Brianna's chest clenched. When was the last time anyone told her that? Such a simple act of caring. "Will do." Brianna climbed into the Jeep, not wanting Dani to see the look on her face.

Dani waved as she pulled from the driveway.

Chapter Thirteen

*B*rianna stepped out of her Jeep and stretched. She'd made good time despite the heavy traffic. Of all places, Molly chose the Gingham Café. It had been Brianna's favorite restaurant as a kid. She'd thought it was so elegant. She chuckled to herself. Wow, had it always been such a dive?

Several lights were burnt out in the sign, which turned the Gingham Café into the "in ham Café." The parking lot had also seen its better days with weeds growing up between the numerous cracks in the pavement. Did she even want to see what the inside looked like?

She pulled open the front door and was pleasantly surprised that the restaurant appeared clean, even if the décor looked to be something out of the eighties.

Molly waved at her from a booth in the corner.

Brianna smiled and waved back.

Molly jumped to her feet and wrapped Brianna in a hug. *Nice.* It was a real embrace, not a polite pat on the back and air kiss. Brianna squeezed her tightly before releasing her. "I cannot believe you chose the Gingham."

Molly smiled. "My mom always laughed when they let us vote on a restaurant. *You* always picked this place."

Brianna glanced around the room. "Wasn't it swankier than this when we were kids?"

Molly shook her head. "I don't think so. We thought it was fancy because it had cloth napkins and real silverware."

"Holy shit." Brianna picked up the butterknife from the table. "They still have the gigantic knives that weigh a ton. Remember how we used to have to use two hands just to hold them to put jelly on our toast?"

"Yeah, and we'd have about ten of those little plastic jelly tubs all over the table because we'd slather our toast so full."

Brianna laughed, remembering the good times they'd shared at the Gingham. "And we thought the food was gourmet. Especially when they put the parsley garnish on the side."

"And we used to fight over who got to eat my mom's, so she'd tear it in half just to shut us up."

"Were we even supposed to eat that shit?" Brianna asked. "I don't think I've seen that on a plate in years."

Molly shrugged. "I'm not sure."

A waitress arrived with two glasses of water and asked if they were ready to order.

Brianna quickly scanned the menu and settled on scrambled eggs with a side of pancakes.

"Their pancakes are still to die for," Molly said.

"Do they still have the syrup that will put me in a sugar coma just smelling it?"

"Yep."

"Sweet."

Molly's face turned serious. "Tell me. How are you liking being back in Flower Hills?"

"This is only my second time. Technically, my third if you count the reading of Donald's will, but I don't."

"Does that mean you haven't formed an opinion or that you're avoiding answering?"

"Good question." Brianna rubbed her chin. "It's a bit surreal."

Molly put her elbows on the table and leaned forward. "How so?"

"I never thought I'd come back here." Brianna paused. "No, more like I never thought I'd *want* to come back here."

Molly tilted her head and raised her eyebrows. "Are you saying you want to be back here?"

Do I? She'd been asking herself that a lot the last couple of weeks. "I've been here two out of the past three weekends."

"Is that something you learned in the city?"

"Huh? What did I learn in the city?"

"Answering a question without really answering it." Molly winked.

Brianna grinned. "Learned behavior, I guess. To answer your question. My last visit was one of the nicest weekends I've had in a very long time."

"What made it so good?"

"The pace. Being outdoors. Seeing you." Brianna paused. "*Dani.*"

Molly studied her for several seconds.

Brianna hoped her face wasn't flushing under the scrutiny.

"I see. And you're sure...?" Molly paused and looked to the ceiling as if trying to find her words. She gazed back at Brianna. "You're sure there's no," Molly raised her hands and made air quotes, "chemistry?"

"Molly Ann, are you asking me if there is anything going on between Dani and me?" Brianna put on a stern face. "You asked me that before."

Molly held up her hands as if in surrender. "Okay, okay. It's just the look you get on your face when you talk about her."

"And what look might that be?"

The waitress dropped off a large bottle of syrup. "Breakfast should be out soon, ladies."

Molly waited for the waitress to leave. "Goofy happiness."

Oh, God. That was a perfect description, but she wasn't about to admit it to Molly. "Really? Goofy happiness? What kind of look is that?"

Molly waved her hand at Brianna. "Never mind. What are you guys up to this weekend?"

"Apparently, I've volunteered to help get the campground ready for opening day."

"What exactly does that entail?"

"Hell if I know." Brianna chuckled. "Dani gave me all sorts of options. I think we're setting out picnic tables and Porta Potties with a skid steer."

"Wow. Look at you and your bad self, throwing around the lingo."

"Impressive, huh?" Brianna smiled.

"You don't actually know what a skid steer is, do you?"

Brianna sat up straighter in her chair and pretended to polish her fingernails on the front of her shirt. "I'll have you know that I do. It's one of those compact tiny tractor thingies with a bucket and a small cab that looks like a cage."

Molly shook her head. "You Googled it, didn't you?"

"No," Brianna said indignantly. "Dani told me."

"She told you it was a little tractor thingy?"

Molly bit her lip, but her eyes danced in amusement.

"It might have been a little more technical than that."

"A little? Do you have a clue how to drive one of those *tractor thingies*?"

"How hard could it be? I drove an ATV."

"Famous last words." Molly grinned. "When is opening day, anyway?"

"Three weeks from tomorrow, so I'm gonna try and help as much as possible this weekend since I won't make it back again until then."

"Cool. Do you think you can talk Dani into taking you to the Spotted Owl?"

"I've been working on her, but she's stubborn. If I can talk her into it, are you free this weekend?"

Molly's face fell. "No, we're going out of town this weekend. But I'll pencil it in for when you're here next."

"Challenge accepted." Brianna pretended to twirl an imaginary mustache. "Dani will succumb to my will."

❧ ❧ ❧ ❧ ❧

Dani finished filling the ATV with gas and leapt into the driver's seat. She'd not expected Brianna to be here so soon, but she'd texted a few minutes ago, saying she'd be there shortly.

The ATV roared down the service road. Skidding around the corner, she spotted Brianna's Jeep parked in front of the store. *Shit. That was fast.* She scanned the area and located Brianna sitting on top of the picnic table near the entrance. Her long blue jean-clad legs dangled from the edge, and she swung them back and forth.

Time to show Bri. She'd lost a little of her ATV cred getting stuck in the mud, but she'd redeem herself with this move. She shoved the gear into high and pushed the pedal to the floor. *Bummer.* The bumpy road made it impossible to see Brianna's face as she bounced along the path. She swung out and headed for the small berm.

She'd made this jump a thousand times, but Brianna wouldn't know that. When she realized she was coming in faster than normal, she tightened her grip on the steering wheel and let off on the gas. *Too late.* Her tires hit the incline, and she went airborne. *Freedom!* She loved how it felt in the air but wasn't as in love with the landing.

The tires hit the ground hard. *Damn!* The jolts shot through her body as the ATV landed, bounced, and slammed down again. Her arms strained to keep control of the steering wheel. After regaining control, she turned sharply and shot off toward the store.

Only a few yards from where Brianna sat, she skidded to a stop and cut the engine.

Brianna's face was a mixture of shock and amusement. "What the hell was that?" Brianna scowled, but her eyes held amusement. "And more importantly, why didn't you let me try that last time?"

Dani smiled and hurried up the steps. "You made good time."

Brianna got to her feet and walked into Dani's hug.

Dani sighed. Any tension left in her body erased.

"Surprisingly, the traffic wasn't bad." Brianna stepped back. "So what the hell kind of move was that?"

"You like it?" Dani strutted back toward the

ATV.

"Are you trying to impress me?"

"Did it work?"

Brianna looked toward the sky and rubbed her chin before shaking her head. "Nope, still seeing you buried in the mud."

"Aw, come on. I got some dope air on that jump."

Brianna curled her lip. "Maybe a smidge."

God, it was nice to have Brianna here. She'd not realized how much she'd been looking forward to it until she'd seen her Jeep. "Ready to get to work?"

"I'm ready for duty, boss."

"Ugh, how many times do I have to remind you, you're the boss?"

☙☙☙☙

Dani pulled the ATV to a stop near the river. She scanned the area. The guys had dropped two piles of tables and Porta Potties on each end of the lot along the river. Hopefully, they'd remembered to leave more up by the clubhouse and the loft, but she couldn't quite see from her vantage point. *Oh, well.* They had plenty of work to do here.

"Where's the skid steer?" Brianna asked.

Dani shot her a glance. *Huh?* Was Brianna screwing with her? She pointed. "Right there."

"Stop messing with me." Brianna crossed her arms over her chest. "That doesn't have a bucket."

Dani put her hand over her face. "Oh, God, I failed at teaching you. That's a skid steer. I just took the bucket off and put forks on it."

Brianna's eyes widened. "You can do that?"

"Obviously." Dani took Brianna's arm and led her toward the equipment. "We have all kinds of attachments for it. A mulcher, backhoe, brush hog, rock grapple—"

Brianna held up her hands. "Really? You expect me to believe that? A brush hog?"

"Honest," Dani said, trying not to laugh. "It's a brush mower, but we call it a brush hog."

"And you connect it to this?" Brianna examined the forks and studied where they attached.

Dani pointed. "See, right there is where it hooks."

"Wow. This shit is even cooler than I thought." Brianna bounced on the balls of her feet. "This is going to be so fun. Can we put the bucket on later?"

Adorable. Oh, shit. Since when did she think of her friend, her boss, as adorable? Brianna's enthusiasm was infectious. *That's all.* Her hair glistened in the sunlight as it flared out with each jump. *Stop.* "If you get your picnic tables and outhouses put in place, I'll let you use the bucket to fill some of the potholes on the road."

"Yes!" Brianna raised her hands over her head as if she'd scored a touchdown.

Dani shook her head. "Once you're done dancing, do you mind getting in?"

"Sorry." Brianna gave her a sheepish grin and climbed into the seat.

After going over the driving instructions, Dani pulled the safety bar over Brianna's lap and shook. *Secure.* "Do you think you've got it?"

Brianna gripped the levers and nodded. "I still don't understand why there isn't a steering wheel."

"You'll get it once you drive it for a while. It can turn on a dime. Something you couldn't do with a steering wheel."

"I'll take your word for it." Brianna smiled. "So

all I have to do is take my forks, pick up a table, and move it to where you have mapped out."

"Yep."

"Sounds pretty simple."

Dani stifled a chuckle. She'd never met anyone who didn't take a while to get used to using hand levers to maneuver the skid steer. "Okay, let's see what you've got." She closed the door and stepped back. "Fire her up."

Brianna punched the buttons in the sequence Dani had showed her, and the engine rumbled to life. She flashed Dani a thumbs-up as Dani pulled her cell-phone from her belt and backed away. This moment needed to be captured on video.

The skid steer leapt forward, then backward and forward again in jerky motions. Brianna's head snapped back as the machine lurched. She looked through the window at Dani, gave her an innocent smile, and shrugged.

Priceless.

In fits and starts, Brianna drove toward the pile of picnic tables while Dani continued to film. As she got nearer, she veered to the right toward the river. In her panic, she must have pulled back hard on her right lever because the skid steer vaulted backward. Brianna let go of the controllers, put her hands in the air, and came to a stop.

Still filming, Dani jogged to Brianna. She was laughing so hard tears rolled down her face. "What the hell was that?" she yelled over the engine.

"This damned thing is possessed." Brianna glowered. "I pushed the right lever, and I went left. Damned thing."

"Remember I told you to pull the lever back

in the direction you want to go, and the other lever forward."

"This is unnatural." Brianna made an exaggerated motion of running her hands through her hair. "I'll never get it."

"Come on, drama queen. You've got a bunch of tables to move before you get a bucket." Dani waved her hand toward the pile of tables.

Before long, Brianna was moving forward, backward, left, and right without much difficulty. It took her longer to master raising and lowering the tines to the correct level to pick up a table. On her first pass, she'd jammed the fork into the wood, splintering it, but soon had it lifted into the air.

Dani clapped and danced on the sideline as Brianna raised her fist in triumph. She pointed to where Brianna needed to take the first table.

With a confident nod, Brianna moved onto the gravel road and went to turn.

Shit. Dani had forgotten to tell her about turning heavy machinery too quickly. The gravel under the skid steer's tires splayed out, and a giant rut appeared. Brianna must have felt the gravel moving under her, so she tried to correct, which only dug a deeper groove.

Once again, Brianna stopped and held up her hands. "What the hell did I do now?" she yelled out the window.

Dani stepped onto the tire and peered into the window. "Now we're gonna have to put the bucket on, so we can clean up your mess."

Brianna stuck out her lip. "I think I'm a better ATV driver."

"No doubt." Dani smiled and winked.

Chapter Fourteen

After only two visits to the loft, it was Brianna's favorite place in Thundering Pines. The view from this high was spectacular. She felt as if she were a bird nestled in a tree. The pine forest was a sight, but it was the view of the water that captivated her.

She strained to see the picnic tables she'd placed today and several areas of road she'd repaired, most of which she'd torn up moving the tables. She took one more look and turned from the windows.

It was so peaceful and relaxing here. She sank into the couch, rested her back against the arm, and stretched her legs out toward Dani, who sat on the other end. "So, tell me, how did you end up single at your age?"

Dani smirked, seeming to measure her response.

"Oh, God," Brianna said. "That came out so wrong."

Dani laughed and pointed at the glass of wine in Brianna's hand. "Do I need to cut you off?"

"Apparently." Brianna slapped her hand against her own forehead. "I'm sorry. I just meant, what's your story? It's unusual for an attractive woman like you to be unattached."

"How do you know I'm unattached?" Dani raised her eyebrows.

"Oh, wow," Brianna stammered. "I'm so sorry. I

just assumed because…"

"Relax." Dani patted Brianna's foot. "I'm single."

Brianna wasn't expecting the wave of relief that washed over her. She didn't have time to analyze her reaction since Dani waited for a response. "By choice?"

"Yep, by choice. No secret broken heart or anything like that."

"You just never found the right one?" Brianna intentionally left her question gender-neutral.

"I guess not." A fleeting look of sadness crossed Dani's face. "I'm not sure I'm built for being in a relationship."

"Come on." Brianna raised her glass to her lips but didn't take a drink. "Aren't we all searching for the one?"

"I suppose," Dani said. "Apparently, you found your one."

Brianna still held the wineglass next to her lips, and she finally took a sip, letting the liquid swish around inside her mouth. "No, you're not changing the subject. It's my turn to quiz you." The low lighting from the setting sun made Brianna bolder.

"Fine, hit me with your best shot." A genuine smile lit Dani's face.

Brianna studied Dani's hazel eyes but found she couldn't hold her gaze. She recovered by making it seem that she was looking toward the ceiling in thought. *Be careful.* She could get lost in Dani's eyes. "Ever been in a serious relationship?"

"Depends on how you define serious."

"Interesting answer." Brianna brushed a wisp of hair off her face and narrowed her eyes as she contemplated Dani's response. "How do *you* define serious?"

"Nope, it's your question, you tell me."

"Fine, any relationship over a year?"

"Yep."

"How long?"

"Let's see." Dani counted on her fingers. "I guess it was around four years."

"Four years sounds pretty serious to me. Tell me about..." Brianna stopped mid-sentence, realizing she didn't know whether to say her or him. She settled on, "Tell me about your love."

"Who said anything about love?" Dani answered.

The response and the unreadable look on Dani's face caught Brianna off guard. "I'm sorry if I'm prying." The dark liquid swirled around inside her glass as Brianna moved her wrist in a circle. "We can talk about something else if this is making you uncomfortable."

Dani's eyes softened, and Brianna could sense the internal struggle raging inside Dani. After what seemed like minutes, Dani said, "You're fine. I guess I'm out of practice having conversations like this."

"Me too. It seems like the older I get, the less real conversations I have with people."

"Very true." Dani nodded. "What was the question?"

"I have a different one now."

"Great." Dani groaned.

"You were in a relationship with someone for four years and you weren't in love?"

"It was complicated."

"Really, you're going to give me a Facebook answer?"

Dani laughed. "It was worth a try. I met him when I was twenty."

"Tell me about *him*," Brianna said, emphasizing

the pronoun.

⚛⚛⚛⚛⚛

Dani's first reaction was to refuse, but when she looked into Brianna's sincere eyes, she found she wanted to share her story. Before responding, she pulled her legs from under herself. Her toes tingled as the blood flowed to them.

Brianna shifted to give Dani more room as she stretched her legs out beside Brianna's.

"His name was Carl Evans, and my dad picked him out for me," Dani began.

"You've got me intrigued," Brianna said.

"As my father's disease progressed, he became obsessed with my future. He wanted to ensure there was a man to take care of me, despite my protests."

Their heated conversations raced through Dani's mind. The more the disease ravaged his body, the more controlling he was with her. It was as if the more dependent he became, the more he wanted to take her independence. No matter what arguments she presented, she couldn't break through his stubborn insistence.

"When Dad took his pickup in for a brake job, Carl was his mechanic. Carl didn't stand a chance. Dad set his sights on him the moment they met."

She still remembered how animated her father was when he came home raving about the bright young man who was a magician with vehicles. Because he was so enthusiastic about Carl, it was one of the last times she was nearly able to forget that he was in a battle for his life.

"By the way Dad talked about Carl, you would

have thought he was courting him," Dani said with a smile. "He told me about the handsome young man with the golden hair, firm handshake, and quick smile."

"Your dad actually said golden hair?" Brianna stifled a giggle.

"Right? He actually did. It was like he was crushing on him."

"Apparently, your dad picked well if you were with him for four years."

"Like I said, it was complicated." Dani let out a long sigh and slowly shook her head.

"Are you gonna leave me hanging?"

"No, but I need a refill." Dani gulped down the last of the wine in her glass, even though there was nearly a third of a glass left. "How about you?"

Brianna held up her half-full glass. "You could top me off."

A feeling of claustrophobia engulfed Dani, and she struggled to breathe. She needed to quell her panic. Before returning to the couch, she painstakingly wiped down the entire countertop, even though she'd only spilled a tiny drop of wine. After emptying the bottle into their glasses, she carried it back to the kitchen and placed it in the garbage can. She felt Brianna's gaze on her when she pulled the not-yet-full bag from the garbage can and slowly tied the drawstring.

"You're running out of ways to stall unless you plan on taking the garbage outside," Brianna said to her back.

"Was I that obvious?"

"Just a little." Brianna held up her thumb and forefinger, so only a single piece of paper would fit between them.

"Where was I?" When Brianna didn't answer, Dani sighed and continued. "Carl was a good man. *Is* a good man, but I was never in love with him. I wanted to be for my dad's sake, but I discovered that's not how love works."

Brianna shook her head and took a sip from her nearly overflowing glass.

"Unfortunately, Carl did fall in love with me and my family. He assured my dad he would take care of me forever, so Dad needn't worry. Ironically, neither of them realized that I didn't join in when they talked about our wedding. I think the two of them had it planned down to the flowers I would carry." Dani looked down at her wine but didn't bring it to her lips; instead, she stared at the liquid as if looking into a crystal ball.

"Your dad's dying wish was for you to marry Carl?" Brianna put her hand on Dani's outstretched leg.

"Yes. It broke his heart that we didn't get married before he died. He kept dropping hints about walking me down the aisle. Then when he could no longer walk, he let me know he could still wheel me down."

"In order for there to be a wedding, didn't Carl need to ask you?"

"He asked me the first day of every month for over three years, and I said no every time."

"Ouch, that's some persistence."

She found herself dreading the end of the month, knowing that she would have to see the look of disappointment in her father's eyes. Then after he died, Carl's despair reminded her anew that she was dishonoring her dad.

"I will probably regret it for the rest of my life."

"Saying no?"

"No, letting him ask me so many times." Pain bubbled inside her. Dani pulled her legs toward her and wrapped her arms around them.

"It's okay, Dani."

Dani's breath caught in her throat, and she struggled to exhale.

Brianna slid down the couch toward Dani.

Tentatively, Dani put her hand over Brianna's and lightly squeezed. When Dani opened her mouth to speak, a sob escaped. She didn't want Brianna to see her this way. Turning away, she put her hands over her face. She needed to get a grip before she embarrassed herself.

It was a mistake telling this story. Why did she think she could do it without emotion? Images of the pained look on her dad's face flooded her mind, and she couldn't make them disappear. Brianna moved closer and put her arm around her.

At first, Dani stiffened but soon relaxed against Brianna's shoulder. Tears silently rolled down her cheeks as her father's face still invaded her thoughts.

Brianna murmured soft reassurance, even though Dani couldn't make out the words. Grief shook her as she tried to regain her composure. They sat together for several minutes until Dani was able to steady her breathing and stop her tears.

"I'm so sorry, Bri." Dani abruptly moved away from Brianna.

How humiliating.

"Dani, talk to me. What just happened?"

Dani bolted off the couch. "I'm so embarrassed. I'm sorry you had to see that. It's probably time we get back to the house." She picked up their still full glasses and took them to the kitchenette, where she frantically straightened up the already clean kitchen while Brianna looked on.

"Nothing to be embarrassed about," Brianna said. "I believe it was me struggling last time here, so it's your turn tonight. It must be something about the loft."

"No, I don't do things like that. I'm not someone who loses control of their emotions."

"Newsflash. You just did."

"What?" Dani whipped around and glared at Brianna. It was bad enough that she'd just lost control, now she had to deal with Brianna taunting her.

"You heard me. Now get your ass back here and sit down." Brianna's normally soft brown eyes held a challenge.

Dani's jaw clenched, and heat spread across her cheeks. When she glanced down at her hand, she was surprised it was steady because she felt as if her entire body was trembling. She settled her stare on Brianna, and her nostrils flared.

Without warning, Brianna burst out laughing. Her perfect white teeth flashed the smile that already had the ability to disarm Dani.

"What the hell is so funny?"

"I never saw someone flare their nostrils when they were pissed. I thought it was only cartoon bulls that did that." Brianna gave her a big smile.

"Damn you." Dani's shoulders relaxed, and she grinned. "Who are you, Brianna Goodwin?" *And why do you have this effect on me?*

"I'm your non-adult friend, remember? Now grab our wine and get over here. I still can't believe you took a nearly full glass away from me. People have lost limbs for less."

Dani laughed, picked up their glasses, and returned to the couch. Brianna had expertly distracted her from her grief, first by making her angry and then making her laugh. Dani suspected it was calculated, which made her appreciate Brianna even more.

Once Dani was seated, Brianna said, "Let me see if I have this straight. You stayed with a man you never loved for nearly four years because you didn't want to disappoint your dad?"

"Pretty much sums it up."

"And you stayed with Carl how many years after your dad died?"

"Three. How fucked up is that?"

"Why?"

"Every time I went to break up with Carl, I'd see my dad's face. Literally, one of the last things he said to me on his death bed was, 'Marry Carl.' Then he put the nail in the coffin and said he would be in heaven looking down on his grandkids. You have to understand, I loved my dad more than I have ever loved anyone in this world."

"Breaking up with Carl was the equivalent of breaking your dad's heart?"

Dani nodded.

"Carl was your way of keeping your dad alive."

"Wow, you're good. The day I finally broke it off was probably the worst day of my life. Worse than the day my dad died. In my eyes, I broke the hearts of two good men that day."

"You do know you did the right thing, don't you?"

"Yes, but that only made me feel worse. I selfishly strung him along all that time. I'm not sure I will ever forgive myself for it."

"You have to." Brianna's voice was full of conviction.

"Want to know the worst part? Carl forgave me long ago."

"What ever happened to him?"

"He's still in town. He's married with two kids."

"See, no permanent damage."

"The dumbass." Affection swelled in Dani. "Every time I see him, he still calls me the one that got away."

"Sounds like a pretty great guy."

"The best, and that's why this is so messed up. Why couldn't I have made it work?"

"The heart wants what the heart wants."

"Isn't that a famous poem?"

"You mean I didn't just make it up?" Brianna winked.

"Afraid not, Shakespeare."

"Did I just quote Shakespeare? Pretty impressive, huh?"

"I think it was actually Emily Dickinson."

"Close enough." Brianna smiled.

⁂

Dani glanced at the clock. "Holy shit. It's two a.m." Why did time disappear with Brianna?

"You talk a lot." Brianna winked. "But I'm glad you did." She picked up her empty wineglass on the table. "I'm afraid neither of us should be driving."

"That's okay. I stay here sometimes. I just need to send Aunt Helen a text, so she'll know where we are when she wakes up in the morning."

"I suppose we should think about getting some sleep." Brianna carried the wineglasses to the sink and began rinsing them. "*Someone* is probably planning on working me all day tomorrow."

"I think I can pull a few strings and make sure you don't have to work too hard."

Brianna had her back to Dani, washing the popcorn bowl they'd used earlier, when Dani said, "Hey, Bri."

"What?" Brianna turned around.

"Thanks."

"For what?"

"For tonight, for talking, just for everything." Dani's face heated, so she busied herself pulling blankets and pillows out of the closet. When she turned from the closet, Brianna stood only a couple of feet away.

Brianna put her hands on Dani's shoulders and looked down at her. "I'm touched. Thank you for trusting me with your story."

"What is this?" Dani waved her hand between them. Brianna's brow furrowed. *Shit.* Did Brianna take what she'd said the wrong way? Heat crawled up her neck. "I mean, I've told you things I've not said to anyone."

The deep furrow in Brianna's forehead disappeared, and she smiled. "And I've done the same."

"And that's okay?"

"Why wouldn't it be?"

"Never mind, I'm just being stupid. Too much alcohol and not enough sleep." Dani broke eye contact and started to turn away.

"No, you're not getting away with that. We've spent the evening talking and laughing. You're not going silent on me now."

"I didn't get the impression this was a place you plan on spending much time once we get things straightened out." Dani ran her hand down the soft blanket she held.

"What does that have to do with anything?"

"You're gonna make me say it, aren't you?"

"I'm sorry, Dani. I'm not trying to be ignorant." Brianna's eyes narrowed.

"You're gonna be gone soon." Dani took a step back, and Brianna's hands slid from her shoulders. She turned toward the couch and began spreading a blanket.

"Aw, are you afraid I'm going to disappear on you?"

Dani was surprised by the tears that welled in her eyes. *Damn it!*

"Dani, no, please. It's okay," Brianna said.

"Fuck. Apparently, I can't hold my alcohol. We just met, no biggie." Dani steeled herself, once again embarrassed by her reaction. It was a bad idea letting herself be drawn into a friendship with someone who would be gone before she knew it.

"I feel it, too, Dani. It's been a long, long time since I've talked to someone like I have to you."

Dani continued fluffing the blankets, trying to think of a lighthearted reply. Words escaped her.

"Dani, I believe this could be the start of a beautiful friendship."

Dani laughed. "That's so *Casablanca* of you."

"You mean that wasn't from *Gone with the Wind*?"

"Afraid not, Scarlett."

Chapter Fifteen

Time at Thundering Pines wreaked havoc on Brianna's sleep. She'd woken at eight a.m., only to find Dani already up. They'd returned to Aunt Helen's for a quick breakfast, shower, and change of clothes before they tackled brush cleanup at Thundering Pines. They'd worked most of the day, but there was still much to be done. Dani would be at it most of the week while Brianna returned to her life in the city.

The lines on the road blurred no matter how hard Brianna focused on them, so she opened her window and let the cold wind thrash her face.

The radio already blared, and she had been singing loudly for several miles, but she still struggled to stay awake.

She probably should have stayed the night in Flower Hills, instead of making the two-hour drive. When Dani tried to convince her to stay, Brianna justified her decision by the hour she saved by traveling at night.

She'd had an amazing time, but sometime late in the day, it was as if the walls were closing in on her, and she just wanted to return to the city. She was too tired to figure out why.

Lake Shore Drive was nearly deserted at this time of night, which was a blessing. She was starting to get jumpy, and the usual fast-moving traffic roaring around the curving roadway would have been too much. When she reached her exit, she slowed and deliberately maneuvered her Jeep onto the ramp.

Relief washed over her when their apartment building came into sight.

Brianna pulled into her parking spot and cut the engine. She ran her hand through her hair and gently slapped her face, hoping to shake the fog from her brain.

Grabbing the duffel bag from the backseat, she fumbled with her access key. Had there been a time she'd been more tired? If she were lucky, Caroline would already be asleep.

All she wanted was a quick shower and to crawl into bed. Or maybe the shower could wait.

Quietly, she opened the apartment door, not wanting to wake Caroline. Without turning on the lights, she tiptoed through the hall.

Sounds came from the bedroom. Caroline must have fallen asleep with the TV on.

Brianna ducked into the bathroom, used the toilet, and brushed her teeth. She pulled off her clothes and contemplated a shower again, but she decided against it. She grabbed her T-shirt and shorts off the hook in the closet and put them on.

The TV got louder.

What channel was Caroline watching? It must be a commercial, they always seemed louder than the shows.

She flipped off the bathroom light and walked down the hallway.

Light came through the crack under the bedroom door.

Caroline must have missed her if she'd gone to sleep with the light and TV on.

Brianna smiled, easing the door open, and abruptly stopped in the doorway.

Caroline lay naked in the middle of the bed. Her fingers were tangled in the hair of the woman between her legs. Her lips were slightly parted, and a moan escaped.

"What the fuck?" Brianna said.

Caroline's eyes popped open, but they were unfocused and glassy. As realization descended, she untangled her fingers from the woman's hair.

When Kylie lifted her head, Brianna gasped. *No!* She stumbled down the hallway, wanting to get away. She needed to find her duffel bag.

"Brianna," Caroline called from the bedroom.

Brianna frantically searched. Where had she put the damned thing?

Caroline came into the living room, tying the drawstring of her silk robe. Her hair was disheveled. A reminder of what Brianna had just seen. "What are you doing?" Caroline walked toward her.

"Where the hell is my duffel?"

"Come here and sit down." Caroline motioned Brianna to the couch.

Brianna ignored her and went into the bathroom. *There it is.* She snatched the duffel from the floor and rushed back into the living room.

"Would you stop, Brianna? For God's sake, what's your problem?" Caroline said, raising her voice.

"Did you seriously just ask me what my problem is?" Brianna glared at her.

"Yes, I did," Caroline said defiantly. "Cut the outrage."

"What is wrong with you? I'm supposed to be okay with this?"

"You agreed to this a long time ago." Caroline waved her hand dismissively.

Before Brianna could answer, Kylie sheepishly walked into the room, carrying her purse and shoes. "I'm sorry, Brianna."

"How the fuck do you expect me to respond to that?" Her face felt as if it were on fire. Adrenaline surged through her body, erasing her tiredness.

"For fuck's sake, leave her alone," Caroline said. "It's not her fault."

"Um, I think I better go and leave you two alone." Kylie ran her hand through her hair, the same hair Caroline's fingers had been entangled in a few minutes earlier.

Brianna watched incredulously as Caroline walked across the room to Kylie and wrapped her arms around her.

Kylie awkwardly returned the hug, keeping her focus on Brianna the entire time.

"I'll call you tomorrow, sweetie," Caroline said.

Kylie hustled from the room, avoiding Brianna's stare.

Once Kylie was gone, Caroline turned to Brianna. "Do you think you can calm down, so we can talk about this?"

"What is there to talk about?"

"Exactly my point." Caroline shrugged. "We've had an open relationship for years, so what's your problem now?"

"An open relationship does not mean sleeping with someone I know in our bed."

"I didn't know you'd written a rule book." Caroline's voice dripped with sarcasm. "Maybe you should have shared it with me, so I didn't have to put up with this bullshit."

"Always a fucking lawyer looking for a loophole." Brianna noticed she still held her duffel bag and slammed it to the floor.

"What's that supposed to mean?"

"I catch you in bed with your best friend, and you're the injured party. Well played, Caroline, well played."

"You're starting to piss me off. An open relationship is an open relationship. You've never complained before, and you certainly never complained when you were out getting some."

All the energy left Brianna's body, and her shoulders slumped. She'd forgotten her earlier fatigue, but it descended now.

Caroline was right. They'd agreed to an open relationship several years ago, when Caroline's eyes had begun to wander. She wasn't about to be like her mother, or her father for that matter. Caroline couldn't cheat on her if she agreed beforehand. *Right?* Standing here now, Brianna wondered if her thinking had been wrong.

The decision had saved their relationship, but for what? Brianna brought her hand to her chest and rubbed it. For what their relationship was always intended. If all went well on the Henning case, Caroline would all but be guaranteed a partnership with the firm. And no doubt, Brianna's promotion should be right around the corner. The power couple would reach the pinnacle.

Like a vulture, Caroline must have recognized her defeated stance because she made her way across the room. "Oh, honey, I'm sorry if you're upset."

"But why Kylie?" Brianna blinked back tears.

Don't hyperventilate. She tried to inhale deeply, but the pain in her chest only allowed her to take a shallow breath.

"It was an accident. The Henning case starts tomorrow, and you know how worked up I get before a big trial."

Caroline approached Brianna and tentatively took her hand. When Brianna didn't pull away, she continued. "You know I always need a release to perform my best, and you weren't here."

"So it's my fault?" Brianna's shoulders tensed.

"Of course not." Caroline put her hand on Brianna's arm.

Brianna wanted to shove it away but didn't.

"I was getting ready to go out, and Kylie dropped by, and…" Caroline stopped mid-sentence and studied Brianna. "And one thing led to another, that's all."

Brianna stared but remained silent.

"I wanted you to come home," Caroline said.

"Why didn't you just ask me?"

"I didn't want to be one of those needy girlfriends." Caroline gently squeezed Brianna's hand and gave her a slight smile. "I know you've got your hands full with the campground, and you're always talking to Danielle. I swear you talk to her more than me."

Brianna's jaw clenched. *Unbelievable.* Now it was her fault. Although there was some truth in Caroline's words, she didn't want to bring Thundering Pines or Dani into this. "I have been focused on the campground."

"No, baby, don't blame yourself. I need to get better at asking you for what I need."

Brianna closed her eyes. Her head felt as if it were full of cobwebs. Wasn't this upside down and backward? She shook her head, hoping to think more clearly. "You and Kylie, is this like a thing, or just…"

Caroline put her hand on Brianna's chest. "Remember, we said we would never talk about what we did when we were with someone else. It's one of the rules."

Brianna's suspicions rose, but before she could respond, Caroline said, "But I'll answer any questions you want if it will help."

"You're right." Relief washed over her. It had to be a one-time thing since Caroline was so readily willing to talk about it.

"Are you sure?"

It wasn't like Caroline to be so accommodating, but Brianna was too tired and too upset to push it. Brianna nodded. "I'm sure."

"Okay, then. No hard feelings between you and Kylie?"

"But…" Brianna started, not knowing what to say.

"You spent the whole weekend with another woman, and you don't see me losing my shit."

Brianna's chest tightened, and she averted her gaze. Was there any difference? She'd cried in Dani's arms. Dani had cried in hers. Which was more intimate? A woman between Caroline's legs or a woman in her arms?

Dani's face invaded her thoughts. Wrapping her arms around herself, she tried to stop the shiver that ran through her body.

Caroline took the opportunity to move closer to Brianna and run her hand down the side of Brianna's body. "Let's not talk about this anymore. I still have my trial tomorrow, and you're home now," Caroline purred.

Brianna froze. Her stomach lurched. Caroline wanted sex. An overwhelming sense of revulsion washed over her, but she wasn't sure if it was for Caroline or herself.

Caroline must have taken Brianna's lack of resistance as consent, so she moved closer and rubbed her body against Brianna. Slowly, she snaked her hand down the front of Brianna's shorts. "Let's have some makeup sex, baby."

She would *never* be like her parents. Especially Donald. Brianna had made the commitment to Caroline and had agreed to an open relationship, so she had no right to renege on it now.

Brianna swallowed down the bile that rose in her throat and let Caroline lead her to the bedroom.

Chapter Sixteen

A knock on the door frame of her office caused Brianna to jump; she looked up from her computer. She hadn't realized anyone else was still in the building.

"Sorry, boss, I didn't mean to startle you." Jason peered in from the threshold.

"What's up?"

"I wondered if maybe I could go home. That is, if you don't need me anymore."

"What time is it?"

"A little after six thirty. I was waiting to see if you needed me to do any more coding."

"Damn, have you been waiting here all this time?" Brianna asked.

"Well, yeah, but it's no big deal."

"Somehow, I don't think Amanda would agree. She hasn't said 'I do' yet, so you best be careful," Brianna teased.

"She understands."

"It's Friday night. You should be taking her out for dinner, not waiting around here."

"That's what she said."

"Tell her I'm sorry and pick up some flowers on your way home."

"What about you? Aren't you going to head home, too?"

"In a little bit. Don't worry about me."

"Don't you and Caroline have dinner plans?"

"Would you get out of here before Amanda starts calling me?" She made an exaggerated shooing motion.

Jason hesitated at the door. By the look on his face, he wanted to say something more. His broad smile replaced the serious look that had been etched on his face. "Okay, I'm going. Have a great weekend."

"You too." She was sure he wanted to ask her why she'd been so uncharacteristically distracted this week. No way would she tell him, but she preferred not to lie.

Her mistakes were piling up as was her guilt. This morning, she'd told him she might have a rush job that he'd need to jump on, but she'd discovered earlier the client wouldn't have the specifications until next week, and she'd forgotten to tell him. This seemed to be happening more often than she cared to admit. She needed to get her head on straight.

Not bothering to slide on her high heels, she stood and walked to the window. Lights all over the city were starting to come on. Her gaze shifted to Navy Pier, where she quickly found the Ferris wheel. She never tired of the view that her forty-eighth-story office afforded her. The minutes slipped by as she watched the Ferris wheel, lost in her thoughts.

Jason was right; she should probably close shop for the night. She walked back to her desk and picked up her cellphone. Nothing from Caroline yet.

Maybe she'd check her email before she left. She sat at her desk and clicked through several that appeared to be junk mail until she spotted an email from Dani. It had only been two weeks since she'd been to Thundering Pines, but today, it seemed like months ago.

Brianna buried her head in her hands, fighting back the tears that threatened. How did she get to this point in her life? More than anything, she needed someone to talk to, who could help her sort out her jumbled feelings.

What's wrong with this picture? Their circle of friends was at least twenty-five deep, so why wasn't there anyone she could pick up the phone and call?

Many times, she'd thought of calling Molly but decided against it. Sad, the only friend she thought she could confide in was one she'd made in grade school and hadn't talked to in years. She'd even contemplated calling one of her old college friends, but why should they want to hear from her after all these years?

She massaged the knots in her shoulders. The face of the person she wanted to talk to more than anyone flashed in her mind. *Dani. Fuck.*

Grabbing her garbage can, she was disappointed to see it had been emptied. Two days ago, she had found herself searching the internet for a counselor. She had been overwhelmed by the number of choices her search brought up. Randomly, she'd chosen ten. One by one, she'd pulled up the websites and had soon become discouraged.

She'd written the names on a notepad, making sure to record the alphabet soup behind their names, LCSW, LMHC, LPC, NCC, ABPP. She had no idea what any of it meant. Her notepad was full of scribbles and notes, but she was no closer to a decision. Eventually, she had crumpled up the list and had thrown it in the garbage. She'd made it this far on her own; she'd just have to suck it up and figure it out for herself.

Brianna quickly read through Dani's email,

typed a response, and hovered her cursor over the send button. Her finger was poised over the left mouse button when her gaze settled on the manila envelope sitting off to the side of her desk.

She removed her hand from the mouse and picked up the envelope. It had come two days ago, but Brianna had yet to thank Dani. She wondered if Dani had received confirmation of its delivery. When she turned the envelope upside down, the contents fell onto her desk. A smile lit her face.

Where in the hell had Dani found these? She didn't think they made scratch-and-sniff stickers any longer until she'd gotten them in the mail.

She lined up the six round stickers on her desk. Cedar, pine, campfire, dirt, fresh grass, and her personal favorite wet dog. Dani must have added that one to the mix since she likely couldn't find a Porta Potty scent.

Using the tip of her fingernail, she lightly scratched a small area on the pine sticker. She'd already scratched it several times since its arrival and was afraid she'd use it all up. Bringing it to her nose, she inhaled deeply. The smell brought tears to her eyes, and she laid her head on her desk.

After several minutes, she sat up. Caroline probably wondered where she was. Maybe she should text her. Brianna picked up her phone and scrolled through her contacts.

☙☙☙☙☙

Damn it. Dani snatched her ringing cellphone from her desk. Brianna's smiling face filled the screen, and her stomach did a flip. She took a deep breath before answering. "Hey, Bri," Dani said, hoping to sound casual.

"Hi, is this a bad time?" Brianna asked.

As soon as she heard Brianna's voice, Dani's chest tightened. "No, not at all, I'm still in the office. I wanted to spruce up our website."

"It's Friday night. You shouldn't be at work."

"Where are you?"

"Work." Brianna laughed. "Okay, fine, you got me."

Dani greeted her response with a genuine laugh. She missed Brianna, especially her laugh, but she certainly couldn't tell her that. "What can I do for you?"

"I just read your email and wanted to respond."

"Oh, okay." Dani hoped the hesitation didn't come out in her voice.

"Is something the matter?"

"No, no, not at all. I just thought you would probably respond via email is all."

"I figured it would be faster, and..." The silence stretched out between them before Brianna continued, "That's not true. It's been a shitty week, and I guess I wanted to hear a friendly voice."

Dani clutched the phone tighter and grinned. "Aw, you just called me friendly," Dani teased.

"Don't get used to it," Brianna said, the smile evident in her voice.

Hope bubbled inside Dani, but she pushed it down. Brianna had been different since she'd visited. It was almost as if the two weekends never happened. If Dani were being honest, which she wasn't going to be, it hurt. It hurt a lot.

Many times over the past two weeks, Dani had

questioned her own perceptions. There had been an undeniable connection between the two, but Brianna's behavior since she'd left Flower Hills said otherwise.

Brianna was never rude to her, but the easy banter was gone. It was all business when they talked, and Brianna relied almost exclusively on email for their communication.

At first, Dani worried she'd done something to offend Brianna, but every time she replayed the time they spent together in her mind, she kept coming up with nothing. For her, their time together had been some of the best she'd had in years. She'd laughed so hard her ribs hurt, and her cheeks ached from smiling so much.

When Brianna switched back to professional mode and began answering all the questions in Dani's email, Dani's shoulders sagged. Was she imagining it or was there sadness in Brianna's voice? She wanted to ask but was afraid her questions would cause Brianna to shut down or, worse, get angry.

They'd finished their business, and Dani knew the conversation would soon be over. She rubbed her chest, hoping to relieve some of the ache. The sad Brianna was better than the cold professional Brianna, but she longed to hear the playfulness in Brianna's voice. *Think.* There had to be something she could say.

⁂

Brianna didn't want the call to end. She felt better than she had all week; just hearing Dani's voice had that effect on her, but she knew the emptiness would descend as soon as they hung up. She had no doubt Dani sensed the wall she'd put up. It was so un-fair, but what could she do? She was not her father's daughter. Donald destroyed relationships. People. Her time needed to be spent repairing her relation-ship with Caroline, not spilling her secrets to Dani.

"Well, I guess I better let you go," Dani said.

"Okay." Heaviness washed over Brianna, and she rested her head on her hand.

"Take care then."

Brianna heard the hesitation in Dani's voice but didn't respond.

After several seconds, Dani said, "Okay, bye, Bri."

"Wait!" Brianna practically shouted into the phone. "Please." Her voice came out in a whisper, and she wondered if Dani heard her.

"Are you okay?"

"No."

"What's the matter? What can I do?"

Brianna could hear the concern in Dani's voice and could imagine the look on Dani's face. During the time she'd spent with Dani, she'd seen it many times. She longed to see the compassion in Dani's soft hazel eyes. "You mean it, don't you?"

"Mean what?"

"You aren't asking just to be nice. You really want to know?"

"Of course I do."

"Thank you."

"Oh, fuck it," Dani said, startling Brianna. "I've been a wreck these last two weeks, trying to figure out what's wrong with you and what I've done to make you push me away." Before Brianna could respond, Dani forged on. "Maybe you'll think I'm the most pathetic person in the world, but I miss you. There, I said it."

Dani stopped talking, and Brianna listened to the silence on the other end of the phone. She hated that she was hurting Dani. She should say something, but what?

"Okay, I get it. I'll stop bothering you," Dani finally said, filling the awkward silence.

"No, I'm sorry," Brianna managed to say through her tears. "I never meant to make you feel bad."

"Bri, it's okay. I just don't understand what's going on with you."

"I miss you, too. I can't remember the last time I've had so much fun or the last time I felt so comfortable talking to someone."

"Me neither. I thought I'd done something wrong."

"No, you didn't. It's me, not you."

Dani laughed. "You did not just use the oldest cliché in the book, did you?"

"I just need a little space." Brianna giggled.

"I hope we can still be friends," Dani countered.

"I'm just not ready for a commitment." Brianna's tears turned to laughter.

"You deserve better."

"I know we've only known each other for a couple months, but I'm afraid we've grown apart," Brianna said.

"Okay, I think it's time I tell you the truth," Dani said. "I've met someone who can drive an ATV better than you."

"No way! But since we're truth telling, if you really cared about me, you would have found Porta Potty scratch and sniffs. I'm afraid wet dog doesn't cut it. Just saying."

"I knew I failed. Now everything makes perfect sense."

"Where the hell did you find them, anyway?" Brianna suddenly felt lighter than she had all week.

With the ice broken, the two fell into an easy conversation. Laughing with Dani was the only therapy she needed. She was grateful Dani didn't push her to talk about what was bothering her.

They'd been talking for some time when another call came in. When Brianna looked at her phone, she cringed. It was after seven forty-five, and she was supposed to be at dinner with Caroline and their friends at seven. So much for working on the relationship.

"Are you getting another call?" Dani asked.

"Yeah, but it can go to voicemail. I suppose I should probably head out because I'm already late for dinner."

"Sorry for keeping you."

"I'm not. I feel good for the first time this week. Thanks for making me laugh."

"Any time."

"I'll talk to you sometime next week then. I'd like to schedule another visit."

"That would be great."

Brianna smiled at the eagerness in Dani's voice.

"Oh, shit, I almost forgot. Are you going to be around on Monday?"

"I should be, why?"

"Aunt Helen has been after me to take her to Navy Pier before the camping season opens, so I told her I'd take her on Monday. I thought maybe we could swing past your office, so I can get you to sign a couple things."

"I'll do you one better. Why don't I meet you two for lunch?" *Presumptuous much*? Maybe they wouldn't want her there. She quickly added, "If you wouldn't mind."

"Mind? Aunt Helen will be thrilled."

"And you?"

"I might be happy, too, but like I told you earlier, I'm not ready to make a commitment."

Brianna chuckled. "It's a date then. Did I ever tell you about the Ferris wheel?"

"No, I don't think so," Dani said.

"Oh. My. God. I can't believe I haven't."

"By your reaction, the Navy Pier Ferris wheel must be something special."

"*Was*," Brianna said.

"It's not anymore?"

"Put your feet on your desk, grab some popcorn and a soda because you are going to learn more about the Ferris wheel than you've ever wanted to know." The tiredness of minutes before was erased as she launched into her story. "I credit the Navy Pier Ferris wheel for bringing my mom back to me."

"Wow, okay, you've got me intrigued. Carry on."

"It was my thirteenth birthday, and my mom hadn't really recovered in the three years since we left Flower Hills. She went to work and took care of me, but there wasn't any joy in our house. I think she felt guilty, so she took me and three of my friends to Navy Pier for the weekend." Brianna walked to the window as she spoke. "I fell in love with the Ferris wheel. My mom says I was obsessed. We must have ridden it at least a dozen times that weekend. It was the first time in years my mom's smile reached her eyes. It was the best weekend ever. And after that, she changed. She started taking care of herself again. Putting makeup on, dressing better, and carrying herself with more confidence. She met my stepdad two months later. I'm sure it was more than the Ferris wheel, but I will always give it the credit."

"Now I'm confused," Dani said. "You said the Ferris wheel *was* something special."

Brianna's chest constricted, and she turned from the window. "It was until the powers that be decided they needed a change. I can still see the *Chicago Tribune* headline. It makes me throw up a bit in my mouth every time I think about it."

"Thanks for the visual," Dani said. "What was the headline?"

"Navy Pier's new Ferris wheel—bigger, taller, faster." Brianna crinkled her nose as she said it. "I wasn't interested in bigger, taller, faster. I loved the smaller, shorter, slower one. I must have ridden it a hundred times over the years."

"Oh, no, they tore *your* Ferris wheel down?"

"Yep, they dismantled it. Right before my eyes."

"You went to Navy Pier to watch it come down?" Dani asked.

"Nope." Brianna looked out the window again. "Guess what I'm looking at right now as we speak?"

"That's a random question," Dani said, her voice filled with confusion.

Brianna chuckled. "I'm staring at the new Ferris wheel out my window."

"What? You can see Navy Pier from your office?"

"Yep."

"Holy shit. That's cool."

Warmth flooded Brianna's chest. "It is pretty cool, except when they were destroying *my* Ferris wheel. I put big ugly curtains over my windows because I couldn't stand to see them doing it. It was a terrible year." Brianna sighed. "The workers tore down *my* Ferris wheel at the same time cancer tore down *my* mom's body."

"I'm so sorry."

"Thank you." Talking with Dani lightened her mood, so she didn't want to go down another path of sadness. "Anyway, the Centennial, that's what they named the new one since it was the hundredth anniversary of Navy Pier, opened for business at high noon the Friday before Memorial Day in 2016. I stood right where I'm standing now watching the people load up for the inaugural ride."

"Since you're a connoisseur, is the new ride any better than the old?"

"I don't know."

"What do you mean you don't know?"

Brianna let out a half snort and half giggle. "You'll think I'm nuts. I've gone to the pier at least once a month with the intention of riding it, and every time, I back out."

"You mean you still haven't ridden the new one?"

"Nope." Brianna gazed out at the Ferris wheel. "Maybe one day."

"Wow, you are a die-hard Ferris wheel loyalist."

"I like it. Die-hard Ferris wheel loyalist. DFWL for short." She smirked. It reminded her of all the letters behind the counselor's names she'd researched. Maybe she could add it to her business cards to see if anyone noticed.

"How did they dispose of a gigantic Ferris wheel?"

"They didn't."

"Did they drop it into Lake Michigan?"

"Swimming with the fishes?" Brianna laughed. "No, they moved it. A company in Missouri bought it for their amusement park."

"At least it had a happy ending."

Leave it to Dani to give it a positive spin. "I'd never thought of it that way. But I miss it. I used to go there a couple of times a month whenever life got too much and ride it. I always came out with a better perspective on things, even if I had to ride it several cycles." *Maybe that's my problem.* The Ferris wheel was her therapy. Maybe she needed to bite the bullet and try a new therapist—the Centennial.

"Sounds like you should give the new one a try."

"I bet you're dying to hear how a Ferris wheel is constructed," Brianna said.

"How'd you guess? My next question was going to be, Brianna, please tell me how they build Ferris wheels."

"You're in luck." Brianna put on her best game show announcer's voice. "I happen to know all about Ferris wheel construction."

Fifteen minutes later, Brianna concluded with, "And that, my friend, is the *Reader's Digest* version of Ferris wheel 101."

"And to think you can see one of the biggest from your office window. Can you see the Sears Tower, too?" Dani asked.

"No, it's west of here. And it's the Willis Tower."

"Never, you can never make me call it that."

"Ah, a traditionalist, I like it." Brianna's cellphone went off again. "Shit, I better let you go, or I might not be alive by Monday."

"Okay. Good night, Bri."

"Night, Dani." Brianna ended the call. She couldn't wait until Monday. Now the weekend wouldn't seem so long.

Brianna looked down at her phone. She should call Caroline back, but instead, she sent a text.

Sorry, got tied up at work. Be there soon.

☙ ❧ ❧ ❧

"I cannot believe that you were nearly two hours late tonight," Caroline said.

Brianna had been bracing for the tirade as soon as the driver dropped them off. She was a little surprised that Caroline hadn't let her have it in the cab, but she'd not spoken the entire ride and stared out the window instead.

"Oh, you're right, I am a horrible girlfriend. Oh, wait, it wasn't me fucking someone else in our bed."

"Are you still harping about that?" Caroline waved her hand as if she were swatting a gnat.

The gesture was like a knife slicing into Brianna's skin, so she turned away and picked up her briefcase.

"Don't you turn your back on me," Caroline said, raising her voice. "You've been sulking around here for the last two weeks."

"I'm sorry I have emotions." Brianna spun around. She tried hard to keep her composure when all she wanted to do was scream at Caroline.

"We've had this arrangement for years. I swear ever since you went back to that Podunk town, I don't even know who you are."

Brianna stared at her a long time, searching for the woman she'd fallen in love with. Their relationship had started as an undeniable sexual attraction. They had sex two hours after they met and spent much of their first year in bed together. Had she ever been in love with Caroline, or was it just lust?

Sex and power. Caroline knew what she wanted; she was driven. Had they not met, Brianna would have left the city. After only a few years at her job, she'd become disillusioned by the corporate grind and had started actively looking for a position in the suburbs.

Caroline's ambition was infectious. She was everything Flower Hills wasn't, at least to the younger version of Brianna. Sophistication. Glamour. Power. Success. They'd been successful. Damned successful. Wasn't that the point?

She'd not questioned it until now. For years, she'd known something was missing, but there was always another party to attend and ladder to climb to give it much thought. Flower Hills and Thundering Pines had made it harder to ignore.

Brianna had no more energy for this argument. "I'm exhausted. I'm going to bed."

"So that's it? That's all you have to say?"

She knew Caroline was goading her, but she had no more fight in her. "Tell me what you want me to say, and I'll say it."

"Tell me that I'm right."

"Okay, you're right."

"About what?"

"I have no idea, but that's what you told me to say, so I said it. Now can I go to bed?"

"No." Caroline's face turned red. "Do you want out of this relationship?"

"That's not what I said." Brianna responded with the line she was trained to say. But tonight, her stomach didn't drop, and her chest didn't tighten. She delivered the line with little effect.

Caroline paused and stared.

Did Caroline sense something different? *Oh, well.* Tonight, she didn't care.

"I'm going to bed," Brianna said, deciding she wouldn't take part in the sick dance they had been doing for years.

Normally, Brianna would be in tears. To add insult to injury, Caroline would detail all the reasons Brianna was lucky. Tonight, she didn't feel lucky, just exhausted.

Before she turned away, she saw the wide-eyed surprise on Caroline's face.

Chapter Seventeen

"What's got you so happy this morning?" Caroline asked. "Big project going at work?"

Brianna hadn't been aware she was humming until Caroline pointed out her mood.

Typical Caroline, thinking a big work project was the key to happiness. Brianna pulled the Grape Nuts from the cabinet while she measured her response.

After their fight on Friday night, they'd spoken little over the weekend. They co-existed in the house but for the most part avoided each other. Caroline had gone out on Saturday night while Brianna stayed in and read the new lesbian novel she'd been wanting to read.

"Nope, I'm only working half a day." Brianna poured a splash of milk over her cereal and stirred in a little honey. She didn't sit, instead preferring to eat standing up while Caroline rushed around the kitchen.

"Really?" Caroline looked at her out of the corner of her eye. "Can I ask what you're doing?"

Brianna thought of being elusive and making Caroline wonder, but she didn't feel like playing the game any longer. "I'm going to Navy Pier."

Caroline rolled her eyes. "I hate that place. I don't know why you go there."

"I didn't ask you to go," Brianna said defensively. If Caroline inquired further about her plans, she decided she would tell her, but she didn't intend to offer up the information.

Caroline didn't ask, already seeming to lose interest in the conversation. "Well, have fun. I probably won't be home until late. I'm sure we'll be working on the case well into the evening."

Brianna took a big bite of cereal and crunched loudly, knowing Caroline hated the sound. *Passive aggressive much?* She felt like an unruly child going for negative attention if she couldn't get positive. "Good luck." Brianna talked around the cereal in her mouth. That should annoy Caroline, too.

"Uh-huh." Caroline picked up her briefcase. She gave Brianna an absentminded kiss on the cheek and was gone.

Brianna stared at the empty kitchen, her emotions churning. Caroline was a beautiful woman, no doubt, but their interactions left Brianna cold. *Fire and ice.* When they'd first met, the fire had burned bright in the bedroom, but everywhere else only ice. Not only was there no fire outside the bedroom, but there wasn't even warmth.

Maybe she wasn't being fair to Caroline; after all, she'd never promised Brianna anything she didn't deliver. Caroline was who she was, and that had been enough for Brianna in the past. So why was she wanting warmth from a woman she knew wasn't capable of giving it? Maybe the question she needed to ask herself was what had changed in her. Why did she crave something they never had? Why was she looking for warmth?

※ ※ ※ ※

Brianna sat on a bench, soaking up the sun and enjoying the gentle spring breeze. She'd been so excited about the day she'd gotten to Navy Pier nearly half an hour early.

Spring was the best season for people watching when they emerged from their houses after a long winter. Some people jogged past in shorts and a tank top while others still dressed in their winter coats and hats. *Leave it to Chicagoans.*

Tilting her head back, she let the sun wash over her. She always loved being outdoors, but it wasn't the same in the city. With the breeze blowing in her hair, she tried to imagine that she wasn't surrounded by giant buildings.

"Imagine running into you here," a voice said.

Brianna excitedly jumped to her feet and engulfed Dani in a bear hug.

Dani seemed surprised by Brianna's reaction but quickly recovered and squeezed her tightly in return.

When they separated, Brianna turned to Aunt Helen and wrapped her arms around the older woman.

"I'm so glad you could join us," Aunt Helen said, hugging Brianna. "Dani's been bouncing around like a kid on Christmas all morning."

Dani blushed and looked away.

"I've been looking forward to it, too." Brianna draped her arm over Dani's shoulders and gave her a one-armed hug.

"What's our plan for the day?" Helen's gaze darted around, taking in the pier.

"Aunt Helen, I told you Bri could only join us for lunch."

"Why?" Aunt Helen frowned.

"She has to get back to work." Dani shook her

head. "I told her not to guilt you, but apparently, I was talking to myself."

"I'm not senile. I can hear you," Aunt Helen said. "It just seems like such a shame that we can't all spend the day together."

"I'm sorry Aunt Helen is not behaving. We'd love to have you, but we understand that you have a *job*." Dani shot a look at Aunt Helen.

"Well, I might be able to arrange something," Brianna said.

Dani's face lit up.

"Actually, I took the rest of the day off, so I didn't have to hurry through lunch."

"We're going to have so much fun." Aunt Helen clapped her hands.

"So what's our first stop?" Brianna asked.

"Dani promised me that we could eat shrimp out of a bucket if it's okay with you."

"Bubba Gump's it is," Brianna said with a smile.

❧❧❧❧

The waiter delivered a large bucket of Cajun shrimp and a smaller basket of hush puppies.

"Oh, my God!" Aunt Helen pulled an enormous shrimp out of the bucket.

"Be careful what you wish for." Dani picked up a shrimp and swam it through the air before she popped it into her mouth.

They were sitting at an outdoor table, and the sun filtered through Dani's hair. Brianna's attention was drawn to the gray streak and the wispy gray hairs at her temples. Brianna didn't agree with Caroline's critical assessment. There was something carefree and natural about it. It was sexy.

She forced herself to look away and concentrate on the conversation.

Dani played with her shrimp and luckily hadn't noticed Brianna's fascination with her hair.

When Brianna glanced at Aunt Helen, the older woman was looking at her with a knowing smile.

"Would you stop playing with your food? We have a day to plan," Brianna said, trying to distract herself from her own thoughts.

"I'm stuffed," Dani said as the waiter cleared the dessert dishes.

"I would hope so," Brianna said. "I have a stomachache just watching you eat."

"She's always had a hollow leg," Aunt Helen said. "Her dad used to say that he knew what it was like to feed a growing boy."

"I wasn't that bad."

"Of course you weren't." Aunt Helen winked at Brianna.

"I saw that. Keep it up, young lady, and we are not going to ride the Ferris wheel." Dani pretended to scold Aunt Helen.

Aunt Helen held up the piece of paper. "Too late, it's already on our itinerary."

Brianna chuckled. "Apparently, agenda-making runs in the family."

Dani peered over Aunt Helen's shoulder at the paper in front of her. "I hope you don't plan on messing up Aunt Helen's agenda like you did mine."

"Nah, but I'm not sure if I can ride the Ferris wheel."

"That's okay, honey." Helen patted Brianna's hand. "We don't have to ride."

"Nope, you have to go and tell me all about it."

"Are you sure?"

"I insist. I want a full report."

"Okay then." Aunt Helen studied the paper in her hand. "That's not until later anyway."

Dani glanced at the list. "We better get moving if we want to make the next architectural tour."

"We're good." Brianna held up her phone. "I already ordered the tickets."

"How much do we owe you?"

Brianna waved her off. "My treat."

"No, you can't buy our tickets."

"I just inherited a million dollars, I think I can afford it."

"So did I," Dani shot back.

Aunt Helen gave her a look. "Danielle Delilah Thorton!"

"Sorry, too soon? Too dark?" Dani said sheepishly.

Brianna laughed. "What's a million dollars between friends? Besides, is there ever anything too dark?"

"Do not encourage her." Aunt Helen tried to give Brianna a stern look, but Brianna winked and flashed an innocent smile.

"Danielle Delilah, really?" Brianna said. "Were your parents on an acid trip?"

"Right." Dani shook her head. "That's what happens when you have two stubborn parents. My dad wanted Danielle and my mother Delilah, so I ended up with both. I don't remember it, but apparently, my mother called me Delilah up until the time she left."

"She did," Aunt Helen said. "The poor girl didn't stand a chance of turning out normal."

"Really? What did I tell you about earning your

ride on the Ferris wheel?"

⁂

They returned to the Ferris wheel near dusk, their itinerary long broken. It was the perfect time of day to view the city from the air. Most of the city lights were aglow while Lake Michigan could still be seen.

Dani sat back and watched as Aunt Helen gently tried to convince Brianna to join them on the ride. Brianna wavered under Aunt Helen's power of persuasion, but Dani suspected she wasn't ready.

"I see the way you've been eyeing it," Dani said. "Are you sure we can't convince you?"

"Not today, but I'll make you a promise."

"You have me intrigued." Dani studied Brianna, trying to figure out what was behind her serious expression. "What are you gonna promise me?"

"If I ever decide to go on the Ferris wheel, it will only be with you."

"Deal." Dani grinned. What an honor that Brianna would reserve a future ride for her. But would it ever happen?

Dani and Aunt Helen joined the line, waiting to board, and Brianna turned to walk away.

"Hey, Bri," Dani called. As soon as she turned back, Dani engulfed Brianna in her arms.

Brianna seemed surprised but quickly recovered and hugged Dani tightly.

"For luck," Dani said. "Ferris wheels can be scary."

"For luck." Brianna squeezed Dani more tightly before letting go.

Dani's mind raced. *What the hell did I do that for?* They were only going to be separated for twenty minutes.

"Don't go running off and getting ice cream without us." Aunt Helen squeezed Brianna's arm.

Dani gave a silent thanks to Aunt Helen, who averted any awkwardness the hug might have caused.

"I wouldn't dream of it." Brianna pointed at a nearby bench. "I'll be right over there, figuring out what flavor I'm getting."

☙❧❧❧

As soon as they disembarked from the Ferris wheel, Aunt Helen was off. Dani weaved through the crowd, trying to keep up with her. In her enthusiasm to tell Brianna about the ride, she'd left Dani in the dust.

When Dani arrived at the bench, Aunt Helen was in the midst of a monologue. A few times, Brianna opened her mouth, apparently to ask a question, but closed it as Aunt Helen prattled on.

Dani smiled and plopped down on the bench next to Brianna.

Brianna listened attentively to Aunt Helen's story and nodded in all the right places, but something seemed off. When Dani had sat, Brianna had slid down the bench, putting a few feet between the two of them. Her normally expressive eyes seemed flat.

Aunt Helen didn't seem to notice as she continued raving about their experience.

Must be my imagination. Maybe the impromptu hug had weirded her out. Dani pushed the thought out of her mind and let herself enjoy Aunt Helen's animated play-by-play.

"Now I'm ready for ice cream," Aunt Helen said as soon as she finished.

"Of course you are," Dani said.

"I am, too." Brianna's tone was flat, without her usual enthusiasm.

"Ice cream it is then." Dani put extra perk into her voice, trying to shake her uneasy feeling.

"Do you girls mind going and getting it? I'd like to take a load off my feet." Aunt Helen sat with a groan.

Dani stopped herself from staring at Aunt Helen but sent her a sidelong glance. Aunt Helen usually ran circles around someone half her age, so her fatigue was concerning. They'd been on the run all day; eventually, she'd have to accept that Aunt Helen would slow down, even though in her sixties, she'd shown no signs of it.

"Give us your order, and we're on it," Dani said.

They made their way across the pier in silence. Dani couldn't read Brianna's expression, and when she tried to make conversation, Brianna's answers were clipped. A distance had descended while they were on the Ferris wheel, and her attempt at playful banter was not returned.

When the ice cream stand came into view, Brianna walked faster, forcing Dani to hustle to keep up with her long stride. Dani struggled to breathe, but not because of the increased pace. Her chest tightened as the gigantic ice cream cone loomed closer. The day couldn't end like this.

Even though she wasn't practiced in open communication, she took a deep breath and plunged in. "Can I ask you a question?"

"Okay," Brianna said, not giving her much to work with.

"Can we sit over there?" Dani pointed to a

nearby sitting area.

Brianna didn't answer but made a beeline for the brightly colored benches.

Silence settled over them once they sat. Brianna looked at Dani expectantly but said nothing.

"Can I ask you something?" Dani rubbed the back of her hand.

"Isn't that why we're sitting here?" Brianna's voice held no edge nor did it have any of her natural warmth. More concerning, she didn't take the opportunity to tease Dani for asking the same question twice.

"Sorry. I'm just trying to figure something out."

"Okay."

"It's just..." Dani started. "It's just..."

"It's just what?" A look of concern finally broke through Brianna's coldness.

"What happened after the last time you were at Thundering Pines?" Dani blurted out. It wasn't what she'd intended to ask. She only planned on asking why Brianna's demeanor had changed today.

"What do you mean?" Brianna said too quickly. A guarded look fell across her face, and she moved away from Dani on the bench.

Now what did I say wrong? Panic rose inside Dani, and her pulse quickened. She couldn't take Brianna shutting down again.

"It's just we had such a good time, well, at least I did. And then it was like a wall came down, and you seemed so distant. Like you really didn't want to talk to me. I wasn't sure what I did wrong. Or maybe you were just pretending to have a good time, and you really didn't like hanging out with me as much as I did with you."

Brianna gazed at her without expression.

Dani took a quick breath and forged on. "But then Friday, when we talked, everything seemed okay again. Then today has been great, but now it feels like your wall is back up. I'm thinking you're sick of me again and just want the day to be over." Dani breathlessly rambled, letting all her fears tumble out. She stopped, shocked and embarrassed at how much she'd said. *What is wrong with me?* How was it that Brianna seemed to bring out this in her when nobody else could? "I'm sorry," Dani said before Brianna could respond. Her face burned. She wanted to hide under the bench or take a flying leap into Lake Michigan to get away from Brianna.

Brianna's eyes softened. "I'm sorry. I never meant to make you feel that way. Something came up at home the night I got back. It had nothing to do with you."

"Is everything okay?" Dani's concern temporarily made her forget her own plight.

"Nothing I can't handle. And definitely nothing I can talk about without having several beers in me." Brianna shrugged and gave Dani a half grin.

Dani tried to decipher Brianna's response. An issue at home might explain why Brianna left so abruptly and why she'd been distant since, but it didn't answer why a switch flipped after the Ferris wheel ride. "You were just preoccupied, nothing else?" Dani said hopefully.

"Yep, that's about..." Brianna broke eye contact and looked down at her lap, suddenly extremely interested in her fingernails. "No, that wouldn't be true."

Dani's stomach lurched. "Then what is the truth, Bri?"

"The truth is, I don't know how to handle this." Brianna waved her hand between them. "I guess I'm afraid."

"Of me?" Dani's words caught in her throat. *What have I done?*

"Yes," Brianna whispered.

"Why?" Dani hoped her voice didn't betray her panic.

"I've had so much fun both times I've been at Thundering Pines. I can't remember the last time I laughed so hard or shared so much."

"And that's a bad thing?" Brianna's words were giving her hope, but the heaviness on her chest remained.

"I was driving and listening to my music, and halfway home, I realized I already missed you. And it scared the shit out of me."

"Would it help if I told you I felt the same way?"

Brianna glanced up and held Dani's gaze. "I'm not sure."

The honesty of the answer struck Dani, the sentiment mirroring her own feelings. The prospect of a friendship with Brianna was both intoxicating and terrifying. Long ago, Dani decided that adults shouldn't share their inner selves with each other, and it had suited her fine for years, but now, Brianna made her question that decision.

"Meaning?" Dani stalled for time to come up with a better response.

"Meaning it wasn't supposed to be this way. I was supposed to be in and out fast. I just needed to figure out what to do with Thundering Pines and then move on with my life."

"And now?"

"I don't know." Brianna gazed out over Lake Michigan. "I really don't know."

"Why do you look so damned sad?" Dani gently put her hand on Brianna's back.

"I don't know what to do."

"What do you want to do?"

"Spend more time with you and Aunt Helen," Brianna answered, seemingly without censor. "Race around Thundering Pines on the ATV. Watch the sunset while drinking wine in the loft."

"So why can't you do that?"

"My life is here, in the city. I left Flower Hills a long time ago."

"Did you? Or did you leave the dysfunctional relationship you had with your dad?"

Brianna shrugged. "It's all so confusing. I put the wall up so I wouldn't do this." Brianna pointed to the tears welling in her eyes. "The last couple of weeks I've asked myself over and over if it was Thundering Pines or if it was you."

"Did you come up with an answer?"

"Thundering Pines isn't here today, you are."

"I'm not sure I'm following."

"I've had another amazing day, and I'm not at Thundering Pines. And Friday when we talked on the phone, I felt right for the first time in over two weeks. I was talking to you, not Thundering Pines."

Brianna fidgeted on the bench while Dani struggled to find words. She wanted to say something witty or profound, but nothing came to her. The silence engulfed her like a swarm of locusts, making it harder for her to concentrate on an adequate response.

"Never mind, I'm just being silly." Brianna stood. "The return to Thundering Pines has just made me overly emotional. Let's get Helen her ice cream."

Dani immediately noticed that Brianna said Helen, not Aunt Helen. She could feel Brianna pulling away again. Without thinking, she grabbed Brianna's hand. "Bri, please sit down and give me a minute to collect my thoughts."

Brianna hesitated but didn't sit.

"Please," Dani said.

Brianna lowered herself cautiously to the bench but sat farther from Dani than she had earlier. She didn't let go of Dani's hand, though.

Dani's stomach was in knots, but she knew she had to say something before Brianna shut down further. "Please don't take my silence the wrong way. I'm not particularly good at this communication stuff, but you make me want to be." She looked at Brianna, who still stared at the ground. "I'm struggling with my words because it feels strange being so open. I definitely don't think you're being silly."

Brianna looked up.

Dani saw hope and fear and knew she needed to continue. "I don't know what's going on, either. But I know that I enjoy the hell out of you. That Sunday night that you left, I missed you, too. And the last couple weeks have been hell."

"I'm sorry I made you feel that way."

"You don't have to apologize. I just want to understand what's going on. I've had an amazing time today, but I'm afraid when we leave here tonight, the wall will be back tomorrow."

"You're right, it's all my fault."

"Stop. We don't need to find blame, just a solution."

"I thought it would be easier, but it wasn't."

"What was going to be easier?"

"Pretending like that weekend meant nothing, like it didn't matter."

"And how did that work out for you?" Dani smiled.

"Obviously, not so good." Brianna returned the smile. "I was miserable and had a lousy week. Every day I thought: just call Dani, she'll make you laugh."

"Why didn't you?"

"I have a lot of friends," Brianna said.

Dani tensed but remained quiet to allow Brianna to continue.

"But I realized despite having all these people in my life, never once did I think about picking up the phone and calling one of them. You were the only one I wanted to talk to."

"Wanting to call me made you not call me?" Dani said with a smirk.

"Stupid, huh? I've only known you for a couple months. And in two visits, I've shared more about who I am with you than I have with anyone currently in my life."

"All still sounding like a reason to want to call me." Dani tried not to show her frustration.

"You would think, but it freaked me out. Maybe I don't know how to have close friendships because I'm sure messing this one up."

"No," Dani said firmly. "You're not messing anything up. You're being open and honest with me. That's a mark of someone who knows how to do friendships right."

Brianna laughed, catching Dani off guard. "You're right, I would never have this kind of conversation with my other friends. They'd run screaming from me. This is far too real and intimate for their liking. Maybe they don't know how to be real friends." Brianna looked at Dani with her eyes wide. "God, I don't have any real friends. I'm thirty-seven years old, and I have no friends."

Dani wasn't sure if she should joke with Brianna or say something supportive. As she weighed her response, Brianna took the choice away from her.

"Dani Thorton, would you like to be my friend?"

"Well, I don't know, sounds like you don't have much of a track record." Dani flashed Brianna a huge smile. "Might be a little risky for me, don't you think?"

Brianna slid closer to Dani and wrapped her arms around her.

Dani's tension drained away as Brianna squeezed.

"Too bad, you're stuck with me now."

"The horror. Don't tell anyone, but I do kinda like having you around."

"It'll be our secret." Brianna released her hold on Dani. "Come on, Aunt Helen is going to be hopping mad if we don't get her ice cream back to her."

❧❧❧❧

Dani grimaced when she looked at her cellphone. When she was with Brianna, time seemed to disappear. "I can't believe it's nearly nine o'clock."

"I'm blaming Aunt Helen," Brianna said.

"Me? You wouldn't want to send an old lady home hungry, would you?"

"Don't try and play the old lady card with us," Brianna said. "You wore us out today."

"Yeah, we tried to get you to stop for dinner two hours ago," Dani said.

"But there was so much to see and do. Besides, our pizza should be out soon. I don't think either of you girls are in danger of starving."

"I think she just called us fat, Bri."

"She did. Unbelievable, and she looks so sweet and innocent."

They were so caught up reliving their favorite parts of the day they didn't notice the waiter until he was at their table. His forearms were rock hard as he squeezed the black metal tongs gripping the sizzling dish. They stopped talking and gaped at the pizza overflowing the three-inch pan.

"That is just wrong." Dani breathed in and enjoyed the aromatic scent of herbs and cheese wafting off the pizza. "Nothing should smell that damned good."

The waiter laughed and set the pizza on the wooden board. He expertly wielded the spatula and removed the first piece, making sure to let the cheese drip off the side before adroitly catching it on the awaiting plate. He smiled at Helen and handed her the first offering. "Beauty before age."

She gave him a flirtatious smile and inhaled deeply before setting the pizza down.

He served up two more slices and picked up their empty glasses. "Another round of soda?"

"I'll take one," Dani said. "What about you guys?"

Both nodded, and the waiter was off.

After they devoured their first slice, Dani brandished the spatula to serve the second piece. With an exaggerated gesture, she jammed her tool into the pizza. She skillfully removed her first piece and plopped it onto Aunt Helen's plate. Her audience clapped as she went in for her second. Once again, with a near perfect motion, she extracted the slice and dropped it on Brianna's plate. Her confidence had turned to cockiness as she snared her own. She raised the pizza triumphantly above her head and twisted her hand dramatically to slam the pizza onto her plate as if she were spiking a football.

At the last moment, Dani realized the spatula suddenly felt lighter right before the empty utensil clanked against her plate. Before the pizza could fall to the floor, Aunt Helen snatched it as it slid down Dani's hair.

"Touchdown!" Aunt Helen spiked the slice onto Dani's plate.

Brianna nearly choked on her drink, swallowing quickly before she burst out laughing.

The waiter had apparently watched the scene because he rushed over with extra napkins. He hurried away, trying to hide his laughter.

"Way to go, Slick," Brianna said. "Now I'm just embarrassed for you."

Dani glared at her, feigning outrage as she wiped her pizza off with the extra napkins.

"Good girl." Aunt Helen patted Dani's arm. She looked at Brianna and winked. "I taught her not to waste food."

✦✦✦✦

They finished their meal with no further mishaps, the laughter and conversation flowing freely. It would soon be time for Dani and Aunt Helen to start home. A twinge nipped at the pit of Brianna's stomach. She pushed it aside when Aunt Helen pulled cheese out of Dani's hair.

Without thinking, Brianna said, "How did you get that?"

"I threw pizza in my hair, smartass."

"No," Brianna said. "That interesting streak in your hair."

When Aunt Helen stiffened, Brianna wished she could take it back.

"It's been there since I was sixteen." A moment of awkward silence ensued, but Dani made no attempt to fill it.

Brianna contemplated changing the subject but knew it would be too obvious, so she forged ahead. "How did it happen?"

"I'll need a lot more beer before I'll talk about it."

"Touché." Brianna smiled. Out of the corner of her eye, she caught Aunt Helen visibly relax. "I guess we have a couple interesting topics for the next time I visit."

"Why don't you come this weekend? After all, it's the first day of the season."

A million thoughts raced through Brianna's head, the loudest one was *YES!* Instead, she said, "I didn't think you did anything special until Memorial Day weekend."

"The big party isn't until then, but it's still kinda fun when people are moving in and getting settled. We usually do something small."

"Let me see what's on my calendar, and I'll let you know."

⁂

Dani insisted on dropping Brianna off at her apartment.

Brianna was glad it was late, so she wouldn't feel bad not inviting them in. She would love to have them up, but she certainly didn't want to subject them to

Caroline.

Dani pulled up to the curb and put her truck in park.

Brianna started to say her goodbyes before exiting the truck, but Aunt Helen interrupted. "Oh, no, you're not getting out of here without a hug." Aunt Helen was standing on the sidewalk before Brianna pushed open her door.

"Thank you for such a nice day, honey." Aunt Helen hugged Brianna.

Dani came around the front of the truck and stood off to the side while Aunt Helen chattered at Brianna.

"I need a hug from you, too, pizza head. Just don't be surprised if I lick your hair."

Dani laughed and drew Brianna in. She hugged Brianna tightly and said into her ear, "You're not going to get all distant and weird on me after I leave here, are you?"

"No, I promise." Brianna sniffed Dani's hair. "I'd miss the smell of your aromatic shampoo too much."

Dani playfully pushed her away. "Aunt Helen, we need to get out of here before she starts chewing on my hair."

❧❧❧❧

"I'm so glad you two talked it out," Aunt Helen said when they pulled away from the curb.

"What?" Dani turned and scowled.

"Did you really think I'm so feeble I couldn't walk to get my own ice cream?" Aunt Helen said indignantly.

"You little scam artist. You set us up."

"Well, somebody needed to. Brianna was acting distant, and I didn't want to have to deal with you moping around all week."

Dani laughed. "Well, old woman, you have some tricks up your sleeve."

"Old woman, my ass. I'm only sixty-five. I'm a hell of a lot younger than Cher, and she's still out there dancing around half-naked on stage."

"Well then, rock on, but please keep your clothes on."

"Maybe." Helen gave her a satisfied smile. "I'm keeping my eye on you two. You've found yourself a good one. Try not to blow it."

Dani rolled Aunt Helen's words around in her mind, trying to decide if she should be offended by Aunt Helen's implication that she might screw something up. Or maybe she should be more concerned by whatever it was that Aunt Helen was implying. When Dani stopped at a redlight, she turned and looked at Aunt Helen for several beats. "What's that supposed to mean?"

"Take it any way you want." Aunt Helen smirked. "I like that girl. I like her a lot. She makes you smile, and I've never heard you laugh so much. Plus, she has you talking about things I don't think you've ever shared with anyone else. It won't be long before she hears the story of your hair."

"We are not having this conversation." Dani reached for the radio knob. There was an eighties song playing, so she cranked up the volume.

Aunt Helen smiled, laid her head back against her seat, and sang along with the radio.

Chapter Eighteen

Brianna swore as she fumbled with her keys, eventually dropping them. She tried again but dropped them a second time. Maybe it was Freudian.

When she finally pushed open the door, she was surprised by the sound coming from the living room. It sounded like the television, but she braced herself in case it was something else. It was rare for Caroline to watch TV when she was absorbed in a big case.

Caroline held a glass of wine in her hand, and her legs were stretched out along the length of the couch. A wine bottle sat on the end table without a coaster under it. "So glad you decided to come home," Caroline said, her voice dripping in sarcasm.

"I thought you'd be working."

"I made supper. The leftovers are in the fridge."

"Sorry, I already ate."

"I guess I made your favorite for nothing." Caroline chugged the rest of her wine before emptying the bottle into her glass.

Something's wrong. Caroline usually didn't pick fights. It wasn't her style. If she was pissed, she'd put it on the table, not beat around the bush.

"You never said anything to me." Brianna was careful not to take Caroline's bait.

"Navy Pier must have been hopping to keep you out this late." Caroline narrowed her eyes at Brianna.

"No, we went out for pizza afterward."

"We?"

"Dani and Aunt Helen were in town, so I met them for lunch."

"And dinner?"

"Yes." She decided short, factual answers were the safest.

"So, it's Aunt Helen, huh? How sweet," Caroline said with a look of distaste. "And how is skunk girl?"

"Please, don't call her that." Brianna's jaw clenched, but she tried to keep the anger out of her voice. She wanted to hold on to the good feelings of the day and not get drawn in by Caroline, who seemed to be looking for an argument.

"Is skunk girl striped down there, too, or does it just smell like skunk?"

Brianna took a deep breath. Her fingernails dug into her palms. "Really, Caroline? Why are you acting like this?"

"I come home and make you a nice dinner, and you don't even show up."

"You never told me, so how was I to know? I thought you'd be working late."

"You're right." Caroline smiled. "Come sit down and talk with me."

Alarm bells went off in Brianna's head. What was with Caroline's sudden flip of the switch? She just wanted to go to bed with her happy glow but didn't want to antagonize Caroline any further. Cautiously, she sat on the opposite end of the couch and leaned back against the cushion. "Did you already finish working on your case tonight?"

"Nope, they took me off it."

Brianna's head jerked around. Caroline had

never been pulled from a case in her life. At least, it explained her foul mood. Her identity was wrapped up in her job. "Why?" Brianna asked with genuine concern.

"Apparently, they wanted someone older..." Caroline's voice trailed off. "And male."

"Ouch, that sucks." She felt herself relax at the news. Caroline didn't experience many career setbacks, so this had to be a blow to her ego. She should have known better than to think Caroline would care about her spending time with Dani.

"Wow. Nice I have such a supportive girlfriend." Caroline hugged a pillow to her chest.

Focus. In her relief, Brianna realized her response hadn't been the best. "I'm sorry, Caroline. You're a great lawyer, so don't let it get you down. You'll get them on the next case."

"Sure, poof, all better because Brianna said to let it go." Caroline took another gulp from her wineglass.

Brianna knew she needed to tread lightly. Caroline drew her self-worth from her job, so being taken off a case was personally devastating to her. "I'm not trying to make light of it."

"Whatever. I just need to get through the next three days without losing my shit."

"Three days? It's only Monday."

"Didn't I tell you that Kylie and Drew rented a cabin in Lake Geneva? You'll need to take Friday off."

"Didn't you think maybe you should have asked me?" How could Caroline think she'd want to spend the weekend with Kylie? *Too soon.*

"What for?" Caroline rolled her eyes. "Have something better to do?"

"As a matter of fact, I do. I'm going to Thundering

Pines to help Dani with opening weekend."

Caroline's laugh cut through Brianna. "Skunk girl definitely isn't very bright, is she? What use will you be?"

So many comebacks swirled inside of Brianna's brain, but instead she said, "I guess she thinks I have some value."

"Self-pity doesn't look good on you, Brianna."

"You know what, you're obviously upset about your day, which I get, but it's not fair taking it out on me. I think we should end this conversation."

Caroline's faced reddened, and Brianna knew she'd picked the wrong thing to say. "Thanks for being so fucking supportive."

"What do you want me to do?" Brianna said, trying to salvage the situation.

"Come with me to the cabin." Caroline slowly licked her lips.

The gesture, which once might have enticed Brianna, only repulsed her. Caroline's attempt at flirtation felt put on, almost creepy. Had it always been that way, or was something different? It almost reeked of desperation, which was unlike the confident Caroline.

"Sorry, I can't. Besides, I'm really not ready to spend the weekend with Kylie and Drew."

"Are you seriously still holding on to that shit?"

Nobody could be that clueless, could they? *Misplaced guilt?* That explanation made more sense. The tension in Brianna's shoulders relaxed. "Sorry if finding you in bed with Kylie threw me off." She kept her voice low and steady.

"Let it go, for fuck's sake. How long have we had an open relationship? Why are you whining now?"

Yep. It had to be guilt causing Caroline to act so

ridiculous. Sure, she could be insensitive at times, but this was taking it to a new level. No sense in fanning the flames. "You're right." Brianna said her practiced line. "Like you always are."

"Glad you finally figured it out." Caroline flashed her a smile. "Why don't you call skunk girl and tell her you can't make it?"

"Stop calling her that," Brianna said between clenched teeth. Guilt or not, she wouldn't allow Caroline to drag Dani into it. "I already told you, I am going to Thundering Pines. I'm not letting Dani down."

"Fuck Dani. Fuck Aunt Helen. And fuck Thundering Pines." Caroline slammed her empty glass onto the table. "Call her and tell her you aren't coming."

Brianna stared. It wasn't like Caroline to lose her temper; she was too controlled for that. "What is wrong with you?"

"I've had enough of you and your little skunk girlfriend," Caroline snapped. "I don't want to catch something."

Wow. The conversation kept getting odder. Was Caroline jealous of Dani? *No.* In all the years Brianna had been with Caroline, she'd never shown any signs of jealousy or insecurity. "What are you talking about?"

"Don't play innocent with me." The vein in Caroline's neck bulged. "I know you're screwing the little bitch."

Brianna stared at Caroline without responding. Where in the hell did Caroline get that idea?

"Is that how you decided to get even with me?" Caroline's lip curled.

Revenge. The pieces fell into place. Caroline thought Brianna was using Dani for payback. "I'm not trying to get even with you."

"I knew it, you aren't denying it." Caroline's lip curled.

"I'm just stunned. I'm not sleeping with Dani."

Caroline studied Brianna before she spoke. "But you want to."

"Why are you so jealous of her?"

Brianna didn't have time to contemplate the meaning of her answer. Without warning, Caroline swept her hand across the end table, sending the wineglass flying. When it hit the floor, it shattered, and shards of glass scattered in every direction.

What the fuck? Never had she seen Caroline act this way. "How much have you had to drink?"

"I am not drunk. And I'm certainly not jealous of that little trailer trash."

"Then why don't you refrain from calling her names?" Brianna said, finally raising her voice. "I'm tired of you degrading my friend."

"Your friend?" Caroline cackled. "Seriously, your friend? What, you've known her for a minute, now she's your BFF?"

Brianna pursed her lips, fighting the urge to say the things raging in her mind. "I never said that. I simply enjoy her company."

"Right. I hear you talking with her on the phone, laughing like a teenage girl. And I always know when she sends you a text or an email because your face lights up."

"So what?" Brianna said. "It's nice to have a friend who doesn't run in our circle. So, yes, it's refreshing talking to her."

"You're bored with our friends?"

"I didn't say that."

"You didn't say you weren't, either."

"This conversation is going nowhere. I'm tired, and I need to be in the office early tomorrow." Brianna stood and walked across the room. She was nearly to the hall.

"You better go call your BFF and tell her nighty night. It's been at least half an hour since you last saw her."

Brianna continued walking out of the room, not bothering with a response.

≈✺✺≈

Brianna held her cellphone in her hand but didn't press her finger against the sensor. Maybe Caroline was right. If she wanted to save their relationship, she should go to Lake Geneva instead of Thundering Pines. She'd not promised Dani anything.

Caroline hadn't suffered many career setbacks, so Brianna understood her frustration, especially since her career meant everything to her, but her reaction to Dani and Thundering Pines had come as a complete shock.

Was Caroline sensing a change in her, the change Brianna had been reluctant to accept herself? Their relationship had been fine for the last ten years, so why was Brianna questioning it now?

Maybe they didn't have deep conversations and share intimate thoughts, but they were known in all the right circles and had built successful careers. Heads turned when they walked into an event, Caroline looked good on her arm, and she knew she looked good on Caroline's.

Most people they knew would kill to have their lifestyle. Brianna snorted. Who was she kidding? The only people who'd want what they had were the superficial and pretentious people they hung out with. She doubted anyone in Flower Hills would be so impressed.

She pressed her finger to the sensor and began typing.

Brianna: I checked my schedule. I'll be there late Friday night!! Looking forward to it!!!

Dani: Awesome. Aunt Helen will be excited too, but she's snoring right now. Lol

Brianna: We wore her out!!

Dani: No doubt. Thanks again for an edible day.

Brianna: Edible. lol

Dani: I'm driving. Voice to text. Not my fault.

Brianna: Supercalifragilisticexpialidocious

Dani: What the hell was that?

Brianna: LMAO. I just wondered what it would sound like when your truck said it out loud.

Dani: Really are you 12? lol

Brianna: Ha Ha. Apparently. I better get to bed. Drive safe.

Dani: Will do. Thanks again for today. Can't wait until Friday!

Brianna: Thank you! I'm looking forward to it.

Dani: Good night

Brianna: Night

Chapter Nineteen

Brianna let out a heavy sigh and fell backward onto the couch. She kicked off her heels and put her feet up. Her suit would probably end up wrinkled, but she didn't have the energy to go to the bedroom to change her clothes. She might make it to the kitchen to get some food, or maybe she wouldn't. After the day she'd had, she was allowed a drama queen moment.

She smiled, imagining what Dani would say about her theatrical flop.

At the thought of Dani, she picked up her phone and pressed her contacts icon. She didn't need to scroll since Dani's picture was at the top, being one of her most active connections. She enlarged Dani's photo with a tap. She loved the picture, and ever since Aunt Helen sent it to her, she found she looked at it multiple times a day.

Dani stood in front of the Ferris wheel with the waning sun casting a surreal light in the background. Her face was flushed, probably from being out in the sun and wind all day. Her smile and the twinkle in her eyes kept drawing Brianna back to it. The picture represented joy and peace, two things lacking in her own life.

Caroline had left for Lake Geneva nearly an hour ago, but her effect on Brianna lingered.

It puzzled her why Caroline showed such deep-seated hatred for Dani. Sure, Caroline could be superficial and shallow at times, but Brianna never heard her speak of anyone with such venom. Considering that Caroline had only met Dani once and Dani spoke little at that meeting, her ire seemed excessive.

If Brianna didn't know better, she would think Caroline was jealous. But it made no sense, either. Caroline encouraged her to enjoy their open relationship, so even if she still believed something was going on between them, it shouldn't matter. Maybe it was simply her contempt for all things rural, and Dani was its representation.

The phone in her hand vibrated, jolting her out of her contemplation.

Shelby's name flashed across the screen. *Could this day get any worse?* She considered not answering but knew it would only give her a temporary reprieve.

"Hi, Shelby," Brianna said, trying to sound cheerful. Shelby called every couple of weeks to inquire about something with the estate, but she suspected it was to berate her for a perceived slight. Brianna always seemed to be guilty of something.

"You need to replace all of the carpeting in Dad's house," Shelby said.

"I'm fine, thank you for asking," Brianna answered.

"Cut the crap. Don't pretend this is a social call."

"Why does the carpeting need to be replaced?" Brianna ran her hand through her hair. She didn't have the patience for this today.

"It's old and gross."

"Really? I reviewed Donald's records carefully, and if I'm not mistaken, it was replaced five years ago. Certainly far from old and gross."

"Fine, then trade me."

"Trade you what?"

"Thundering Pines for the house."

"I don't need a house."

"You sure as hell don't need a campground, either."

"We are not having this conversation again." Exhaustion settled over Brianna.

"Why don't you just trade me? I'm the one that loves it, not you."

"I'm starting to really enjoy Thundering Pines." Brianna knew her words would antagonize Shelby, even though that wasn't her motive. Wasn't the truth supposed to set you free? In this case, it would probably only get her screamed at.

"Are you fucking kidding me?"

Got that one right. Keeping her voice calm, Brianna replied, "Nope, actually, I'm not."

"You're letting that little conniving bitch play you? I thought the big-city girl would be more savvy than that."

"If you are referring to Dani, I would suggest you watch your tone."

"Or what?" When Brianna didn't respond, Shelby continued. "You are such an idiot. Do you think she's your friend?"

"Yes, as a matter of fact, I do."

Shelby's laugh cut through Brianna. She knew she shouldn't take the bait, but the combination of her tense exchange with Caroline earlier and Shelby's shrill laughter had her on edge.

"We had a lovely time on Monday when we spent the day at Navy Pier." Brianna rolled her eyes. When did she become someone who used the word "lovely"?

"The little gold digger obviously has her claws in you. Do you really think her act is real? How precious. I can't wait to see the look on your face when her true colors shine through."

Brianna took a deep breath. "I'll take my chances."

"She already ripped us off for a third of our inheritance. Keep on being a dumbass, and she'll take us for more."

"Did you need anything else, other than new carpet?" Brianna was done and wanted off the phone.

"Yeah, let this serve as a warning. That bitch is going down, and I'm taking you with her."

"Thanks for sharing."

"I'm serious. If you think you and your friend can get away with this, think again."

Brianna considered asking what they were trying to get away with but didn't want to spend another minute on the phone with Shelby. "Since it seems you have nothing new, I'll talk to you later."

Before Shelby could respond, Brianna ended the call. She held the phone, fighting an internal battle. Maybe she should go to bed and end this perfectly lousy day, but it was only eight p.m. If she fell asleep this early, she would be wide awake at four in the morning and potentially ruin tomorrow night with her sleepiness.

She would see Dani tomorrow, but more than anything, she wanted to hear Dani's voice, or more accurately, her laugh. She knew that Dani would lift her mood without having to try.

Tired of debating with herself, Brianna clicked on Dani's photo.

Chapter Twenty

When Brianna pulled into the driveway, Dani and Aunt Helen were sitting on the porch.

Before she was out of the Jeep, Dani bounded down the stairs and handed her a beer.

Brianna laughed, opened it with a flourish, and took a large gulp. She made an exaggerated sound of satisfaction and wiped her shirt sleeve across her mouth. "Now if only I could burp on command."

"Amateur." Dani let out a loud burp.

"Danielle," Aunt Helen yelled from the porch. "Would you stop being so crude?"

Brianna giggled and wrapped Dani in a bear hug. "I am so glad to be here."

If Dani was surprised by Brianna's reaction, she recovered quickly. She squeezed her tightly. "Me too."

The stress of the week faded as Brianna clung to Dani. She should probably let go, but she held on until the last of the tension left her body. "God, I needed that."

"I'm sorry you've had such a rough week." Dani's eyes were soft and comforting. "But it's over and you're here now."

"Where's my itinerary?" Brianna pretended to look around for one.

"What?"

"My itinerary. You did make us one, didn't you?"

"I thought we could wing it." Dani winked.

Brianna jumped back into her Jeep. "Unacceptable, I'm heading back to the city."

"Get your ass out here."

"Sheesh, I thought you'd put a little preparation into my arrival, but I see how it is. Third time here and already being taken for granted." Brianna hopped back out of the Jeep and grabbed her bag.

"Yep, hospitality is gone. You're on your own."

"Well, at least you can take my bag." Brianna tossed it to Dani. "I have to say hi to Aunt Helen."

Before Dani could protest, Brianna ran up the stairs, taking them two at a time.

⁕⁕⁕⁕

"You're gonna help me with this," Dani said. It should be interesting watching the city girl build a fire.

"But I don't know what I'm doing," Brianna said.

"You gotta learn some time." Dani pointed to a large pile of wood. "Grab five or six logs."

Brianna walked to the covered area under the loft, where all the wood was neatly stacked. She nudged a couple with the toe of her boot but made no move to gather it.

"What are you doing? Cutting the logs?" Dani called.

"Which ones do you want?"

"What do you mean? Just grab a few."

"But they're not all the same," Brianna protested.

Dani joined her. Brianna's brow was furrowed in concentration as she examined the wood. Impressive, most people wouldn't have noticed. "Good eye. But they're all hardwood, so any will do."

"As opposed to softwood?" Brianna giggled.

Dani considered making up an outrageous story about the differences but decided against it. "Yep, as opposed to softwood."

"You're just screwing with me, aren't you?" Brianna narrowed her eyes at Dani.

"Actually, for once, I'm not, but I thought about it." Dani picked up a log. "All this is hardwood, which is better for fires."

"What kind of wood is that?" Brianna pointed at the log in Dani's hand.

"This one is oak." Dani picked up another. "This is ash, and that one over there is maple."

"Where is the cedar?" Brianna asked. "I love the smell of cedar."

"Cedar is a softwood, so I don't have any here."

"But I've smelled fire that smells like cedar."

"You can burn softwoods, too, but I only do it when I'm looking for the scent."

"What about pine?"

"It's soft, too."

Brianna began picking out logs, taking two of each type, then paused. "Wait, can I mix the different types, or do I need to get all the same wood?"

Watching Brianna learn about the campground made Dani smile. She was like an excited ten-year-old. "You can mix them. My favorite is ash."

"Wow, you're a geek. I've never met anyone who has a favorite firewood." She cradled the wood and started back toward the firepit.

Dani grabbed an armful and followed. "You're just jealous." She dropped her wood next to the pit and puffed out her chest.

"Yep, you're on to me." Brianna dropped her

own wood. "Where did you learn this stuff?"

"My dad. Didn't your...?" Dani stopped. That was stupid. "Sorry, Bri."

"It's okay." Brianna patted Dani on the back and gave her a cheesy smile. "I guess you'll have to teach me."

"Great." Dani groaned. "Let's find some kindling and tinder, so we can start your first lesson."

"Tinder? Isn't that a creepy dating app?"

Dani shook her head. "This is going to be more difficult than I thought."

She led Brianna into the woods and helped her pick out small sticks for the kindling, showing her how to tell if a stick was dry enough to catch fire easily. After that, they found dry leaves and cattail fluff for tinder.

When they returned to the firepit with their loot, Dani flipped open the cooler and pulled out two beers. She twisted the caps off and handed one to Brianna before pulling her folding chair out of its bag. "Okay, let's see what you've got."

"Are you just going to sit there and watch?"

"Yep." Dani raised the bottle to her lips and tilted her head back. "That's exactly what I'm gonna do. Would you like me to hold your beer?"

Brianna glared and took several long pulls from her beer before handing it to Dani. "Okay, I'm ready. What's next?"

"I think I'll start you off with a teepee fire." Dani quickly went over the design and structure of the fire. When she finished, she asked Brianna to repeat the steps back to her. Dani was impressed when Brianna ticked off the instructions with few prompts.

"Looks like the student is ready to fly solo." Dani

put her feet up on the cooler. "I'll be enjoying my beer should you need me."

"Gee, thanks."

Dani grinned as she watched Brianna kneeling by the firepit, carefully arranging her tinder in the center. It was hard to believe this was the same woman she'd met a little over two months ago.

Her hair, no longer pulled back severely, settled loosely on her shoulders, moving in the breeze. Her distressed jeans gave her a carefree appearance, a look that Dani never could have imagined from the buttoned-down woman she met at Thomas's office. When Brianna stood to get her kindling, Dani marveled at the length of her legs and how well her jeans hugged her body. Dani quickly diverted her gaze, hoping her cheeks hadn't colored.

"Hey, are you watching this?" Brianna called. "If I start a forest fire, it will all be on you."

"Sorry," Dani stammered. She turned back and looked into Brianna's expressive brown eyes. *Damn, looking into those eyes isn't going to help.* Humor was the only way for her to get back on solid ground. "I wasn't sure if you'd ever get done building that nest, so I got bored."

"I wanted to make sure I had my tinder just right," Brianna said with smug satisfaction as she used her new vocabulary. "Now pay attention while I get my kindling in place."

"Yes, ma'am."

"Look." Brianna held up an ash log. "I'm making sure to use your favorite firewood." She fought to keep a straight face but ended up snorting as she held back her laughter.

"Just build your damned fire." Dani laughed.

She finished her beer and grabbed another out of the cooler. She needed to get a grip on her conflicting emotions. Maybe another beer would help.

In some regards, she was more relaxed and at peace than she'd ever been. The easy interaction between them felt right, and the playful banter only enhanced that feeling. On the other hand, it also scared the hell out of her. How had she gotten so close so fast to someone she'd known for such a short time? Bri had become a part of her world, and on the days they didn't talk, something was missing.

Dani unsuccessfully tried to push her fears aside. *What if Brianna decides not to keep Thundering Pines?* As much as she loved the campground, she could find another job, but she couldn't find another Brianna. The thought of Brianna disappearing from her life terrified her.

Was this normal? They were just friends, after all. She always hated that expression, *just friends*. Not sleeping with someone didn't make the relationship less intimate. *Fuck.* Should she think of intimacy and Brianna in the same thought?

It wasn't as if she wanted to jump her bones. So what if she appreciated Brianna's beauty? For fuck's sake, she wasn't blind. She took another swallow of her beer. *Shit.* She'd drank nearly half already. She was not a big drinker, and this could turn out to be a mistake.

Dani detected Brianna's gaze on her. When she glanced up, Brianna was studying her. "Care to tell me what's going on?"

"I'm watching you build a fire," Dani answered.

"Care to tell me why you're slamming down the beer?"

"Because I'm watching you build a fire," Dani teased.

Brianna stared at her a couple more beats but apparently decided not to push. "Very funny. Just you wait, you're going to be so impressed by my fire-building skills."

"You did have a good teacher, just saying."

"Of course you're gonna try and take the credit." Brianna rolled her eyes and made another pass around her teepee. She added a little more tinder and pulled the lighter from her pocket. "Here goes."

After several tries, she had a roaring fire. It required all of Dani's willpower to stop herself from jumping in to help. Brianna hadn't yet developed a feel for the fire's movement, so several times, she threw the kindling into the wrong place, delaying the blaze.

It sputtered a few more times and finally took.

Brianna let out a scream and danced around the fire. On her second pass around it, she raised her arms over her head and strutted as she sang, "This girl is on fire."

Dani admired the pure joy on her face. It made her even more beautiful. *Stop it!* "Congratulations, I bow to your fire-building prowess."

"I bet you didn't think I could do it." Brianna pulled her phone out of her pocket and snapped several pictures.

"I had no doubt." Dani pulled her phone out and took several more photos. "You must have a picture with your first fire. Something a girl is gonna want to commemorate."

"Let me see." Brianna practically hopped over to Dani.

"Look at that goofy grin. You look like a ten-year-old that just won the science fair."

Brianna squeezed Dani's arm. "Look at it, isn't it beautiful?"

"Yes, very beautiful." Dani stared at the picture. A loud pop from the fire made her flinch.

Out of the corner of her eye, she caught Brianna studying her. Did Brianna catch the change in her tone? She needed to get on firmer ground quickly. "Do you know why the fire pops like that?"

Brianna looked at Dani for a few beats with a smirk on her face. "No, why?"

Dani swallowed hard and cleared her throat before she broke into her teaching voice. "When the water and sap in the log heat up, it produces steam or gas that pushes out and makes the sound."

"Of course, anyone that has a favorite firewood would know that." Brianna put her arm over Dani's shoulders and bumped her with her hip.

※ ※ ※ ※

Brianna edged closer to the fire, hoping to combat the cold night air. A shiver ran through her body, but the blaze immediately caused her face to flush. She leaned back in her chair and closed her eyes, listening to the sounds of the night.

Life was so strange. If someone had told her two months ago that she'd be sitting out under the stars enjoying a campfire she built, she would have told them they were crazy. When smoke drifted her way, she deeply breathed in. She detested cigarette smoke but was coming to appreciate the smell of the campfire.

"You learned all this from your dad?" Brianna

asked.

"Yep, I can't remember how old I was when he started teaching me, but I'm sure I was pretty young," Dani said. "I was in awe of how much he knew. I thought he was a genius because he could just look at a tree from a long way off and tell me what it was."

"And I bet you can do the same now."

"I can." Dani grinned. "You can't have a favorite wood unless you can identify trees."

"Obviously." Brianna opened the cooler and pulled out a beer. "Do you want another one?"

"Sure, why not? I already told Aunt Helen we were going to stay at the loft tonight."

Brianna handed Dani the beer she'd just opened and pulled out another one for herself. She popped off the bottle cap and took a big gulp. "Is there anything better than an ice-cold beer?"

"I could think of a couple things."

"I wasn't thinking of *that*," Brianna said.

"Thinking what?" Dani put her hand on her chest as if she were clutching her pearls, but her smirk gave her away. "I was referring to my favorite wood. What are you referring to?"

"Very funny," Brianna said but decided this wasn't a path she wanted the conversation to go down. The beer might be making her feel too relaxed. She'd caught herself studying Dani's face more than she was comfortable with.

She put her hands out toward the fire and rubbed them together. Warmth penetrated her skin. The fire cast an eerie glow on the surrounding woods.

"So are you going to tell me what's been going on with you these last couple weeks?" Dani asked.

Brianna held up her beer. "Whoa, you're two or

three ahead of me. You have to go first."

"How could I have gotten that far ahead?"

"Remember kicking back watching the fire-building show? I believe you were drinking the entire time. I, on the other hand, was busy with the task at hand."

"Okay, fine, I'm not even going to try and argue with you. What do you want to know?"

"How did you get that gray streak in your hair?"

"Wow. Okay, you're going to jump right to the point."

"It's how I roll." Brianna held up her beer and brought it to her lips.

"It happened when I was sixteen."

"Was it an accident?" Brianna asked when Dani didn't continue.

"No." Dani took a deep breath and let it out slowly. "It was one of the worst days of my life."

Brianna saw the struggle on Dani's face. "You don't have to talk about it if you don't want to."

"It's okay. I've never told anyone this story, except Aunt Helen. But I want to tell you."

Brianna put her hand to her chest as the warmth spread. "I'm honored."

"I was sixteen. I was curious and wanted to experience everything life had to offer." Dani cleared her throat and stared into the fire. "My best friend's name was Julie. We were inseparable. We could talk about anything and laughed at the most stupid things. I loved her. We started experimenting." Dani stopped speaking and rubbed her hands together.

Brianna's mind jumped to what Molly had told her about Dani sleeping with several of the lonely women at the gym. Was she referring to sexual experimentation, or was it the typical high school drugs and alcohol?

"I loved her," Dani said again, making Brianna more convinced of the type of experimentation she was referring. "And she loved me, I think. We'd hang out after school while my dad was at work. It started out with goofing around and wrestling, then one time, we kissed. To this day, I couldn't tell you who initiated it. It just kinda happened. And it progressed from there, kissing became touching, and...I guess I don't have to explain the progression to you."

"I get the picture," Brianna said when it was clear Dani was waiting for a response.

"One day, my dad came home early from work, and we didn't hear the garage door open. He walked in on us."

"Oh, shit."

"Oh, shit, is right. He caught me with my face between Julie's legs. I have no idea how long he was there before he yelled my name." Dani ran her hands through her hair. "We threw on our clothes, and Julie ran out. It was a blur, but I'll never forget the look on his face. It was so full of contempt. I was daddy's little girl, and I never thought I'd see such hatred blazing in his eyes. At least not directed at me."

Brianna wanted to reach out to her but sensed that touching her would be a mistake, so she kept her hands in her lap. "It's okay, Dani."

"I'd never seen him so angry. When he walked toward me, I backed up against the wall. I didn't know what to say, so I just said, 'Dad.'" Dani shook her head as if trying to clear her mind. "That seemed to enrage him. He slapped me so hard across the face that I fell to the ground."

Brianna gasped and took Dani's hand, no longer able to sit and do nothing.

Dani squeezed her hand. "I was so scared. When he stepped toward me, I curled into a ball and covered my head, afraid he'd hit me again. The next thing I knew, I felt him beside me. He was crying. No, sobbing. I'd never even seen him shed a tear before that."

Brianna's heart ached for Dani. She wanted to take her pain away but knew she couldn't. The only thing she could do was sit quietly and let Dani tell her story.

"He kept saying my name over and over. I wanted him to stop. Then he grabbed me hard and held me against him and wept. I was so scared." Dani's body tensed as she spoke. "Eventually, I relaxed and started sobbing, too." Dani finally glanced at Brianna. Tears streamed down her face.

Without hesitation, Brianna knelt in front of Dani and put her arms around her. Brianna wasn't sure how long they stayed in this position, but it must have been a while since her leg was starting to cramp from kneeling.

"I'm sorry, Bri." Dani loosened her grip. "I don't know where that came from."

"Nothing to be sorry about." Brianna let go and sat back on her heels, trying to work the cramp out of her leg. "I think that pain was buried pretty deep. It needed to come out."

"I didn't need to blubber like a damned fool, though." Dani brushed at Brianna's shoulder. "Sorry if I got tears on your sweatshirt."

"I'm not worried about the tears. It's the snot I'm concerned about." Brianna hoped to lighten the moment and erase the embarrassed look on Dani's face. Relief washed over her when Dani smiled.

Dani pretended to pick something off Brianna's shirt. "There. I think I got it. Well, except what got in your hair."

Brianna laughed. "You okay now?"

"Yes." Dani squeezed Brianna's hand one last time. "You might want to get off your knees before you get stuck down there."

Brianna made an exaggerated groan as she stood and stretched her legs. "The pain I put myself through for you."

"Not my fault you're old and out of shape."

"For the record, I heard that, but I'm choosing to ignore it because I want to hear the rest of the story." Brianna returned to her chair. "He got that upset from seeing you in bed with a girl?"

Dani threw another log on the fire. A few embers broke off and rolled away. She kicked them back with the toe of her boot. "That night, he told me that my mom left us for another woman. Apparently, he caught her in the same compromising position he'd found Julie and me."

"Ouch," Brianna said.

"I will never forget his face. It was so full of hatred." Dani stared into the flames. "I know he hated my mom, but it sure felt like he hated me, too. He made me swear that I'd never turn out like her."

"Oh, Dani," Brianna said, the reality finally setting in. "Hence Carl Evans."

"Yep, poor Carl got caught in the crossfire of my dad's hatred. I never felt what I should have for him, but I wanted to please my dad. How messed up is that?" Dani went back to the pile and pulled out a few more logs.

The fire seemed big enough to Brianna, but she sensed that Dani needed to keep moving. "I'm so sorry, but at least you didn't make that mistake."

"What do you mean?" Dani turned around, the logs still in her grip.

"You didn't marry Carl, so you can be who you are now."

"Who do you think I am?"

"Well, gay, I guess."

"I'm not gay." Dani's jaw clenched, and her eyes narrowed.

"Oh, I just assumed..."

"No, I'm not." Dani slung the log onto the fire, causing the embers to scatter. She went back to her chair and sat, making no move to straighten the disorder that her haphazardly thrown log had created. "Just because I was experimenting when I was sixteen doesn't make me a lesbian."

"My mistake." Brianna searched for something to defuse the situation. The conversation was obviously making Dani defensive. "I just thought since you'd not been interested in Carl that maybe that was the reason."

"Not wanting to marry Carl doesn't make me a lesbian," Dani said.

That didn't work. Should she ask if Dani had been attracted to any other guy, or would she take it as provocation? She settled on the safest response. "Of course, that's true."

Brianna stared straight ahead, suddenly extremely interested in the fire. She felt Dani's gaze boring into the side of her head.

"What aren't you saying?" Dani asked.

It was Brianna's turn to busy herself cleaning up

the embers. She wanted to get back on solid ground with Dani but wasn't sure how. Was she angry because Brianna assumed she was a lesbian or because her father's reaction had caused her to live a lie? Did Dani even know who she was? Brianna turned away from the blaze and made eye contact with Dani. "Why are you tense with me all of a sudden?"

"Wasn't it presumptuous of you to just figure I was a lesbian?"

Brianna wrestled with her answer. She didn't want to upset Dani any further, but it was refreshing how openly they communicated about everything, and she didn't want to start holding back now. "There is one more thing that made me think maybe you were."

"Okay," Dani said hesitantly.

"The other day when I was talking to Molly, she'd mentioned that you might have had some..." Brianna stopped, unsure how to finish. She kicked a few of the embers back into the fire. "That maybe you might have had some romantic relationships with a couple of women from the gym."

A shadow crossed Dani's face. "Are you going to listen to all the local gossip? I guess you've forgotten what it's like to live in a small town. Everyone has something to say about everyone else." Dani got up and joined Brianna. "We're starting to get a little too much smoke. Try and push those two logs back into the center of the pile."

It wasn't lost on Brianna that Dani hadn't answered her question, but she wasn't going to push the issue. Why should it matter to her how Dani identified? Brianna followed Dani's instructions and soon had the blaze back under control. "How's that?"

"Looks good." Dani smiled. "Although I'm not

sure how much longer we're going to be able to enjoy the fire."

"Why?"

"Haven't you seen the flashes off in the distance?" Dani pointed to the west.

"Nope, I guess I'm not very observant."

"Lightning," Dani said. "And if you listen, you can hear the faint sound of thunder. So we better not add any more logs."

"You never answered my question," Brianna said. She felt Dani stiffen beside her. "How did you get the streak in your hair?"

Dani let out the breath she'd been holding. "About two weeks after that night, I noticed that my hair was coming in white, just in that one spot."

"It didn't turn white overnight?"

"No, I'd always heard that when people had a traumatic event that it happened that way, but my hairdresser said it wasn't true. She said the hair that we can see already has pigment, so it only affects what comes out of the follicle after the trauma."

"So it's come out white ever since?"

"Yep."

"Did you ever think of coloring it?"

"My dad wanted me to, but for a long time, I was stubborn. I guess I wanted him to be reminded of what he'd done."

"What about now?"

"I think even if I had the choice, I would leave it. I'm kinda used to it now."

"Why don't you have a choice?"

"About a year after it turned, I gave in to my dad and agreed to have it dyed. But the universe had other ideas. For some reason, it won't hold dye for any longer than a couple days, no matter what I do with it."

"Brutal," Brianna said.

"My dad always tried to sit on the other side of me, so he didn't have to see it."

"I like it." Brianna reached out tentatively and touched the strand of hair. It felt a little coarser than the rest, but that could just be her imagination. "I mean, I don't like how you got it, but I like the way it looks. It's unique. Does that make sense?"

"Yes." Dani laughed. "I already knew you were weird."

༄༅

Dani felt exposed after her emotional revelation but also relieved. She'd finally shared her story with someone other than Aunt Helen. Brianna had handled it well, even though the exchange had gotten tense at the end. She was grateful Brianna hadn't pushed it any further. So what if she slept with a woman every now and then? It didn't make her a lesbian. Not sleeping with men didn't, either.

They sat in silence, watching the dark clouds roll in. The distant thunder was getting louder, and the wind picked up, swirling the smell of campfire through the air. Occasionally, the smoke wafted in their direction, but neither tried to move away from it. The smell was a reminder that summer was coming.

Brianna sat facing the fire. The flames danced, casting a surreal shadow on Brianna's face.

"Thank you," Dani said, breaking the silence.

"For what?" Brianna turned to her.

"Listening. Caring. Making something that has

haunted me for years seem not so horrible."

"I don't feel like I did much."

"You did. I appreciate it more than you know."

Brianna smiled. "I'm honored you entrusted your story to me."

Dani reached into the cooler and pulled out two dripping bottles. "Looks like we're down to our last two."

"Think we'll have time to finish them before the storm gets here?" Brianna took the bottle from Dani, brought it to her lips, and took a long pull.

"I'm sure we will if you keep drinking like that." Dani chuckled. "You know it's your turn now."

"My turn for what?" Brianna looked at the fire intently, as if trying to remember what she'd forgotten. "Oh, shit, you're right." She jumped up and grabbed the bag sitting next to the cooler.

"What are you doing?"

"Getting out the stuff for s'mores. Isn't that what you wanted?"

"That's not what I meant, but I'll never turn down s'mores."

Brianna peeked into the large sack. "Holy hell, how many were you planning on us eating?"

"I bought enough for the whole season. It shouldn't go bad. We can keep it in the loft in case of emergency."

"Isn't that pretty presumptuous, assuming I'll be back enough times to get through all this?" Brianna held up the bag and smiled.

Dani smirked. "Who said you were the only one I plan on sharing my s'mores with?"

"Really, just like that, you're already replacing me?"

"You're the one that said you weren't coming back. Am I supposed to sit around pining for you?"

"Yes." Brianna faked a frown. "I'm pine-able."

"Is that even a word?"

"It is now."

"Well, get your pine-able ass over here with the goods," Dani said. "I'm ready to hear your story."

"Do I really have to tell it?"

"Wasn't that the deal we made at Navy Pier? We ply each other with beer and tell our stories?"

"Yes." Brianna spread the contents of the bag onto her chair. "But I need a couple promises before I do."

"What am I promising?" Dani reached for the bag of marshmallows.

"Don't touch those." Brianna slapped at Dani's hand. "Stipulation number one: If I have to tell this story, I need to keep busy, so hands off my stuff."

"Done." Dani withdrew her hand and took a swig from her beer. "I have no problem sitting here drinking beer while you do all the work."

"Isn't that how the evening started?"

"It is, but this is our last beer, so I'm going to have to savor it."

"Uh-huh." Brianna grunted.

Dani sensed Brianna's discomfort and wished she could say something to put her at ease. Dani's heart went out to Brianna as she watched her dig through the bag. "Is there another stipulation?"

Brianna stopped rummaging in the sack and turned. She pointed. "That's number two. No looking at me like that."

"Like what?"

"No concerned looks. If I even sense you're pitying me, I'm leaving."

"I don't understand. I get not wanting pity, but I can't be concerned, either?"

Brianna stood, put her hands on her hips, and stared down at Dani. "You can be concerned, but don't show it. I'm serious, I'll walk."

"Whoa, how am I supposed to not react if it's something that has you this upset?"

"Come here." Brianna motioned Dani to stand.

Dani was puzzled, but she complied.

Once Dani rose to her feet, Brianna hugged her tightly. "Okay, you've shown your concern. No more," Brianna said after they separated.

They'd shared a lot over the last couple of months. What could be so bad to cause Brianna to act like this? *Oh, God, she's sick.* Dani's heart raced. *Stop.* Now wasn't the time to overthink. She took a deep breath. "You're serious, aren't you?"

"Completely." Brianna ripped open the bag of marshmallows, poured them onto her chair, and began putting them into two piles.

"What are you doing?"

"Duh, looking for the most perfect marshmallows." Brianna pushed the larger pile back into the bag and examined the smaller stack. "I only need four, so I have to eliminate more." She tossed a few more into the bag and continued studying them until she'd whittled it down. She held them up for Dani to inspect.

"I'm good with those."

"You didn't even look."

"I defer to your marshmallow prowess. Besides, they're gonna melt anyway, so what does it matter?"

"I'm going to pretend that you didn't just say

that." Brianna gave Dani a serious look. "You have to promise."

"Apparently, I have no choice."

"That's not a promise." Brianna set aside the chosen marshmallows and spun the bag before wrapping the tie around the neck.

"I promise, Bri." Dani gave her a slight smile.

Brianna pointed at Dani. "Watch that look, it's bordering on concerned." She ripped open the bag of graham crackers and laid them out. "Wait until I finish getting this set up. I'm not talking when I'm standing this close to you."

Dani subtly wiped her sweaty palms on her jeans. She suspected being nervous wouldn't be allowed, either. "Are you sure you don't want me to help?"

"After your disregard for the perfect marshmallow, I'm afraid I can't trust you with the chocolate squares." Brianna unwrapped the candy and carefully snapped it into uniform pieces before placing them on the graham crackers.

"I could roast the marshmallows."

"Nope, that's part of the deal." Brianna placed the fluffy pillows on two sticks and walked around the fire, so it stood between them. She didn't look up; instead, she stared at the marshmallows. "Remember I told you I was having a rough time after the last time I visited here?"

"Am I supposed to answer, or is that rhetorical?"

Brianna looked up and smiled. "You can speak when I ask you a question, but that's it."

"Well then, yes, I do remember."

"When I got home that night, I thought Caroline had already gone to bed because the living room was dark." Brianna stopped to take a drink of her beer. "I didn't want to wake her, so I was quiet when I slipped into our bedroom." Her voice was near a whisper.

Oh, shit. Dani leaned forward straining to hear. Did she really want to know what Brianna discovered? And could she keep her face from showing any reaction?

"When I opened the bedroom door, I found Caroline in bed with her best friend, Kylie."

Blood rushed in Dani's ears, but she hoped her face gave nothing else away.

"And yes, that meant they were having sex," Brianna said.

Dani's chest tightened. She bit back the "I'm so sorry" that was on the tip of her tongue. Why did she agree to these stupid rules? She stopped herself from rushing to Brianna and thought better of crossing her arms over her own chest. That would probably break the rules, too.

Brianna studied the marshmallows, holding them far enough from the fire that they roasted slowly. "I wasn't completely surprised. We've had an open relationship for the past five or six years."

Don't react. Don't react. It took everything Dani had not to say anything. She took a deep breath, trying to show no expression.

Brianna slowly turned the marshmallows at a consistent pace, ensuring they cooked evenly. "But she's never brought anyone into our bed or slept with one of our friends, at least that I know about. Do you want to know what was worse?"

"Yes," Dani said tentatively.

"She acted like it was my fault. That I shouldn't have been upset. That somehow I was breaking our agreement by my reaction."

Dani gripped the arms of her chair, hoping Brianna couldn't see her white knuckles. The thought of Caroline belittling Brianna caused the vein in her neck to throb.

"Not that she's ever validated my feelings, but her callousness caught me off guard." Brianna continued to robotically roast the marshmallows, showing no reaction to her own plight.

Apparently, it wasn't just Dani who wasn't allowed to react. It all seemed so unnatural, but Dani remained silent.

"The worst part, as I stood there feeling completely humiliated, Caroline said she was still horny. Apparently, I'd interrupted her before she'd gotten her release."

Dani's stomach clenched. Part of her wanted to hug Brianna, and the other part of her wanted Brianna to stop talking since she suspected where the story would go next.

Brianna pulled the golden-brown marshmallows out of the fire and brought them to the waiting graham crackers and chocolate. Carefully, she placed a marshmallow on the cracker and put another cracker on top. She squeezed down, letting the marshmallow ooze out the side.

When she handed one over, their fingers brushed.

Dani shivered, hoping her reaction didn't betray her feelings. She could still feel Brianna standing next to her, not moving.

"This isn't fair to you, is it?" Brianna asked.

"It's hard. I'm trying to keep my promise."

Brianna moved away and went to the other side of the fire.

"I'm sure you've already figured this out. But I

let her take me to our bedroom and have me. The same place that I'd just caught her with Kylie." Brianna was back to calmly rotating the marshmallows, watching them as she slowly spun them.

Bile churned in Dani's stomach. She wanted to vomit, but it would certainly be against the rules. She knew her eyes would betray her concern, which was the look Brianna strictly forbade. How could someone treat someone they loved that way? And why did Brianna put up with it?

"After she was done, she rolled over and fell fast asleep. I went into the bathroom and vomited." Brianna said nothing more, putting her entire focus on the fork in her hand. Once she was satisfied with the results, she made her way to her chair and created another perfect treat.

Dani held hers uneaten, not having taken a single bite. She wasn't sure if she could eat.

Brianna methodically packed up the ingredients littering her chair and sat.

A million questions flooded Dani's brain as she fought against showing how much she ached for Brianna's pain. Even though Brianna sat next to her, there was too large of a gap to be able to accidentally touch. At this point, she wasn't sure which of them needed to be comforted more.

"So that's the story of your new friend," Brianna said with contempt. "Still want to hang out with me?"

"Of course I do. I can't handle this not doing or saying anything, but I don't want to break my word."

Brianna sat with her feet on her chair, and her arms wrapped around herself as she rocked slightly. "I'm sorry. It was wrong of me to make you promise that, but please, I can't handle pity."

"Oh, Bri, I don't pity you. I might hate Caroline, but I don't pity you. Can I come sit next to you?"

"Yes, please."

Dani slid her chair next to Brianna's. Gently, she wrapped her arm around Brianna, who let her head drop to Dani's shoulder.

Questions swirled around in Dani's mind, but she chose not to ask any of them; instead, she kept her arm around Brianna, letting her presence speak for her. Brianna's body relaxed as they silently watched the fire.

The distant thunder was getting louder, and the lightning cut across the sky. Dani figured they only had about ten minutes before the storm was on them, but she hesitated, not wanting to disturb Brianna. She wasn't sure how long they'd been sitting this way but thought it had been nearly half an hour. Brianna's breathing was rhythmic, and Dani suspected she'd fallen asleep.

She scanned the area, making a mental note of what to grab should the storm blow up. Their cooler was empty, so she would pour the ice and water onto the campfire, and then use the cooler to put the odds and ends into. With a plan formulated, Dani tilted her face to the sky. When the night lit up, she noted the clouds moved faster than she had realized. The tree branches whipped around in the fierce wind.

"Bri," Dani said softly. When she didn't get an answer, she spoke louder, "Hey, Bri, the storm is almost here. I think we better get inside before it hits."

"Huh?" Brianna said groggily, blinking several times.

"The storm's coming. We need to get into the loft before it hits."

Brianna lifted her head.

Dani rotated the shoulder that Brianna had been leaning against. It tingled as the blood began circulating again.

A loud crack of thunder reverberated off the trees, bringing Brianna out of her chair. "What the hell? That sounded close," Brianna said.

"It's coming in quicker than I thought." Dani sprang to her feet and picked up the cooler. She checked inside to ensure there was only ice before using it to douse the fire. The sizzles and crackling were drowned out by the rolling thunder. "Normally, we would put the fire out much more methodically, but I think Mother Nature will take care of it for us." As if on cue, the first raindrop hit Dani's cheek.

It was followed by several larger drops, which put Brianna in motion. "What do you need me to do?"

"I'm putting everything into the cooler." She'd already packed the s'mores ingredients and was scouring the area for any loose items.

Brianna struggled with the roasting sticks, unable to get them to retract.

"There's a little button on the side. Brute force won't do the trick," Dani said.

Brianna found the button, collapsed the sticks, and stashed them in the cooler. The wind surged and knocked over their chairs, sending them tumbling toward the fire. Brianna lunged and snagged them before they landed in the ashes.

"Damn, you have quick reflexes." The rain was coming down harder, and the wind was whipping around. "I hope you can run fast, too."

"Why?"

"I think the downpour is just about on us. Bring

the chairs, I've got the cooler."

"Got 'em, let's go."

Before they could make their move, the skies opened.

❧❧❧❧❧

They were drenched and panting when they pushed into the loft. The wind lashed the trees, and the thunder rattled the windows. Dani smiled at the look of awe on Brianna's face. Water dripped off Brianna onto the floor, but she was too mesmerized by the light show to notice.

Dani removed her wet shoes and wrung out the front of her shirt into the sink. She went into the bathroom and returned with a towel. "You might want this," Dani said, bringing Brianna out of her trance.

"This is amazing." Brianna took the towel and vigorously rubbed it over her hair. "I have never witnessed a thunderstorm quite like this before."

"It never gets old." Dani smiled. "I've watched many a storm from here, but it still draws me in every time."

"It's breathtaking." Brianna wrapped her arms around herself and shivered.

"Why don't you get out of those wet clothes? I have a pair of sweatpants and a T-shirt you can use." Dani rummaged through her overnight bag.

"I don't want to miss anything." Brianna moved closer to the windows.

The trees danced in the wind, and the lightning acted as a strobe light capturing their movement.

"I'm sure the storms on the forty-eighth floor beat this," Dani said.

"It seems more intense here. Up that high, the only sign of the ferocity is the choppy water on Lake Michigan, so the effect is muted. Here, with the trees only a few yards away, I feel like we're in the midst of a tempest."

Dani handed Brianna the garments. "I'm pretty sure this storm isn't close to done, so you can probably spare a few minutes to change."

Brianna perched the clothing on the windowsill and without warning pulled her shirt off in one quick motion.

Dani tried not to look, but it was hard not to gape at her long lean torso. The muscles in Brianna's arms and shoulders rippled as she reached around to unhook her bra. As if on cue, a flash of lightning lit up the loft as Brianna's bra fell to the floor. The damp cold clothing caused Brianna's nipples to protrude from her perfectly formed breasts.

Dani swallowed hard and looked away. *Holy shit.* Brianna's body was nearly flawless.

"Where do you want me to put my wet clothes?" Brianna said.

Dani flinched. "Um, I can take them." She put out her hand but didn't shift her gaze to Brianna. The clothes touched her hand, and she squeezed her fingers around them. One of the garments slipped from her grasp and fell to the floor.

Dani and Brianna bent at the same time and almost bumped heads. Their faces were inches from each other. Dani stumbled backward and nearly fell over her overnight bag. Righting herself, she stammered. "Um, sorry."

"Are you okay?" Brianna touched her arm.

Electricity surged through Dani. "I better

change, too." She rushed to the bathroom and closed the door between them, then put her back against it and breathed in deeply. *Slick!* It wasn't as if she'd never seen a half-naked woman before. It must just be the beer and the alluring way the storm lit her body. *Alluring? Stop!*

Dani peeled off her wet clothes and wrung them out. Standing naked, she glanced in the mirror and thought of Brianna again. She diverted her gaze and yanked a T-shirt over her head.

Get a grip. Even though Brianna was into open relationships, she wouldn't be someone Dani would tap for a one-night stand. Brianna was her friend, her close friend, which made her off-limits.

⚘⚘⚘⚘

Brianna pulled the blanket Dani had given her up to her chin. A contented sigh escaped her lips as she snuggled into the warmth. She sipped on a cup of tea as she watched the storm pull away.

"Can I ask you a question?" Dani said.

"About?"

"What you told me earlier."

Brianna's shoulders sagged. Did she have anything left in the tank? "Do we have to talk about that?"

"Not if you don't want to."

"Go ahead. Ask."

"How do you do it?"

"Well, you know lady parts are the same, but—"

"No, that's not what I meant, smartass."

Brianna laughed. "So what's your question?"

"How do you handle it? Isn't it strange sleeping with someone else and then going back home to

Caroline?"

"I don't." When she saw Dani's puzzled look, she added, "I mean, I don't sleep with other people."

"But you said you have an open relationship."

"We do, I just don't exercise my option," Brianna said with a sad smile.

Dani pursed her lips and studied her. "Then why did you agree to it?"

Brianna stared at the retreating clouds. She sighed and blew on her tea. "We'd been together for a few years, and I could tell Caroline was starting to get restless. I wasn't sure if we'd stay together, and then she suggested we try an open relationship." She paused and took another drink. "I suppose if someone psychoanalyzed me, they'd say I didn't want to turn out like my mother."

"I'm not following."

"Caroline can't cheat on me if I give her permission."

"That seems like some fucked-up logic."

Brianna shrugged. "Probably."

"Doesn't it hurt when she does it?"

"It used to, but now I think I'm mostly numb." Numb was the perfect word. Until walking in on Caroline and Kylie, she'd not given it much thought in years.

"She doesn't deserve you."

"Thank you. But it's as much my fault as it is hers."

Dani frowned. "How do you figure?"

"I'm an adult. She isn't doing anything to me that I didn't consent to."

"But she backed you into a corner."

Brianna shook her head. "Nope, I'm not a victim

now or ever. I had the choice to say no, and I didn't. I still do."

"What happens next?"

"I don't know."

"Are you happy?"

"No," Brianna answered without hesitation. There, it was finally said. Somehow, verbalizing it wasn't as devastating as she thought it would be. Just sad. "I haven't been happy for a while." How could she explain to Dani that she'd not given it much thought until recently? They were too busy working fifty- to sixty-hour weeks. She'd spent more time talking to Dani in the last two months than she had Caroline in the last two years. They were rarely home, and when they went out, it was always with others. "Can we talk about something else?"

"Of course," Dani said.

"Did you and your dad ever talk about that night?" Brianna asked.

"Not really," Dani answered.

"He never apologized?"

"No." Dani shifted uncomfortably. "He thought he was justified since he stopped me from walking down the horrible lesbian path."

"What about Julie?"

"She was never allowed at our house again." The sadness was evident in Dani's hazel eyes. "Not that she wanted to come back, anyway. Our friendship was pretty much over after that humiliation."

"I'm sorry." Brianna wished she could erase the pain in Dani's eyes. "Did your dad ever soften his stance?"

"Nope, he was a homophobe to the bitter end."

"Do you ever wonder about your mom?" Brianna

asked.

Dani stared out the window but didn't respond.

"I'm sorry. I ask too many questions."

"You're fine," Dani said. "I'm just feeling raw. It's like the top couple layers of my skin have been peeled away."

"Wow, that's not the way I wanted to make you feel." Brianna's stomach knotted. Had she pushed Dani too far?

"No, I meant it in a good way."

"Layers of skin being peeled off." Brianna shook her head. "Nope, having trouble interpreting that in a good way."

Dani smiled. "Sorry, I guess I'm not very poetic. I meant I'm feeling a little exposed and raw but exfoliated at the same time."

Brianna burst out laughing. "Don't quit your day job. I'm thinking Hallmark wouldn't go for the slogan *you exfoliate me.*"

"Why not?" Dani joined the laughter. "If *you complete me* became a big thing, why not *you exfoliate me?*"

Chapter Twenty-one

Brianna stretched her legs in the passenger seat of Dani's pickup and yawned. Maybe one day they wouldn't stay up talking half the night, so they wouldn't be tired the next day. She wanted to be fresh for opening day.

At Thundering Pines, Brianna normally didn't wear much makeup, but she'd put some on this morning. She'd noticed that Dani did, too. Brianna sneaked a peek at her. Dani looked good. *Damned good.* This early in the season, she'd already developed a tan that highlighted her love of the outdoors and gave her a sporty look.

Brianna had pitched million-dollar deals, so why was she nervous meeting a few campers? Dani had assured her that it was a low-key affair. Some of the campers liked to arrive in mid-April to get their campsite in order, while many others wouldn't come until Memorial Day weekend, which was why the big party wouldn't happen for a couple of weeks.

No activities were planned since everyone would be busy setting up. Thundering Pines sprang for a catered meal that would be served around three, but after, the campers would be right back at it opening their units, cleaning, and getting their site ready for the season.

"How many of the campers will be there?" Brianna asked.

"About half, give or take." Dani turned down the road to Thundering Pines. "It's a real casual affair. We'll drive around on the ATV, checking in and saying hi."

"That's it?"

"Basically. Every now and then, they have a question or need a little help, but it's pretty chill, so relax."

Am I that transparent? "Who said I'm not relaxed?"

Dani glanced in her direction and nodded at Brianna's lap. "Yep, picture of relaxed."

Brianna shifted her gaze to her lap, where she'd clenched her hands into fists. She unclenched them and wiggled her fingers. "Fine. I might be a little nervous."

"They're just people." Dani patted Brianna's leg. "Just be you."

"You mean the city girl? Don't most country folks hate my kind?"

Dani shot her a look. "First, country people aren't that judgmental. And second, you're far from the city girl I met two months ago." She smiled. "If that version of you showed up, then maybe they would give you a hard time."

Had she really changed that much? Or had she just let who she truly was show? She'd asked herself that question many times recently but still had no answer.

Dani pulled into her parking spot. The buzz of activity had already begun.

❧❧❧❧❧

"Last stop before we make sure the food is ready. I don't know about you, but I'm getting hungry." As if to drive the point home, Dani's stomach growled. Opening day usually went fast, but with Brianna here, it flew past. It had been a good day. Brianna was a natural with the campers who reveled in telling Brianna stories about Dani. They'd laughed so much that her cheeks hurt.

"Who are we visiting?" Brianna asked.

"The Turners."

"Do you want to fill me in on the *Reader's Digest* version of your notecard?"

"The Turners are my favorite. I can't lie." Dani smiled. "They're good people, but I have to warn you, they're eccentric. Whatever you do, just roll with the punches. They're harmless, but they are characters."

"You're making me nervous. Any other tips?"

Dani wished she could video this as she'd done with the skid steer experience. She couldn't wait to see Brianna's face when old man Turner got to going. They pulled up outside an immaculate campsite with a fully landscaped yard. "As you can tell by the setup, they've been at Thundering Pines since the beginning."

Lulu burst out of the camper door. Her white hair looked as if it hadn't seen a brush in several days. "Dani! We've been wonderin' when you'd come around." She scampered to Dani, who'd just stepped from the ATV.

"Lulu. How the hell have you been?" Dani wrapped her arms around the tiny woman and laughed. They hugged for several beats before they separated. "I don't think you've had the pleasure of meeting Brianna Goodwin."

Lulu turned and her face lit up. "I'm so glad to

meet you in person." Without warning, Lulu lunged at Brianna and wrapped her arms around her. Dani had to look away, so she wouldn't giggle. The tiny woman's head was right at chest level, so her face nestled against Brianna's breasts.

Brianna recovered and hugged Lulu back. "It's nice to meet you, too," Brianna said once she was released from the iron grip.

Lulu giggled. "In person, your head looks a lot smaller."

Brianna laughed, despite it being at least the twentieth time she'd heard it from any of the campers who'd met her at the virtual meet and greet.

The screen door rattled, and Lester stepped outside. "Just in time. The hooch is just about ready." He tottered down the stairs and made a beeline toward Dani.

"Lester, you're getting more handsome every year."

He waved at her and laughed. He hadn't aged much since last year. He still had several patches of white hair, which he refused to cut off, even though it made him look like a poor man's Albert Einstein. His skin was leathery from too much sun without sunscreen. Despite his advanced age, his eyes were piercing blue and crystal clear.

"Who do we have here?" He smiled at Brianna.

"This is Brianna Goodwin." Dani swept her hand in Brianna's direction. "Donald's daughter."

"Well, I'll be damned." Lester squinted and looked up at her. He was not much taller than Lulu, so he had a long way to look up. "Head's not near as big as I thought." He chuckled at his joke. "We'd heard you'd inherited the campground and pissed off that sister of yours."

"Half." Brianna delivered her usual response.

"I've got a treat for you, young lady." He reached into his back pocket and pulled out a flask.

Dani couldn't take her focus off Brianna. She wanted to see how this would play out.

"Um, thank you," Brianna said. "Can I ask what it is?"

"The finest hooch you'll find in Thundering Pines." He lowered his voice and leaned in. "Don't tell those vultures out there that I've made my first batch, or they'll be all over me like flies on shit." He twisted the cap off the flask and held it out to Brianna.

Brianna tentatively took it from him but didn't move it toward her mouth. "That's awfully nice of you, but I've never had hooch."

He cackled. "You hear that, Lulu? She's never had hooch." His toothy smile was bigger when he turned back to Brianna. "You're in for a treat."

Dani held her breath as Brianna brought the flask to her lips. *She's a sport.* Her esteem for Brianna increased when Brianna tilted her head back and took a swig. *Oh, shit!* It was more than a swig. It was more like a gulp.

Brianna's face went white, then turned bright red. She swallowed hard and immediately broke into a coughing fit.

"Damn it, Lester." Lulu handed Brianna a bottle of water. "Here, hon. Drink some of this."

"What's in this?" Brianna croaked out between coughs.

"Plain old water, darlin'."

Brianna gulped the water, and her coughing finally stopped. "Thank you." She turned to Lester.

"Holy shit, that packs a punch. What's the proof on that?"

Lester shook his head. "I'm embarrassed to say it's probably only about one hundred eighty proof. Still trying to hit that sweet one hundred ninety."

Watching from a distance had been entertaining, but they needed to get moving, so Dani stepped up. "Lester, I won't be happy if you try and kill off my friend with your nasty hooch."

"Nasty!" Lester pretended to scowl. "Those are fighting words, young lady."

❧❧❧❧

The meal was over, and most of the campers had returned to their sites. Brianna sat back in her chair and admired Dani's charm. *They adore her.* She was seeing a whole new side of Dani. Well, not entirely. She'd seen her in action during the virtual meet and greet, but watching it in person was different.

Had she been wrong about the rapport she thought they had? Dani was easy with everyone. *Maybe I'm not special.* The thought hurt her more than it should. *Stop.* She wasn't seriously getting jealous of the campers because her friend had other friends. Was she in grade school now?

Dani sauntered over, but she stopped short when she looked at Brianna. "Is everything okay?"

"Yeah, fine," Brianna stammered. "You have quite a following. They all love you."

Dani eyed her. "They're good people."

"All the ones I met sure seem to be." Brianna knew her demeanor had changed, but she hoped Dani wouldn't notice.

"Spill," Dani said. "What's going on?"

Damn. That plan didn't work. Without giving it any more thought, her mouth opened, and words poured out. "You've got all these people in your life. Why would you want to bother with an uptight city girl?"

A puzzled look came across Dani's face. Her eyes twinkled, and the corner of her mouth twitched upward. "Brianna Goodwin, are you jealous?"

"No." Brianna tried to glare but felt her gaze softening. "Not exactly jealous."

"Then what are you, exactly?" Dani smirked.

"Okay, fine." Brianna shook her head. "It must be all this fresh country air that's messing with my brain. I just thought our friendship was deeper, but then I see you have it with everyone."

"Oh, Bri." Dani put her hand on Brianna's arm. "No. That's not true. I love these guys, but it's not the same."

"How is it then?"

"You not only make me laugh, but you also make me want to talk about stuff that I don't talk about with other people."

"But everyone here seems to know your story, so I'm not sure I get the difference."

Dani smiled. "I might tell some of my story to people, but..." She patted her own chest. "Not many people get the feelings behind the story. Besides, it's not any of them that I'm taking to the Spotted Owl in a few hours."

"Really?" Brianna clapped her hands and grinned. "You're not just screwing with me, are you?"

"Nope, but this may be the worst decision of my life." Dani put her arm around her. "Just know, I'm doing this strictly for you, and if you hate it, you can't blame me."

"Deal." Brianna gave Dani a quick hug. "I need to text Molly to let her know the good news."

Dani groaned.

Chapter Twenty-two

 ven though Dani had been joking about not wanting to go to the Spotted Owl, Brianna suspected there was some truth to it. Brianna was looking forward to it, so hopefully, she could get Dani to relax.

Dani parked her truck but didn't turn off the engine. "Are you sure you don't want to go to a movie or something?"

"Why are you so against bringing me here?"

"It doesn't seem like your thing. You're a long way from the city."

Brianna bristled. "Ah, now I get it. Stuck-up city girl won't fit in?"

"That's not what I meant." Dani met Brianna's gaze. "Never mind."

"What?"

"You're gonna think I'm stupid." Dani turned away and peered out the windshield.

"I already do, so why will this change anything?"

Dani laughed. "Fine, smartass. The Spotted Owl is a dive bar. You're gonna get country music and line dancing."

"You think I can't handle a little local flavor? Besides, I went there with Molly."

"Different crowd. The old men hang out in the afternoon. There's going to be a lot of testosterone. It's certainly not going to be like the clubs you go to in the city."

"I'm nearly six foot tall, and I don't look like what men think a lesbian should. Trust me, I've handled plenty of men hitting on me. I won't break."

Dani sighed. "Okay, let's go in."

When Dani led her to a table in the far corner, Brianna considered making a joke but changed her mind after she noticed the set of Dani's jaw. Apparently, she wanted to remain inconspicuous.

While they waited for the waitress, Brianna told stories about life in the city, in hopes that Dani would relax. It seemed to work until she noticed the looks from other patrons.

Dani must have noticed, too, because her posture stiffened.

"Would you be more comfortable if we continued this conversation under the table?" Brianna asked.

Dani smiled. "Possibly. Sorry, I'm trying."

"I know you are." Brianna reached across the table, patted Dani's hand, and laughed. "How many people do you think just saw that?" She couldn't help messing with Dani. She was so cute when she got flustered. *Cute?* Probably not a word she should be using. But Dani's reaction to her own discomfort was endearing.

"Everyone, and those that didn't will probably get the text soon."

"What do you say we act like we would if we were in any other bar in the world?"

"And how would that be?"

"Since it looks like the waitress is covering the entire floor by herself, maybe one of us should go to the bar." Somehow, she didn't think Dani would let her go, but it was worth a try.

"Now you're just talking crazy. Can't we start with something easier?"

"Nope, shall we flip for who goes?"

"No," Dani said a bit too fast. "I'll go."

"Suit yourself, but don't be surprised if I'm not alone when you return." Brianna wriggled her eyebrows.

Dani groaned. "I think you're enjoying this a little too much."

"I just want you to calm down and have some fun."

Dani rose from the table. "Let's see if a beer will loosen me up."

"Just so you know, I plan on dancing before the night is over."

"You're killing me. Maybe I should order myself two beers."

Brianna took in the bar once Dani walked away. In the twenty minutes they'd been there, it had become more crowded.

Dani's overreacting. Sure, most of the men wore cowboy boots and big shiny belt buckles, but they appeared respectful. She'd been in bars during college that she'd never want to step foot in now, but the Spotted Owl wasn't one of those bars.

The women dressed similar to what she'd see in the clubs in the city. There was an abundance of short, black dresses with lots of cleavage.

A group of four men glanced her way. Eventually, one broke from the rest and strutted across the floor.

Brianna watched him, trying not to smirk.

His perfectly groomed beard hugged his face. He wore the standard bar uniform, gray cowboy boots, a pair of faded blue jeans, and a blue plaid shirt. A beer bottle swung between his beefy fingers. As he approached the table, he flashed a smile. "Hello, little lady. I believe you must be Donald Goodwin's daughter." He extended his hand.

"You got one of the two right." She stood, and his mouth fell open. With her boots on, she had at least six inches on him. She looked down at him and extended her hand. "I'm Brianna, Donald's daughter, but I'm afraid I'm not so little."

He stepped back but didn't take her outstretched hand.

She pushed her hand out farther. "And you are?"

"Matt Foster." He recovered enough to take her hand.

Dani returned to the table with Brianna's beer. "Matt, what are you up to?"

"Uh, hi, Dani," he said. "I just came over to introduce myself to this lovely lady."

"Matt and his dad built the loft," Dani said to Brianna.

"You do beautiful work. I love the loft." Brianna gave him a smile.

"Thanks. Can I buy you a beer?"

"Sorry, Dani just bought me one."

"Maybe later then?"

"It looks like Cindy is watching you." Dani tilted her head in the direction of a group of women staring from across the room. "Maybe you should go buy her a beer instead."

"Come on, Dani," he said. "I don't see a ring on Brianna's finger or Cindy's."

"No ring, but I'm taken," Brianna said before Dani could respond.

"Well then, he's a lucky fellow."

"Yes, she is lucky. It was nice meeting you, Matt."

"You too." He walked away, shaking his head.

"Great, Bri," Dani said. "Won't be long until everyone knows."

Brianna fought back her frustration with Dani. "Am I supposed to stay in the closet here?" She knew Flower Hills was far from the city, but she thought Dani was overreacting. Did Dani think they would come after her with pitchforks or what?

"I'm sorry. I just need to keep my mouth shut tonight." Dani plopped into her seat.

"Do you think you could lighten up? I can deal with any backlash I get from being a lesbian."

"It's not the lesbian thing, as much as it's…well, it's just that you're a beautiful woman, and I know how these guys can be."

Beautiful woman, huh? Dani didn't seem to register what she'd just said, so Brianna wasn't going to point it out. "I work in the city with plenty of vultures, and I'm still standing. Do I need to ply you with shots?"

Dani laughed. "No, you're right. If I don't chill out, I'm going to ruin all your fun."

"Exactly, and I plan on learning how to do one of those line dances you were telling me about."

"Ugh, can we at least wait until Molly gets here? I need reinforcements."

An hour later, the earlier tension was long forgotten. After Matt had broken the ice, several locals, both male and female, stopped by their table to introduce themselves. After the first couple of visitors, Dani seemed to relax, which made it easier for Brianna to enjoy herself.

Molly's arrival sealed the deal. She insisted they join a group of women they'd gone to grade school with. Brianna didn't know them well, but nobody would have guessed by the laughter coming from the table.

Brianna had been on the dance floor several times, much to her surprise. *Caroline would be pissed.* She was always self-conscious in the city, as if she'd be judged, but here she felt free. She recognized the irony but was having too much fun to analyze it.

It was a treat to watch Dani dance. On the dance floor, she held nothing back. She let the music wash over her and moved as if her body were directly connected to it. There was something sexy, even though none of her moves was overtly sexual. The unbridled way she responded to the music made it impossible for Brianna to look away.

They finally returned to the table to catch their breath and enjoy their beer, which had gone untouched for nearly an hour. Brianna crinkled her nose when the warm liquid glided down her throat.

A tall blond man eyed them from the bar while Molly told Dani a story about their childhood. Before Brianna could point him out to Dani, he gave her a dimpled smile and headed their way. *Great.* She didn't want another uncomfortable repeat of the Matt encounter. Beer had been flowing freely; she hoped it hadn't lowered the man's inhibitions.

He stopped behind Dani and wrapped his arms around her from behind. "I thought that was you. How's the girl who got away?"

Carl Evans. Shit. Brianna's stomach clenched. It had been a great night, but this could ruin everything.

Dani smiled and turned around. "Well, I'll be damned. I haven't seen you around for a while, stranger."

He wrapped Dani in a bear hug and lifted her off the ground.

Dani playfully slapped his back. "Put me down, you brute."

Brianna couldn't help but notice his good looks. The two made an attractive couple. Her stomach dropped. Why did thinking of Dani and Carl together make her uneasy? She pushed the thought aside.

"I heard you had another little one," Dani said.

"Yep, our third, our first boy." Carl beamed. "He's three months old. It's our first night out since he was born." He set Dani down and released her from his grip.

"Are you kidding me? The first night out, and you bring Sara to the Spotted Owl?"

"Hey now, I took her out for dinner." He unleashed a killer smile. "Besides, this was her idea. It's her friend's birthday."

As if on cue, a group of women started a loud rendition of *Happy Birthday to You.*

"Seems like she's having a good time," Dani said.

"No doubt." He grinned. "And what are you doing here? The Spotted Owl isn't normally your thing."

"Oh, shit, where are my manners? Hey, Bri." Dani motioned to Brianna. "Carl, I'd like you to meet Brianna Goodwin."

"Well, hello." He took her hand. "I'd heard you were in town. It's nice to meet you."

"It's nice to meet you, too," she said and meant

it. Meeting Carl, she better understood Dani's anguish and guilt. There was something sweet and genuine about him, which must have made it harder for Dani.

They'd been talking for a few minutes when a scream came from the other side of the room followed by laughter.

Carl's eyebrows shot up. "Oh, no, Sara hasn't had a drink for over a year. Doesn't look good." He nodded in the direction of the commotion. "I think I best go check on her. I'm sorry I have to rush off."

Dani smiled and gave him a quick hug. "Duty calls. I get it."

He turned to Brianna with a big smile. "It was mighty nice to meet you." He started to reach out his hand but stopped and opened his arms instead.

Brianna walked into his hug.

"Dani's a keeper," he whispered so only she could hear. "Don't let her be the one that gets away from you, too."

What? Did he think they were a couple? What was it with the people in Flower Hills? Molly had made the same mistake. Brianna fought to keep her expression neutral. She gave him a warm smile. "It was nice meeting you, too, Carl."

After Carl left, Dani leaned over. "What did he say to you?"

"He seems like a sweet guy," Brianna said.

Dani's eyes narrowed, but before she could quiz Brianna, the music changed. "You're up," Dani said.

"Up for what?"

"You said you wanted to learn to line dance." Dani held out her hand.

The dancers began to line up.

Brianna held up her beer. "I'm not sure I've had

enough to drink."

"Too late. You wanted me to chill out. Well, I'm chill, so let's do it."

Molly laughed. "She's got a point."

"Whose side are you on, anyway? Never mind, don't answer that." Brianna smiled. "You're coming with us."

Molly started to protest, but Brianna grabbed her hand.

"Sorry, folks, we have a virgin with two left feet," Dani said, raising her voice.

Brianna shot Dani a look. "You just watch, I might be a natural."

Brianna turned out not to be a natural. The more she and those around her laughed, the worse her dance moves became.

Dani finally moved in front of Brianna. "Just follow my moves."

Ugh! She tried to mimic Dani's movements, but many times, she stepped in one direction while everyone else went in the opposite. She accidentally bumped into several fellow dancers, who good-naturedly tried to right her and get her back in rhythm.

When the music faded, Brianna sighed. She took one final step back and felt herself being shoved forward. She slammed into Dani and nearly lost her balance.

"What the fuck are you doing?" Dani said loudly. Her eyes blazed.

Brianna took a step back and put her hands up. She'd never seen this side of Dani. She struggled with how to respond.

"Sorry, Bri, I wasn't talking to you."

"Sis," a very drunk Shelby said. "I'm so sorry, I

didn't see you and your lap dog."

Brianna spun around.

Shelby stood flanked on each side by her cousins Nicky and Tommy.

"Sure, it's hard to see a six-foot woman dancing badly," Dani said as she stepped between Brianna and Shelby.

"What the hell was that?" Matt pushed his way into the circle that was forming. "I was watching from over there, and Shelby just crossed her arms, lowered her head, and rammed right into Brianna's back."

"Of course she did it on purpose." Dani stood to her full height and took a step toward Shelby.

Brianna put her hand on Dani's shoulder. "Don't let her get to you. I'm having too much fun to let someone like her ruin it."

"Oh, the princess is having fun and doesn't want the peasants destroying her party," Nicky said with a sneer.

Shelby shoved past Dani and grabbed Brianna in a hug. "I'm just wanting to say hi to my sister," she slurred. "I can't believe you came into town and didn't look me up."

Nicky and Tommy snorted.

Brianna pushed Shelby away.

"The bitch thinks she's too good for you. For us," Nicky said.

"Check it out. My sister seems to have a thing for Dani." Shelby turned toward Dani, pressed up against her, and ground her pelvis against Dani's leg.

Brianna bit her lip, knowing she needed to let Dani handle Shelby on her own.

"Doesn't everyone or should I say every woman?" Tommy said.

The three went into another round of laughter.

Dani pushed Shelby away and glared.

Brianna took a calming breath. Things could easily get out of hand. "Come on, Dani." She took her hand. "I think it's about time to call it a night."

"Don't leave on their account," Matt said. "I'd be happy to escort them out of here."

"Thanks, Matt," Brianna said. "I don't think it's worth starting a fight over."

"Oh, bitch, you ain't seen nothing yet," Shelby yelled. "You think you can come here and take my campground, invade my bar, and get away with it?"

"I didn't realize you'd bought a bar, congratulations." Brianna knew her sarcasm would only serve to infuriate Shelby, but in the moment, she didn't care. She'd had enough of Shelby's antics.

Shelby lunged at Brianna, but Dani stepped between them. Shelby's lowered shoulder caught Dani under her breast. The blow caused Dani to let out a loud exhalation before she doubled over coughing.

"Enough, Shelby." Brianna stepped up and got in Shelby's face. "You better never lay a hand on her again."

"Or what?" Shelby said, defiantly looking up at Brianna.

"Grow up, Shelby. And keep your hands off Dani."

Shelby smirked. "Maybe you want your hands on Dani, or should I say mouth?" For emphasis, she flicked her tongue.

Brianna grabbed Dani's hand. "It's been a great evening. Don't let her ruin it. Let's get out of here."

Chapter Twenty-three

*B*rianna's hand shook as she put the key in the lock. She took a deep breath to steady her nerves. Had it only been three weeks ago? It seemed like much longer that she'd found Caroline in bed with Kylie.

Spending time in Flower Hills was an anomaly. On one hand, the time she spent with Dani seemed to go way too fast, while on the other hand, time stood still. An hour conversation with Dani held more meaning than a month's worth of conversation with her other friends. If she were being honest, the conversations were more intimate than any she'd had with any of her current friends. Plus, she laughed more than she had in years. Dani got her sense of humor, and she never made Brianna feel stupid because of the things she laughed about.

She needed to get Dani out of her mind. The weekend had been amazing, but she was home now and had to face whatever lay behind the closed door.

The door flew open, and she screamed. Her keys dropped from her hands and went skittering across the floor. "Jesus, you scared the shit out of me." Brianna's heart raced in her chest.

"Welcome home," Caroline said with a smile.

Brianna scrambled to pick up her keys. "Uh, oh, hi."

"Here, let me help you with this." Caroline

picked up her bag and disappeared into the apartment.

What the hell? She must have entered an alternate universe. She took another deep breath before she followed. "When did you get home?" Brianna said, deciding on a neutral topic.

"I've been home since about one." Caroline kissed her and let the kiss linger. "I'm glad you're home."

"Did you have fun at Lake Geneva?" Since she wasn't sure what was going on with Caroline, she decided staying on safe conversational ground was the best choice.

"It was all right. How about you?"

Edit. Edit. She certainly couldn't tell Caroline about her amazing time. "Not bad. What did you guys do?"

"We went on one of the boat tours, ate too much, and shopped in those cute little shops. Oh, that reminds me…" Caroline rushed out of the room without finishing.

Brianna was still standing, puzzled when Caroline returned.

Caroline grinned and handed her a bag.

"What's this?"

"I got you something."

She couldn't remember the last time Caroline had bought her a present. Was it a guilt offering? *Stop being a cynic.* Caroline seemed genuinely happy to see her. "Oh, how nice." Brianna hoped she didn't sound as artificial as she felt. She pulled a tiny roller coaster made from distressed metal out of the bag and rotated it in her hand, examining it from all angles, trying to determine its purpose. She hoped the confusion didn't show on her face.

"I know you love roller coasters, so when I saw it, I had to get it." Caroline beamed.

It was the thought that counted, right? This wasn't the time to react the way she would if her cat brought her a mouse. "It's so cute." Brianna studied the piece. "Wow, did you see the workmanship? I wonder how they get the metal formed this way." God, she needed to shut up. She sounded fake to herself, Caroline would surely pick up on it.

"Isn't it great? I knew you'd love it with your fascination with carnival rides. Not that I understand, but to each his own."

Wow. Apparently, Caroline thought her obsession with the Ferris wheel translated into a fascination with carnival rides. She wasn't sure how to respond. "I know just the place for it in my office, thank you."

"Great. I was about to have a glass of wine. Join me?"

She was exhausted and just wanted to crawl into bed. "I'll just have some water. I need to hit the bathroom after the long drive. Meet me in the living room?"

Brianna walked into the bathroom and closed the door. Once she sat on the toilet, she put her head in her hands. Caroline almost seemed perky, which wasn't a word anyone would use to describe her. Questions swirled around in Brianna's mind, and she wanted them to stop. Was Caroline feeling guilty? Or did absence make the heart grow fonder? She couldn't sit here much longer, or Caroline would wonder what she was doing.

Reluctantly, she rose and flushed the toilet. When she washed her hands, she splashed some of the cool water on her face, hoping it would revitalize her. After leaving the Spotted Owl, she and Dani had gone to the loft and talked until three in the morning. They were back up by eight o'clock and spent the day working on Thundering Pines's grounds. It had felt good to use her body for a change, instead of just her mind. The combination of fresh air and manual labor had her longing for her pillow.

"Did you fall in?" Caroline called.

"Coming."

Caroline's feet were tucked under her on the couch. Two glasses of wine sat next to each other on the coffee table. Apparently, Caroline decided she needed wine instead of water.

No sense arguing. Brianna picked up one of the glasses. "Thanks." She raised it in Caroline's direction, then sank into the recliner across the room and propped up her feet.

Caroline pursed her lips and grimaced.

"Um, sorry, my feet are killing me." Brianna braced herself for Caroline's reaction.

"Rough weekend?" Caroline asked without any hint of attitude.

"No, just a rough one for my feet." Brianna reached down and rubbed her arch. "I spent the day cleaning up fallen limbs. I had no idea how many trees lose branches over the winter. And my poor feet were already sore from too much dancing the night before."

"I didn't know there was dancing involved in campground work." There was no mistaking the edge in Caroline's voice.

Shit. Being tired caused her not to think straight. Telling Caroline about Saturday night was the last thing she wanted to do. "Yeah, didn't I tell you Molly asked me to meet her at the Spotted Owl on Saturday night?"

"Oh, so it was just you and Molly?"

Fuck. She didn't want to have this conversation, but she refused to resort to lying, even though the mention of Dani normally seemed to infuriate Caroline. She took a sip of her wine, hoping to stall the inevitable. "No, Dani went, too."

Fire burned in Caroline's eyes, so she forged on before Caroline could start calling Dani names. "We met up with a group of women that I went to grade school with. It was nice catching up with them. And they taught me how to line dance. Not that I was particularly good, but it was kinda fun."

Brianna hoped if she kept rambling that Caroline would forget the mention of Dani, but so far by the look on her face, it wasn't working.

"Oh, yeah, I forgot to mention that I ran into Shelby, well, actually, she ran into me. Literally. She rammed into me in the middle of the dance floor." If anyone could distract her from Dani, it was Shelby.

"Skunk girl dances?"

Nope, it didn't work. Brianna got to her feet. "I've had enough of the name calling. I'm done with this conversation."

"Sorry," Caroline said. "Please, sit. I just couldn't imagine her dancing up a storm with that twangy shit you've been listening to lately."

A brief image of Dani on the dance floor invaded Brianna's thoughts. She hoped her cheeks didn't flush in response. Brianna sat. She didn't have the energy to argue with Caroline tonight. Deflection was her best bet. "Did you guys hit any of the bars in Lake Geneva?"

"Nope, we were in bed by ten."

Alone? Don't go there. All she wanted was to curl up in bed with the good feelings from the weekend at Flower Hills still with her. She raised her arms over her head, stretched, and yawned. "Damn, all that fresh air has me tuckered out."

"Wow, tuckered out. Are you going to start talking like those people now?"

Brianna couldn't think of a suitable response, so she took another sip of her wine and laid her head back against her chair. It would be best if she could just go to sleep, but it probably wouldn't work. She took another sip of her wine and let it swish around in her mouth before swallowing. *Change the subject.* "This wine is good."

"Drew and Kylie missed you this weekend."

Whew, it worked. She couldn't very well say she missed them, though. She still had no interest in seeing Kylie. "I'm glad you guys had a nice weekend." That was about as civil as she could be about Kylie.

"They're looking forward to seeing you on Memorial Day weekend," Caroline said.

"You know that's the big party at Thundering Pines. I won't be able to make it."

"Then surely you'll be able to make their party the weekend before?"

Something's off. Was she being set up? Caroline handled Memorial Day too easily. "What's the occasion?"

"Kylie's birthday."

Hell, no! "I'm afraid I won't be able to make it. I leave for Missouri that Friday and probably won't be back until Sunday."

"Missouri? St. Louis?"

"I'm not sure of the town."

"You're going to a conference, and you don't even know where it's at?" Caroline brought her glass to her lips and eyed Brianna over the rim. "Is that new assistant of yours going with?"

Brianna braced herself. "It's not for work. It's for Thundering Pines."

"What the hell are you going to Missouri for?"

"An auction."

"You're kidding me, right? Are you going to buy tractors?"

"Yes."

"No way. Seriously? What the hell do you know about buying tractors?"

Should I go there? Why not. "Dani's going, too."

"Of course she is."

Brianna looked at her half-empty glass. "Do you want any more?"

"More what?"

"Wine. I'm going to bed." Caroline started to protest, but Brianna held up her hand. "I'm tired. I've had a very nice weekend, and I'm not going to let this conversation ruin it." Brianna stood and set her wine-glass on the end table next to Caroline. "Good night."

Caroline called after her, but she continued to walk from the room.

Chapter Twenty-four

*B*rianna wasn't an expert on auctions, but she was puzzled why they'd traveled all the way to Missouri for this. Dani halfheartedly bid on a few items but didn't purchase anything.

While Dani filled the pickup with gas, Brianna leafed through the program again. Nope, still couldn't find anything worth the trip.

Dani strolled across the lot before disappearing into the mini mart.

Brianna shifted her attention back to the brochure. Maybe she should ask Dani when she returned; she must be missing something.

The driver's side door flew open, and Brianna jumped.

"Oh, sorry, I didn't mean to startle you." Dani held out a bottle of water and a bag of Doritos.

"You must be a mind reader. I was nearly out."

"Good thing, or you probably would've sent me back to get ya one."

Brianna smiled, knowing it was true. She would have given Dani a pathetic look, and Dani in turn would have trudged back into the store.

"I'm trying to learn, so I've been poring over this program, and for the life of me, I can't figure out why we drove all this way." Brianna held out the program, thinking Dani would take it from her.

Instead, Dani buckled her seat belt and started

the truck. "It's kinda complicated. I'll have to explain it to you when we get back to Thundering Pines."

Brianna eyed her. She'd been acting a little strange all day, and this was even more uncharacteristic. Dani always took the time to answer all her questions, so it surprised her that Dani brushed her off now. It was a long drive; maybe she was tired.

"Ya know, I'm probably going to be too tired to drive all the way home," Dani said as if reading her mind. "I'll need you to relieve me in an hour or two. Why don't you lay back and take a nap, so you'll be rested?"

"I'm not tired. I'll be fine to drive when you need me."

"No, driving can wear you out," Dani said. "I'd feel better if you took a little nap."

Is Dani trying to get away from me? She'd never felt that before, but she couldn't deny the feeling now. Her chest contracted, and she struggled to inhale. Was Dani sick of her? Brianna opened her mouth to protest but thought better of it. "Okay, maybe I could use a little rest." She pulled the lever, and her seat reclined. *Did Dani just visibly relax?* Maybe she did need some rest, she seemed to be sensing conspiracies everywhere.

She shifted in her seat trying to get comfortable, and Dani covered her in a blanket.

"Where did you get that?" Brianna asked, looking directly at Dani.

"I had it behind my seat. I thought you might want it."

Now she was sure Dani had this planned. *Who has a blanket right at their fingertips?* It wasn't as if they had any trouble talking for hours, so Dani couldn't be concerned about running out of things to say. Or maybe her constant chatter on the drive down was too much. Whatever the reason, it was obvious that Dani didn't want to talk.

They hadn't been moving for long before Brianna's eyelids became heavy. The combination of the motion of the truck, the warm blanket, and the whir of the tires against the pavement created the perfect scenario for a nap.

❧❧❧❧

Brianna didn't know how long she'd been asleep when Dani lightly shook her. "Huh?" Brianna mumbled. "Are we there? Do you need me to drive?"

"I had to take a little detour," Dani said, shutting off the truck.

"Detour? Was there an accident?" Brianna finally opened her eyes and yawned. "How long have I been asleep?"

"Only about forty-five minutes or so."

Brianna's mouth was dry, and she ran her tongue over her lips to moisten them.

Dani twisted the cap off the water bottle and handed it to her.

Brianna took a big gulp. The fog from sleep started to lift. "Where are we?" She reached for the lever to bring her seat upright, but Dani stopped her.

"There's something I didn't tell you." Dani smiled and winked.

What the hell was that sound? Brianna strained to hear. It almost sounded like circus music. "What didn't you tell me?"

"I wanted to surprise you. You were right. I didn't really care about the auction."

"Then why in the world did we drive all the way to Missouri?" Could it be her grogginess that made this conversation hard to follow? "You're confusing me."

"Go ahead and sit up."

Brianna grasped the lever and pulled. She must have yanked too hard because the seat shot her into an upright position. They were in a crowded parking lot, where a weather-beaten sign read: *The Track Family Fun Parks*. Why did that name sound so familiar?

Dani eyed her expectantly, but Brianna drew a blank. "You might have to clue me in."

"Really? Bri, look over your right shoulder." Dani pointed for emphasis.

As Brianna turned, she caught a large structure out of the corner of her eye. "Holy fuck." She looked back at Dani. "Is that what I think it is?"

"I do believe it is." A large smile lit Dani's face.

Brianna sat staring, not saying a word. Tears streamed down her face. She couldn't believe she was looking at her Ferris wheel.

"Are you okay?"

She heard Dani's voice, but the blood pumped in her ears, muffling Dani's words. Finally, she reached across the console, wrapped her arms around Dani, and pressed her face against her shoulder. "You did this for me?"

"Yep, I wanted to surprise you. Did it work?"

Tears continued to roll down Brianna's face, but she laughed, too. "That auction was pathetic. I thought you'd lost your mind."

"It was pretty pitiful. I was afraid you were gonna fire me before I got you here."

Brianna turned from the Ferris wheel and met

Dani's gaze. "I believe this is the sweetest thing anyone has ever done for me."

Dani's face reddened. "Enough of the sappy stuff. Are you going to take me for a ride?"

"Four."

"Four?"

"At least four rides, maybe six." Brianna stared at the Ferris wheel and beamed.

⚘⚘⚘⚘

Dani practically sprinted to keep up with Brianna as she weaved between the people. "Jesus, it's not going anywhere."

Brianna's reaction had been priceless. It made enduring the horrible auction worth it just to see the pure joy on her face. At times, Dani still couldn't believe Brianna was the same woman she'd met in Thomas's office in February.

"Hurry up," Brianna called, having gotten even farther ahead of Dani.

Dani grinned and slowed down. She exaggerated swinging her arms in slow motion as she meandered through the crowd.

Brianna circled back. Her face pinched in a scowl. "Danielle Delilah Thorton! You are not funny." Brianna grabbed Dani's hand. "Come on."

Dani chuckled and allowed herself to be pulled along by Brianna's enthusiasm. "You know we have all day, don't you?"

"I don't." Brianna picked up the pace. "Do you know how long I've been waiting to ride?"

"I'm sure you could tell me down to the minute." Dani swerved around a small child who ran into her path. "Crap. You're going to have me injure a kid if you don't slow down."

"Well, watch where you're going."

"How can I? Everything's a blur since we're moving so fast."

"You are such a drama queen." Brianna flashed a smile. "But I'll give you a pass for bringing me here."

When they'd almost reached the Ferris wheel, Brianna stopped in the middle of the crowd. Several people brushed past them, muttering about their abrupt stop. While Brianna stared at the ride, Dani's gaze never left Brianna.

Brianna's misty eyes shone as she looked into the sky toward the top of the wheel. Her flushed cheeks, likely caused by a combination of the sprint across the park and her excitement, gave her a healthy glow. She turned to Dani and squealed.

Dani jumped and then laughed. "I can't believe you just squealed like a little girl."

"But this is so freaking exciting." Brianna grabbed Dani by the shoulders and shook her. "Aren't you excited?"

Dani let her arms swing like a rag doll, making it appear as if Brianna shook her harder than she actually did. "If you give me a concussion, I'm not going to be able to ride."

"You'll be fine." Brianna grabbed Dani's hand. "Let's go."

Warmth spread across Dani's chest as she let Brianna pull her forward.

❧ ❧ ❧ ❧ ❧

True to her word, they'd ridden the Ferris wheel six times throughout the afternoon and into the evening. Brianna's infectious smile and pure joy attracted the attention of several people standing near them in line. Dani lost track of the number of times Brianna told the tale of seeing the Ferris wheel dismantled. By the third time they rode, the ride operators greeted them by name.

Dani found her gaze constantly drawn to Brianna, instead of the breathtaking view of Branson, Missouri. Brianna refused to let her miss the sights, though. Several times, she grabbed Dani's knee, shook it, and pointed out various parts of the city.

Time flew. Brianna dragged Dani around the entire park until closing time. They exited with the straggling families, the weary parents carrying or practically dragging their exhausted children to the parking lot.

Their exit was different. Brianna bounced along, skipping, talking rapid-fire about their adventures.

Dani simply smiled, unable to get a word in.

Brianna chattered all the way to the truck, reliving their experience on the Ferris wheel, along with everything else they'd done. Dani especially enjoyed the go-karts, getting a little vindication from her humiliating ATV experience.

"I'm just glad you don't like roller coasters," Dani said.

"Why?"

"Because you forced me to eat so much, I would have hurled." Dani patted her overly full stomach. "I'm gonna have a stomachache for a week."

Brianna laughed. "What's next?"

"Seriously?" Dani was tired, but Brianna's energy was contagious. "Okay, I admit I anticipated this. Well, not closing down the park, but I figured we wouldn't want to drive home. I got us a room. A female country singer is doing an acoustic set at the bar that's just around the corner from our hotel."

"You thought of everything." Brianna clapped and bounced in her seat. "This is the best day ever."

"Put your seat belt on so we can get moving then." Dani smiled.

Brianna reached for her seat belt but instead put her hand on Dani's arm. When Dani turned and made eye contact, Brianna said, "Thank you. You're the best."

Heat rose up Dani's neck. "I just wanted to do something that would make you smile and forget everything for a little bit."

"You succeeded."

Dani's heart fluttered as she started her pickup truck.

⁂

Brianna linked her arm through Dani's as they strolled along the sidewalk. Just like the park, they'd stayed at the bar until closing. The music had been phenomenal, and since it was a small venue, they'd gotten the opportunity to talk with the lead singer after she finished her sets. Brianna couldn't have written a better script if she'd tried.

They only had a couple of blocks to their hotel, so they took their time, enjoying the crisp night air. "I don't want the night to end," Brianna said. It was perfect.

"I know." Dani glanced around the streets. "I'm not sure it's a smart idea to walk too far in unfamiliar territory at one a.m."

Brianna sighed. She knew Dani was right. *Bummer.* "It's just been such a relaxing evening."

"That's just the Long Island iced tea talking." Dani playfully bumped her hip against Brianna's as they walked.

"Oh, come on. You're acting like I'm a lush. I only had two drinks all night."

Dani smiled. "Yeah, but that iced tea packed a punch. I think I might be buzzed."

"Lightweight." Brianna bumped her shoulder against Dani's.

They arrived at their hotel too soon. After entering the elevator, for the first time all day, neither spoke. Brianna replayed the day in her head. She still couldn't believe Dani pulled off the surprise and more importantly cared enough to want to.

When the elevator doors opened, Brianna took Dani's arm again.

Dani jerked.

"Did I startle you?" Brianna asked.

"Sorry, I was just lost in my thoughts."

"What had you so engrossed?"

Dani fumbled with the keycard, having to run it across the scanner several times before the green light came on. She pushed open the door and motioned for Brianna to enter.

"Ya didn't answer my question," Brianna said. "What were you thinking about?"

Dani busied herself with emptying her pockets and kicking off her shoes. "Just thinking about what a nice day it's been."

Brianna moved closer. "I just want to thank you again."

When Dani turned, she flinched. Dani's face flushed, probably from the drink. "You're welcome."

Their gazes met.

Brianna's heart leapt. *Damn, that drink was strong.* "You might never understand how much I appreciate it and you."

Dani took a step back, bumping into the dresser. "It was my pleasure."

The word *pleasure* reverberated in Brianna's brain, and she licked her lips. *It's warm in here, or maybe it's the drink.* "The pleasure was all mine." Her voice came out huskier than she expected.

Their gazes locked. Dani touched Brianna's cheek.

The sensation from Dani's fingertips caused Brianna to shiver, and a moan escaped.

As if sensing her chill, Dani closed the gap between them and wrapped her arms around Brianna.

Heaven. Warmth spread through her as Dani pulled her closer.

Brianna melted against her. She lowered her mouth toward Dani's. Their lips met.

Dani's lips brushed Brianna's and moved away.

Brianna longed to feel them again and moved closer.

Their lips touched again. The kiss started out soft and gentle with an unhurried quality to it. It was unlike the lustful kisses she'd experienced in the past. The light touch was driving her crazy.

Dani slid her hand up Brianna's arm past her shoulder until she cupped the back of Brianna's head. Gently, Dani pulled her deeper into the kiss.

Their lips explored each other until Dani gently pressed her tongue between Brianna's lips.

Brianna gasped, her eyes sprang open, and she stepped back. *Shit!* What did they just do? What did she do?

❧❧❧❧

Oh, fuck! Dani stumbled backward and slammed into the dresser. Her heart raced, and her face felt hot; it was likely as flushed as Brianna's. She needed to say something, but what?

Brianna spoke first. "I'm sorry. I didn't mean to...I shouldn't...we can't."

When they'd arrived back at the room, Dani had been exhausted, but now she was wide awake. *Say something. Anything.* But instead, she stared at Brianna, who'd taken several more steps back.

"Dani, I shouldn't have." Brianna looked as if she might cry.

Maybe they shouldn't have, but Brianna's words still stung. She could still feel Brianna's soft lips against hers and the electric shock that ran through her body.

"You're right." Dani tried to mask her hurt. She picked up her shoes. "Which bed do you want?"

Brianna stared.

"If you don't mind, I'll take this one." Dani put her shoes next to the bed nearest the door and opened her duffel bag. "I brought us both something to sleep in." She threw a set of clothes onto Brianna's bed, picked up her own, and walked toward the bathroom. "I'll go ahead and change first."

"Wait," Brianna said right before Dani disappeared into the bathroom.

Dani steeled herself before she turned back. She didn't think she could handle the pain of Brianna's rejection. "What?"

"Don't you think we should talk about it?"

"Nothing to talk about." Dani shrugged, hoping it came off nonchalant. "Chalk it up to too much alcohol and two tired people."

Brianna winced.

Dani knew her words hurt, but she couldn't take them back now. They were walking on dangerous territory. Someone needed to be sensible, and it would have to be her. "Did you need anything else? It's late, and we have a long drive in the morning."

Brianna shook her head.

Dani escaped into the bathroom. When the door shut behind her, she rested her back against it and squeezed her eyes shut. Images from the day, the kiss, and Brianna's hurt look flooded her mind. Tears threatened.

Things had gone terribly wrong. Sure, Dani had slept with other women, but they meant nothing to her. This was Brianna. Someone who meant the world to her. *Shit.* She'd screwed everything up.

A cold shower was all she needed. It would stop the fire burning in her and cut off the thoughts she didn't want to have. She stripped off her clothes and stepped under the spray. The cold hit her in the chest, taking her breath away. Goose bumps covered her body. She reached for the temperature control, but her hand dropped. With her arms pinned against her sides, she let the water continue its assault.

When Dani emerged from the bathroom, Brianna was under the covers in her bed, her eyes shut.

Dani flipped off the light switch and climbed into her own bed.

Chapter Twenty-five

The weekend rolled like a film in Brianna's head. The near perfect day ruined by the kiss. Her feelings for Dani were a jumbled mess. She'd never felt more at ease, at home, with anyone in her life, but now she'd ruined it. Why had her body betrayed her? They could have gone on being the best of friends, but she doubted they could now after crossing the line. *Past the point of no return. No going back.* There must be a dozen more clichés she could come up with.

Dani had made it clear on numerous occasions that she'd never have a relationship with a woman. Besides, Brianna would *never* be her father. She made a commitment to Caroline, and she intended to honor it.

Brianna pulled into her parking space, hoping her two hours of torture were over. She'd been trapped with only her thoughts on the long drive from Thundering Pines, and now she just wanted to escape herself.

She pushed open the door, and her ears perked up. A low murmur came from the living room. It sounded like the TV. *Shit.* Caroline was awake. Would guilt show on her face? Heat coursed through her body. Why should she feel guilty when Caroline had slept with her best friend, and she'd just shared one little kiss?

She carried her overnight bag inside and found Caroline reclined on the couch. "Hi," Brianna said.

"Hello," Caroline responded, staring at the TV.

Okay. Caroline was still angry. Should she engage or just go to bed? If she thought she could sleep, she'd choose the latter. "Watching something interesting?" That should be a safe topic.

"Not really." Caroline turned off the television.

There went her choice. Apparently, Caroline wanted to engage. "How was Kylie's party?"

Anger flashed in Caroline's eyes. "It sucked."

She wasn't expecting that. "Oh." *Really?* Was that the best she could do?

"You're not going to ask me why? Or do you still hate Kylie so much you're glad her birthday was ruined?"

Don't take the bait. "What happened?"

Caroline turned up her nose. "Drew."

"Oh, God, what did she do?" Brianna sat on the chair, happy to have a diversion from thoughts of Dani.

"I got Kylie one of the cakes she loves from the bakery around the corner from my office."

"Red velvet?"

Caroline cocked her head. "You remembered?"

Brianna nodded. "What does red velvet have to do with Drew?"

"Kylie was cutting the cake, and Drew leaned over, patted her ass, and told her she shouldn't make the pieces so big." Caroline's fists clenched. "Kylie didn't react, but when she was eating it, she went to take a bite and Drew pulled the cake away from her."

"Why?"

"She told her she'd never get rid of those extra

pounds at that rate." Caroline sat up. "What a bitch."

Brianna bristled. Even though Kylie wasn't high on her list right now, she didn't deserve to be treated that way. "What did Kylie do?"

"Typical Kylie. She laughed it off." Caroline's eyes blazed. "Then she picked at her cake and wasn't right the rest of the night."

"Wow. Why does she stay with her?"

Caroline threw her arms into the air. "God only knows. She could do so much better."

At least she hadn't been thinking about Dani the last couple of minutes, but this was still weird. They were talking about Kylie as they would have before Brianna caught the two of them in bed together. "Maybe someday she'll figure it out."

Caroline studied her for a couple of beats. "How was your trip to Missouri?"

"It was a bust." Brianna hoped she sounded casual. "We got outbid on everything."

"Too bad," Caroline said without an edge.

Did she mean it? This was getting weirder, first talk of Kylie, now the auction. If anyone were observing, they'd think it was normal conversation. Both topics would usually bring out animosity, but there was none. "Thanks."

"What time do we leave next weekend?"

Shit. Now what did she forget? "For what?"

"Isn't the Memorial Day party next Sunday?" Caroline leaned forward and rested her elbows on her knees.

"You're going?" Brianna blurted out without thinking. Did Caroline detect her panic? "I mean, I didn't think you'd want to go."

"Why wouldn't I?"

Loaded question. "Um, well, I didn't think you were really into Thundering Pines."

"I'm not, but it's important to you, so I should be there."

"Oh, how nice." She hoped her voice didn't come out as flat and insincere as she felt. The last thing she wanted was to have Caroline there after what had happened with Dani. Talk about putting the nail into the coffin. Dani wouldn't understand; she'd be hurt.

Caroline stood. "I've got an early morning. I think I'm going to take a shower and head to bed. You coming?"

"After the drive, I just need to unwind, so I think I'll watch a little TV."

"You never told me when we need to leave on Sunday."

"Probably ten," Brianna answered. Her stomach dropped.

Caroline gave her a quick kiss before walking out.

Ugh. Brianna slammed her head against the back of the chair. Could this weekend get any worse? How was she going to break it to Dani?

Dani's face filled her mind. *No.* She'd thought about Dani all the way home and couldn't do it anymore. It made her head hurt, actually her heart. Brianna grabbed the remote control. Netflix should have a good thriller for her to get lost in.

✦ ✦ ✦ ✦

"Is that you, sweetie?" Aunt Helen called from the kitchen.

Shit. Dani had hoped she'd stayed out long

enough for Aunt Helen to be in bed. She walked into the kitchen. "Yep. What are you still doing up?"

Aunt Helen sat at the kitchen table with an iced tea in front of her, thumbing through a food magazine. "I couldn't sleep, so I thought I'd see if I could find a new recipe for the party next weekend."

Dani opened the fridge and pulled out the iced tea. "Why couldn't you sleep?"

"I was worried about you." Aunt Helen paused before adding, "And Brianna."

She didn't have the energy for this tonight. Should she play dumb or flat out deny it? She settled on dumb. "Why would you be worried about us?"

"Bri was crawling out of her skin when she said goodbye. She couldn't get out of here fast enough, and you weren't much better. It was like someone lit a fire under both of your asses."

"She had a long drive, and I had more work to get done for next weekend." She wasn't lying.

"Right. Nice try. Care to try again?" Aunt Helen closed her magazine and patted the table. "Sit down and tell me what's going on."

Dani hesitated. Her heart hurt, but she wasn't ready to talk about it. She set her glass down and pulled out the chair. "Everything will be fine. We just had a little misunderstanding."

"Did you tell her how you feel?"

"What?" Dani glared at her.

"Or did she tell you how she feels?" Aunt Helen returned Dani's glare. "Don't try the evil eye on me. It won't work."

"I don't know what you're talking about." Dani started to get up from the table.

Aunt Helen put her hand over Dani's. "No,

you're not running away from me."

Dani slumped against the back of the chair. "What do you want me to say?"

"That you have feelings for the girl." Aunt Helen patted her hand.

Dani leapt to her feet. "We're friends. Can't I have a close friend without you putting a spin on it?"

"Danielle Thorton, cut the melodramatics with me." Aunt Helen narrowed her eyes, and her brow furrowed. "I think thou dost protest too much."

"What the hell is that supposed to mean?" Dani clenched her jaw shut before she said more.

"Go ahead and be angry, but that doesn't change anything," Aunt Helen said with conviction. "She's a gem. Don't get in your own way."

"Just stop." Dani threw her hands into the air. "I don't know what you're getting at, but I don't like it."

"How can you not like it if you don't know what I'm getting at?" Aunt Helen gave her a satisfied grin.

Wow. It was so unlike Aunt Helen to push her like this. "For one thing, Brianna is in a long-term relationship." *Nope.* She wasn't going to say more.

"And the other thing?"

"Why does there have to be another thing?" Dani said.

"Because people don't usually say, 'for one thing,' if there isn't a second thing."

"Fine." The tips of Dani's ears were warm. "I am *not* a lesbian."

Aunt Helen held her gaze. "The heart wants what the heart wants."

The words were like a knife stabbing her in the chest. They were the same words Brianna had used when they'd talked. Dani turned to leave.

"You can't run away from yourself, Dani."

Dani didn't turn back. "I'm going to bed." *And I'm done thinking about Brianna.* The kiss was simply a culmination of a great day and too much alcohol, nothing more.

Chapter Twenty-six

Dani lifted the mallet over her head and swung it down hard on the skid steer forks. The impact barely moved them, so she swung again. Cursing under her breath, she kicked the forks with the heel of her boot, and her leg tingled from the reverberations.

The forks remained immobile. She gripped the mallet with both hands and brought it down hard on the stuck piece of metal. In a frenzy of motion, she hammered at the tines, the clanking of metal rang in her ears. With one final wild swing, the mallet glanced off the forks and flew from her hands.

Dani dropped to the ground with tears streaming down her cheeks. She leaned her back against the tire of the skid steer and buried her head in her hands. What the fuck was the matter with her? She'd just lost her shit on an inanimate object.

The tears overtook her, no sense trying to keep them at bay. She wrapped her arms around her knees and drew them to her chest. Her sobs wracked her body, and her tears fell onto the dusty shop floor creating dark spots of dirt.

Ever since they'd returned from Missouri, Dani hadn't been able to do anything right. Her jumbled thoughts made it impossible to concentrate. No, that wasn't true. They weren't jumbled. They were laser focused on one thing. *Brianna.* Brianna and that stupid kiss.

They'd only communicated via email since then, and the messages were short. She longed to talk to Brianna about it but didn't know what she'd say. Was Brianna hurting as bad as she was, or had she written it off as a drunken mistake?

The kiss had been a gigantic reality bomb in her head. Maybe she should have admitted it to herself before, but now there could be no denying it. Her attraction to Brianna was real and strong.

"Oh, God." Dani groaned and put her chin on her knees. If it had just been her body wanting Brianna, that would be easy, but when her heart and soul got in the act, things became much more complicated. Sure, Brianna was easy on the eyes, but it was so much more. Nobody had made her feel the way Brianna did. It had been building for months, so why hadn't she seen it coming?

Denial. Courtesy of her dad. She wasn't betraying his wishes as long as she never got attached to any of the women she slept with. Sex was sex. Nothing more. Sleeping with a woman didn't make her a lesbian. But what if she wanted more from Brianna? *No!* She'd broken her dad's heart once by not marrying Carl. No way would she dishonor him by becoming just like her mom.

Dani stood with conviction. They'd find a way to mend their friendship, and these crazy thoughts would go away. Her chest ached, but she needed to put the pain aside. She had a campground to run and a skid steer to fix. She picked up the mallet and swung it at the forks.

❧❧❧❧

Brianna stared out her office window toward Navy Pier. The sun had slipped beyond the horizon several minutes ago, and night descended. She gazed at the lights of the city and sighed.

A lone tear ran down her cheek, and she brushed at it with the back of her hand. She wouldn't do this again. Her tears had to be nearly dried up after how many she'd spilled since they'd returned from Missouri.

The last three days, this had become her ritual. Fly through the day so busy that she could barely think straight, but then at the end of the day when everyone had left, she'd stare at the Ferris wheel and cry.

Not tonight. Dani made it clear that the kiss was a mistake. They both had. Now they just needed to find a way to get their friendship back on solid ground. The thought of losing Dani's friendship felt like a noose tightening around her neck.

Stupid. The friendship was all that mattered. She couldn't lose Dani because of a moment of indiscretion. Dani made it clear that she would never be in a lesbian relationship, so Brianna couldn't push.

What the hell was her problem? Of course she wouldn't push. *Caroline.* She was already in a committed relationship, and she would never become her father.

She needed to forget the stupid kiss and focus on the friendship. That was the only thing that truly mattered. If she could go back in time, she would.

She turned away from the window and returned to her desk. Tears streamed freely down her cheeks. Dropping her head into her hands, she let the drops splatter on the papers. The crinkled paper would be a reminder tomorrow of her pain, but right now, she didn't care. She lost her battle with keeping her tears at bay. Sobs wracked her body, and she lowered her head to her desk.

Chapter Twenty-seven

*B*rianna didn't want to make this phone call. She'd put it off all week. It wasn't fair to Dani to wait any longer. She shouldn't be dropping it on her on Thursday afternoon, but it was too late to change now. She took a deep breath and tapped her finger on Dani's face. The phone rang, and she let out a loud exhale before Dani answered.

"Hey, stranger."

Dani's familiar voice made her smile, even though the statement was loaded.

Since last weekend, they had only communicated via email. The return trip from Missouri had been awkward, and their normal easy communication was strained. Before the kiss, they shared their most intimate thoughts, but on the drive back, they stuck to the weather, traffic, and Thundering Pines. So many times during that long drive, Brianna wanted to break down the wall between them, and she sensed Dani did, too, but neither found the courage.

"Hey, so is everything set for Sunday?" Brianna said.

"Yep, we're ready. Are you coming in Saturday night? Aunt Helen wants to make sure she has enough food." Dani chuckled. "Ya know, she's in danger of running out."

Brianna laughed. Aunt Helen had the fullest pantry Brianna had ever seen; she had a backup to the backup of her backup. "That's what I wanted to talk to you about." Brianna's chest tightened.

"Yeah." Dani hesitated.

"*We'll* be coming in Sunday morning." *Really?* She'd practiced what she was going to say all week, and this was not how she intended on doing it.

"I see." Dani's voice turned businesslike. "I will tell Aunt Helen to prepare for an extra guest."

"No, I would never impose on her that way."

There was a long pause before Dani spoke. "So you'll be staying at the loft?"

"God, no. That's our place. I would never dream of..." Brianna cut herself off. She didn't expect this to go well, but she'd hoped not to botch it this badly. "We're driving back Sunday night."

"Okay, so when can I expect you?" Dani's tone was frosty.

Brianna started to respond with a time but stopped. "Oh, Dani, I'm so sorry. I didn't mean for it to come out this way."

"And what way did you want it to come out?" Dani said with an unmistakable edge. When Brianna didn't respond right away, Dani continued. "It's your campground. You can bring anyone you want to opening day. Is there anything else you need?"

"No."

"Okay, I'll see you Sunday. Goodbye, Brianna."

Before she could respond, the line went dead.

Brianna looked at Dani's picture, still on display on her screen. *That didn't go well.* What did she expect? They'd been planning the party since March. They'd been like two kids anticipating the fun they would have, and Brianna had turned that upside down without giving Dani any say in it.

With Caroline being there, everything would be different. Caroline didn't exactly scream fun nor would she want to participate in much of what Dani planned.

Would she have agreed so readily with Caroline had it not been for the kiss? *Probably not.* It would keep her from being alone with Dani. She hadn't been sure if it was a good thing or a bad thing. Right now, the tightness in her chest told her it was awful.

She laid her head on her desk, suddenly tired.

❧ ❧ ❧ ❧

Dani tossed her phone onto a pile of papers on her desk and stood. *What the fuck?* That had been a shit move from Brianna, but her reaction hadn't been much better. It was that damned kiss. Since it happened, Brianna behaved like a stranger or simply a business associate.

Her stomach had been in knots all week, and she'd barely eaten.

Brianna's absence left her feeling empty. All week, it consumed her. She wished they could go back to the way it had been before. If they hadn't gone to the bar afterward. If she hadn't drunk that damned iced tea.

Now the party they'd talked about for months would be ruined. Obviously, Brianna was doing this on purpose to send her a clear message. *Back off.* Why else would she bring Caroline when she'd never come before or mentioned her coming? It still was a shit move. Brianna should have just set her boundaries, not sling Caroline at her.

She sighed. There was no turning back the clock.

They'd ruined everything. Wasn't a kiss supposed to create intimacy? In this case, it had destroyed it. She'd never been closer to anyone in her life, and now a hole gaped in the middle of her chest.

The weekend she'd been anticipating for months was now something she just wanted to get over with. The only silver lining was being the manager, she could keep herself busy and spend little to no time with Brianna. The thought made her heart hurt. She'd imagined greeting the campers together and all their playful banter. Then at the end of the long day, they would retire to the loft and talk into the early morning hours. A tear ran down her cheek at the thought of what wouldn't happen.

She swiped at the tear with the back of her hand. *Enough!* Brianna owed her nothing. The kiss wouldn't have happened if they hadn't been dangerously close to crossing lines that never should have been crossed. Brianna had Caroline. Dani had no one, except for an occasional one-night stand when she needed a release, which was how she preferred it. So why did she feel so empty?

It was for the best this way. Brianna would never have stayed. She'd sell the campground and leave Dani with her heart ripped out, just like her mother had. Her dad had been right. Nothing good could come from this.

She was headed for the door when a vibration came from her desk. Her phone slid on the loose papers. She walked across the room, picked up her phone, and looked down at Brianna's face.

❧ ❧ ❧ ❧

Brianna thought she might vomit. Maybe she should leave well enough alone, but she couldn't. Apparently, Dani could because she wasn't answering. *Should I leave a message or not?* Her thought was interrupted by a click on the other end.

"Brianna?" Dani's voice sounded small and far away.

"I'm sorry. I couldn't. I can't. I don't know. I just…" Brianna's hand trembled, and her words made little sense.

A chuckle came from the phone, and relief flooded over Brianna.

"Don't most people learn to talk when they're two?" Dani said. "I think you may need to go back and take a few more lessons."

Brianna's chest opened, and she could breathe again. She laughed. "I was exceptionally bright, and they let me skip ahead. Seems like it might have been a mistake in hindsight."

"I'm sorry, Bri. I shouldn't have hung up on you."

"You're sorry? I think hanging up on me was the kindest thing you could have done. You should yell at me."

"I'm not a yeller."

"I can't handle the chasm between us."

"Me neither. But I don't know how to fix it."

"We need to talk."

"Isn't that what we're doing?"

"I can't do this on the phone. I have to see your face."

"Oh, God, do you want to do a Zoom call?"

"No, I need to see you face to face."

"The day of the party is always crazy busy,

and..." Dani didn't finish her sentence.

"Tonight."

"It's Thursday."

"We'll meet halfway."

"But what about...? Won't...?" Dani's voice trailed off.

"It's Thirsty Thursday. Caroline will be out."

"You're sneaking out to see me." The edge was back in Dani's voice.

"No, if she asks, I'll tell her. But I can't do Sunday with things feeling so weird between us. I'd rather not come at all."

"Okay," Dani said without hesitation. "I'll meet you in Lombard."

"That's not halfway."

"You'll have heavier traffic. Besides, I have an absentee boss, so I can slip out any time I want, and the bitch won't notice."

Brianna laughed. "When and where?"

"Five o'clock. The Greek Islands?"

Brianna looked at the clock. It was only two thirty. It would give her plenty of time. "I'll be there. And, Dani?"

"Yeah."

"Thanks."

"Don't thank me, you're paying."

Brianna smiled. No matter how bad things were, Dani always made her feel better. They had to find their way past what happened in Missouri. "Deal. See you at five."

Chapter Twenty-eight

*B*rianna was early. She couldn't concentrate on her work, so she'd wrapped up and called it a day. With the extra time, she'd decided not to take the highway and wound her way through the Chicago streets into the suburbs. Despite her meandering route, she still arrived half an hour early. Her restlessness made it impossible to sit in such a confined space. She'd go inside and hit the restroom before Dani arrived.

When she walked into the Greek Islands, she was greeted with the familiar "opa" as one of the waiters lit the saganaki with his lighter. The brandy-soaked cheese burst into flames, burned for a few seconds, and was extinguished when the waiter squeezed a lemon over the remaining fire.

She made a beeline through the bar area to the restroom. She felt jittery and needed to get it under control before Dani arrived. *That damned kiss.* She didn't want it to ruin everything between the two of them. Surprising her with the Ferris wheel was the most thoughtful thing anyone had ever done for her, and she didn't want to taint the memory because of a moment of indiscretion.

In their brief friendship, they'd talked about everything and shared so much. Surely, they could figure this out. Dani was her best friend, and the thought of losing her was terrifying. At all costs, she needed to save the friendship. It was pure. *Without drama.* The kiss had turned everything upside down, so they just needed to find a way to get past it and right things.

Brianna gazed into the mirror and steeled her jaw. Failure was not an option. Their friendship was too valuable to let a stupid kiss derail it.

When she returned from the restroom, she decided to get a table. She wanted to soak up the atmosphere, plus she could really use a drink.

She nursed the ouzo she'd ordered. It was strong. She should probably add a little more water. *No.* The overpowering taste of anise and alcohol might clear her muddled thinking.

She ripped a chunk of bread off the larger loaf and dipped it into the melitzanosalata. A word she'd butchered when she ordered, so she'd changed tactics and simply said, "The eggplant dip." The waiter smiled and returned shortly with what she wanted.

Brianna was so intent on piling the dip on the bread, the waiter startled her when she approached the table. "Here you are, ma'am," Brianna looked up, and her heart skipped a beat.

Dani stood in front of her with the smile she'd come to adore. *Adore.* Was that an appropriate word for a friend? *Stop!* They needed to talk this out.

It was obvious Dani had gone home to clean up before coming. She wore her hair down, and the silver streak glistened in the lighting. The black pinstriped tailored shirt made her shoulders look broad and her waist slim. Her gray slacks hugged her in all the right places.

This was not starting out well. She needed to put her eyes back into her head before Dani caught her gaping.

"Not used to seeing me cleaned up, are you?" Dani smirked.

Shit, too late. Brianna rose from the table and tried to put on the aloof façade that used to come easily to her. "Thanks for coming." She quickly hugged Dani and stepped away. "Please, sit down." She waved her hand toward the seat across from her.

"Sure, boss." Dani winked. "I can't do this. I can't deal with whatever it is you're trying to be."

Brianna's shoulders relaxed. She couldn't keep up this charade. "Fine, smartass. Is that better?"

"Much." Dani pulled her into another hug. This time, it was genuine. "Okay, now that we got that out of the way, I need a drink."

"The waiter should be around soon." Brianna sat.

"What is this?" Dani picked up Brianna's glass and started to raise it to her lips.

"Be careful." Brianna reached for the glass. *Too late.*

Dani took a big gulp, and her eyes got enormous. Brianna couldn't stifle her laugh as Dani's face turned red. Dani swallowed and immediately choked. "What in the hell is that? Kerosene?" she said between coughs.

"Ouzo. I tried to warn you." Brianna no longer tried to hide her laughter. "I guess that will teach you to ask before you steal someone's drink."

"Who the hell thought making a black licorice drink was a good idea?"

"The Greeks. And it's anise."

"I don't care whose anus it is. It's disgusting." Dani pretended to wipe her tongue with her napkin.

"Good God, remind me not to bring you out into civilization again." It felt so good joking with Dani, she wanted to pretend that this was just two friends meeting for dinner.

Apparently, Dani thought the same and continued complaining about the ouzo while poking at the eggplant dip with her fork. "And what's this?" She picked up the menu and pretended to scan it. "Nope, I don't see anything that says baby poop."

"Really? Anus and baby poop. I see how this evening is going to go."

᪥᪥᪥᪥

The banter and laughter were just what Brianna needed. The conversation was light, and it seemed to put both at ease. Neither brought up the reason they were sitting in a restaurant on a Thursday evening.

Dani slid the last bite of baklava into her mouth, and Brianna tensed. They would have to talk about the elephant in the room eventually, but Brianna didn't want to spoil the mood.

"What do you say we move to the bar?" Brianna asked.

"Is that code for the fun is over, we need to talk?"

Brianna took a deep breath. "I'm afraid so."

Dani reached for the check, but Brianna slapped her hand away. "Remember, you told me I was paying."

"Damn, I forgot. I would have ordered double if I'd remembered."

The waiter arrived, took Brianna's credit card, and they fell silent.

Brianna met Dani's gaze and held it. Behind the twinkle, there was a hint of fear or maybe hurt. Brianna realized that soon what lay behind Dani's eyes would rise to the surface, and she wondered if she was ready for it. She had to be. "Do you need to use the restroom?"

"Well, yes, Mom, I do."

Brianna grinned. "Why don't you go ahead and find us a table in the bar? I'll wait for the waiter to bring back my card."

"It's getting uncomfortable looking into my eyes, huh?"

"Yes." She wasn't going to lie to Dani, and if she did, Dani would know it anyway. "I need to get my bearings before we talk."

"That's fair." Dani rose from the table and turned to walk away. She stopped, turned back, and put her hand on Brianna's shoulder. "We'll figure this out. This..." She waved her hand between the two of them. "Us. It's too important not to."

Before Brianna could respond, Dani was gone.

Brianna put her hands on each side of her head and massaged her temples with her fingertips.

The waiter returned and silently set her credit card next to her plate.

As difficult as the conversation was going to be, there was no one in the world she trusted more than Dani. That had to count for something, right? They'd figure it out. They had to.

⁂

Dani splashed water onto her face. The cold water needed to stop the fire burning in her brain. She was scared. *No, terrified.* Brianna had become an important part of her life, and she couldn't imagine it without her. Why was she being so fatalistic? If dinner was any sign, Brianna felt the same way; they just needed to clear the air.

With a final glance in the mirror, she steeled herself. *I can do this.* Ignoring the doubt on her own face, she turned away.

She'd been in the bathroom longer than she realized; Brianna had already found a table in the corner. Dani slid into the booth across from her. "Do you need to go before we start this?" Dani motioned toward the bathroom with her head.

"No, I think I'm good. Besides, I might not come out once I go in."

"I thought the same, but there weren't any windows to climb out." Dani smiled.

"Then I definitely don't need to go." Brianna returned the smile and put her hand over Dani's. "Where do we want to start?"

Brianna's warmth burned into her skin. Part of Dani wanted to yank her hand away while the other part was comforted by the contact. "You called the meeting. Isn't it customary for you to start?"

Brianna pulled back and picked at her cuticle but remained silent.

"We kissed," Dani blurted out.

"Okay, I guess we're jumping right in."

"I've been wracking my brain trying to figure out what happened, but I still don't know."

Brianna shifted her gaze away from Dani. "We had a wonderful day. Surprising me with my Ferris wheel was probably the sweetest thing anyone has ever done for me. The day was magical. I had a blast. Then we had a few drinks. I don't even know how it happened or who made the first move."

"It was an accident? A perfect storm?"

"I guess you could say that."

"So it was a mistake, and we really have nothing more to talk about. It was a waste of time coming here tonight when there's such a simple answer." Dani tried to keep the anger from her voice. Judging from Brianna's words, the kiss had been a mistake and meant nothing to her. Apparently, Dani had been the only one agonizing over it the past few days. She crossed her arms over her chest.

"You seem upset."

"Oh, fuck it, Bri." When Brianna flinched, Dani stopped. "No, I didn't mean it that way. I'm just so messed up in the head right now. Since the first time you came to Thundering Pines, I've never had a problem talking to you, but I can't now."

"I know. I feel it, too, and so much more."

What did *so much more* mean? Dani couldn't ask, so she remained silent but gave an encouraging nod.

Brianna ran her finger along the crease in the tablecloth but then returned her gaze to Dani. "You're my best friend. And the thought of losing you terrifies me. I've been closed for so long. I'd stopped having real conversations with people a long time ago, and you opened me back up. If I lose you, I'm afraid I'll lose me again, too. Does that even make any sense?"

Dani's heart ached for Brianna and for herself. Brianna was so far from the uptight woman she met in Thomas's office only a few short months ago. And Brianna had just credited her for the transformation. No doubt, Brianna had also had a profound effect on her life, but would she have the same courage to admit it? *Be fair.*

"I do understand. And I feel it, too." Dani fought to keep her voice even. "It's been so long since I've had someone I trust enough to let in. No, that's a lie. I have never connected with anyone like I do you. It's scary as fuck. Do you want the truth?"

"Always."

Dani couldn't look at Brianna any longer, so she became interested in her fingernails. "Some days, the only thing I want to do is talk to you and have you in my life forever." She stopped, unsure if she could finish.

"And other days?" Brianna asked in a flat voice.

"Other times, I want to run away and hide and never see you again." Dani exhaled. It was out. For better or worse.

Hurt flashed in Brianna's eyes.

It was worse.

"I cause you that much pain?"

"No, I cause me that much pain. The truth. You scare the hell out of me. There's so much that could go wrong with us. And now we've made it even worse."

"And what exactly could go wrong?" Brianna's voice held a definite edge.

Dani wanted to retreat. Retreat from Brianna. Retreat from this conversation, but somehow, she knew she'd be hiding for the rest of her life if she did. "You could leave," Dani said in a voice barely above a whisper.

Wow. Where had that come from? She'd agonized over the kiss all week, but this new reality hit her between the eyes. People left Dani. Her mom. Her dad. Why would Brianna be any different? Besides, Brianna had been gearing up to leave ever since they met.

"Did you say I could leave?" Brianna leaned forward.

"Yes," Dani said with more force.

"Why would I do that?"

"Seriously? You never wanted to come back to Flower Hills, and you certainly didn't want Thundering Pines. Six months will be up before you know it, then you can sell. And now we just complicated things with that kiss, so why would you stay?"

"Oh, Dani." Brianna put her hand on top of Dani's. "Why do you think I'm sitting here with you now? You matter to me. This matters to me. Yes, it is complicated, but if there is anyone I can talk this through with, it's you."

A flicker of hope rose in Dani. Ironically, she felt more confident since she revealed her biggest fear. Her cards were on the table, and Brianna knew her most vulnerable place, and it wasn't as scary as she expected it to be. She looked at Brianna and realized she trusted her completely.

"How do we get past the kiss?" Dani asked.

"We just do."

"Well, that clears things up." Dani smiled. "Call me a planner, but I need a little more to go on than that."

"It happened. As much as we'd like to take it back, we can't. It was a mistake, nothing more."

Ouch. That hurt worse than Dani expected. Was it really that simple for Brianna? She'd thought about that kiss for days. She would never consider it a mistake. That simple kiss felt more intimate than anything she'd done with any of the other women she'd slept with. Bravado was her best defense. "Yeah. No biggie. Besides, you have an open relationship, so no harm, no foul." Dani sat back and crossed her arms over her chest.

"No, that's not an excuse. And it's not fair to Caroline, either."

Dani pulled her arms in tighter against herself and tried not to flinch. Over the years, she'd developed a poker face; she hoped she was pulling it off now. She wanted to scream, *I don't give a fuck about Caroline,* but she steadied herself. "Then it's simple. It never happens again." Her heart sank at the words she knew she had to speak.

Brianna studied her but didn't speak for some time. "I'm sorry that I had to bring Caroline into this, but it's all tied together."

Obviously, her poker face wasn't working. "You're right. It just hurts," Dani found herself saying. *Where did that come from?*

"It's not fair to you, either."

"I'm a big kid." Dani's tone was more defensive than she'd intended. She softened it before continuing. "I mean, you can't be responsible for me."

Pain filled Brianna's eyes, and Dani could tell she was wrestling with her response. "When I agreed to an open relationship, in my mind, it was physical thing—sexual, nothing more."

"She had sex with her best friend. We didn't do that. Like you said earlier, it was a mistake." The words slipped out before Dani could censor herself.

Brianna winced. "Trust me, I've thought of that a million times since last Saturday. I've tried to justify my actions in a thousand different ways. And I've come to peace with what I did to Caroline. I won't become my father. I'm better than that."

"What aren't you saying?"

"Damn it, I can't get anything past you, can I?" Brianna gave Dani a sad smile. "I haven't been able to find peace with what I did to you."

"To me? I'm here, aren't I? I dropped everything and came running, so I don't think you have anything to worry about on that front."

This time, there was no mistaking that her words cut into Brianna. She ran her hand through her hair and suddenly became interested in studying the rest of the patrons sprinkled around the bar.

"Brianna," Dani said, trying to draw her back. "What did I say wrong?"

Brianna's jaw was set. "Are we going to keep beating around the bush, or is one of us going to have the balls to speak the truth?"

"I spoke my truth earlier," Dani said louder than she intended.

"Did you speak the whole truth?"

"Maybe not, but I haven't heard any truth from you. It's your turn." Where was her anger coming from? Probably because she could no longer deny what had been building for some time. Even though it would be a mistake, part of her wanted more from Brianna, but that wasn't possible. Brianna seemed hellbent on not being like her father, which meant she'd stay in a loveless relationship to prove she wasn't. Besides, even if Brianna wanted it, could Dani betray her father? There were too many complications to risk their friendship.

"Fine." Brianna threw her hands in the air before settling them on the table in front of her. She fumbled with her napkin as she spoke. "The truth is, my feelings for you are a jumbled mess. You've become the person I rely on more than anyone else in my life. The person I want to talk to first when something good or bad happens. The person who makes me laugh harder and longer. The person I open up to and have conversations like this with. And it feels wonderful and horrible all at the same time." Brianna paused but didn't give Dani time to respond. "I see the question in your eyes, so I'll answer it. Yes, I mean the first person, the only person. You, not Caroline. And I don't know what the fuck to do about it. So I can't pretend that if I kiss you, it's just sexual because it's the most intimate thing I've ever done in my life. But I don't want to risk our friendship. I can't lose you. So I want to pretend the kiss never happened and go back to being your best friend."

Dani's heart jumped into her throat. Was it possible to feel exhilarated and annihilated at the same time? Her thoughts were interrupted when Brianna threw the napkin on the table and stood. "Don't go," Dani said, the panic evident in her voice.

"I need to go to the bathroom."

"You're coming back?"

"Yes, just give me a couple minutes, please."

Dani's chest tightened as she watched Brianna walk away.

⁂

What the hell just happened? Dani let the emotions wash over her. They felt the same, but it wasn't going to happen. She needed to push aside any thoughts of romance and take charge when Brianna came back...if she came back. Brianna was right, they couldn't risk their friendship over something so complicated. It was just a silly crush; it was their friendship that was real. How many times had she heard stories about friends who crossed lines and lost the friendship forever? She'd also heard stories of people who'd turned their friends into lovers and said it was the best of both worlds. *No, I can't think that way.* They couldn't take the chance.

Dani sat for several more minutes, becoming stronger in her conviction. Worry also crept in the longer she waited for Brianna to return. Despite crawling out of her own skin, she resisted going in search of Brianna. She needed to come back on her own terms.

Every few seconds, her gaze would drift in the direction of the restroom, even though she tried to resist it.

Finally, Brianna emerged. She seemed composed as she took long strides across the bar. Her eyes were red, but she'd done a good job of hiding it. If Dani weren't scrutinizing her, she'd never have noticed.

"Are you okay?" Dani asked as Brianna slid into the booth.

"I think so." Brianna flashed her a smile. "Are you?"

Perceptive. "I'm hanging in there." Dani returned the smile. "I have to say this, and then I am never going to say it again because it will be too painful."

"That sounds mysterious." Brianna's voice came out lighthearted, but her eyes betrayed her.

"I feel the same way you do." Dani's chest tightened. It was only fair to tell the truth since Brianna had laid so much of herself on the line earlier. "But we know it can't be, so we have to pull our heads out of our asses and not ruin the best friendship either of us has ever had."

"All righty then." Brianna laughed. It was a real laugh this time. "That's one of the things I appreciate about you, your eloquence."

Dani chuckled. "Just keeping it real. Are we in agreement? We do whatever we need to do to preserve our friendship."

"Definitely!"

"So you're going to keep your hands off of me." Dani's eyes twinkled. "And your lips."

"Good thing you added that, you'd have left the door wide open for me."

Dani relaxed. *Crisis averted.* She would ignore her disappointment, and she would stop staring at Brianna's lips.

Chapter Twenty-nine

*B*rianna turned up the radio to hear it above the wind rushing in her open window. She knew Caroline's gaze was on her but pretended not to notice. The music and the open window made conversation impossible, which was exactly how she wanted it.

The day was gorgeous, not a cloud in the sky, with the temperature in the mid-sixties. Hopefully, the trees in the campground would block the breeze. *Perfect for opening day.*

Even though Caroline seemed to be trying, things still felt stilted. Caroline was doing her best to fit in, wearing a pair of jeans, albeit designer, and a University of Illinois sweatshirt. Her outfit didn't exactly scream campground, but it was an attempt.

Whenever Caroline had brought up opening day, Brianna answered her questions but had tried to change the subject as quickly as possible. She felt guilty while at the same time a touch angry. Caroline had spent the last three months belittling Thundering Pines and Flower Hills, but now that she'd been supportive the past week, Brianna was supposed to be jumping with joy to have her with.

Brianna's mind wandered to Dani, a thought she should probably avoid. After they'd talked on Thursday night, at least Brianna no longer feared her world was collapsing, but her chest still ached. They'd left the restaurant on a high note, enjoying a few laughs before they'd called it a night.

The kiss played out in her mind often. It was more than just the kiss; it was the entire day that invaded her thoughts. No doubt, it was a nearly perfect day. What would have happened if they hadn't stopped? It was a question she asked herself often.

Stop thinking! Her thoughts were painful, so she cranked up the radio and sang loudly. Caroline was yelling something to her, but she pretended not to notice and kept singing.

The music suddenly stopped when Caroline turned the stereo off.

Brianna glanced at her with an annoyed look. "Why'd you do that?"

"We're almost there," Caroline said loudly to be heard over the open window. "I have a couple questions before we get there."

"Okay," Brianna said noncommittedly.

"Tell me the schedule again. What are your duties?" Caroline asked.

"At two o'clock, Dani and I will do a brief welcome to the campers. After that, there are games, hayrides, and other fun things planned until dinner at six."

"That's when they do the barbaric pig thing?"

"Yes, the pig roast," Brianna answered, trying not to get annoyed. "Everyone will also bring a dish to pass, but you won't have to eat it."

"Good." Caroline crinkled up her nose. "Then after dinner?"

"I will have to say a few more words to thank everyone for coming out. Then there'll be a couple local bands playing and dancing into the night." Brianna's mind wandered back to her failed attempt at line dancing at the Spotted Owl. Despite her lack of coordination, she'd had a blast. Somehow, she didn't think the experience tonight would be quite as fun.

"Once they start playing, then we can go home?"

Brianna's shoulders tightened. *Don't react.* "We should probably stick around for a little while before we make our exit."

"But everyone knows we have a drive home, so I wouldn't think they'd expect us to stay long."

Brianna fought back the desire to say she'd mentioned renting a room in a nearby motel on multiple occasions, but Caroline had shot the idea down. Brianna sighed; she wasn't going to have a confrontation now. *In and out.* "We should be able to leave by eight or nine."

"Great." Caroline flashed a smile and turned the radio back on.

❦❦❦❦

Despite the volume in the nearly packed clubhouse, the strains of music could be heard as the band warmed up outside. Brianna checked her watch. They'd be on in fifteen minutes. She glanced around the crowded room. Most of the campers had finished eating and milled around the tables. The laughter and good cheer filled the large room.

Brianna picked at the food on her plate. Everything was tasty, especially what Aunt Helen had made, but she didn't feel like eating.

"What's wrong with you?" Caroline asked. "You've barely touched your food."

"I guess I'm not hungry." Brianna pushed her

plate away.

"Does that mean you're done?"

Brianna nodded.

Caroline stood and picked the plates up off the table.

Was she seriously going to clean up? Brianna watched in stunned silence as Caroline made her way across the room to the trash cans. Hopefully, the shock she felt didn't show on her face.

A sudden sensation of being watched made her turn her head. Her gaze met Dani's; she sat three tables over with a group of campers. All she saw etched on Dani's face was pain. Dani turned away, suddenly interested in her tablemate's conversation. Had Dani misread Brianna's expression when she watched Caroline? She'd been gaping because Caroline bused the table, not because she was lusting after her.

What the hell? Why did she care if Dani thought she was ogling her own girlfriend? Wasn't that what couples did? Brianna crossed her arms over her chest.

Caroline stood near the garbage, having an animated conversation with one of the campers.

Brianna had to admit, generally, Caroline had behaved herself. She'd made her share of snide comments about the locals but only to Brianna. She'd directed her worst commentary toward Dani until Brianna snapped at her and cut off any further attacks.

Dani. She peeked back at where Dani sat, but she was gone. For months, she and Dani had talked about the fun they'd have, but for the most part, Dani had stayed away from her. Dani had kept busy attending to the party details. Brianna suspected Dani would have asked her to help if Caroline weren't there. But this gave her an excuse to be too busy for Brianna.

Many of the campers drifted outside as the band heated up. She should rescue Caroline.

She crossed the room, but several campers stopped her before she made it to where Caroline stood. "Hey, we should probably get outside since I have to introduce the band."

Caroline gave her a grateful smile. "Certainly." She turned back to the camper. "It was so nice to meet you, but I'm afraid I'm needed elsewhere."

Before Brianna could react, Caroline took her arm and led her outside. "Looks like you have an admirer."

Caroline glared. "God, he wouldn't shut up about the new tractor he just bought."

Brianna chuckled. "He hopes you think his tractor's sexy." She had the world's worst timing. Dani stood in a group only five feet away staring straight at her. Brianna's stomach clenched when Dani abruptly made a retreat.

"Who thinks a tractor is sexy?" Caroline's forehead creased.

"It's a song. You know. About a guy thinking his girlfriend thinks his tractor's sexy."

Caroline gave her a blank stare.

"Never mind." Brianna waved her hand. "I need to get to the stage, so I can do my thing."

"Break a leg," Caroline said.

Brianna breathed in deeply. Caroline was trying, so she smiled. "Thanks. Go ahead and find a seat. I should be back soon."

Brianna made a beeline to the stage, in particular to where Dani stood off to the left. Surprisingly, Dani was alone.

Dani fought with a microphone, tapping it on

her hand several times.

"Hey, Dani." Brianna tried to keep her voice light.

Dani started and nearly dropped the microphone.

"Sorry." Brianna reached out to grab the mic, and their hands met.

Dani pulled back as if she were burnt. "Shit. You scared me."

The electricity from touching Dani surged through her. She breathed in deeply. More than anything, she wanted to wrap Dani in her arms but couldn't. Caroline wouldn't like it, and more importantly, Dani might pull away. She felt miserable enough without adding to it. "Sorry again."

Dani took a couple of steps back and appeared to have regained some composure. "No worries. Are you about ready to take the stage?"

"I can't stand this," Brianna said.

"No, don't. I can't. I just want this day to be over."

"Oh, Dani." Brianna fought the desire to step closer. "You love opening day. I've ruined that for you."

Dani's eyes were full of pain. "I can't have this conversation with you. Not here."

A man walked toward them. He carried drumsticks and pounded the air as if playing an imaginary drum.

Shit. He must be with the band, which meant she had little time left with Dani alone. "I've missed you today. I miss our fun."

"Looks like you were having plenty of fun." Dani's voice held an edge.

"Please. It's not that way."

"No, you have no right to talk to me about this.

Your girlfriend is over there. You need to join her as soon as you make the introduction." Before Brianna could respond, Dani stepped toward the man. "Howard, are you about ready to get started?"

❧❧❧❧

Dani's heart clenched. Why had she acted that way toward Brianna? They'd agreed this was for the best, but why was it so painful to watch Brianna all day with Caroline? Luckily, opening day was hectic, or she wasn't sure she would have survived.

She admired Brianna's long legs as she walked up the steps to the stage. *God.* She missed Brianna, too. She'd meant what she'd said. She wanted the day to be over, so she could go home and sleep.

"Hello, everyone," Brianna said from the stage. "I want to thank you again for coming."

The cheers were louder than earlier. The free-flowing beer probably had a hand in that. Brianna talked for several minutes, and Dani never looked away until she finished. Then Dani hurried back into the clubhouse.

❧❧❧❧

Brianna sat next to Caroline.

"What bug crawled up Skunkie's ass?"

"Enough. Just fucking stop it." Brianna raised her voice and popped up out of her chair.

Caroline grabbed her arm. "Relax, I was joking."

Reluctantly, she sat back down.

The band struck their first chords, and the crowd erupted.

Brianna's muscles were still tense, but she sat back against her chair. How long before they could slip out? She agreed with Dani; she wanted this day to be over.

The band's volume climbed, so Caroline leaned over and said into Brianna's ear, "At least you won't have to drag me off the dance floor. Who in the hell can dance to this shit?"

Brianna bit her tongue. "Ya know, I'm getting pretty tired. Maybe listen to a couple songs, and then we can hit the road."

"Oh, thank God, my ears are starting to bleed."

She shot Caroline a glance but didn't respond. A loud cheer from the dance floor diverted her attention.

Dani and one of the male campers were in the middle of a large circle, dancing wildly.

Running her hand over her chest, Brianna hoped to alleviate the tightness. No doubt, Dani could dance. The entire day, Brianna marveled at how many people seemed to love Dani. She didn't seem to know a stranger. Seeing Dani interact and laugh with so many people made her feel empty. As if she had room to talk, sitting next to Caroline.

"I'm about ready to call it a night," Brianna said, not wanting to look at Dani any longer.

❧ ❧ ❧ ❧

Brianna glanced over at Caroline, whose head was resting on Brianna's coat that she'd placed between her head and the window. She'd fallen asleep shortly after they'd left Thundering Pines, which suited Brianna fine.

There had been a mixture of pain and relief on

Dani's face when they'd stopped to tell her goodbye. The entire drive, she'd not been able to stop the endless loop of Dani in her mind. She'd visualized how the day would have been if she'd been able to spend it with Dani. The day with Caroline hadn't been horrible, just lifeless and flat.

She needed to stop. None of this was helping her mental health. They'd agreed they would be friends, but it certainly didn't even feel as if they were friends today. She turned on the radio low, so it wouldn't wake Caroline. Looking at the beautiful woman sleeping next to her, she felt nothing.

The beckoning lights of Chicago were usually something she enjoyed but not tonight. They were a reminder she wouldn't see the stars again until the next time she returned to Thundering Pines, and she didn't know when that would be. Chicago was feeling less like home.

Brianna gazed over at the sleeping Caroline. She sighed. Caroline was feeling less like home, too. Or maybe she never did.

Chapter Thirty

$\mathcal{D}$ani trudged down the stairs of the loft. She'd thought of spending the night but found she didn't want to anymore. The walls closed in around her, and she needed to escape. It no longer felt comforting, just empty.

Everywhere she turned, something reminded her of Brianna. Tonight, she'd looked in the cupboard for a snack and stumbled upon the bag of ingredients for s'mores. She'd lost her appetite and never regained it. Time to go back to Aunt Helen's, maybe then she'd be hungry.

It had been nearly three weeks since the Memorial Day party, and Brianna hadn't been back. Maybe she never would return. It would probably be the best thing for both of them. Not having Brianna around hurt, but having her there with the chasm between them was even more painful.

They'd exchanged a few emails about campground business and even talked on the phone a couple of times, but it was weird. Their conversations were strained, and despite their best efforts, their easy banter was stilted.

They never discussed the uncomfortable turn their friendship had taken. She thought back to the evening at the Greek Islands, when they vowed that they wouldn't let anything come between them. It seemed so long ago, even though it had only been three weeks.

Would it have been different if Caroline hadn't come to the Memorial Day party? They'd had no time to reestablish their connection after the kiss. Then they were thrown into the painful party where the chasm widened.

Dani's heart ached. She'd hoped, with time, things would go back to the way they were before, but her hope had diminished with each awkward interaction. She wondered often if Brianna felt as bad as she did, but she couldn't bring herself to ask. What if it was just her?

She pushed through the door at the bottom of the stairs and turned to make sure it was closed and latched before leaving. She started across the platform but turned back a final time to make sure it was locked.

The breeze was surprisingly cool after a day in the eighties. Maybe a storm was brewing. The wind soothed her face, so she pulled up a chair, deciding to stay a little longer. Hopefully, Brianna wouldn't haunt her thoughts outside on the deck.

The new moon was high in the sky. She tilted her head back and studied the stars. As a kid, she and her dad would lay outside on the lawn and identify the constellations. Orion. Cassiopeia. Ursa Major. Ursa Minor.

The sound of an engine jolted her out of her stargazing. The wind was blowing toward her, but the campsites were far enough away she normally didn't hear the sound of vehicles that clearly.

She stood and went to the railing facing the pine forest where the sound originated. *Nothing.* She strained to see out into the night with little success.

The new moon afforded her little light. The darkness enveloped her.

Was that a car door slamming? *Another?* Probably teenagers. She was always having to chase them out. They'd sneak in by convincing another camper they belonged. It was late, after midnight, and quiet time began at eleven.

She closed her eyes, hoping it would heighten her sense of hearing. Was it just the sound of the wind rustling through the trees or did she hear voices? *Damn it.* She should probably call the night guard and have him meet her. Occasionally, trespassers became belligerent. She'd made the mistake of confronting a group on her own several years ago, and she'd been fortunate that another camper had come along before she was injured. She'd learned her lesson since then.

As she took out her phone, a flicker of light came from the grove. *Great.* The idiots appeared to be setting up camp and starting a campfire. She leaned out over the railing and squinted as if that would help.

Lights bounced along behind the trees and moved fast. The roar of an engine reached her, followed by the squealing of tires. *What the hell?* Another door slammed.

Raised voices drifted to her. Something in the tone made her think the newcomer was angry about something, but she was struggling to hear the words.

The campfire appeared to be growing. Damned kids, they were going to start a forest fire if they weren't careful. She grabbed her phone out of her pocket. Before she could call for backup, a scream pierced the night air. "No. Stop. Please."

Crap. Quickly, she made the call to security. The guard was on the other side of the campground.

Dani needed to get there now. She ran across the deck and rushed down the stairs. On her descent, the voice cried out again. It sounded like a female. Dani thought she heard, "I didn't mean it." But she couldn't be sure.

When she arrived at the bottom of the stairs, blood rushed in her ears, and she breathed heavily. She sprinted to her ATV and hit the ignition. The engine roared to life.

The fire seemed to be growing.

She gunned the engine and headed toward the pine forest. Luckily, she knew the terrain well because she was going too fast for her headlights to keep up in the dense woods. She wove between the trees, letting her instincts guide the way.

She was about one hundred yards from the fire, and by now, she could tell the blaze was bigger than she'd realized—too big to handle on her own. She slammed on her brakes and called 911.

"Nine-one-one," the dispatcher said. "What is your emergency?"

"This is Dani Thorton at the Thundering Pines Campground. There's a fire burning out of control in our pine forest."

"May I have the address?"

Dani rattled off the address and gave directions so the firetrucks could get to the location.

"Thank you, ma'am. If you could stay on the line while I dispatch help."

"I need to go to the fire." Dani's heart raced, and she struggled to keep her breath even.

"Ma'am, you should not approach the fire. Our engines will be there shortly."

Dani opened her mouth to protest when a

bloodcurdling scream pierced the air.

"Ma'am, are you okay?" the dispatcher asked.

"You heard that, too?"

"Yes. Please communicate what occurred."

Another scream rang out. "I have to go." Dani disconnected the call. She pressed down hard on the accelerator and sped toward where the fire raged.

About fifty yards from the fire, she was beginning to see the scene better. Several trees were on fire, and two figures ran from the area toward two pickups that were parked on the road. Both leapt into one and squealed their tires as they drove away.

Fuck. They were going to get away. Without much thought, she made the decision to chase them. The fire department would no doubt be able to find the blaze without her help, so she needed to get a license number of the escaping truck.

She stepped hard on the gas and shot toward the road. An agonizing scream rang out. Dani looked over her shoulder, then back at the retreating truck. *Damn it.* She gave one last look at the truck before spinning around. Someone or something was injured. She needed to give up her pursuit.

A figure writhed on the ground a few yards from the fire. If the wind shifted or the fire spread, it could mean danger for the person. Dani needed to pull them out of harm's way. Skidding to a stop, a safe distance from the fire, she cut the engine. All her focus landed on the down figure as she vaulted out of the ATV and ran toward the shape that had stopped moving.

Hopefully, the person wasn't big, or she'd have trouble moving them. The closer she got to the fire, the more distinct the smell of gasoline became. Her urgency increased. If there were an accelerant, she needed to get the person to safety straightaway.

She fell to her knees beside the prone body that lay face down on the bed of pine needles. The hair was long and wavy. A woman! Gently, she turned her over. *Shelby!*

Chapter Thirty-one

*W*as that the phone? Brianna felt around in the dark. *What the fuck time is it, anyway?* In her grogginess, she nearly dropped it but finally got a grip and pulled it toward her. When she saw Dani's picture, she was wide awake.

"Dani?" Brianna said into the phone.

"I need you to come to Thundering Pines," Dani's voice was businesslike.

"Who the hell is that?" Caroline asked.

"It's Dani," Brianna whispered.

"What?" Dani said.

"Sorry, Caroline woke up and asked who you were." Caroline flipped on the light, and Brianna was suddenly blinded. "Holy hell, why did you do that?"

"Why is she calling at one in the morning?" Caroline asked at the same time as Dani spoke.

"Because we have a situation here," Dani said.

"Why aren't you telling me what's going on?" Caroline glared at Brianna.

"Stop!" Brianna waved her hand at Caroline.

"You don't want to hear about it?" Dani asked.

"Not you, Caroline. Hold on one second, Dani." Brianna covered the phone and got out of bed. "I'm going to take the call in the living room. Sorry for waking you."

Caroline started to speak, but Brianna held up her hand. "No, there's a situation at the campground, and I can't hear both of you at the same time." She didn't give Caroline time to protest before she left the room.

"Okay, sorry," Brianna said into the phone. "I didn't mean to cut you off. Now what's going on?"

"I need you to come here as soon as you can." Dani's voice was controlled, but Brianna could hear the panic under the surface.

"Mind telling me why?" Brianna flipped on the living room light, plopped onto the couch, and pulled a blanket around her. She hadn't thought to put on a robe, and her tank top and shorts weren't cutting it with the air conditioner blasting cold air.

"There's been a fire."

"Oh, God, is everyone all right?" Brianna's heart raced.

"Except for the person who tried to stop the arsonists."

"Did you just say arsonists? Oh, my God, are you hurt?"

"No, I'm okay." Dani breathed in deeply. "It's Shelby."

"Shelby?" Brianna rubbed her eyes. "Shelby tried to stop the arsonists?"

"Nicky and Tommy."

"Oh, fuck, are you serious?" Brianna shivered and pulled the blanket more tightly around herself. Caroline was staring at her from the door, but Brianna pretended not to notice. "Wait, you said she was injured."

"She'll survive, but she has third-degree burns on her hands and arms. Apparently, the fire ran up the gas can when she tried to take it from Nicky."

"Fuck. Which hospital did they take her to?"

"She was just airlifted to OSF hospital in Rockford."

Brianna's stomach clenched. "Airlifted, that doesn't sound okay to me."

"Her skin was practically melting off her arms. It was the most horrendous thing I'd ever seen. I tried to take care of her, but she was screaming. And the smell of charred skin. It was…"

"Are you all right?" Brianna asked, finally realizing how traumatic it must have been for Dani.

"Yeah."

"Are you truly all right?" Brianna asked again, not believing Dani.

"I guess I'm a little shaken up."

"Do you want me to come now?"

"Would you?" Dani sounded hesitant. She quickly added, "I can handle it on my own. I'm just being silly. You don't want to come."

Brianna stood from the couch. "I'm going to get dressed now. Will you be at the loft?"

"Yes."

"I'm on my way."

"No, I never should have called you," Dani stammered. "It was a weak moment. I panicked. I'll be fine."

"I'm coming," Brianna said forcefully. "I'm hanging up now and will see you soon."

"Okay, thanks. I'll be waiting. Goodbye." Then the line went dead.

Caroline stood with her hands on her hips. "What the hell was that all about?"

Brianna gave Caroline a rundown as she hurried around the room tossing clothes into her bag.

"You're not going there in the middle of the

night, are you?"

"It's my responsibility." Brianna continued gathering her things.

Caroline followed her to the bathroom while she pulled out her toiletries. "How long are you planning on being gone?"

"I'm not sure. I need to assess the situation. Tomorrow's Friday, so I'll probably stay through the weekend." Brianna stripped out of the clothes she had been sleeping in and pulled on a pair of jeans and a T-shirt.

"Do you want me to come with?"

"No." Brianna thought of elaborating but didn't have time for an argument. "Shelby was severely injured. I may need to deal with that, too."

"Aren't you going to need a lawyer?"

"I'll call you if I do." Brianna had all her stuff together and was standing near the door. She gave Caroline a quick kiss. "I'll call you later to let you know what's going on."

❧❧❧❧❧

Brianna had her window down as she sped down the sparsely traveled road. There were more semi trucks at this time of night than anything else.

She was racing toward Thundering Pines, to Dani. Would the crisis bring them back together, or would it highlight the depth of the wedge between them? She couldn't think about that now, so she pushed the thoughts from her head. Dani needed her.

Since the roads were nearly empty, Brianna was making good time. The conversation with Dani ran through her mind. *What the fuck were the twins think-*

ing? And what was Shelby's role? Shelby had been so angry for so long and made threats to anyone who would listen. Brianna had thought they were just letting off steam. Had Shelby known what the twins were up to and had gotten cold feet, or had she seriously not known?

Brianna tried to be kind to her, but sometimes, Shelby made it hard. Maybe this would bring Shelby to her senses, and she would stop letting the pain her father inflected come out as hatred toward Brianna.

How much damage had Shelby done to herself? She'd heard burns were the worst pain imaginable and realized Shelby would likely have a long road of recovery ahead.

After hearing about Shelby, she'd forgotten to ask Dani how severely damaged the pine forest was. She'd thought of calling but decided against it. Dani was probably tied up with the police and firefighters. It could wait until she arrived.

❧❧❧❧

Dani slumped against the side of the ATV. It was after three a.m. She'd functioned on pure adrenaline earlier, but it had mostly worn off now.

She'd talked to so many people that the conversations were beginning to blur together. Every volunteer firefighter from Flower Hills and all the nearby towns had descended. She was glad they had because it appeared the damage to the forest was kept to a minimum, but she couldn't be sure until she saw it in the light of day.

She shuddered. More than likely, the whole forest would have been destroyed if she hadn't been awake and in the loft. Left unchecked, it could have reached some of the campsites, where unsuspecting campers may not have woken up in time to escape.

The thought made her angry at Shelby all over again. Sure, she'd come through at the end, but without her hatred for Brianna, it wouldn't have happened in the first place.

The flashing lights from the police cars and fire-trucks continued to illuminate the woods like an insane discotheque. The colors bouncing off the pines might have been pretty if she didn't know why they were there. Finally, having enough, she'd turned away, walked to the edge of the forest, and stared out over the water. The reflections of the strobes bounced off the river. *No escape.* The longer they pulsed, the more claustrophobic she became.

Crazy, but she just wanted Brianna to get there, then maybe she could breathe again. In hindsight, maybe it was stupid waking Brianna in the middle of the night, but hearing Brianna's voice had calmed her.

When everything blew up, she'd forgotten the wall between them. She'd panicked. It wasn't as if Brianna could do anything. *That's not true.* Brianna made things better just by being there. She hoped for no awkwardness tonight.

Was it a mistake asking her to come? Dani was already wrung out, and she didn't know if she could take it if Brianna was cold and distant.

Arms wrapped around her from behind, wrenching her from her thoughts. *Brianna?* Her heart soared, but the male voice brought it back down.

"How are you holding up?" the familiar voice asked.

She relaxed against him. "Carl. Thank you. I knew

when I saw you on one of the trucks that the good guys were gonna win."

"That was some crazy shit," he said.

"It's been building for a while, but I wasn't expecting this." She continued to lean against him, and he made no move to let her go. His gesture was comforting. If any other man were to have put his arms around her like this, she would have been uncomfortable, but Carl was the purest soul she'd ever met. And right now, she needed a friend, and she knew Carl was happy to be that for her.

"Were you there when they took her away?"

"Yes." Dani shivered. "I know you're used to seeing things like that, but I think I'll have nightmares for months."

"She'll be okay, but she's gonna have some painful rehab in front of her."

"I'm so pissed off at her right now."

"But she tried to stop them."

"Yeah, but she's the one that stirred them up in the first place. I didn't want this for her, though."

"I know." He hugged her tighter.

≈≈≈≈

Flashing lights lit the sky from at least a mile off. Brianna stepped on the gas and covered the final distance quickly. Slowing, she turned into Thundering Pine's entrance. She stuck her arm out the window and waved at several campers who were huddled together talking among themselves.

The smell of smoke was heavy in the air, causing her eyes to water and her lungs to burn. *Damn it, that can't be good.* She tried to calm herself, knowing a pile of burning leaves could make a whole neighborhood smell as if it were on fire. *Don't panic yet.*

The strobes blinded her as she rounded the curve. The fire was long extinguished, but several firefighters scoured the area, probably searching for evidence. The trees were still standing, but a few appeared to be in bad shape. Dani would be able to better assess than she could.

As soon as she brought the Jeep to a stop, she jumped out. Her eyes were having trouble adjusting because of the chaotic flashes. She wasn't having any luck locating Dani with the disorienting light show.

A man with an air of authority walked up to her. "You must be Brianna Goodwin. I'm Chief Talbot."

"Hello, Chief," Brianna said, breaking into her professional mode. "Thank you so much for the work you've done here tonight."

"You have your manager to thank. If Dani hadn't acted so quickly, we'd be looking at a serious situation." He pointed to the west. "Those campers just down the hill might not have escaped the fire. Who knows, it could have taken them all out."

"I don't even want to think about it." Brianna shivered and wrapped her arms around herself. "Speaking of Dani, do you know where she is?"

He pointed toward the river. "Last I saw, she was heading that direction. I reckon she'd had enough and needed to get away for a spell."

"If you don't mind, I'd like to go check on her."

"No, ma'am, I don't mind at all."

"It was nice meeting you, Chief Talbot. I just wish it could have been under different circumstances."

"You as well. Take care." He started to turn away and stopped. "I think Dani's more shaken up than she's letting on. I just thought I should tell you that."

"Thank you." Brianna's heart raced. She wanted to run off in the direction Chief Talbot indicated, but she tried to keep her pace steady.

Brianna hurried toward the edge of the woods. The farther she walked, the smoke in the air cleared, and she was able to breathe again. Poor Dani had been in it for hours. She quickened her pace. She needed to find Dani. *Now!*

Brianna neared the edge of the woods when she saw a man with his arms wrapped around Dani. Their posture seemed intimate. She froze and took a deep breath. Obviously, Dani had a guest in the loft, and he was still with her. *I can do this.* It stung more than she cared to admit. The loft was their place, and the thought of Dani sharing it with someone else made her angry. Really, she was hurt, but it was easier to be angry. Why the hell did Dani drag her out here if she had her boyfriend with her? *Only one way to find out.*

Brianna coughed and cleared her throat, pretending that the smoke was bothering her to alert the couple of her arrival.

The man turned, and Brianna's breathing evened. *Carl.*

"There you are." Carl sported a huge smile. "I've been trying to keep Dani company until you arrived."

Before she could say anything, Dani turned and hurried toward her. "Thank God you're here." She flung her arms around Brianna and buried her head against Brianna's shoulder.

Brianna hugged Dani tightly and glanced over her head toward Carl.

He was smiling and nodding. "Now that you're here, I best be heading home." He looked at his watch.

"I have to be up in a few hours for church."

Brianna felt herself relax. "Thanks, Carl."

"You'll look after our girl? She's had one hell of a night. I think she could use a little sleep and a lot of understanding."

"I'll take care of her." Brianna continued to hold Dani, who still said nothing.

"I know you will." He smiled his million-dollar smile. "I'll be seein' you around, Dani."

Dani finally let go of Brianna and turned to him. "Thank you again. You know I appreciate everything, don't you?"

"I do," he said, and then he was gone.

Brianna studied Dani for the first time since she'd arrived. Her face was smudged with soot, and most of her hair had escaped her ponytail. Tiny branches and leaves clung to her hair, and her clothes were covered in ash. Brianna's gaze settled on her lifeless eyes.

"You look beat," Brianna said.

"It's been a long night," Dani answered.

Brianna wiped a black splotch off Dani's cheek. "Why don't you go to the loft and clean up? I'll see if the guys need anything more."

"You'll come up after you're done?" Dani sounded panicked.

"Of course." Brianna brushed debris out of Dani's hair and then left her hand resting against the side of her face. "Are you going to be okay?" She'd never seen Dani looking so defeated, and truth be told, it made her uneasy. Dani was always so strong, but tonight, she was shaken.

"Now that you're here, yes." Dani finally gave her a smile.

Brianna exhaled. "Ah, now that's what I needed to see. I've missed that smile."

Dani smiled bigger. "I've missed yours, too."

"Get your ass up there and clean up. You smell like an ashtray," Brianna said, trying to lighten the mood. "I'll be along shortly."

⚜⚜⚜⚜

The warm water from the shower had felt good on Dani's skin. She'd scrubbed herself for nearly half an hour and washed her hair three times in hopes of ridding herself of the smell of fire. The stench was embedded in her brain, so she'd have to rely on Brianna to tell her if she'd gotten rid of the odor.

She held on to her bottle of water with both hands to steady it. The bottle jiggled in her grip, but it was manageable. She took another drink and laid her head back on the pillow.

The door clanked, and her eyes popped open. "Bri?" she called out.

"It's me." Brianna threw her duffel bag on the floor. "I've got to go to the bathroom."

"You might want to take a shower. I can smell you from here."

"Really? That shit sticks to everything. I wasn't out there for long."

"It doesn't take much. We're lucky the wind wasn't blowing in this direction, or everything in here would smell hideous."

Brianna walked to the couch. "Will you be awake when I come out?"

"Wake me if I'm not."

"Okay," Brianna said.

Dani suspected it was a lie. Knowing Brianna, she'd let her sleep.

Brianna reached down and brushed the hair away from Dani's face. "Thank you for calling me."

"You own the place, of course I'd call you."

"That's not what I meant." Brianna paused and seemed to be searching for words. "Thanks for wanting me here."

"I need you here," Dani answered in a voice a little over a whisper.

"And I need for you to need me here." Brianna laughed. "Was that just a Hallmark moment?"

"I think it was." Dani grinned. "Get your ass in the shower. You're smelling up the place."

❧ ❧ ❧ ❧

When Brianna finished showering, she found Dani lightly snoring on the couch. She pulled the blanket over her and lightly kissed her forehead. "Sleep tight, Dani," she said aloud. She pulled one of the recliners toward the couch, careful not to make too much noise. It was silly, but she wanted to be close to Dani.

She stretched out in the chair and pulled the blanket to her chin. It was the last thing she remembered.

Chapter Thirty-two

*B*rianna's face felt warm. She opened her eyes and blinked. The sun was streaming in through the bank of windows. It took her a couple of seconds to figure out where she was. To her left, Dani still slept.

She wanted to study Dani's face but was afraid she would sense her stare and awaken. Her hand fumbled around beside the chair until her fingers found her phone. *What the hell?* Five missed calls.

The blue light blinked. When she punched in her code to retrieve her messages, she had five voicemails from OSF Medical Center concerning Shelby. After listening to them, she sighed. She wasn't going to wake Dani for this. It could wait until Dani came to.

Quietly, she got up, tiptoed to the windows, and forced herself to look toward the pine forest.

A sigh of relief escaped her lips. A small corner of the forest had been damaged, but from this vantage point, it was a relatively small patch. Probably a few trees would need to come down. She'd leave that to the experts.

She didn't know how long she'd been staring out the window when Dani said, "You didn't wake me."

Brianna turned and smiled. "I thought you needed your sleep more than you needed my witty repartee."

"Oh, so that's what you're calling it nowadays."

Dani winked. "Is that the same thing as your witty bullshit?"

"Look who woke up full of piss and vinegar."

"How bad is it?" Dani asked, her face suddenly serious.

"I don't think it's too bad, but come see for yourself." Brianna held out her hand, as if welcoming Dani.

Dani rose tentatively and took the few steps across the room. She looked down and shuffled to the window.

Brianna draped her arm over Dani's shoulder and pulled her close.

Dani wrapped her arm around Brianna's waist and relaxed against her. Maybe she should keep her distance, but right now, the need to be close to Brianna won out. "I'm afraid to look." She slowly lifted her head and let out a loud exhalation. "Oh, thank God."

"From that reaction, I'm taking it that my assessment was an accurate one."

Dani leaned toward the window, squinting, and didn't respond right away. "From here, I can't be sure, but it looks better than I thought it was going to. Do you realize what could have happened?"

Brianna squeezed her shoulder. "Yes, and it scares the hell out of me. If you hadn't been here…"

"But I was."

Brianna didn't know if she wanted to ask the question, but she did anyway. "Why were you out here at one in the morning?" She held her breath waiting for the answer.

"Do you really want me to answer that?" Dani shifted uncomfortably.

No, I don't. But she needed to. "Yes." She let her

arm fall from Dani's shoulder. They were still standing close enough that their arms brushed against each other's.

"It's the place I feel closest to you. And..." Dani stopped.

Brianna felt her heart surge. "Meaning?"

"Do I really have to say this?" Dani shifted again and broke contact with Brianna's arm.

"No, I think it's time I say something." Brianna moved closer to Dani, so their arms were touching again. "I've fucking missed you so fucking much."

Dani laughed. "Such a wordsmith. I'm touched. I think."

Brianna turned to Dani. "I had a lot of time to reflect on my drive here last night. I realized I'd kept myself so busy these last three weeks, so I didn't have to think. I've put in seventy-hour weeks at my job, so they love me. It might even get me the promotion I thought I wanted. But there's something about a drive in the middle of the night that leaves you with nothing to do but wrestle with yourself. And the only thing that was clear is I need my best friend back. I hate the weirdness between us."

"I panicked, and when I did, it was you I called. That told me everything I needed to know. But then I was afraid you would come, and it would feel like you were just an acquaintance. I don't think I could have handled that. So thank you for not doing that to me."

Brianna went to hug her but was interrupted by the sound of her cellphone. "Oh, shit, there's something I hadn't gotten around to telling you. Let me answer that."

☙ ☙ ❧ ❧

In three strides, Brianna was across the room. "Yes, this is Brianna Goodwin," she said into the phone.

Dani looked on in interest. *What has Brianna neglected to tell me?*

"Yes, she is," Brianna said in a professional voice. She listened for some time. "I see. And when are visiting hours today?" Brianna nodded. "I believe it's a couple hours' drive from where I am. Do I have to specify a time?" She inhaled. "You're sure she's asking for me?" Again, Brianna listened for some time before answering. "Okay, then I will be there sometime this afternoon."

Brianna ended the call and let her hand holding the phone drop to her side.

"Shelby?" Dani asked.

"She wants to see me."

"Why?" Dani said without thinking. "Sorry, that came out wrong. What did they say?"

"The nurse said she keeps asking for me. And then she went into a long spiel about how advantageous it is for the patient to have their loved ones around them. I didn't bother to tell her I wasn't exactly a loved one."

"How is she doing?"

"The nurse said it wasn't near as bad as it could have been. It will be a few days before they know if she'll need surgery or skin grafts, depending on how it heals. For now, she's in a lot of pain but still wants to see me."

Dani rolled her response around in her head. *Be diplomatic.* "Do you think it's one of Shelby's, um…"

"Manipulations," Brianna said, finishing Dani's

sentence.

Dani smiled. "Yeah. With her talking revenge all over town, she could still possibly be implicated. Arson isn't exactly a small charge."

"Trust me, I thought of that, but I have to go." Brianna's gaze met Dani's. "Would you go with me?"

"Of course."

"But you have so much to do around here. I shouldn't have asked."

Since the call, Brianna was edgy, and their earlier connection seemed in danger of being broken. Dani wasn't going to let that happen again. "There's nowhere else I'd rather be. Besides, I have employees that can handle what needs to be done here." Dani could feel Brianna's distance, so she added, "If you didn't invite me, I'd just follow you in my truck, anyway."

"Stalker." Brianna laughed. "Thanks."

"What do you say we convince Aunt Helen to make us some breakfast before we go?"

Brianna's smile lit up the room. "I would love that."

"She's missed you, too, so be prepared for a feast."

❧❧❧❧

Despite Brianna's apprehension about the visit, she was thankful the drive to the hospital was good. Much better than the awkward drive they'd taken home from Missouri. They were back to their easy banter, but more importantly, they were able to share their thoughts the way they had in the past. Dani urged Brianna to talk about Shelby, so she could go in with an open heart and mind.

"I was an only child," Brianna said. "At least in my mind. But there were times I wished I had a brother or sister. And I guess I still kinda do. Did you ever feel that way?"

Dani smiled. "All the time. I loved my dad, but I was always envious of my friends that had siblings. Sure, they fought sometimes, but they always seemed to come together. Do ya want to know the thing I'm saddest about?"

"Yes."

"I'll never have any nieces or nephews. I always dreamed about sitting around the campfire with a big family. Three generations all together. Stupid, huh?"

"Not stupid at all." Brianna smiled. "Do you think if Shelby ever has kids, they will call me Aunt Brianna?"

"Do you want them to?"

"God, I don't know. I guess we'll have to see if she gets some help."

Dani nodded. "You know she's probably going to try and take credit for being the hero."

Brianna groaned. "I know. Forget the fact she stirred the twins up in the first place. Her hatred caused this, but I doubt she'll see it that way."

"Can you forgive her?"

Brianna's hands tightened on the steering wheel. The thought had rolled around in her mind ever since she'd gotten Dani's call. When she'd looked at the burned trees, she didn't think she could forgive her, but now she wasn't certain. Shelby had done so much damage.

"I know that wasn't a fair question," Dani said. "I'll rescind it and allow you to withhold judgment a little longer."

Brianna flashed to one of Shelby's drunken calls. One that burned in her brain, no matter how hard she tried to push it aside. "Thanks. Since you're asking the hard questions, it's my turn." Brianna glanced at Dani for her reaction.

"I don't like the sound of this. Go ahead, hit me with your best shot."

"Why did you sleep with Shelby?"

Dani practically choked on the water she was drinking. "How did you know?"

She hadn't until now. Her chest tightened. She'd wanted it to be another Shelby lie. "During one of Shelby's drunken tirades she told me, but I wasn't sure I could believe her."

"You mean I just outed myself?"

"Afraid so."

Dani's face was strained, and she didn't speak for several beats. "I'll answer. If you really want to know."

Do I? "Yes, even if it might be painful to hear." *Oh, God, did I just say that?*

"Painful?"

Brianna could feel Dani's gaze on her but pretended to be intent on her driving. She didn't want things to go back to being stilted between them, so she decided on honesty. "You're the person I confide in and tell everything. But you've had the most intimate experience anyone could have with my sister, somebody that hates me."

"Oh, Bri. There was nothing intimate about what we did together. This conversation, all our conversations are way more intimate. It was just sex."

"And you were okay with that? Knowing you, it doesn't seem to fit."

"It fit Dani BB."

"BB, what's that?" Brianna squinted her eyes.

"Before Brianna." Dani snickered at her own joke.

"Smartass!"

"I'm only partially joking. I've been pretty shut down all my life. Probably ever since my mom left. For God's sake, I slept with Carl for years, and it didn't mean anything. Sex was just sex. So that's all it was with Shelby and all the other women."

"God, you and Caroline should compare notes." Brianna stopped, mortified. "Wow, I'm sorry. My filter seems to be broken today." Brianna glanced at Dani. "Now you're admitting to sleeping with the other women?"

Dani snorted but then grinned. "I'm glad your filter is gone. I'd much rather have this Brianna than the guarded one." She ran her hand through her hair. "Yeah, I'm admitting it. Although for the record, I never lied to you. I just avoided the question."

"I noticed. I let you get away with it." Brianna smiled. "But I'm not going to now."

Throwing her hands up as if in surrender, Dani turned toward Brianna. "I'm a collector of people. I have hundreds of friends, yet I have no one. And I've slept with...with...more people than I care to admit but never found someone to love."

Brianna's chest ached for Dani. More than anything, she wanted to pull off the road and hug her but knew it wouldn't be received well. "How can you have sex without...without...I don't know, not feeling anything?" *Wow!* What a hypocrite. As if she had any room to talk.

"People do it every day."

"Nice try, but I'm not talking about people.

I'm talking about you. How can you do it?" Brianna glanced at Dani before turning her attention back to the road.

"You're tough today. For me, sex is only about my body. It doesn't touch me here." She touched her forehead. "Or here." She rested her hand on her chest. "This probably won't make any sense, but I've thought a lot about it since you came along. Maybe I found a loophole."

"A loophole?" Brianna glanced at Dani.

"To be a lesbian and dishonor my dad, I'd have to be in an emotional and physical relationship with a woman. I've never had that. It's just sex. So I'm good."

"You know it doesn't work that way, don't you?"

"It does in my world." Dani crossed her arms over her chest. "When did you become the sexuality police?"

"Point taken." Brianna held out her hand. She'd hit a nerve. It wasn't like Dani to be so defensive. Time for her to back off. It wasn't her place to give Dani a label that she wasn't ready to accept. "So all these women were just sex?"

"You mean you've never had emotionless sex?"

What a loaded question. She'd been asking herself that a lot recently. She'd been going through the motions lately with Caroline, probably longer than she cared to admit. Between her thighs was completely disconnected from the rest of her, especially her emotions. "I suppose I have." If Dani sensed there was more to her words, she didn't say anything.

"Then see, you understand. That's been my experience my whole life. I've never had anything different."

"How sad." Brianna stopped herself from

looking at Dani, afraid her look would be one of pity.

"Who knows, maybe one day I'll find someone who rocks my body, mind, and emotions all at the same time." Dani tried to put a teasing note in her voice, but Brianna could hear the pain. "Shelby has her good traits, she just hides them well."

"No doubt." Brianna nodded, happy to move on to a different conversation, even if it was about Shelby. "I've spent a lifetime hating her, and I hardly know her. And I'm sure she's hated me just as much. Probably more."

"If last night is any indication, I'd say more."

❧ ❧ ❧ ❧ ❧

Brianna looked out the window and saw Six Flags Hurricane Harbor in the distance, reminding her of their trip to Missouri. They were on I-90 and would soon be exiting on Business 20, which would put them only ten minutes from the hospital and Shelby.

Dani must have sensed her apprehension because she'd stopped talking and gave Brianna the space she needed to prepare.

"We're almost there," Brianna said as she took the exit.

"I know. Are you ready?"

"Will I ever be ready?"

"Probably not, but you've got this."

Brianna smiled and went back to concentrating on the road. The traffic was heavier than she expected on a Sunday afternoon, but it was a gorgeous day, so maybe everyone decided to get out and enjoy it.

The hospital loomed in the distance. "Isn't life strange? Look at all these people out enjoying their day while there are people fighting for their lives a mile down the road." She fell silent.

Dani nodded.

They drove onto the campuslike setting of OSF St. Anthony Medical Center. The building was formidable and dwarfed everything surrounding it.

Brianna pulled into a parking spot and stared at the large building in front of her. She continued to hold on to the steering wheel, even after she'd turned off the Jeep. Her palms were sweating, and she knew she'd leave damp fingerprints on the wheel when she removed her hands. "Okay, we've been here. Time to go home." She pretended to reach for the ignition.

"Nope, we're going in. I have to pee."

Brianna laughed, realizing she couldn't do this without Dani.

☙ ☙ ☙ ☙

Their footsteps echoed in the polished corridor. Brianna hated the smell of hospitals but expected the burn unit to be worse.

The woman at the information desk directed them to the third floor.

When they stopped at the bank of elevators, Dani reached for Brianna's arm. "You know, you have to take the last part of the journey on your own."

Brianna looked at her in horror. "You're not coming with me?"

"I'm afraid not. You need to talk to Shelby alone. It changes the dynamics if I'm in the room."

"That was my plan." Brianna smiled. "At least go up to the floor with me. I'm sure there will be a place for you to sit."

"I can do that." Dani pushed the up arrow.

They rode in silence. The elevator dinged open much too soon. Brianna took a deep breath and stepped through the door.

⚜⚜⚜⚜

Brianna rubbed her hands together as she followed the nurse. *I'm not ready for this.* Hospitals already made her uncomfortable, but this was unbearable.

As they walked down the hall, moans and whimpers came from behind the patients' doors.

The nurse seemed accustomed to it and didn't flinch. She must have sensed Brianna's discomfort because she said, "I'm sure your sister will be glad to see you."

"Half," Brianna said on instinct.

"Pardon?"

"Half sister. Shelby is my half sister." Brianna stumbled over her words.

"Regardless. Family is the key to people's recovery, so it's good that you're here."

Brianna decided it would be in poor taste to explain her history with Shelby. Better to let the nurse have the illusion of a caring sister. "Thank you. I've heard wonderful things about your burn unit, so I know she's in good hands."

The nurse smiled. "How kind."

Brianna was about to ask her how she was able to handle doing such difficult work, but they'd stopped outside of room 326.

"Here we are. Let me check to be sure she's not undergoing any treatment before I take you in." The nurse disappeared before Brianna could respond.

It gave her time to collect her jumbled thoughts. What would she say to Shelby? Would it turn into an ugly confrontation as it always did?

The nurse stepped out of the room. "Shelby is ready. Be warned, she's a little groggy since she's on heavy pain medication."

"Um, maybe I should come back later then." Brianna felt relief at the thought of escape.

"Nonsense." The nurse pushed the door open.

Brianna had no other choice than to enter. She stopped inside the door and let it close behind her. The short hallway blocked her view of Shelby's bed, so she had a couple of beats before coming face to face with her.

She wasn't sure what she had been expecting, but it wasn't this.

Shelby looked small and frail, nothing like the boisterous woman who'd gotten in her face multiple times. "Hi, Brianna," Shelby said in a soft voice.

"How are you?" Brianna walked to the side of the bed.

"I did a number on myself." Shelby held up her heavily bandaged hands. She dropped her hands to her chest and winced.

"Hurts?" Brianna knew the conversation was forced, but it wasn't as if they were used to having long heartfelt talks.

"Just a bit." Shelby gave her a weak smile. "Thanks for coming. I didn't think you would."

So many ways to respond. "I wasn't sure I would, either, but Dani convinced me." Obviously, she was going with honesty. What had gotten into her? She needed her polished reserve back.

"Is she here?"

"In the waiting room."

"Why didn't she come in?"

Brianna hesitated. "She thought we needed to talk alone."

Shelby laughed.

Brianna braced herself, waiting for Shelby's venom to spew out.

"Figures. Leave it to Dani to push us to do the right thing."

Brianna relaxed when she realized Shelby's comment was sincere. "Yeah, I fought her," Brianna said with a smirk. "But you can see who won."

Shelby made eye contact with Brianna. "I'm sorry."

Brianna hoped shock didn't register on her face. Did her "I'm sorry" mean she saw her part in what happened? Miracles never ceased. Brianna waited for her to say more, but she didn't. Sadness washed over her. "Why do you hate me so much? I never did anything to you."

Shelby's eyelids closed for several seconds. At first, Brianna thought she might have fallen asleep, but she opened them. It was the first time Brianna realized just how pretty her eyes were. Brianna held back a smirk at the backhanded compliment because they were nearly identical to hers, just a little darker. They'd gotten them from their dad.

"I was so angry," Shelby said. "I hated you because I didn't know how to hate him."

Without any ire, Brianna answered, "The feeling was mutual."

"I know. But this is where it got us." Shelby glanced around the room, and then her gaze settled on her bandaged hands. "Look where it got me."

"You know this is exactly what he wanted, don't you?"

"This?" Shelby tried to raise her hand but immediately lowered it back to her chest.

"I know you loved Donald, but he was an evil man. Maybe not evil, but he was a small man. A selfish man."

"I know, but I just wanted him to love me." Tears welled, but she fought them back. "But he always loved you more."

Brianna's back stiffened, and she wrinkled her nose. "No, he didn't. I don't think he was capable of love. At least not real love. All these years, I've resented you because you and your mom took my dad, but maybe I was the lucky one because I got away. Don't get me wrong, I still have my demons because of him, but I escaped."

The hard set of Shelby's mouth softened. "I chased him around my whole life, grasping at whatever crumb he would throw my way. And I got to be the bastard child of Flower Hills."

Brianna fought back tears, and her chest unexpectedly opened. She'd been closed to Shelby for so long, she wasn't sure what to do with this newfound emotion. "He's gone now, and it's only us."

Shelby eyed her. Brianna saw suspicion, but there was something else, too. "Meaning?"

"You're my sister," Brianna said.

"Half," Shelby responded with a smile.

Brianna laughed. "You're my sister. The only one I have, I think. Oh, God, do you think we have other siblings out there we don't know about?"

It was Shelby's turn to laugh. "I think two of us

is enough. Let's say we don't go looking."

"Deal." Brianna touched Shelby's shoulder. "We could try to be sisters or at least try and get to know each other."

Shelby closed her eyes, and the tears escaped the corners. "I'd like that. But why after everything I've done?"

"Honestly?"

"Please."

"He fucked up both of our lives, but we let him. Maybe it's a way to give him the ultimate fuck you." Brianna's words came out a little more forceful than she'd intended.

"Okay then." Shelby's eyes widened. "I was hoping for 'because I see how wonderful of a sister you could be, Shelby,' but I'm okay starting here."

"What do you say I bring Dani in for a bit?"

"Definitely, I think we've had enough sisterly bonding for one day."

Brianna laughed.

Chapter Thirty-three

*B*rianna looked down at her phone. Dani still hadn't called. She was supposed to call nearly two hours ago. It wasn't like her to be so late. Brianna had tried her an hour ago but had gotten no answer. Dani always called her Thursday to give her an agenda for the weekend, so she'd know what to pack.

Should I try to call her again? No, just wait.

She could check on Shelby, but as soon as she did, Dani would call. *Wow.* What a difference a month made. Who would have thought she'd willingly be calling Shelby? Things hadn't been perfect between them, but they were working on it, much to Caroline's disgust.

When was Shelby's next appointment? Brianna brought her calendar up on her phone. *Tomorrow.* She needed to check on her afterward. Hopefully, Shelby wouldn't have to have another painful surgery on her hand. She shivered. The thought of fused fingers freaked her out, so she pushed it out of her mind.

Ironic how a little thing like arson could bring a family together. She laughed out loud and made a mental note to tell Dani. She'd find the dark humor hysterical.

Brianna carried her supper dishes to the kitchen. Maybe she'd start packing and add whatever else she might need later. She felt edgy tonight, she wasn't sure why, and needed to keep moving.

Things were almost back to normal with Dani, but Brianna was reminded of the tenuous nature of their relationship by the butterflies that danced in her stomach. There was still the elephant in the room. *The kiss.* They hadn't talked about it again, and they had kept the underlying physical attraction heavily under wraps.

With Dani's missed call, the elephant grew. She hadn't admitted to herself, until now, an underlying fear hiding in the corner of her mind. Her heart still feared that the unspoken attraction would destroy their friendship. Neither wanted to jeopardize their emotional connection for a night of ecstasy. It wasn't worth losing the best friend she'd ever had.

Damn it, Dani. Brianna picked up her phone again, thinking maybe she'd missed a text. *Nope.* She set it down on her nightstand and went into the bathroom to collect her toiletry bag. She'd finally broken down and bought an extra set of everything so she could leave her bag packed. Dani told her to just leave it at Aunt Helen's, but it seemed too intrusive, so she carried it back and forth.

She'd just walked back into the bedroom and her phone rang. *Finally.*

"It's about time," Brianna said into the phone.

"Brianna, I need you to come quick," Aunt Helen said on the other end, her voice cracking.

Brianna's stomach lurched. "Is Dani okay?"

"I'm not sure," Aunt Helen said with a sob.

"Oh, my God, how bad is she hurt?" Brianna felt the panic rising in her. She threw the toiletries into her bag and zipped it.

"No, I'm sorry, Bri. There hasn't been an accident, but she left."

"Left?" Brianna sat on the bed. "What do you mean left?"

"She's gone."

"Aunt Helen," Brianna said, trying to keep her voice calm. "You're going to have to explain a little better than that. Where did she go?"

"I don't know." The despair was clear in Aunt Helen's voice.

"Why did she go?"

"She's upset with us."

"Us?" Brianna was trying to remain patient but was getting increasingly frustrated as she pulled the information out of Aunt Helen.

"You and me."

She should be conscientious and ask about Aunt Helen first. *Fuck it.* "Why would she be mad at me?"

"The appraiser came today."

"What appraiser?"

"The one you sent, so you could sell Thundering Pines."

"What? I never sent an appraiser."

Papers rustled on the other end of the line. "Let me find it. Sorry, I'm so shaken up I can't think straight."

"It's okay, just relax. We'll figure this out," Brianna said in her most calm voice. Aunt Helen was obviously mistaken and overreacting. She was surprised to hear Aunt Helen rattled; it wasn't like her.

"Here it is. The appraiser's name is Jonathan Wilson."

"Nope, never heard of him."

"There's a Realtor's card here, too. The name's Drew Mulligan."

"Oh, fuck," Brianna said. "I forgot all about

that. Drew's a friend of mine. I talked to her back in February when I thought I wanted to sell." *Why in the hell hasn't Drew checked with me?* "It probably just popped up on her calendar, and she wasn't thinking. No worries, I'll call Drew in the morning."

"No, she's not coming back."

"She can't be that mad over this. I'll give Dani a call and explain."

"No!" Aunt Helen said forcefully and launched into the rest of the story.

❧❧❧❧

How many late-night trips would she make to Thundering Pines? As soon as Brianna hung up the phone, she'd grabbed her stuff, left a note for Caroline, and headed out the door. She'd tried to call Dani again, but she didn't pick up. She'd explained on Dani's voicemail what had happened with the Realtor but still no response.

As she drove, she imagined the scene Aunt Helen had described.

❧❧❧❧

Dani slammed the door harder than she'd meant to when she'd stormed into the house.

Aunt Helen called from the other room. "Dani, are you making all that noise?"

Dani walked into the room as Aunt Helen blinked and brought her chair to an upright position. "Sorry, I didn't mean to shut it so hard. Go back to sleep."

Helen studied her. "What's wrong? You don't

look so good."

Dani sat on the couch and ran her hands through her hair. "Do you trust Brianna?"

"Of course. What's this about?"

Dani pulled two business cards from her pocket and handed them to Aunt Helen.

"What are these?"

"An appraiser came to Thundering Pines today. Apparently, he needs to do an appraisal, so Brianna can sell the campground. The second card is from some hotshot Realtor in Chicago."

"There must be some mistake." Helen tossed the cards onto the coffee table. "She wouldn't put it on the market without talking to you first."

"Are you sure?"

"Absolutely, and you know it, too. Did you call Brianna and talk to her about it?"

"No."

"Danielle, you know Brianna would never do that to you." Aunt Helen squinted her eyes and pursed her lips. "What is this really about?"

Damn it. Aunt Helen picked up everything.

"And don't give me that shocked look, either." Aunt Helen's voice softened. "The last couple of weeks, it seems to me you've been looking for something to get upset about."

"That's ridiculous. Why would I do that?"

"I've wondered the same thing," Aunt Helen said. "But I've noticed it always seems to be directed at Brianna."

"Now you're just imagining things." Dani went into the kitchen and came back carrying a beer. "I've not been upset with Bri."

Aunt Helen's raised eyebrows told Dani that she

was surprised by her beverage choice, but it seemed
Aunt Helen decided not to say anything. "Let's see,
last week, you were upset because she couldn't drop
everything and come to Thundering Pines."

"But I needed her help. It is *her* campground
after all."

"It was Caroline's birthday. And you've been
pouting around here all week because she invited
Shelby and Molly to dinner on Friday night."

"She should have asked me first." Dani took a
pull from her beer. "Besides, I never said anything to
her, just you."

"And I ask again. What is this really about?"

Dani glared and took two more swallows of
beer before answering. "Nothing." When Aunt Helen
stared at her without saying anything, Dani continued.
"She's being thoughtless and self-centered."

Aunt Helen laughed. "I think you can come up
with something better than that. What say you try
again?"

Dani started to protest but stopped and took another gulp of her beer. "I need another one. Do you
want one?"

"Not before dinner."

Aunt Helen was probably right. She set the
empty bottle on the table but didn't go for another
one.

"Want to know what I think?" Aunt Helen asked.

"I'm sure you're gonna tell me, whether I want
to know or not." Dani gave her a half smile.

"You're in love with her."

"What? Where did you come up with that?"

"Answering a question with a question isn't going to fool me." Aunt Helen's gaze remained steady

on Dani.

"She's been with Caroline for over ten years."

"You still haven't denied it."

Dani's face fell. "I can't be."

"Well, you are."

"No," Dani said loudly, causing Aunt Helen to jump.

"You're going to look me in the eye and tell me that you're not in love with her?" Aunt Helen never broke eye contact.

Dani sat heavily on the couch. She looked down at the floor. "I can't. I promised Dad."

Aunt Helen put her hand to her chest. "Oh, Dani. That stupid promise has sentenced you to a life of loneliness. I can't continue to ignore what it's done to you all these years. Now it's threatening the most worthwhile relationship that you've ever had." Aunt Helen clutched her chest and massaged it.

"Are you okay?" Dani didn't like the pallor of Aunt Helen's skin or the way she'd been rubbing her chest.

Helen ignored the question. "Are you really going to let that promise hold you back? It was one that never should have been asked of you."

"Maybe so, but it's too late to take back. He's gone."

Helen took a deep breath. "This may be the hardest thing I've ever done. I don't want to lose you."

"Lose me?" Dani studied Aunt Helen. "You're starting to scare me."

"I promised your dad something, too." Tears misted her eyes. "And I've regretted it every day of my life since."

It was rare that Helen cried, so when she did,

Dani took notice. "What did you promise?"

"Something I never should have. And like you, even though I knew how much damage it was causing, I felt too guilty to break my word to your father."

"Why won't you tell me?"

Aunt Helen slowly got up from her chair. Her movements were normally spry, but today, it appeared her limbs were heavy. She sat back down next to Dani and put her hand on Dani's cheek. "You know I love you more than anything, don't you?"

"I love you, too. But you're scaring me."

"I'm about to tell you something that might change everything, so I just needed you to know that before I do. Stay right here, and I'll be back." Helen turned away before Dani could say anything.

She returned in a couple of minutes carrying a box and set it on the table in front of Dani.

"What's this?" Dani eyed the box but made no move toward it.

"Letters from your mom," Helen answered.

Dani's face froze. "My mom?"

Helen picked up the box and held it out toward Dani. "Yes. She wrote to you every month until you were thirteen."

"Why until thirteen?"

"Your dad sent her a threatening note. He told her he'd turn you against her. He told her that you didn't hate her, but he could change that if she didn't leave you alone. She stopped writing after that."

Bile rose in Dani's throat, and she fought to breathe. "You've been keeping them from me for the last thirty years?" Dani hugged the box to her but didn't open it.

"The last thirteen." Tears freely rolled down

Helen's cheeks. "I didn't know about it until right before he died. He gave me the box and told me what he'd done. He wanted me to burn them."

She stared at Aunt Helen. Did the contempt she felt show on her face? The disdain was soon replaced by pain.

"It was his deathbed confession. He wanted to be absolved of his guilt before he passed. I begged him to tell you, but he wouldn't."

"Why in the fuck didn't you tell me?" Dani asked, finally raising her voice. She'd never sworn at Helen, even in her worst teenage years. Even when her dad had been dying.

"I wanted to. But you were in so much pain when he died. I couldn't throw this on top of your grief. I didn't know what it would do to you. Then after a couple years, you started to heal, but then I was afraid to set you back."

Dani touched the streak in her hair. "But why didn't you tell me the day I told you about this? It was only five years ago."

Helen dropped her gaze to the floor. "I wanted to. I was a coward. It was huge for you to tell me about your hair. I thought it meant you were healing. You'd been so hurt and angry as a teenager, and you'd finally come out of it. I was afraid it would spiral you downhill again."

Dani opened her mouth to speak, but Helen held up her hand. "I know, it's no excuse. I should have told you, even if it meant breaking a promise to him that I never should have made. Now I've broken the hearts of the two people I love most in this world. And I'll have to live with that for the rest of my life."

Dani pointed her finger. "No, Helen. You don't

have the right to feel sorry for yourself after what you did to me."

Aunt Helen flinched. "I thought maybe you'd understand since you made a promise to him, too, that you never should have."

"No! I'm not going to let you get away with that. I was a teenager when he got sick and only twenty-one when he died. But you were a grown adult. It's not the same."

"You're an adult now, and you've let it stand in your way, so don't claim otherwise."

"There is one big difference," Dani shouted. "I never hurt anyone else, just myself. I never hurt the person I professed to love."

Aunt Helen flopped back into her chair. "You're right. And tonight, when I realized you were going to end up hurting the person you love, Brianna, because of your promise, I couldn't let you go down the path I did. I'm sorry. I know that's not enough, but I am truly sorry."

"You're right. Sorry isn't enough." Dani held up the box. "What did she say?"

"I don't know. I never read them," Helen admitted. "They weren't mine to read."

Dani walked out of the room, carrying the box. Ten minutes later, she walked back into the room. She still clutched the box to her chest but pulled a suitcase behind her.

"Are you leaving?" Aunt Helen asked.

Dani walked out the door without answering.

Chapter Thirty-four

Brianna watched the rain pelt the window and trickle down it like tears. The rain matched her mood. She'd spent part of her drive talking with Aunt Helen, trying to convince her that Dani would come around. Aunt Helen seemed to be comforted by her words. Too bad she didn't believe them herself.

The last half hour, she'd been left with her own thoughts. She'd tried multiple times to call Dani with no luck. She'd left her a message about what happened with Drew, but so far, there had been no response.

Her thoughts returned to Aunt Helen. When they'd talked, Aunt Helen's normally enthusiastic voice sounded old and defeated. Her heart ached for Aunt Helen, too. She'd been put into an impossible situation and somehow convinced herself that it was for Dani's own good. People made the strangest decisions out of love.

Brianna turned into Thundering Pines and made her way down the narrow road. The lightning streaked across the sky, and the thunder rattled her windows. The storm battered the pine forest, bending the large trees, but never breaking them. She felt bent just like the trees. *But will I break?*

She pulled her Jeep as near as she could to the loft. She left her suitcase in the back but grabbed her raincoat. If it were possible, the rain came down harder than before. With a kick of her foot, she pushed the door open and leapt out of the Jeep. Not bothering to put her arms in the sleeves of her raincoat, she draped the hood over her head and wore it like a cape.

Lowering her head, she dashed to the loft stairs. In the driving rain, she couldn't make out if there were any lights on. She could only hope.

❧❧❧❧

Dani sat up on the couch and turned down the music. She strained her ears, almost certain she'd heard the door at the bottom of the stairs rattle. *Footsteps.* They got louder as they ascended. Then the door slowly opened.

"Dani?" Brianna's voice called out.

"Bri."

"Oh, thank God you're here." Brianna rushed in, slinging her rain-soaked coat aside. She abruptly stopped a few feet from Dani. "Did you know I'd come?"

"I thought maybe."

"Did you want me to?"

"I don't know. Maybe." Dani shifted her gaze to her lap. "Maybe not."

Brianna gave her a half smile. "Well, that clears things up."

Dani returned the smile, but she didn't speak.

"Did you get my messages?" Brianna asked.

Dani nodded.

"I didn't mean for the appraiser to come. I'd talked to them months ago and forgot all about it. I would never have done that without talking to you."

"I know. I believe you."

Brianna's shoulders visibly relaxed. "Mind if I

sit down?"

Dani motioned for the chair, sure that Brianna would get the point. "Have a seat."

Brianna pulled the chair closer to the couch but still left plenty of distance between them. Dani studied her for the first time. Brianna looked haggard. Her eyes were puffy, and her hair looked as if it hadn't been brushed in a while.

Brianna took a deep breath. "Why didn't you answer my calls?"

The truth was all Dani had left. "I thought maybe you'd come. If you hadn't, I planned on calling before I left in the morning."

"You're leaving?" Brianna stiffened, and her voice came out measured.

"Yes."

"I see." Brianna leaned back in her chair, almost as if she wanted to get as far away from Dani as possible.

It stung, but who could blame her? "I need a little time to get my head on straight. I'd like to request a leave of absence. One of the crew could cover Thundering Pines. I'd recommend Shawn."

Brianna sprang to her feet. "Seriously, I drove all the way out here in a raging storm, so my *employee* could ask for a leave of absence. That's fucked up, Dani."

Dani flinched. She knew Brianna was right. "Sorry. That came out wrong. Please, sit."

Brianna lowered herself back into her chair, but her posture remained guarded.

Dani ran her hand through her hair. "I need to go away for a little bit. Please, can't you respect that?"

"I want to, but I don't understand. You know I

wasn't trying to sell the campground, so why are you running from me?"

Great question. It had been one Dani had been agonizing over for the past several hours. When she'd run out of Aunt Helen's, she'd done it without thought. Once she'd gotten to the loft, she'd had time to think through everything. Her conviction grew. She needed time and space. "I have things I need to sort out. Figure out."

"But can't we do that together?" Brianna's jaw relaxed, and her gaze softened.

"No." Dani pointed at the box of letters she'd placed on the counter. "I've been afraid to open that."

"Is that the box of letters?"

Dani nodded.

"We can read them together." Brianna's voice was full of hope.

Dani shook her head. "I can't."

Brianna grimaced. "You're my best friend. I want to be here for you, and I don't understand why you won't let me. Why are you shoving me away for something I had nothing to do with?"

"I'm not shoving you away for that."

"But you're admitting you're shoving me away?"

Dani sighed and broke eye contact with Brianna. "Yes."

"I'm not trying to be dense." Brianna's tone was measured, as if she were trying to hold her exasperation at bay. "But I'm having trouble understanding. I get that Aunt Helen delivered some turn-your-world-upside-down news, but why wouldn't you want to walk through it with your best friend?"

"You're right. Helen kicked the final leg out from under the stool I was sitting on. But that's the thing, I was already balancing precariously on one leg. The other legs had already been kicked out from under me. I just didn't know it until I ended up flat on the floor."

Brianna ran her hand through her hair. "Whoa. Now I'm really confused. Why was your stool balancing on only one leg?"

"Oh, come on. You have to know that things have been messed up ever since Missouri."

"But we worked through it. Things have been better."

"You don't get it, do you?" Dani's limbs felt heavy, and she sank farther into the couch.

"I guess I don't, but I want to. How can I fix something I don't understand?"

Maybe it was the wrong time to have this conversation when Dani's thoughts and emotions swung in one direction and then another. *No.* This conversation was long overdue. "You kicked the other legs out from under me."

"What?" Brianna practically shouted. "You said you believed me."

"I do. The appraiser wasn't one of the legs."

"For God's sake, Dani. Can you just tell me what I have done so wrong, instead of making me figure out this puzzle?" Brianna leaned forward in her chair. Her gaze locked on Dani.

"Fine. Your friendship kicked out one leg. Up until you, I had all the friends I needed, and I didn't take the time to analyze how superficial they all were. I happily believed I had tons of friends. When, in reality, I had none. And now that I know what true friendship feels like, I can't pretend that I'm not alone."

"Damn it, Dani." Brianna crossed her arms over her chest and glared at Dani. "You are *not* alone. How many damned times do I have to tell you that? Am I fucking chopped liver? You know I get it. I feel the same way. You are the first real friend I've had in forever, too. We are two peas in a pod."

"The next leg got kicked out with the kiss," Dani said, moving on without responding to what Brianna said.

"What about the kiss?" Brianna's brow furrowed. "We talked it out. Everything was fine."

"Maybe for you." Dani's heart pounded. "I'm glad you were able to put it in a nice little box, put a ribbon on it, and toss it onto the shelf. It wasn't that easy for me."

"Who said it was that easy for me?"

"You acted like it," Dani said.

"So did you," Brianna shot back. Her face reddened.

"Touché." Dani sighed and rubbed her temples. "You're right. I thought it was what I was supposed to do."

"We did what we needed to do to make it right."

"Right for who?"

"Both of us. You have a mouth. If you weren't happy, don't you think you should have told me instead of running away from me?" Tears welled in Brianna's eyes, but she blinked them back.

"Yes." Dani's voice was barely over a whisper. She didn't want to be causing the pain on Brianna's face. "It isn't fair to you, and I'm sorry."

"I don't want your 'I'm sorry.' I want us to come up with a solution. Just like we did that night at the Greek Islands."

"And that is the third leg of the stool."

"What is?"

"Our conversation at the Greek Islands."

"How can that be a leg kicked out from under you? We talked things out and cleared the air." Brianna waved her hands in the air. "What in the hell am I missing?"

"I agreed to something I never should have. We pretended the kiss meant nothing, and so we went on acting as if everything was fine. We're just *buddies*." Dani said "buddies" as if it were a dirty word.

"Really? Just buddies. Listen to yourself." Brianna's fist clenched. "You are so much more to me than a buddy."

"Then why is a tiny piece of my heart torn off every time I'm with you? Bit by bit, the damage is done. Can someone survive if too much of their heart is removed?"

"Not fair," Brianna snapped. "How do I tear a piece of your heart off?"

"You don't. I do it to myself." Dani kept her voice low. She bit down hard, hoping to stem the tears that wanted to escape. Brianna rubbed her chest and gazed at Dani. Her eyes were so full of sadness that it threatened to break Dani. "I'm sorry."

Brianna opened her mouth and closed it. An internal battle raged in her eyes. Eventually, her gaze fell to her lap. "I think the same is happening to me," she said in a near whisper.

Dani exhaled. "Thank you for being honest."

"So what do we do?"

"You let me take a leave of absence, and I go find my mother."

"But I want to be there with you."

"You can't." Dani wished it weren't true, but she knew it was the best choice. "I know it probably hurts you, but I can't be around you. Not right now."

"But why? I can support you."

"I know you would, and you would make it so much easier for me. But it would only make my ties to you deeper than they already are."

"And that's a bad thing?"

Dani nodded. "Unfortunately, yes. Things are complicated enough between us. We can't add another layer to it. And I can't be dealing with everything between us and my mom at the same time. It would be too much. I'm barely hanging on now. I'd short-circuit."

"Fix us first. Would a couple months make that big of a difference?" Brianna said in a rush. She put her hand over her mouth and stared in horror. "God, that was selfish. I'm sorry. Of course you want to see her as soon as possible."

"It's okay. I've been wrestling with the same question for the past couple hours." Dani leaned forward. "But it has to be this way."

"But why?" Brianna's voice quivered.

"I'm not a whole person right now, and I didn't even realize it until you came along." Dani let the tears well in her eyes, tired of fighting them.

Hurt registered in Brianna's eyes. "What did I do so bad to you?"

"No!" Dani moved to the edge of the couch. Despite wanting to touch Brianna, she kept her hands on her own knees. "You've opened my eyes and made me realize I want more in my life. Nine months ago, I would have told you I was happy. Content."

"But now?"

"You've opened me up in ways I didn't even know I needed to be opened. I feel so alive when I'm with you. I've never been happier." Tears streamed down Dani's cheeks.

"Yeah, you look pretty damned happy to me." Brianna grinned, but her eyes didn't hold their normal sparkle.

Dani wanted to hug her for her attempt to lighten the mood, but she held back. "I just need to sort out how I got so messed up. I need to fix me."

"Both of us have our demons. Why can't we fight them together?"

Dani shook her head. "You don't know how tempting that is. But it won't work that way. Things are too complicated."

"Life is messy!" Brianna sat on the edge of her chair, so they were closer together.

Dani watched Brianna's lips move and quickly sat back against the couch to put distance between them. "It's not forever, Brianna. I'm doing this so I can come back and be the friend you need me to be. I just need to get my head on straight."

"What if I leave Caroline, and we give it a try?" Brianna's eyes widened, and she clamped her hand over her mouth.

Holy shit. Dani's pulse quickened. She needed to get this under control before things spiraled any further. She'd resort to what worked best between them. Humor. Dani chuckled. "Apparently, that one shocked you as much as it did me."

A shadow crossed Brianna's face, but then she smiled. "I just don't want you to go. I don't want to lose you."

Dani smirked. "Throwing yourself on me in a fit

of desperation probably won't improve the situation."

"Why? It worked so well in Missouri." Brianna sat back in her chair and put both hands on the top of her head. "Damn it, we're too good together to end things like this."

"Haven't you been listening? I'm not trying to end things. I'm trying to save them. If we keep impulsively reacting to every emotion we have, eventually, something bad is going to happen."

"Like the kiss?" Brianna's eyes narrowed.

Dani averted her gaze. "Yes. Like the kiss."

Brianna winced. "How can you say that was bad?"

"Because it's almost destroyed our friendship. It still could."

"Only if we let it." Brianna abruptly stood and went to the window. "This is all our choice. We're creating unnecessary problems for ourselves."

"Maybe so." Dani shrugged. "But we both have complications we can't ignore."

Brianna spun around. "Who said I wanted to ignore them?"

"That's what we've been doing for months. Now is the time that we both need to face our issues."

"And what issues would that be?" Brianna put her hands on her hips.

Dani let out a joyless chuckle. "I do believe we both have daddy issues."

Brianna's jaw clenched, and her eyes blazed. "Seriously?"

Dani stood and walked to the kitchen area. She no longer wanted to be seated while Brianna stood but also didn't want to be anywhere near her. It wouldn't take much for her to rush to Brianna and wrap her in a hug, which would be the worst thing she could do. "Do you want to hear what I think?"

"Sure, why the hell not?" The anger and sarcasm were evident in Brianna's voice. The daddy issue comment evidently hit a nerve.

"I've run around my entire adult life trying to appease my dead father. I broke his heart with Carl, so I sure as hell can't do it again by turning out like my mother." Dani took a deep breath. "So I've created an elaborate ruse. As long as I screw anyone and everyone, without emotion, then I don't dishonor him. How fucked up is that?"

"Oh, Dani." Brianna started toward her.

"No!" Dani held her hand up.

Brianna stopped. "But you can work on that. Figure it out."

"And that's what I'm trying to do, but I don't know how it will turn out. My promise to my dad messed me up. Bad. His disappointed face may haunt me forever and prevent me from having the relationship I want."

Brianna's eyebrows raised. By her reaction, Brianna knew Dani was talking about her. Brianna nodded. "I see."

"I'm hoping meeting my mom will help me work through some of it. I know I'm grasping at straws. But I can't deal with everything all at once. It's too much."

"But why are you letting your dad ruin everything for you because of something that happened so long ago?"

"You didn't just say that, did you?" Dani tried to keep her voice in check. "Come on, you've done the same."

"What do you..." Brianna dropped her gaze to

the floor. When she looked up, tears welled in her eyes. "You're right. I've stayed in a loveless relationship because I didn't want to be like that asshole. I've gone along with things I never should have, just so I wouldn't be like my parents."

"Yes. And after everything we've been through the last few months, you'd never once mentioned leaving Caroline until today. When you were desperate. And even now, I'm not sure you meant it."

Brianna's shoulders sagged. "But what about our friendship? Isn't it worth working on?"

It wasn't lost on Dani that Brianna switched back to the safer topic of their friendship. "Definitely. I'm not going away forever. I want to give *us* both time to get our heads on straight. Donald's death stirred up a lot of emotions in both of us. I suspect that once we get a little space between us and deal with our own shit, we'll discover that this was all a perfect storm."

"Meaning it's not real?" Brianna wrapped her arms around herself. "The hits just keep coming."

Dani sighed. "I didn't say it wasn't real. Circumstances brought us together, but we have things we need to work on. For ourselves."

"I still fail to understand why we can't work together." Brianna hugged herself tighter.

Dani threw up her hands. "Okay. I'll tell you. What if I decide that I'm going to ignore my father's wishes and be with a woman, but then you decide to stay with Caroline?"

Brianna's face fell.

"On the other hand, what if you leave Caroline, and then I decide that every time I kiss you that I see my father's disappointed face and run away?" Dani rubbed her face. "I'm not a good person, Brianna. I hurt a wonderful man for years, and I'm not about to do that to you."

Tears welled in Brianna's eyes, but she didn't speak.

"Now do you understand? We can't work on these things together. We have to figure our own shit without influencing each other."

"But what about our friendship?

Dani's chest ached. "I don't want to lose you. That's as real as I can get."

"But?"

Dani nodded. *Perceptive.* "But if we aren't careful, we could blow everything up. A little while ago, you almost made the knee-jerk decision to throw away your long-term relationship. What if we crossed those lines, and it didn't work out? Then we lose *everything.* I'm not willing to take that chance. Are you?"

Brianna's shoulders slumped, and she cast her gaze down. Dani waited for her to speak, but she didn't. Brianna wrung her hands in front of her but remained silent.

"Are you okay?" Dani asked tentatively.

Brianna shook her head, and her shoulders shook. "No."

Dani fought the urge to go to her, knowing she couldn't trust herself if they touched. "It'll be okay. We just need some space to get our heads on straight." Dani waited for Brianna to respond. When she didn't, Dani continued. "All I know is that I'm leaving here tonight to figure things out. Find my mom. And maybe find peace with my dad."

Brianna's gaze shot up. Her eyes wide. "You're leaving tonight? I thought you said in the morning."

"I did, but I don't think anything good can come out of me staying here." Dani rubbed her chest. "The pain is already too much."

"So that's it then? You're just going to walk out of here?" Brianna turned away and went back to the window.

The storm had moved off, but there were still traces of lightning in the distance. Dani approached the windows but went to the side opposite Brianna. "Yes. But it's not like that."

"What is it like then?" Brianna gazed up. She no longer tried to hide the hurt in her eyes.

"I just need to go away for a little while."

"How long?

"I don't know." Dani tried to smile but couldn't manage one. "However long it takes me to get my head screwed on straight." She gave Brianna the perfect chance to tease her. Would she take it?

"I wish you luck." Brianna continued to stare out the window.

Ouch. Pain stabbed into Dani's chest. Anger would have been better than Brianna's resignation. She wanted to rush to her and at least hug her, but that wouldn't be fair to Brianna. There was nothing more she could say. All the cards were on the table. She'd be back. They'd find a way to resume their friendship, but she wouldn't promise Brianna anything. She'd done enough damage. "Thanks."

Brianna didn't answer.

Dani picked up the box of letters off the counter and tucked them under her arm. She glanced at Brianna's back one last time. Tears streamed down her face. *Just go.* She needed to leave Brianna in peace.

Dani opened the door and descended the stairs.

Chapter Thirty-five

*B*rianna stumbled out of her Jeep. She couldn't remember when she'd ever felt so defeated. The weekend at Thundering Pines without Dani had been tortuous. She'd stayed an extra day to get everything set up for the week before heading home. The conversation with Dani left her raw. She'd picked up the phone so many times to call her, but she knew she had to let her be.

Dani was gone, and she'd left Thundering Pines in someone else's hands. She wasn't sure if it was a good idea or not, but she was left with little choice. Brianna still had her own job in the city. Her own life.

She hoped Caroline had already left for Kylie's house because she couldn't handle a confrontation tonight. She closed her eyes as she waited for the elevator. She refused to cry anymore; instead, she needed time to think. Dani couldn't be gone. She felt a hole in the middle of her chest just thinking about it.

A man pushed past her into the elevator before she realized the door had opened. It began to close as she stepped forward, but he held out his arm to stop it from closing on her.

She gave him a quick smile of thanks but couldn't bring herself to speak.

He must have sensed her mood because he flashed her a smile and turned away.

When she put her key in the door, she realized

that she didn't shake anymore when she did. It had been a while since she'd had that reaction. Maybe she finally trusted Caroline again, she thought, and then laughed at her own deception. The truth was, she didn't much care who Caroline slept with.

She pushed the door open and stiffened when she heard the television coming from the living room. The last thing she wanted to do was talk to Caroline. She doubted there was any chance Caroline accidentally left it on. She set down her bags and kicked off her shoes.

"Brianna? Is that you?" Caroline called from the other room.

"Yeah, I didn't think you'd be home." Brianna made her way into the living room, where Caroline was stretched out on the couch. She was wearing a pair of sweatpants and appeared to have removed her makeup. "Aren't you going to Kylie's for dinner?"

"Nah, I thought I'd spend the evening with you." Caroline turned off the television and looked at Brianna for the first time. "Holy shit, rough weekend?"

"That obvious?"

"No doubt." Caroline smiled. "You know I'm not the most observant, but even I can see you look like hell."

"Gee, thanks." Brianna sat in the recliner. She just wanted to be alone, but Caroline ruined those plans. Should she feign a migraine and crawl into bed?

"Care to talk about it?"

Had the world turned upside down? Since when did Caroline want to hear about her day or what was bothering her? "Didn't you have a big case today?"

"I was supposed to, but they settled first thing this morning, so I slipped out a little early."

Now she was sure she'd stumbled into the Twilight Zone. "Since when did you become someone that cuts out of work early?" She hoped it hadn't come out as snarky as she feared it might. "I mean, it just surprised me is all."

"You know, ever since the Henning case, things have changed. I don't see myself staying there much longer."

Brianna nodded, not sure what else she could offer the conversation. She closed her eyes and laid her head against the back of the chair. Maybe Caroline would be okay with her taking a little nap.

"You never answered why you look so bad," Caroline said.

"Lots of stuff to take care of at Thundering Pines." She certainly wasn't going to get into it with Caroline. She wasn't sure how she would handle it if Caroline called Dani names tonight.

"I've been thinking..." Caroline began and stopped.

Oh, God, words that nobody ever wants to hear. Can this day get any worse? "Yeah, thinking about what?"

"I think we should discuss our current arrangement."

Was Caroline breaking up with her? *Do I care?* "What arrangement is that?" Brianna said, her voice full of hesitation.

"Our open relationship."

"Wanting to expand the parameters?" Brianna was calm, as if she'd just asked, "What's for dinner?" She realized that was the level of emotion she felt.

"No, I think we should close it."

Am I being punked? When she had walked into

the apartment, she was sure the day couldn't get any weirder, but she'd been wrong. She struggled with a response and decided a non-response was the best. "And what brought that on?"

"I know how bad the Kylie thing hurt you."

A calm washed over Brianna. "Why do I love Ferris wheels?"

"What?"

"Answer the question. Why do I love Ferris wheels?"

Caroline's eyes narrowed, and she studied Brianna's face. "I don't know, something to do with when you were a kid."

Brianna smiled. "Why does Kylie have a koala tattoo on her ankle?"

"Did you just have an aneurysm?"

The expression on Caroline's face would have made her laugh any other time. "Just answer the question. Why does Kylie have a koala tattoo on her ankle?"

Caroline shook her head but answered. "Because her Grammy Marge always said she looked like a koala bear when her hair got all fuzzy and out of control."

"Who's Grammy Marge?"

"She was Kylie's mom's mom."

"Did you ever meet her?"

"What in the hell does this have to do with anything?"

"Humor me. Did you ever meet Grammy Marge?"

A smile crossed Caroline's face as she looked into the air. "She was the sweetest, kookiest lady I ever met. I remember how she used to chase us around the kitchen trying to feed us whenever we stopped by. She said I was too skinny."

"When did she die?"

Caroline glared at her. "What the fuck is this about, Brianna?"

"Answer," Brianna said more harshly than she intended.

"Fine, it was three years after we graduated from college. I had just started my new job in the city."

"I want to break up." A sense of relief washed over her as the words tumbled out of her mouth.

Caroline jumped up from the couch, her eyes wild, and she stood over Brianna. "What the fuck is wrong with you? You don't want to give up skunk girl, is that it?"

Wow. How had she missed it? "So that's what this is all about? You think I'm sleeping with Dani?"

"Aren't you?"

Brianna sighed. It was time to be honest. "Nope. We only shared one kiss."

"I don't fucking believe this. So you're going to sit there and calmly admit it?" Caroline's face reddened, and spittle flew from her mouth as she yelled.

Brianna pushed down the footrest on her chair and stood. Having Caroline tower over her was starting to feel uncomfortable, and she preferred not to have Caroline's spit raining down on her. "Yes, it was the agreement we had, remember? I'm done playing games."

Caroline smirked. "Hey, wait. You said one kiss. Does that mean skunk girl decided she didn't want you after all? Is that why you look like hell tonight?"

"This isn't about Dani. It's about us." Brianna was exhausted, but she knew she owed it to Caroline to finish the conversation. Suddenly, everything was clear. "I'm going into the office tomorrow and filing for a leave of absence, then I'm heading to Thundering Pines."

"What have you been smoking? You're leaving me for her?"

It wasn't lost on Brianna that Caroline hadn't called her skunk girl. "No, Dani is gone, and I need to run the campground."

Caroline's tears welled, but none spilled. She walked away from Brianna and plopped back onto the couch. Brianna almost felt sorry for her but knew Caroline would recover. "You're making absolutely no sense. So you're not leaving me for her?"

Brianna sighed and walked to the opposite end of the couch and sat. "Not in the traditional sense, no."

"What the hell kind of legalese is that?" Caroline's eyes flashed, and a little life returned to them.

Brianna smiled. "Sounds a little like something you would say, huh?"

"Actually, yes." Caroline returned the smile.

They sat not saying anything for several minutes, both lost in their own thoughts. Brianna wondered what Caroline was thinking. If they were honest, the relationship had been dying for years. *Who am I kidding?* It had always been based on making an impression, creating an image of the perfect couple. There was never anything real about their relationship, except it kept her from feeling like the shameful ten-year-old who sneaked out of town in the middle of the night.

A stab of pain twisted in her gut. It had been so easy for her to think of herself as the wronged party, especially with Caroline's powerful personality, but she realized it wasn't true. She wasn't a victim; she'd played her own part in everything. Hadn't she used Caroline, too? How better to feel worthy than have someone like Caroline on her arm?

Brianna broke the silence. "So where do we go from here?"

"How the hell should I know? This seems to be your show, not mine." The earlier venom was gone from Caroline's voice. It seemed that the original shock had already worn off.

"Maybe you should be with Kylie," Brianna said, recognizing the truth in her own words.

"Is that what this is about? I told you, I'm done with that." Caroline relaxed against the back of the couch. "Here I thought you were serious."

"I'm serious about it all. I love you. I once thought we had something, but it's been long in the past. I'm not in love with you. It's time for both of us to move on." It wasn't necessary for her to tell Caroline that she loved Dani on an entirely different level. It would only hurt her and serve no real purpose; besides, she may never have Dani. She knew it was no longer right to be with Caroline, regardless of what happened with Dani.

"But you said Danielle was gone." Caroline stared into her eyes. Brianna was sure she was trying to figure out if Brianna was telling the truth. It was also the first time she'd used Dani's name; progress was happening.

"She's gone, and I don't know if she'll be back. But this isn't about her, it's about us. It's about you. Believe it or not, I want you to be happy. And Kylie is the only person I have ever known that truly makes you happy. Why didn't you ever date her?"

"Are we really having this conversation?" Caroline

looked down at her hands that rested in her lap and picked at her fingernail.

"Yes, we are." Brianna patted her knee. "Tell me why you didn't."

"She didn't have the right look."

"Seriously?" She was caught off guard by Caroline's shallow answer.

"Not for me, for my family." Caroline continued to study her fingernails. "Ironic, isn't it? My family was fine with me being a lesbian as long as I picked the right woman, but Kylie wasn't that woman."

"And I was?"

Caroline smiled. "You were perfect. Beautiful, cold, and guarded, just like my family."

"Ouch," Brianna said and then laughed. A real laugh that came from her gut. Caroline's eyebrows shot up, but she was soon laughing with her.

"I was so excited my junior year when I brought Kylie home to meet my family. We were just friends, but I wanted them to love her like I did. They didn't. They found her crude, unpredictable, and beneath me."

Brianna's eyes widened. "They told you that?"

"Yep, my father pulled me aside before we left while my mother kept Kylie busy. I never told her about it. We were best friends, and I'm fairly sure she wanted more, too, but I pulled back after that. She never complained, and she's been by my side all these years."

"She makes you a better person," Brianna said, surprised by her own honesty. "You smile more. You laugh more. You're full of life when she's around. We've never had that."

"Don't say that." Caroline frowned.

"It's okay. It's true."

Caroline nodded. "Dani does that for you, doesn't she?"

It was Brianna's turn to nod. "She does."

"You're in love with her." Caroline said it as a statement, not a question.

Brianna felt tears welling in her eyes. "Yes," she said in a near whisper. But she'd waited too long to admit it to herself, even though she'd known for longer than she cared to admit.

"Maybe things would have been different if we'd been able to talk like this before."

"No, we can't think that way." Brianna held up her hand. Even though Dani was gone, she couldn't allow herself to cling to Caroline for fear of being alone. "You need to tell Kylie how you feel."

"What about you?"

"It's too late for me. I wasn't lying when I said Dani is gone. But I need to rebuild my life, and you need to be happy."

"Do you want me to stay home with you tonight?"

"No, I want you to go and find Kylie. And I'm going to tell you now, I don't want you coming home tonight."

Caroline started to protest, but Brianna stopped her. "No, Caroline. You will feel obligated to come home, and I don't want you to have to make that decision. You've broken her heart for too long. Tonight, you choose her."

Brianna watched Caroline struggle with a response, but Caroline settled on the simplest. "Thank you."

Brianna stood from the couch. "I'm going to pack a few things tonight. Is it okay if I leave most of my stuff here until I figure out what to do with it?"

"Certainly." Caroline stood and walked to where Brianna stood. "Can I give you a hug?"

"You better," Brianna said with a genuine smile and stepped into Caroline's arms.

Chapter Thirty-six

A voice called Brianna's name, and she looked up from Dani's desk. "Hey, Molly. Sorry, I was trying to get this damned checkbook to balance." She stood and gave Molly a hug. "What brings you here?"

"I stopped by Helen's to see you, and she said I'd probably find you here." Molly gave her a concerned look. "Says you're here most of the time. Which might explain the lack of response to my texts and calls."

Brianna lowered her gaze to the floor and mumbled, "Sorry." When Molly touched her arm, she flinched. "Sorry," she said again.

"Brianna, what's going on?" Molly squeezed her arm. "It's time to give up the tall, dark, and mysterious vibe."

Tears puddled in Brianna's eyes, and she blinked several times, hoping to stop the flow. It only seemed to make it worse as a drop escaped down her cheek. *Damn it.* She wasn't going to do this in front of Molly. That was what the loft was for. She went there most nights and got this out of her system, so she could continue to function during the rest of her day.

"Please, talk to me," Molly said. "I know you're in pain. Helen knows you're in pain, but we don't know what to do."

Brianna's heart ached. She rubbed her chest, hoping to alleviate some of the pressure. She finally shifted her gaze to Molly. *Mistake.* Her heart seized. Molly's kindness and concern were almost more than she could take. If she allowed herself to let go, she wasn't sure when she would stop.

It was as if Molly sensed she was teetering because she moved closer and put her arm around Brianna's shoulder. "Brianna, it's okay. You're hurting. You've got lots of shit going on. You need to talk about it. Get it out, so you can figure out how to move forward."

The words, the touch, and the kindness were too much. Brianna buried her face in her hands, and the floodgates opened.

Molly gripped her shoulder tighter and moved toward the couch.

Brianna followed, her resistance gone.

Molly maneuvered her onto the couch and sat next to her.

Brianna kept her hands over her face, and the tears flowed harder.

"It's okay." Molly lightly rubbed her back. "Get it all out of your system, and then we can talk."

Brianna wasn't sure how long they sat on the couch, but when the tears finally stopped, she felt relieved and wrung out all at once. She shot a sideways glance at Molly. "I don't know where that came from."

"Let's see. Maybe I can help you with that." Molly put her hand gently on Brianna's chin and turned her face, so she was looking at Molly. "Over the last five months, your dad who you'd not spoken to in years died, you inherited a campground, you've left your job in the city to run it, your sister's hatred almost caused it to be burned down, you're trying to forgive her and begin anew, you've returned to your hometown that you left in disgrace, you broke up with your long-term girlfriend, you fell in love, and then she walked out the door." Molly put her hand to her chin and shook her head. "Nope, I can't figure out why you'd be struggling. Apparently, you just can't handle stress."

"When did my life turn into a fucking soap opera?" Laughter broke through her tears.

"I'm thinking two or three of those things would be enough for a mere mortal, but apparently, you feel the need to one-up everyone." Molly smiled. "You've built up one hell of a shield, but, my friend, it's time it comes down."

The pain flooded back into her chest. "The shield had come down. I was handling all the other stuff because Dani was here, but now she's gone and might never come back."

Molly put her hand on Brianna's leg. "And notice, you didn't deny that you fell in love."

Brianna clutched her chest and said in a near whisper, "I can't deny it. Fuck me! I'm in love with Dani."

"Wow, really? Shocker," Molly said with mock surprise. "Nobody saw that coming. Oh, wait, maybe someone noticed the first time she saw you two together. Who was that brilliant woman?"

Brianna smiled. "Fine, smarty. You called it. But what do I do about it? She's been gone for over three weeks. She may never come back."

"You're right." Molly nodded.

"Gee, thanks. That was reassuring."

"But you didn't let me finish." Molly's face was a mask of determination. "Or you can take charge of the situation."

"How?"

"You're both in pain. Scared. One of you must be courageous. And since I'm sitting here talking to you, not Dani, I'm nominating you."

Brianna's breath caught. What the hell was Molly suggesting? "What if I reach out, and she doesn't respond? Or worse, rejects me?"

"Then your heart gets ripped out, and you're driven to your knees."

Was this supposed to be a pep talk? Brianna shot Molly a look.

Molly continued. "And then you stand back up, let your friends brush you off, and eventually, you get back out in the world and try again."

Brianna started to protest, but Molly held up her hand. "On the other hand, maybe Dani needs you to reach out, and if you don't, you may be letting the best thing that has ever happened to you walk out the door because you were afraid."

Brianna put her hand on the back of her neck and rubbed the tight muscles. "You make it sound so easy."

"Nope, it won't be easy." Molly smiled. "I'm returning the favor you did for me years ago. It changed my life, even though I was pissed at you. You had the courage to tell me the truth. To tell me I could do better." Molly stood. "So you can be pissed at me and not talk to me for over a decade like I did you, but I'm willing to take that chance. You need to open your heart and take the risk of rejection. The choice is yours." Molly waved her hand at Brianna. "But this is no way to feel. Pull the Band-Aid off and get your answer."

"But she asked for space. Maybe I haven't given her enough."

"Or maybe she's embarrassed and doesn't know

how to reach out to you now."

"But which is it?"

Molly shrugged. "No way to know. I can't make you any promises. But I'll be here to cheer you on or to pick up the pieces."

"Thank you." Brianna looked up at Molly and held out her hand.

Molly took it and helped her to her feet.

Brianna wrapped her arms around Molly. "I'm not going to run away for a decade."

"Oh, thank God." Molly exhaled. "You did not want to be in my brain. All I could think is, 'what in the fuck are you doing, dumbass?'"

Brianna laughed. "Thank you for your dumbass advice." She bumped Molly's hip with hers. "You know if I get my heart stepped on, I'm going to be on your doorstep."

"I wouldn't want it any other way."

⊰⊰⊱⊱

Brianna pushed her food around her plate but hadn't eaten much of it. Aunt Helen continued to make amazing meals, but neither seemed to have much of an appetite. It wasn't lost on Brianna that Aunt Helen continued to make all Dani's favorites.

Brianne looked across the table, and her heart clenched. Aunt Helen had aged ten years in three weeks. She'd broken Dani's heart but broken her own worse. Her shoulders were stooped, and her normally lively eyes were flat. Dani's absence was ripping them both apart.

"Molly stopped by Thundering Pines today," Brianna said.

"She's such a sweet girl." Aunt Helen smiled.

"She stopped by here looking for you. I hope it was okay I told her where you were."

"Of course."

They ate, or rather pushed their food around in silence, for several minutes.

"What was she up to?" Aunt Helen broke the silence.

Do I go there? "She's been worried about me. I haven't been very good at returning her calls or texts."

Aunt Helen nodded. "I think she's a good friend for you. Don't let what's happening with…with…the situation mess up your friendship."

Sad. She couldn't even say Dani's name. Neither of them had. It was too painful, but Molly was right. "She told me that I need to be courageous and not let Dani get away."

Aunt Helen flinched at the sound of Dani's name, but she remained silent.

Brianna sighed. "She's right. I wanted to get your opinion."

"About?" Aunt Helen asked, hesitation evident in her voice.

"I want to reach out to Dani and ask her to talk."

"She might say no." Aunt Helen blinked back tears.

"I know."

"Can you handle that?"

Brianna shrugged. "I don't know. But I do know that we can't sit around here pushing our food around our plate night after night."

Aunt Helen's gaze met hers. "I have to tell you how proud I am of you. I know your heart is broken, but you've been a champion."

Brianna looked away. "I do what I have to do."

"No," Aunt Helen said with more force. "You've rolled up your sleeves and did what you needed to do to run the campground."

"What choice did I have?" The conversation made her uncomfortable. She wasn't used to having someone saying they were proud of her.

"You could have turned it over to the staff to run and had the Realtor put it on the market, but you didn't."

No. "Dani loves Thundering Pines, so I could never sell it."

"I think you're falling in love with it, too."

Yep. But which did she fall in love with first? Dani or Thundering Pines? "I am."

"Would you keep it even if she never comes back?" Aunt Helen swallowed hard a couple of times. She'd still not been able to say Dani's name.

"I think I would." Brianna put her hand on the table hard. "But Dani not coming back is not an option. If she doesn't want me around, I'd be a silent partner and let her run it."

"We're not gonna talk like that." Aunt Helen stood and carried her barely eaten plate of food to the garbage. "I want her to come back, and I want you here, too."

Warmth spread over Brianna's chest. "It's settled. I'm going to reach out to her and see what happens."

Aunt Helen blinked back tears. "I never meant to hurt her. I want to get the chance to make it up to her."

"I know." Brianna took her plate to the garbage.

"Bring our girl back." Aunt Helen had hope in her eyes for the first time in three weeks.

"I'm gonna do my best."

Chapter Thirty-seven

*B*rianna peered out the window at the Ferris wheel, trying to calm her jagged nerves. She'd checked into the Sable at Navy Pier an hour ago and quickly regretted arriving so early. She'd unpacked her suitcase and put her clothes in the drawers. It was a ridiculous gesture since she was only staying one night, but she had to keep herself busy.

The butterflies danced in her stomach. This was the first time she would ride it, but that wasn't the reason for her nerves. Would Dani show up?

Dani had been gone for nearly a month. Since she'd left, she'd only heard from Dani once. It was a simple text that read: *I've made contact with my mom. I'm doing okay. I didn't want you to worry.*

Brianna responded back with: *I'm so happy for you!!!!!*

Dani responded with a smiley face.

She was reminded of Dani everywhere. She'd been staying with Aunt Helen, where Dani hung in the air like a mist. She used Dani's office and left all of Dani's personal items on the desk and walls, not replacing them with her own. She was afraid if she did, it would mean that Dani was never coming back. It was the loft that was the hardest place for her to be, but she went there often. She watched the sunset every evening, but tonight, she would watch it from the Ferris wheel. Would Dani?

Brianna couldn't stand it any longer. Life was strange. If someone handed her a script that first day in Dunhurst's office of what her life would be from that day forward, she would have laughed at them and told them they were crazy. She wasn't laughing now. Her life had been turned upside down and inside out, mostly for the better. But she wanted someone to write a happy ending.

Three days ago, she sat at her computer and spent two hours composing an email. She wrote and rewrote it at least a dozen times. In the end, she kept it short and simple.

Dani,

I miss you. There are so many things I need to say to you. So many things I want you to hear. I have rented one of the gondolas in the Navy Pier Ferris wheel (I know, I'm braving it) on Tuesday from 7 to 9 p.m. I will be there and hope you will join me.

Love, Bri

There had been no response from Dani. She couldn't even be sure she'd read it. She knew Dani was diligent about checking her email several times a day, so she had to hope she'd seen it. What if Dani didn't show up? She pushed the thought away; it was too late to change her mind. It could be the most excruciating two hours of her life.

It was six thirty. She only had half an hour; she should probably make her way to the pier. A quick check of her reflection in the mirror reminded her of the work she'd been doing at the campground.

Working outside gave her the best tan of her life. It gave her a healthy glow, the same look that Dani always sported. She ran her fingers through her hair that fell loosely to her shoulders. *This was more nerve-wracking than a blind date.* She took one last look and turned away.

⚜⚜⚜⚜

Brianna's gaze darted around, searching all the faces in the crowd. She hoped to see Dani but didn't. Having arrived fifteen minutes early, she sat on the bench, so she could scan the crowd easier. The minutes ticked by with no Dani sightings. *What did I expect?* Dani standing by the Ferris wheel with her big grin, but that wasn't happening. She wasn't going to feel dejected yet. There would be two hours for her to ride alone with her thoughts.

She stood and took a deep breath. It was time. With a half-smile, she greeted the ride operators. "I'm expecting another party to join me, but she might not be able to make it." That should cover herself, so she didn't have to deal with their looks of pity two hours later if Dani didn't show.

"You will have to wait here for the VIP gondola to arrive. Have you ridden before?" the ride operator said.

"Not this one. I loved the old one," Brianna answered.

"This one's a beauty," he said. "You'll love it, especially having the glass floor. There's been lots of marriage proposals in the car you're about to ride in."

Was he fishing for information? She needed to calm down. He was just making conversation. She nodded.

"When it arrives, you'll go up those stairs, and the doors will slide open. You're not afraid of heights, are you?"

"No," Brianna said, surprised by the question.

"You just seemed a little jumpy, so I thought maybe you were."

She put on her best smile, hoping this conversation would end soon. "Nope, just excited to get in and start my journey."

"Only be a couple more minutes." He pointed. "There's your gondola there."

She climbed the stairs, and when the door slid open, she entered. She glanced around once more, hoping to see Dani. She didn't.

The gondola started its ascent while she continued to scan the crowd, until she could no longer make out the faces on the ground no matter how hard she strained. She pulled her gaze from the ground and took in the breathtaking view of the city. Chicago from this vantage point had always been her favorite, so she focused all her attention on it. She located all the familiar buildings. The Sears Tower. *Not the Willis Tower*. Then she shifted her gaze to the Hancock Building.

A familiar ache settled in her chest as she remembered the day she'd spent with Dani and Aunt Helen at the pier. *Don't cry. Breathe*. The glass floor under her drew her attention. She breathed in deeply, not wanting to cry. It had only been five minutes, so she couldn't start crying already, or she'd be a hot mess when she exited.

The Ferris wheel completed its first rotation, so she stared at the ground again, searching the people milling around. Would she be able to spot Dani in the crowd? She wasn't sure from this height if she could, but it didn't stop her from trying.

Her gondola approached the loading area. She didn't realize that she held her breath until the loading gate passed and she made a loud exhale. One rotation and no Dani. She sat back in her seat. How many circles were left? She did a rough estimate in her head. About twenty more trips around. Plenty of time.

After the third rotation, she was beginning to lose hope. She no longer examined the buildings but stared out over the lake instead. The water was calm tonight, unlike her insides. She tried to draw on the serenity of Lake Michigan, needing to find peace somewhere. She was lost in her thoughts when she heard the gondola door slide open.

Dani entered, and Brianna froze. She was dressed in a pair of jeans and a long-sleeved denim shirt. Her hair hung loose, and the silver in her hair glistened in the waning sunlight. She gave Brianna a tentative smile, but it was her eyes that captured Brianna's attention. While her expressive hazel eyes were still beautiful, they were strained.

I need to say something. Or should she get up and hug Dani? Instead, she sat speechless.

Dani pointed off to the west. "Sunset was always our time of day, so I thought I'd wait for the perfect moment."

"You've got to be kidding me," Brianna said. "You've let me ride around all by myself, going in circles waiting for the freaking sunset."

Dani smirked. "That and I might have been working up the courage to hop on."

Brianna leapt to her feet and wrapped her arms around Dani. She didn't even try to hide her tears.

She clung to Dani and cried. She didn't realize how many pent-up emotions she had until the floodgates opened.

Dani hugged her back, but she shed no tears. "Bri, it's okay. Please don't cry."

"Dani Thorton, I've missed the fuck out of you."

Dani laughed. "I've missed your eloquence."

Brianna smiled. "Would you like to have a seat?"

Dani's gaze traveled between the seat next to Brianna and the one across from her. Dani sat across from her.

She doesn't want to sit next to me. That's okay, she's here. "How have you been?" Brianna said, not knowing what else to say.

"Okay. And you?"

"I'm surviving."

"Looks like you've got yourself quite the tan."

Brianna raised her hand to her face. "That's what running a campground does for you."

Dani's eyebrows shot up. "You're running Thundering Pines?"

"Yep." Brianna wanted to say something clever but was afraid it would come out wrong or accusatory.

"Isn't it hard managing from the city?"

"I'm living in Flower Hills." *Should I tell her the rest?* "With Aunt Helen."

"I see."

Brianna searched Dani's face for a negative reaction; when she didn't see one, she continued. "It's been good for both of us."

"What about Caroline?"

"We broke up."

Dani sat up straighter, and her eyes widened. "Wow. Lots happened since I walked out."

Brianna nodded. "What about you? What have you been up to?"

Dani glanced out the window as the sun continued to set. "I love twilight. We can still see the buildings, but the lights are starting to come on."

Brianna looked in the same direction. "The view is beautiful this time of day."

"That's why I waited. There's something magical about it." Dani turned back to Brianna. "Why did you break up?"

Dani hadn't answered Brianna's question, but she was going to let Dani decide how the conversation would play out. "I broke up with her right after you left."

"I see. Strange timing."

"I realized I didn't love her anymore, so there was no sense pretending. Besides, I knew she was better matched with Kylie."

"Holy shit. So she's with Kylie now?"

"Yes, has been since the day I cut her loose."

"Wow, I've only been gone for a month."

"Three weeks and five days, but who's counting?" Brianna said, trying to lighten the mood.

"I'm sorry." Dani's eyes turned sad.

It wasn't the reaction Brianna was going for. "No, Dani. I didn't say it to make you feel bad. I was hoping to make you laugh. But you don't seem to be in the laughing mood."

"No, I guess I'm not."

Brianna's stomach roiled. *Did Dani come to say goodbye?* The thought never occurred to her until now. When she had seen Dani standing in the door, she hoped it meant she was coming back. *What if that wasn't it?* Brianna suddenly felt vulnerable and crossed her arms over her chest.

Dani must have noticed the change in Brianna. "I'm sorry."

"Why did you come?" fell out of Brianna's mouth. She hoped it didn't sound harsh, but the walls were closing in on her. They were nearing the bottom of a rotation, and one of them could get out if she needed to.

Dani looked up and held Brianna's gaze. "I fucked up. I hurt the two people I love most in this world. And I didn't know how to fix it."

"No, you had a lot to deal with. You didn't fuck up."

"The first week, maybe not. But letting it go on for three weeks and five days..." Dani gave her a hint of a smile. "That was too long. You guys deserved better from me. I made you both worry. Then I didn't know how to make it right."

"You're here now." Hope rose in her.

"I am. But I should have been the one reaching out to you. And to be honest, I almost didn't come."

"What changed your mind?"

Dani smiled a real smile for the first time. "My mom."

"So you made contact?"

"Yep. I found *my mom.*" Another goofy grin crossed her face. "Do you know how long I've wanted to be able to say those words?"

Without thinking, Brianna crossed the gondola and wrapped her arms around Dani. "I'm so happy for you. Tell me about it."

"After I left, I spent three more days holed up in a motel room reading and rereading my mom's letters. Then I found her house. It took me a couple of days to approach her. I hung around the neighborhood and watched."

"Stalker."

Dani laughed. "Right? Luckily, I didn't get pulled in by the police. I finally got up the nerve to knock on her door."

"And?"

"Phyllis answered."

"Phyllis?"

"Her wife."

"The same woman she left your dad for?"

"Yep. They've been together for thirty-one years. Phyllis took one look at me and screamed."

"You have that effect on people," Brianna said, patting Dani's leg.

"God, I've missed you." Dani put her hand on top of Brianna's. "No matter how intense something is, you always know how to make me smile."

"Okay, enough of the sappy shit. I want to know what happened." Brianna winked. For the first time since Dani arrived, she felt hope.

"Phyllis screamed, and then called out 'Lydia.' As soon as I saw her, I understood. She could have been my older sister. I can't remember what happened next. It was a blur. Hugging and crying." Dani stopped and looked into Brianna's eyes. "It was amazing."

"I'm so happy for you." Brianna blinked back tears.

"I have a brother and a sister."

"Seriously?"

"And I'm going to be an aunt."

"And you said I had a lot going on in three weeks and five days. Holy fuck, you have an entire family."

Dani couldn't contain her smile. "I have a family.

I never thought I would say those words. And how fucking cool, I'm going to be an aunt?"

"You'll make a great one." Brianna couldn't stop smiling. "How did your mom react?"

"She cried and hugged me and cried some more and hugged me some more. I've been staying with them and getting to know everyone."

"I want to hear everything about them."

Dani pointed out across the water. "We can't miss that." She held Brianna's hand, and they sat in silence as the last light faded from the sky.

The Ferris wheel made a complete rotation before either spoke. "What are your brother's and sister's names?"

"Karen and Andy."

"Tell me about them. What do they do? What are they like?"

Dani turned toward Brianna. "There's something else I need to talk to you about." Dani's demeanor was suddenly serious.

Brianna tensed. She wanted the happy playful Dani back. *Oh, shit, did she go in search of her high school girlfriend, too?* Brianna's heart sank. "Why so serious?"

"I have to tell you this, or I probably never will." Dani paused and looked down at the glass floor, no longer able to look at Brianna. "I'm in love." It came out in a rush, so it took Brianna a moment to realize what she said.

Brianna closed her eyes. "Julie?"

"Who the hell's Julie?" Dani asked.

"From high school."

Dani laughed. "No! Seriously?"

"I just thought. Well, since you were revisiting

your past and all. I thought maybe you searched her out, too." Brianna held her breath. Could she allow herself to hope?

"Are you serious? Oh, for fuck's sake, I'm in love with you." Dani groaned. "That didn't come out like I imagined it."

"And how did you imagine it?" Brianna felt a rush of adrenaline but was trying to remain calm.

Dani smirked. "I thought maybe you'd throw yourself into my arms and tell me that you were in love with me, too."

"Pretty cocky, aren't you?" Brianna smiled and slid closer to Dani. Before Dani could reply, Brianna put her hand against Dani's cheek and leaned toward her. She whispered, "I love you, too," before their lips met.

The kiss started out slow and soft. It was tender, and their lips barely brushed together. Dani pulled her closer and ran her hand up the length of Brianna's back. Brianna's heart beat out of her chest, and her hands trembled.

Their lips pressed together harder. *Slow down.* Brianna reduced the pressure and lightly ran her tongue along Dani's lower lip.

Dani let out a throaty moan that sent a spark to Brianna's center.

Brianna slipped her hand inside Dani's shirt and touched the soft skin along her side. Brianna's face was warm, and she was having trouble catching her breath.

Dani thrust her tongue between Brianna's lips, and Brianna lightly sucked it in.

"Oh, fuck," Dani said, breaking the kiss. Her face was as ruddy as Brianna's.

"I'm sorry. Did I do that wrong? I was supposed to leap into your arms."

Dani chuckled. "Your version was okay."

"Just okay? I need to do better than that," Brianna said, moving toward Dani again.

"No!" Dani held up her hand. "I can't promise what happens next if you do that again."

Brianna's heart clenched. In her joy, she'd let herself hope, but she still needed to be sure. "But when we talked...three weeks and five days ago..." She hoped the joke would hide her nerves. "When we talked, you said you might be too broken to ever be able to have a relationship with me. You made it pretty clear. What's changed?"

"Time. Perspective," Dani said, but Brianna could sense her nervousness. "I was a wreck when we talked. Everything was so fresh. I was hurt. I was scared. When you said you'd leave Caroline for me, I almost rushed across the room and professed my love."

Brianna put her hand on Dani's arm. "What stopped you?"

"Fear, mostly." Dani rubbed her chest. "I didn't get out of bed for two days. I cried, read letters, and slept. When I got up, I knew I couldn't come to you. I'd backed you into a corner when you said you'd leave her for me. I didn't want it like that because I never would know if it was truly what you wanted. If we were going to give this a try, it couldn't be a knee-jerk reaction just to stop the pain we were feeling."

"I know we both needed space to process everything, but..." Brianna grabbed the front of Dani's shirt and pulled her toward her. "Don't you ever do that to me again, Danielle Delilah Thorton."

Dani raised her hands in surrender. "I got it. I got it. Sheesh."

"Apparently, this is the proposal gondola." Brianna raised her eyebrows. "I'm sure there have been other interesting things happening here." Brianna dragged her hand down Dani's arm and intentionally brushed against her nipple when she did.

Dani jumped.

Brianna giggled and said, "Oops, my bad."

"Jesus, you can't do that. I already feel like I'm going to explode." She glanced around the car helplessly. "And it's gonna be awhile before I can release some of this tension."

"Maybe not as long as you think." Brianna moved in, and Dani didn't stop her. Their lips met. Brianna sucked Dani's lip between hers and ran her tongue over it. The move was supposed to inflame Dani, but Brianna felt the sensation travel down her body to her center. She gasped and moved away.

"That was mean," Dani whined. "Can someone die from sexual tension?"

"I think I can take care of that for you."

"Not here." Dani eyebrows shot up.

"I have a room in the hotel right over there." Brianna pointed at the Sable.

"You tramp. You planned to seduce me all along." Dani winked.

"Truthfully, I was afraid you wouldn't come. I planned on going straight to Bubba Gump's and drink myself silly. Then I'd stumble back to my room and pass out."

"Wow, that's pathetic," Dani teased. "Good thing my mom made me come."

"Yeah, we got sidetracked by that kiss. But I

want to hear what your mom told you."

Dani grinned. "I didn't tell her about you until last week." She looked away. "She caught me on the patio one morning with tears streaming down my face. I had to tell her what I'd done. She wanted me to call you right then and there. She nagged me for days until your email came."

"And you still thought of not coming?"

"For about five minutes. I felt horrible about how I'd handled things. I figured you and Aunt Helen hated me." Dani's eyes filled with tears. "Does she know you're here?"

"She does."

"And she approves?"

"Of course she does. She loves you more than anything."

"But I broke her heart."

She wasn't going to lie to Dani. "Yes, you did. But she figured she deserved it for what she did to you."

"It wasn't all her fault. Once I calmed down, I understood what a tough choice she had. I think she chose wrong, but it's easy for me to sit back and play armchair quarterback." Dani's face was full of pain. "As much as I loved my dad, what he did to all of us was wrong."

Brianna wasn't sure how to respond. Dani worshiped her dad, and she didn't feel comfortable criticizing him, but she needed to say something. "He let your mom leaving him poison everything."

"No doubt. And I let it poison everything I touched, too."

"It poisoned Aunt Helen, too. You might forgive her, but I'm not sure if she'll ever forgive herself."

"There's a lot of healing that needs to be done yet. But I love my mom, and I love Aunt Helen, so we'll figure it out."

"There's someone else who you need to show some love to."

"Really? Who?" Dani pretended to scan the gondola.

Brianna grabbed Dani by the shirt and pulled her close. "By the way, nice outfit. I don't remember seeing it before." Was Dani blushing?

"My mom helped pick it out."

Brianna threw her head back and laughed. "Your mom helped you pick out your date clothes?"

"Is this a date?" Dani smiled. "In that case..." She pulled Brianna to her and brought her lips to Brianna's.

When they separated, both were breathless. "We need to get off this thing," Brianna said.

Dani glanced at her watch. "But we've got nearly forty-five minutes."

"I don't have forty-five minutes." Brianna wriggled her eyebrows. "Unless you want me to explode."

※ ※ ※ ※

Dani subtly ran her sweaty palm down the side of her jeans. She didn't want Brianna to know how nervous she was.

Brianna fumbled with the keycard. Dani made her task harder by running her hand across Brianna's stomach.

"Would you stop that, or we'll never get inside?"

Dani moved her hand higher and gently touched Brianna's breast.

Brianna smiled. "Didn't I tell you to stop that?"

"You told me to stop touching your side," Dani said, pretending innocence.

"I swear if you don't stop, I'm going to do you right in the middle of the hallway."

As she said it, an older couple rounded the turn and gave them a disgusted look.

Dani stifled a laugh and pulled her hands back, letting Brianna unlock the door.

They tumbled into the room, both laughing.

Their laughter soon stopped when Dani moved toward Brianna. Brianna let herself be pushed against the closed door.

Dani felt as if she'd run a sprint. Her heart pounded, and her breathing was ragged. She'd had sex with more people than she could count, so why was she so damned nervous?

Brianna's hand snaked under Dani's shirt, and she raked her fingernails over the small of Dani's back.

Dani shuddered, her nerves forgotten.

Their lips found each other. Dani rubbed her nipple while Brianna caressed Dani's buttocks. The kiss increased in intensity, and they continued to explore each other's bodies.

Dani stepped away.

"What are you doing?" Brianna's voice was breathy.

"If we don't stop, I'm going to cum."

"What's wrong with that?" Brianna moved toward Dani but stopped, a look of understanding crossed her face. "You want this to be different."

"It is different." Dani's voice was barely over a whisper. "As much as I want you, I want more."

Brianna smiled. "Okay." She took Dani's hand. "Let's have ourselves a drink and get undressed. What would you like?"

"I'll just have a bottle of water. I don't want alcohol to cloud anything I'm feeling."

"Two waters coming up." Brianna twisted the caps off the water and handed one to Dani. She kicked off her shoes, turned down the bed, and sat.

Dani stood stock-still by the window, taking tiny sips from her water bottle.

Brianna went to Dani. "It's okay."

"I've never made love with anyone. It's always just been sex." Dani studied Brianna.

The wheels spun behind Brianna's eyes, and a smirk played on her lips. "I've always wanted to make it with a virgin."

Dani laughed and felt the tension leave her body.

"Oh, good, you've got your sense of humor back. Dark and brooding doesn't become you." Brianna licked her lips with an exaggerated flick of her tongue.

"Are you planning on jabbering the whole time we do this?" Dani shot back.

"Maybe."

"Remind me again why I thought this would be a good idea."

"Because you love me."

Dani gently brushed Brianna's hair off her face. She let her palm cup her cheek. Brianna's skin felt like silk under her fingertips. "I do love you, Brianna. I love you so much it scares me."

"We can be scared together." Brianna took Dani's hand in hers, brought Dani's palm to her lips, and planted featherlight kisses in the center.

An electric charge ran up Dani's arm, followed by goose bumps. Her lips parted, and a soft moan escaped.

"I love you, too," Brianna said,

They started tentatively, slowly undressing each other. Dani fumbled with the buttons on Brianna's shirt.

Brianna put her hand over Dani's to calm her tremble. "Let me help."

Dani let Brianna guide her to each button. When the last was undone, Brianna's shirt fell to the floor.

With one hand, Dani adeptly unhooked her bra.

"I guess you're a little better at that than buttons," Brianna said, her lips inches from Dani's ear.

Brianna's hot breath made Dani's heart race. Dani ran her hand up the length of Brianna's naked torso. She lingered as she admired her long, lean muscles. Dani brought her hands to Brianna's breasts and gently cupped them. They fit perfectly in her palms. She caressed Brianna's nipples with her thumbs.

Brianna moaned. She slowly unbuttoned Dani's shirt while Dani continued her gentle teasing of Brianna's nipples. Soon Dani's shirt and bra were in a pile on the floor with Brianna's. Naked from the waist up, Dani pressed her body against Brianna's.

As their warm skin touched, Dani closed her eyes and moaned. The heat from Brianna's body coursed through her. She slid her hands down Brianna's smooth back and lightly massaged her buttocks.

Their lips met and their tongues danced until Brianna trailed her tongue down Dani's neck.

Dani moaned, pulling Brianna closer. She fumbled with Brianna's jeans.

Brianna stopped her. "Let's get in bed." She slid out of her jeans and panties while Dani did the same.

Dani reached for the light switch.

"No," Brianna said. "I want to see you when you

make love to me."

"Now you're talking crazy," Dani said with a smile. "Aren't virgins supposed to do it in the dark?"

Brianna gave her a seductive smile and nudged her toward the bed.

They began in earnest exploring each other's bodies. Despite her need, Dani took it slow, caressing Brianna's shoulders and arms before moving to her breasts. When she arrived at Brianna's nipple, she ran it gently between her fingers.

Brianna inhaled sharply.

Brianna seemed to be touching everywhere on her body all at once. The sensations of Brianna's touch were almost too much, so Dani brought her lips to Brianna's.

Their kiss lingered. They explored each other's mouths with their tongues. Dani's lips tingled with anticipation. The kiss continued while they increased their exploration.

As the kiss intensified, Brianna rolled on top of Dani, straddling her leg.

Dani arched her back and pressed into Brianna's leg. They moved in rhythm as they kissed.

Brianna broke the kiss and put her fingers against Dani's cheek. "I want to touch you. Are you ready?"

"I've been ready for months."

Brianna reached between Dani's legs. She shifted, allowing Brianna better access.

When Brianna's fingers brushed across her clitoris, Dani closed her eyes.

"No, Dani, I want you to see me," Brianna said.

Dani met Brianna's gaze, the intimacy deeper than anything she'd ever felt before. This wasn't just sex. "I'm not sure I can do this."

"You can." Brianna continued running her finger in a circle.

Dani began stroking Brianna's clitoris.

Brianna moaned and kept her eyes open.

Dani increased the intensity of her strokes. She could tell by Brianna's breathing she was close. The look of bliss on Brianna's face was pushing Dani closer to her own orgasm. Brianna's beautiful body writhing under her touch was enough without the rhythmic pressure on her own clitoris.

Brianna locked gazes with Dani as her climax overtook her.

Seeing Brianna in the throes of an orgasm sent Dani into her own. Dani cried out and clung to Brianna. The wave of pleasure washed over her, and she ground against Brianna to intensify the throbbing.

Brianna collapsed onto Dani, trying to catch her breath. She rested her head on Dani's chest and hugged her. "Holy fuck," Brianna said. "Not bad for a virgin."

When Dani didn't respond, Brianna lifted her head. "Are you okay?" Brianna brushed the hair off Dani's forehead.

"Better than okay." Dani ran her fingers down Brianna's back. "I'm not a virgin anymore."

"Confession. I think I was a virgin, too. I just didn't know it."

"Seriously?"

"Seriously. That was intense."

Dani wanted to say more but knew there would be many more nights like this that she could share all that she was feeling. For now, she just wanted to bask in the glow.

Epilogue

Beginning of next camping season

"You've got to take a shower," Dani said. "You look like you just had sex."

"I did." Brianna rolled over.

She'd fallen asleep while Dani had been in the shower, despite the bright sunlight coming through the loft windows. When Dani left their bed, she'd been tempted to get up and look out over the river, but it would have required her putting on clothes if she didn't want to flash anyone that might be outside. In her satiated state, it sounded like too much work.

She smiled at Dani. Her hair was still damp from the shower, and her face glowed. *Maybe another round?*

"Do not look at me like that." Dani flipped the sheet over Brianna's head and walked over to the bank of windows. "Our guests are probably already arriving, and we can't be up here, going at it like rabbits."

"Why not?" Brianna peeked her head out from under the sheet.

"Because my mother will be here," Dani said, faking outrage.

Brianna laughed. "Well, that just threw a bucket of cold water on my libido."

"Glad to know something could." Dani bent down and kissed Brianna but pulled back before they got in too deep.

Brianna was happier than she'd ever been. Finally, her dad had done something right. Tonight was the night before the new season of camping kicked off, and they'd invited their family and friends for a special gathering outside the loft. A year ago, who would have believed Brianna would be living in Flower Hills, running Thundering Pines with Dani?

Dani slipped on her sweatshirt. "I'm going to go out and greet our guests while you take a shower."

"Can't I go like this?" Brianna ran her hands through her hair, messing it up further.

"No. Then they'll definitely know what we've been doing."

"I'm pretty sure they'll figure it out when I come sauntering down with a satisfied look on my face."

"Would you stop? My mom might be down there."

Brianna chuckled. It was a new game for her to threaten to embarrass Dani in front of her family, especially her mother. She never did it, but just watching Dani's reaction was reward enough.

"That's it. I'm going down." Dani crossed the floor and gave Brianna one final kiss. "Would you please get your butt up?"

"I suppose." Brianna threw off the covers and stood.

"Oh, God, you don't have any clothes on."

"I believe you took them off me a couple hours ago."

Dani laughed. "You're screwing with me, aren't you?"

"Whatever gave you that idea?" Brianna winked. She went to Dani and wrapped her arms around her. "I just want you to relax."

Dani grinned. "You did a pretty good job of that earlier."

"Everything will be fine tonight."

"But it's the first time *everyone* will be together. It's freaking me out."

"I know. Why do you think I kept you distracted earlier? You would have been climbing the walls otherwise."

"You mean it wasn't because you couldn't keep your hands off me?"

"Well, that too. Now get your butt down there and let me take my shower. Or do you want me to continue standing in the middle of the room naked?"

Dani eyed her and pretended to think about it.

"I can stand here all evening while your mother is down there waiting."

"Stop." Dani covered her ears. "I'm going."

Brianna watched Dani leave before she went into the bathroom. She looked at herself in the mirror. No wonder Dani was panicking. She did look as if she'd just had sex.

❧ ❧ ❧ ❧

Brianna stopped at the second-floor landing and looked out. The sun still reflected off the river, even though it was getting lower in the sky. Now that it was April, the days were getting longer, so there would still be another hour before dark.

Some of their friends and family had already arrived, and their lawn chairs were scattered in clusters with no particular order. A perfectionist's nightmare. Most of the chairs were empty since everyone stood around talking. There were two large tables nearly full of food. They might have to bring another table out if it got any fuller.

Her gaze settled on Dani, who was meticulously positioning the wood to start a fire. Her heart swelled. Her life had changed so much in the past year, and she marveled at how full of love it had become. It wasn't just Dani who filled her life, it was everyone gathered tonight. *My friends. My family.*

When one of the guests noticed her arrival, she waved and began walking down the final flight of stairs.

"Look what the cat drug in," Shelby said as she walked toward Brianna. "Hey, sis."

Brianna wrapped her arms around Shelby and squeezed her tight. "Where's Curtis?"

"Over talking to Dani's brother about football or something equally uninteresting." Shelby eyed Brianna. "What do you want him for?"

"Now that Dani's gonna be an aunt, I'm getting jealous. I think you need to find a husband and settle down."

Shelby smirked. "Patience. Do you really want to find out what raging hormones might do to my personality?"

"Oh, God, I hadn't thought about that." Brianna chuckled.

"There you are." Aunt Helen wrapped Brianna in a hug. When she let go, she winked at her. "Dani said you took a nap and overslept."

Brianna's face heated. Dani was paying her back. She probably deserved it. Wanting to change the subject as quickly as possible, she pointed at the food table. "How much of that food did you bring?"

"Just a couple dishes."

"Did you bring that spinach dip?" Shelby asked.

"As a matter of fact, I did. A little birdie told me it was your favorite."

"Sorry, Brianna, but you're just not as interesting as spinach dip, so I'll catch you later."

"Don't eat it all," Brianna said to the retreating Shelby before turning back to Aunt Helen. "So how many dishes did you make?"

"I wanted to make sure there was enough," Aunt Helen said without answering the question. "Is Dani still crawling out of her skin about her mama meeting everyone?"

"Yep. I'm not sure why. She's already met almost everyone here."

"She's just excited." Aunt Helen's face dropped. "I just wish she hadn't had to wait all these years."

"No." Brianna pointed her finger at Aunt Helen. "What did Dani tell you? She's lost enough. You loved her when she wasn't loveable. She can forgive you for your mistakes."

"Easier said than done, but I'm trying."

Brianna didn't want to dampen Aunt Helen's mood, so a change of subject was in order. "Didn't you bring Mr. Dunhurst?"

Aunt Helen grinned. "He hates it when you girls call him that."

"Maybe we'll call him Uncle Dunhurst one day." Brianna grinned.

"Stop it." Aunt Helen playfully swatted at Brianna's arm. "We've only been seeing each other for a few months. You'll scare him away."

"Is that why you didn't bring him?"

"He's here." Aunt Helen pointed toward a group of people standing about twenty yards away. "He's talking law with Dani's sister and Caroline."

"Oh, shit, Caroline's here already? I didn't think they were going to be here until later. I should go say hello."

"And call him Thomas, will you?"

"Maybe." Brianna gave Aunt Helen a quick hug before heading across the open area. She waved at Molly, who was engrossed in a conversation with Carl's wife, Sara. She passed Carl, as well, and gave him a quick hug before moving on.

Dani remained bent over the fire, so Brianna leaned down. "Hey, Caroline is here already. I'm going to say hi. Do you want to come?"

"I'll be over in a minute," Dani said. "I want to make sure this fire is going good before I leave it."

"Your mom's not here yet?"

"Nah, she texted a little bit ago and said they'd be here soon."

Brianna made her way to where Caroline stood. "I didn't see you guys over here. Dani's big pile of firewood blocked my view."

She greeted Mr. Dunhurst by his first name, even though it made her cringe, and exchanged pleasantries with Karen, Dani's sister, before turning to Caroline.

"I didn't think you two would be here until later."

"Surprise," Caroline said with a big smile. She stepped toward Brianna and wrapped her arms around her. "About time you show up for your own party."

Kylie playfully slapped at Caroline's arm. "Leave her alone, she's in love."

Brianna wrapped her arms around Kylie and enjoyed her exuberant embrace.

"Speaking of love..." Brianna let go of Kylie.

"How was your honeymoon?"

Kylie launched into a story of their misadventures in Hawaii and had Brianna laughing so hard that tears ran down her face.

"Sounds like I'm missing out on the party." Dani moved beside Brianna.

"Dani," Caroline said and stepped forward for a hug.

Brianna smiled as they hugged and draped her arm over Kylie's shoulder. "I'm so glad you could make it."

"We were so happy when you called and invited us. We wouldn't have missed it for anything. Besides, it's good for Caroline to rough it for one night."

Really. Brianna grinned. "You're staying at a hotel. I wouldn't exactly call it roughing it."

"To Caroline it is." Kylie rolled her eyes.

Caroline and Dani were having their own conversation when Dani turned to Brianna. "Hey, would you mind grabbing a few more logs for the fire?"

"What kind do you want?" Brianna asked.

"Your choice. Pick your favorite."

"You know it's maple. Are you sure you don't want ash?"

"Did you just say you have a favorite firewood?" Caroline eyed Brianna.

"She does, but it's the wrong one," Dani said.

Kylie turned to Caroline. "I think their relationship is in trouble. How can they survive when they can't even agree on the right firewood?"

Everyone laughed.

They stood talking for another fifteen minutes as people filtered in and out of the conversation.

Brianna held Dani's hand, hoping to keep her

calm, as she waited for her mom and Phyllis to arrive. She knew the moment they showed because Dani tightened her grip on her. "Relax," Brianna said into Dani's ear. "Let's go greet them."

Brianna turned to Caroline and Kylie. "Dani's mom just arrived. So we'll catch up with you later."

"Sure thing. You owe me a ride on that whatchacallit." Caroline pointed.

"ATV?"

"Yeah, that's it."

Brianna shook her head and rolled her eyes. "I'll put you on my schedule." She turned to Dani. "Let's go."

They'd only taken a few steps when Dani stopped without warning.

"What's the matter?" Brianna asked.

Dani's smile lit her whole face. "We're going to greet my mom."

Brianna returned the smile. Her heart overflowed seeing Dani's face. She started to move forward but Dani didn't. "Now what?" Brianna asked.

"I'm going to greet my mom with the woman who took my virginity."

Brianna laughed. "Would you come on? We don't want to keep your mom waiting."

About the Author

Rita Potter has spent most of her life trying to figure out what makes people tick. To that end, she holds a Bachelor's degree in Social Work and an MA in Sociology. Being an eternal optimist, she maintains that the human spirit is remarkably resilient. Her writing reflects this belief.

Rita's stories are electic but typically put her characters in challenging circumstances. She feels that when they reach their happily ever after, they will have earned it. Despite the heavier subject matter, Rita's humorous banter and authentic dialogue reflect her hopeful nature.

In her spare time, she enjoys the outdoors. She is especially drawn to the water, which is ironic since she lives in the middle of a cornfield. Her first love has always been reading. It is this passion that spurred her writing career. She rides a Harley Davidson and has an unnatural obsession with fantasy football. More than anything, she detests small talk but can ramble on for hours given a topic that interests her.

She lives in a small town in Illinois with her wife, Terra, and their cat, Chumley, who actually runs the household.

Rita is a member of American Mensa and the Golden Crown Literary Society. She is currently a graduate of the GCLS Writing Academy 2021. Sign up for Rita's free newsletter at:

www.ritapotter.com

If you liked this book...

Share this book with your friends or post a review on your favorite site like Amazon, Goodreads, Barnes and Noble, or anywhere you purchased the book. Or perhaps share a posting on your social media sites and help spread the word.

Join the Sapphire Newsletter and keep up with all your favorite authors.

Did we mention you get a free book for joining our team?

sign-up at - www.sapphirebooks.com

Check out Rita's other books.

Broken not Shattered - ISBN - 978-1-952270-22-2

Even when it seems hopeless, there can always be a better tomorrow.

Jill Bishop has one goal in life – to survive. Jill is trapped in an abusive marriage, while raising two young girls. Her husband has isolated her from the world and filled her days with fear. The last thing on her mind is love, but she sure could use a friend.

Alex McCoy is enjoying a comfortable life, with great friends and a prosperous business. She has given up on love, after picking the wrong woman one too many times. Little does she know, a simple act of kindness might change her life forever.

When Alex lends a helping hand to Jill at the local grocery store, they are surprised by their immediate connection and an unlikely friendship develops. As their friendship deepens, so too do their fears.

In order to protect herself and the girls, Jill can't let her husband know about her friendship with Alex, and Alex can't discover what goes on behind closed doors. What would Alex do if she finds out the truth? At the same time, Alex must fight her attraction and be the friend she suspects Jill needs. Besides, Alex knows what every lesbian knows – don't fall for a straight woman, especially one that's married…but will her heart listen?

Upheaval: Book One - As We Know It - ISBN - 978-1-

952270-38-3

It is time for Dillon Mitchell to start living again.

Since the death of her wife three years ago, Dillon had buried herself in her work. When an invitation arrives for Tiffany Daniels' exclusive birthday party, her best friend persuades her to join them for the weekend.

It's not the celebration that draws her but the location. The party is being held at the Whitaker Estate, one of the hottest tickets on the West Coast. The Estate once belonged to an eccentric survivalist, whose family converted it into a trendy destination while preserving some of its original history.

Surrounded by a roomful of successful lesbians, Dillon finds herself drawn to Skylar Lange, the mysterious and elusive bartender. Before the two can finish their first dance, a scream shatters the evening. When the party goers emerge from the underground bunker, they discover something terrible has happened at the Estate.

The group races to try to discover the cause of this upheaval, and whether it's isolated to the Estate. Has the world, as we know it, changed forever?

Survival: Book Two - As We Know It - IBSN - 978-1-952270-47-5

Forty-eight hours after the Upheaval, reality is beginning to set in at the Whitaker Estate. The world, As We Know It, has ended.

Dillon Mitchell and her friends are left to survive, after discovering most of the population, at least in the United States, has mysteriously died.

While they struggle to come to terms with their devastating losses, they are faced with the challenge of creating a new society, which is threatened by the divergent factions that may tear the community apart from the inside.

Even if the group can unite, external forces are gathering that could destroy their fragile existence.

Meanwhile, Dillon's budding relationship with the elusive Skylar Lange faces obstacles, when Skylar's hidden past is revealed.

Other Sapphire books from Sapphire Authors

Greenish: A Romance of New Beginnings - ISBN - 978-1-952270-44-4

Harley Hewitt is living the dream. She's about to wed her fiancée, Tracey, when her best friend suddenly bails as her maid of honour. Her night job as a nurse and her lack of contact with anyone in her hometown make her realize that she has no friends of her own, so she goes to a speed dating event in hopes of catching a maid of honour, rather than a future bride-to-be.

Denise North thought she had everything. Her own home, a good job with great friends, and zero debt. At her best friend's wedding, she soon realizes that her aspirations of being someone's one and only have been put on the backburner. She throws herself back into the dating pool, expecting to find the perfect man of her dreams but accidentally shows up at a lesbian speed dating night instead.

When Denise and Harley cross paths, it seems like the stars have aligned. Denise needs to get out of her shell, and Harley needs "someone borrowed" for her big day. They both have similar interests and senses of humour. What could go wrong? As the wedding approaches and Harley's best friend returns with a secret, both women find out just how green they've been at love and life so far.

Curtain Call - ISBN - 978-1-952270-42-0

What do you do when you come from a long line of

dancers that spans the globe and generations, yet you
can't tell your right foot from your left? You fall in love
with a dancer, of course!

Gray Rickman is an awkward seventeen-year-old
when she first sets eyes on Christian Scott at the dance
studio/theater Gray's parents own and run in Denver,
Colorado.

Though only a handful of years older than Gray,
Christian carries herself with poise and wisdom far
beyond her years. A woman of few words, she speaks
volumes with her body.

Before Gray even really knows what her type is,
Christian stars in endless daydreams and even fulfills
a couple of her fantasies before vanishing out of thin
air, leaving Gray in an empty bed with nothing but
bittersweet memories and broken dreams.

With no choice but to move on, Gray attempts love,
even moving with her college girlfriend to New York
City to pursue a career in journalism. But her standard
has been set, the bar way too high for any other woman
to reach or clear. It's an unexpected encounter in an
obvious place when Gray sets eyes on her dancer again.
Will the bright lights of Broadway illuminate the way
back to the woman of her dreams? Or will they blind
her to any other possibility of happiness?

Break a leg, Gray. The Great White Way calls.

Diva – ISBN – 978-1-952270-10-9

What if...you were offered a part-time job as the personal assistant to someone you have idolized for years? Meg Ellis has just completed the school year as a nurse in the Santa Fe school system. It isn't her first choice of profession, but a medical problem derailed her musical career years ago. The breakup of a bad relationship is still painful. The loving support from her close-knit family and good friends has buoyed her spirits, but longing still lurks below the surface. She can't forget the intoxicating allure of the beautiful diva who haunts her dreams.

Nicole Bernard is a rising star in the world of opera, adored by fans around the globe. When Meg learns that Nicole is headlining a new production at the renowned New Mexico outdoor pavilion—and then is asked to accept a job offer to be her personal assistant—she is beside herself. After a short time learning the routine and reining in her hormones, Meg discovers that Nicole's family will be visiting for the opening. Her responsibility to the charismatic singer immediately becomes more difficult when Nicole's young husband Mario shows up and threatens the comfortable rapport between Meg and the prima donna.

The two women brace for a roller-coaster interlude composed by fate. Will the warm days and cool nights, the breathtaking scenery, and the romance of the music create summer love? A heartbreaking game? Or something very special?

Laying of Hands - ISBN - 978-1-952270-49-9

Nestled in the Adirondack Mountains of upstate New

York lies a picturesque retreat for the conservative young women of the Sanctity Covenant religion, surrounded by crisp, pine-scented breezes and the endless blue shimmer of Coyote Lake. But dark secrets lurk behind closed doors at Valley of Rubies, and what emerges from the summer shadows is nothing less than terrifying.

Adel Rosse, an investigative journalist for Vanity Fair looking for a way to stand out in the cutthroat world of Manhattan journalism, has just been handed an assignment that will catapult her career—if she can survive as an undercover Creative Writing tutor at Valley of Rubies and get the scoop on what really happens there. Just as she starts to uncover the gritty truth behind the shadowy cult running the organization, she falls in love with the one woman who holds the key to the story.

Grace Waters is an old maid at twenty-six, at least by Covenant standards, and her annual idyllic summers spent teaching at Valley of Rubies are suddenly imperiled by the news that she must marry the man chosen for her at the end of the session. If she refuses, she risks being excommunicated—or worse—but a mysterious new writing instructor at camp makes her wonder what would happen if she dared to write her own story.

Pushing their boundaries in search of answers, Grace and Adel seek to redefine themselves to save their futures—and maybe each other.

Made in the USA
Las Vegas, NV
10 July 2022

51334584R00270